Storm Warning

Also by Wilma Wall

Forbidden
The Jade Bracelet

A NOVEL

Storm Warning

Wilma Wall

Storm Warning: A Novel

© 2009 by Wilma Wall

Published by Kregel Publications, a division of Kregel, Inc., P.O. Box 2607, Grand Rapids, MI 49501.

All rights reserved. No part of this book may be reproduced, stored in a retrieval system, or transmitted in any form or by any means—electronic, mechanical, photocopy, recording, or otherwise—without written permission of the publisher, except for brief quotations in printed reviews.

The persons and events portrayed in this work are the creations of the author, and any resemblance to persons living or dead is purely coincidental. Springton and Fairdale are fictitious towns set in the Central San Joaquin Valley of California.

Scripture is taken from the King James Version, although many verses in thoughts and sermons are paraphrased.

ISBN 978-0-8254-3932-2

Printed in the United States of America

09 10 11 12 13 / 5 4 3 2 1

*To my husband,
Dave Wall,
my strong, gentle rock
of support*

Acknowledgments

Thanks to all the peach farmers who gave me suggestions and advice—Charles Neufeld, Steve Goossen, Delbert Wiest, and others. Any mistakes are mine and not theirs.

Thanks to nurses Jean Reimer and Margie Kuffel for medical advice.

Thanks to Bob Suderman for tips on ambulance use.

Thanks to Ed Reimer for motorcycle information.

Thanks to my husband, Dave, and my family for their patience and encouragement.

Thanks to my editors and publisher at Kregel Publications.

And special thanks to my dear friend and mentor Elnora King and the Tuesday workshop for all their good advice and critiques.

Chapter 1
Monday, April 3, 1995

"All rise! The Honorable Grover Trent presiding."

In the courtroom, Velita Stanford scrambled to her feet and grabbed the back of the seat ahead to steady herself. She felt as though she were back in high school assembly, standing at attention. The United States and California flags were on the platform—what if they'd have to recite the flag salute? It'd been nine years since she'd dropped out of high school back in Chockamo, Oklahoma, and she couldn't even remember it.

A door opened at the front of the room, and the judge marched in, his black robe swirling.

Velita thought frantically. *One nation, under God, indivisible . . .*

"Be seated."

Whew. Settled back in her chair, Velita peeked up at the judge, hoping he wouldn't notice. He had bushy salt-and-pepper eyebrows to match his thin hair, and his mouth was pinched as though he'd just tasted something bad. He slipped on a pair of half-rimmed glasses and stared at the group in the courtroom. *Like a king deciding whose head to chop off,* thought Velita. His eyes reached hers, and her stomach cramped, her face growing as hot as if she were the one on trial.

The clerk announced: "Department seventeen of the Superior Court of the County and City of Springton, California, is now in session. *The State versus Duane Jackson.*"

The judge nodded at a young black man sitting at the lawyers' table directly ahead of Velita. "Mr. Jackson has been charged with murder of the first degree with special circumstances."

That's the guy? Velita stared at the back of the young man's head. His clothes were nice, his hair trimmed short, and he wore a sports coat. She'd thought he was one of the lawyers and that, when the trial finally started, guards would bring in a wild-looking prisoner shuffling in chains and wearing an orange jumpsuit.

This man could be anyone you'd see behind the counter in a nice store, even a teacher at a PTA meeting. But a murderer? How could the judge let him loose in here with all these innocent people around?

The man turned and looked at the people waiting to be chosen for the jury.

Velita's heart skipped a beat. All these people were here to decide his fate. He could look right into their eyes and know what they were thinking. What if he went crazy and attacked everyone in reach before guards could get to him? The only thing separating him from her and the others was that little bitty railing with its tiny swinging door.

The judge kept on talking, and Velita dragged her thoughts back to him. He introduced the lawyers: prosecutor James Pettigrew, young and handsome in a classy navy suit and shiny shoes, and defense attorney Arnold Torrance, an older man, tall, skinny, and a little stoop shouldered.

"A policeman has been killed, and two other officers have been injured. This trial will probably last two weeks. Perhaps three." The judge turned to the clerk, and they murmured together over a stack of papers.

Three weeks? thought Velita in a panic. No. Oh, no. She *had* to get out of here.

This whole day hadn't seemed real. Ralph had been right: he'd said it was a dumb thing to do, her coming to the courthouse. She didn't belong here. What did she know about law?

But she knew that wasn't her husband's real reason. He'd claimed that the judge and lawyers asked people questions about their jobs and families, nosing around in their private lives. Ralph always said what he did in his own house was nobody else's business, and she'd better keep her trap shut.

What would happen if I just walked out? Velita glanced over her shoulder at the entrance. A big, hulking man in uniform stood there, teetering on his feet, his arms folded across his chest. Just daring anyone to sneak past him.

"Been on a jury before?"

Velita jumped, although the woman next to her had only whispered. "Uh-uh," she answered, clamping her shaking fingers on her purse. "And I better not get on this one." Her own life was in such a mess; how could she be responsible for someone else's?

"I've been on three," said the woman. She had short dark hair and wore jeans with a T-shirt that said, *Nurses call the shots.* "Two civil and one criminal. It's not that bad."

Easy for her to say. She doesn't have to answer to Ralph. Velita glanced at the clock. One fifteen. "What time do you think we'll get off today? My kids are out of school at two."

"It'll be a while. Did you explain that to the clerk?"

"Tried to." All morning she'd sat in the assembly room, waiting for her turn, and they'd brushed her off right smart. "She told me to get a sitter. As if I could afford one."

"Don't you have a friend or some relative that could help out?"

"Ralph's mother, clear across town. She's not much for watching grandkids." *Not much for doing* any *favors for her daughter-in-law.*

"What about a neighbor?"

"Lady next door'll check on them today if I'm not home in time. But I hate to bother her. I . . . don't know her that well." She'd talked to the woman several times over the fence. Rhonda Avery seemed friendly and easygoing, but once Ralph caught her at it, that was the end of any possible friendship.

The woman next to her shrugged. "Might be good to get acquainted real quick. If you're not chosen this time, you're home free. But if you are, you're stuck until it's over."

Velita chewed her lip. Ralph wouldn't like that one bit. She was supposed to be at home, tidying up, washing his clothes, and setting a nice dinner on the table by five thirty sharp.

The judge rapped his gavel. "The court will now select a panel of twelve, with three alternates."

The clerk reached into a plastic cylinder, brought out a slip of paper, and called, "Laura Crutchfield!"

A woman in a classy pantsuit went to the jury box and sat down in one of the seats.

Velita listened carefully to the judge's questions. Was the woman married, had she any children, what was her occupation?

Laura Crutchfield was single, had no children, and was a furniture store owner. She sounded smart enough to run the whole show herself.

The judge motioned to the wall at his right, where a whiteboard showed a row of names printed in thick black. "Do you know any of these police officers?"

The woman looked at the board and shook her head. "No."

What did she do in her free time? Did she drink, do drugs, was she racially prejudiced? What did she think of the death penalty?

Just like Ralph said—prying into stuff that is nobody else's business. Even into their thoughts!

As each person went up, Velita tried to figure out which answers would get her out. But there didn't seem to be any set pattern. Some people were excused for no reason she could see, and those she thought would get off easy had to stay.

One woman said Jackson *had* to be guilty; she knew how hard it was to bring someone to trial.

The judge smiled and asked, "Do you think you could listen to the witnesses with an open mind?"

The woman answered, "I guess so," and the judge kept her up there.

"Hiram Anderson!" called the clerk.

A shriveled old man hobbled up to the jury stand.

"Do you have teenage sons? Do you own a gun? Have you ever smoked marijuana?"

Mr. Anderson answered each question with a "Huh?" and the judge had to repeat everything.

Velita frowned. *What dumb things to ask the poor old guy.* Even she could see that.

Finally the man shook his head. "I don't hear so good."

"I gathered as much," said the judge dryly. Some people snickered, and he rapped the gavel. "Excused."

Maybe she could pretend to be deaf. Ralph would like that; he'd think it was a big joke.

An hour later, they still hadn't called her name, and the jury box was almost filled. Velita began to relax. They probably wouldn't need her, and she'd worried all for nothing.

"Jacob Franzen!"

The man walking up looked about Ralph's height, only broader in the shoulders. He wasn't movie-star handsome, but there seemed to be something different about him, something special. His hair was the color of ripe wheat, thick and curling a little below his ears, his face tanned and rugged with little laugh crinkles on the sides of his eyes.

"Age thirty-five," he said. "A farmer. Widower, raising three children." His voice was deep and warm, almost like music.

Velita couldn't imagine Ralph raising kids by himself. He even groused about watching them when she went to the supermarket, so to keep the peace, she usually took them along. If anything happened to her, he'd farm them out and find a new woman right quick.

Jacob Franzen told the judge he'd never used marijuana. He didn't know any policemen personally. Didn't own a gun.

The judge glanced down at a sheet of paper. "I see here that you are a Mennonite." He peered at the man over the top of his glasses. "You don't look like one."

Mr. Franzen smiled. "You may be thinking about the Amish. There are many kinds of Mennonites. I'm Mennonite Brethren."

"And what does that mean?"

"Clothes aren't that important. We believe in the Bible. And nonresistance."

The judge lifted his eyebrows. "Well, Mr. Franzen, what would you do if someone threatened your children?"

The man looked at the ceiling and worked his mouth.

Velita wondered what the judge meant. She sneaked a peek at Duane Jackson. Would the guy get back at the jurors and their families in revenge? What if *her* kids were in danger?

But the defendant just sat there scribbling in a tablet, like all this had nothing to do with him. He didn't act dangerous.

Finally Mr. Franzen answered, "It's hard to say. Try to talk them out of it, I guess. But I wouldn't let anyone hurt my family. If it came down to the wire, I'd do whatever I had to."

What kind of man was this? He seemed so different from Ralph and his friends. So kind. And he believed in the Bible. Ralph said the Bible was just something preachers used to hold over people's heads and make them put money in collection plates.

Velita suddenly realized she was staring at this man and felt guilty. She glanced around—what if Ralph had sneaked in after all and caught her at it? But he hadn't, and she shuddered with relief.

"How do you feel about capital punishment?"

The man stroked his jaw. It was square and clean-shaven and looked strong. "I . . . I'm not sure. It depends."

"On what?"

"Well, the Bible says if you live by the sword you will die by the sword. I think government is ordained by God. It has the power and obligation to punish wrongdoers and protect the innocent."

The judge lifted his bushy eyebrows. "Do you always agree with the government?"

Mr. Franzen smiled. "No. But I think God can use it no matter who is in command."

The judge nodded. "Hmmm. Very interesting." He looked at the lawyers.

"No objection," said one. "No objection," said the other.

Finally the jury box filled up, and Velita breathed more easily. She was safe. If she'd hurry, she could make it home before the kids got off the school bus.

Then the judge asked the lawyers if they had any questions.

The defense attorney asked Jacob Franzen to talk a little more about alcohol, drugs, and the death penalty.

"Well, I'm not against the *use* of alcohol. Just its *abuse*. Drugs are another matter. I believe they should only be in the hands of medical doctors, for diseases and pain." He stopped and studied the wall across the room, then said, "The death penalty? I don't like it, but maybe sometimes it is necessary. In extreme cases, like, oh, serial killers and such."

The lawyers questioned a few more jurors and then seemed satisfied. Velita gripped her purse and waited to be excused.

Then the judge said something about a challenge.

The prosecution said, "Excuse juror number seven," and a woman left the stand.

The clerk drew another name out of the cylinder.

"Velita Stanford!"

Chapter 2

Velita's heart pounded so loud the noise seemed to echo off the walls. Her hands were sweaty, and as she stumbled through the little gate in the railing, it slapped back at her. She grabbed it and caught her thumb in the hinge, breaking the nail. A million eyes stared at her.

She'd been so close. Now her only hope was to convince the judge to let her go. But her throat squeezed shut, and when she tried to answer his questions, her words came out all tangled.

"Speak up," said the judge.

The room was too hot. Velita's pulse throbbed in her neck and sang in her ears. She cleared her throat and tried again.

"I'm t-twenty-four years old. Um, married."

"Do you have children?"

"Two."

"What are their ages?"

"Suanne's eight and TJ—no, TJ's eight and Suanne, she's um, six. That's why I—"

"What is your husband's line of work?"

"Mechanic. But I—"

"Where does he work?"

Velita gulped. Ralph wouldn't want her to say. The judge leaned forward, waiting, his eyebrows raised.

"Ca–Carter Machine Shop."

"And your education?"

"What?"

"Your education. How far have you gone in school?"

"High . . . high school." Velita hugged her elbows and wished she could disappear. She couldn't admit in front of all these people that she hadn't even finished her sophomore year because she'd been pregnant.

"Do you have a job?"

"No. I've gotta be home for the kids . . ." But then the questions came faster, and she had to admit that no, the neighbor didn't work, but . . . well, Rhonda *might* be willing to watch the children, but—what? Policemen? No, she didn't know any policemen.

Velita's face grew hot. That wasn't a lie, not really. She'd seen quite a few but didn't know them personally. Not the ones named on the board.

The judge stabbed her with stern gray eyes. "Have you or any of your family members ever been arrested?"

That felt like a punch in the stomach. Did he know about the times the neighbors had called the cops?

But Ralph had never actually been arrested. He'd always talked the cops out of it, telling them she'd started the fights, and she'd never dared to argue or file charges.

"N–no," she finally answered.

"Have you or your family members ever been the victim of a crime?"

Oh, Lordy. This is getting too close. What would Ralph want me to say? Velita looked down at her hands and picked at the broken thumbnail. Stalling, she asked, "Like what?"

"Robbery, mugging, shooting?"

She thought back. *Robbery.* "A kid stole my son's lunch money at school."

The judge shook his head and smiled. "If that's the worst that's ever happened to you, you're very lucky."

Lucky? If he only knew.

"Do you drink alcohol or smoke marijuana? What about hard drugs?"

"No. Never done drugs. Well . . ." That wasn't exactly true. "I tried pot once at a party, just one drag." She cringed, remembering how Ralph had kept after her, bugging her, until she finally gave in. And everyone laughed when she ran to the bathroom to throw up.

She heard whispers and snickering, and the judge rapped his gavel. Now, for sure, he would let her go. Anybody could see she wasn't smart enough to be on a jury.

The judge turned away from her, and she waited, twisting her hands together. After a minute, one of the lawyers said, "Excuse juror number three."

Velita looked to the end of the row. She was number three! Her heart beating fast, she started to get up, but the man on her right left the jury box. She sat back down, confused. That had to be a mistake— it was supposed to be her!

She glanced at the woman on her other side, and the woman mouthed, "You're number four," and then she realized—the numbers had started from the other side.

The clerk dipped into the cylinder again. "Wallace Takashi!"

That's it? Velita wanted to say, *Wait—you've got to listen to me—I can't stay!* But the judge was busy questioning Mr. Takashi, and then the lawyers excused two other people.

"Marsha Lewis!" called the clerk.

The woman who had been sitting next to Velita before Velita had been called now came up. She smiled at Velita, then turned to the judge.

"What is your occupation?" he asked.

"I'm a nurse. Mercy Hospital."

"Are you married?"

"Divorced."

"Do you have children?"

"One daughter, seventeen years old."

"Does she live with you or your husband?"

"With me."

"How do you two get along?"

"Okay. The usual." Marsha gave a lopsided grin. "She's a teenager."

Velita had to admire the woman; nothing seemed to bother her. One would think she was just talking to the paper boy.

"Does your daughter see her father often?"

"About once a month."

"Do they get along all right?"

Marsha shrugged again. "Fine."

"Do you drink?"

"Rarely. Maybe a small glass of wine on special occasions."

"Use marijuana or other controlled substances?"

"No."

It was getting even hotter in the room, and the judge took a sip of water. "Do you know anyone with drug problems?"

Velita glanced at Duane Jackson. The scribbling on his tablet looked like a face. Was he drawing pictures of the jurors? Had he drawn her, too?

"Only professionally."

"Please explain."

"I work in ICU—that's the intensive care unit—"

"Yes; go on."

"Sometimes we have cases of drug overdose."

Duane Jackson stared at Marsha for a minute, then went back to his drawing.

"Do you get personally involved?" asked the judge.

"I don't understand."

"Do you stay in contact after they are released from the hospital?"

"No."

"Are you acquainted with or related to any police officers?"

Marsha didn't answer right away. She stared at the opposite wall and rubbed the side of her nose. Then she said, "One. Sergeant Jerry Mitchell, Fifth Precinct."

Duane Jackson's eyes flashed up at Marsha. Then he whispered to his lawyer. The lawyer shook his head.

The judge asked, "And what is your relationship?"

"He was my friend, once. Not anymore."

"Please explain."

"We . . . dated for several months. But it didn't work out. Personal differences."

Duane Jackson looked worried and kept on whispering to his lawyer.

"Are you acquainted with any of the officers involved in this trial?"

Marsha squinted at the whiteboard. "No."

"Would you give more credibility to a police officer's testimony than to, say, a street person?"

She slowly shook her head. "No way."

"Do you think your previous friendship with Sergeant Mitchell would influence your judgment in this trial?"

Marsha looked straight at Duane Jackson and shook her head. "I don't see any connection."

Jackson and his lawyer argued some more, but in the end, Marsha stayed up.

The clock's minute hand twitched past three. Velita hoped the kids had gotten on the right bus. That Rhonda had remembered to check on them.

In spite of the heat, cold sweat trickled down the inside of her blouse. The judge could still excuse her, couldn't he? One of the lawyers still object to her? She closed her eyes and crossed her fingers, her nerves on edge.

Back when she was little, the neighbors had taken her to Sunday school. The teacher had said if you prayed, God would answer. Was it true? With all her might, Velita tightened her fingers and breathed, *Please, God, make them let me go.*

The judge said, "Let the records show that Panel Thirty-one has been selected for the trial of *The State versus Duane Jackson.*"

That was it. Velita slumped into her chair.

Her Sunday school teacher had been wrong. Prayer didn't work. She was a gone goose.

Chapter 3

Velita listened numbly while the court chose three alternates and the judge talked about duty and privilege, serving the community.

Velita's mind raced in circles. What would she tell Ralph? Why hadn't she tried harder, made the judge understand? *Oh, Lord, why did I mess up again?*

How could she leave the kids for three whole weeks? If it was just TJ, he could probably stay home alone. But he'd been picking on Suanne lately. If the Child Protective Services got wind of it and thought the kids were neglected, who knew what would happen? Especially after the teacher had reported TJ's black eye. Nobody had believed he'd run into the bathroom sink.

There was no other way; she would have to depend on Rhonda. Velita sighed. Bad enough she was caught on the jury, but cozying up to the neighbors—Ralph would pop his balloons.

The other jurors got up, and she followed them out past the platform, through a back door, down the hall, and into a little room. The bailiff said the door would be locked from the outside and he would call them when it was time.

The room was filled with a long table and wooden chairs. One whole wall was a whiteboard, with a clock above; the other had cupboards over a sink and a counter with a big coffeemaker in one corner. At each end were restrooms.

By now, it was nearly four. How late would they have to stay? If Ralph got home first . . .

Velita slid a fingertip over her jagged thumbnail. How stupid of her to get it caught in that little gate. She tried so hard to keep them nice, but keeping up the house and yard work and all, she was forever chipping them off. Ralph liked long nails, said they turned him on.

She sighed. Ralph was going to be steamed anyway; a broken nail wouldn't make much difference.

Some of the jurors sat down by the table and settled down to read paperbacks they'd brought, and one woman got out some knitting. The rest stood around by the windows at the far end, chattering away.

The voices echoed in Velita's head, louder and louder. She shrank into a corner and stared at her feet.

Then she thought of the woman who had sat next to her earlier. Marsha Lewis. So calm, the kind who could handle anything. Friendly, too. If she could just latch on to her, it might not be so hard.

But Marsha and another woman were digging around in the cupboard. They'd found a can of coffee and some paper cups and now were talking and laughing, arguing over how much of the grounds to use.

Velita couldn't hold back anymore. Looking around, she saw her only refuge. She hurried into the room marked Ladies, sat down on the toilet lid, flushed to cover the sound, and bawled like a baby.

Three weeks ago, Ralph had brought in the mail as usual. He always had to be the first to look through it.

He'd said the official-looking letter was junk mail, some politician asking for money, and was about to toss it. Then he'd laughed, a weird, high giggle that she'd learned to recognize as a warning sign.

"Hey, this one's got *your* name on it! Who'd be writing you?" He tore it open and whipped it out of her reach. "Well, whatta you know? Says here, report for jury duty, April 3. Forget that!"

Velita's skin prickled. "Jury duty? Me? How'd they get my name?"

"The phone book, the census, who knows? Don't worry about it."

"Won't they put me in jail if I don't go? I saw on the news—"

"Naw, that was different. All we gotta do is say we never got the notice."

"But that's a lie! We keep telling the kids not to lie. We can't just—"

"What's a lie?" Ralph's friend from work, Tom Dolan, poked his curly red head around the back door.

Velita told him, "I got a thing in the mail about being on a jury."

"No big deal," said Tom. He flipped a kitchen chair around, straddled it, and leaned his thick arms across the back. "They call a lot of people, choose twelve, and send the rest home. The judge'll take one look at you and say, hey, what does that little blond airhead know? And then you're home free."

"She better be," said Ralph. "I can't take a lotta time off to cart her around. Hey, Vel, we got some more Coors in the fridge?"

She'd hoped that was the end of it. Ralph and Tom took their beers into the living room and watched the football game on TV.

She called the kids in to wash up, kissed Suanne's freckled nose, and fussed about the fresh rip in the knee of TJ's jeans. Listened with one ear to their ruckus at the bathroom sink in case she'd need to step in. When dinner was ready, she took filled plates in to Ralph and Tom, and they ate in the living room while she and the kids dished up at the kitchen table.

"Good dinner, Velita," shouted Tom.

"Yeah, my old woman's a great cook," said Ralph. "You gotta give her that."

Velita smiled and breathed easier. Everything would be okay. She stopped pushing her mashed potatoes around and dug into the slice of meat loaf.

But after Tom left and she was cleaning up the kitchen, Ralph stomped in and grabbed her arm. He hissed, "Whatta you mean, putting me down in front of Tom?"

She stared at him, not understanding. "I never!"

Ralph squeezed her arm harder and gave it a quick twist. "Don't give me that! You called me a liar just when Tom came in. And you had to blab about the jury."

"So?" She tried to pull away, but his grip was too strong.

"*So?* So now we can't get out of it!"

Velita looked around for the kids, but they'd already gone into their bedroom. They knew better than to stick around when Ralph got mad.

His dark eyes flashed, and he gave her arm another jerk. "Don't get any ideas around all them hotshot lawyers, y'hear? You let me do the talking. I'll tell that judge our kid's sick. No—I'll say you got cancer and gotta go to the hospital. You're so skinny he'll believe it." He shoved her away, and she spun against the table.

The pain cut through her lower back like she'd been sliced in half, and she screamed, "Ralph, no! You promised—"

He came after her with a clout on her ear. "Shut up, stupid. Just remember what I said, and keep your yap shut."

She nodded, biting back accusing words, blinking back the tears he hated. Anything to make him stop. "Okay, okay. I will."

Ralph gave her one last push, then went back to the living room and his TV program.

All that evening, her ear ringing and her back sore, she kept quiet, patching TJ's jeans. During commercials, she noticed Ralph glancing at her, but she wouldn't meet his eyes. As if the physical pain wasn't bad enough, it made it worse to be called *stupid*. Back in school, the teachers had told her she was smart, had given her stars and hundreds. But then she remembered TJ's last school conference; Mrs. Dorsey had used all kinds of big words, and half the time she didn't know what the woman was talking about. She'd gone home and looked up the word *cognitive* in TJ's dictionary and found it meant *understanding*. Maybe Ralph was right. She was stupid, stupid.

Later in bed, he pulled her close to him, pawing all over her, kissing the sore spot by her ear. "Baby, I'm sorry. I swear I won't do that again. You know I'm crazy about you."

He'd said that before. And for a while, he'd kept his promise. But she wondered how long it would last this time. One thing she knew: if she pulled away now, it would only set him off again. Best to grit her teeth and go along with whatever he wanted. If there was an Oscar for pretending in bed, she'd be a winner.

After he rolled over and went right off to sleep, she lay awake a long time, thinking. It had been so good in the beginning, her and Ralph, even in the one room his mother had let them use. What had come between them first, she wondered—the babies or the booze? Or was it that Ralph couldn't hang onto his jobs and they had to move from town to town? She tried so hard, but some days, nothing she did was right. She didn't even have to open her mouth, and he'd get crazy.

Sometimes when Ralph was weepy drunk, he'd talk about how miserable he'd been as a kid, his dad long gone without even a card for his birthday, his mom working day and night. Velita couldn't help feeling sorry for him about that, thinking maybe that was what boiled inside of him. Her own daddy had died when she was five, but then three years later, her mama had married again. Her stepdad yelled a lot and was pretty free with his fists or the paddle, but at least he'd stuck around.

Since she and Ralph—and his mom—had settled in Springton, he'd calmed down some, and she'd been real hopeful. He liked his job, liked fixing almost every make of car. Now that he'd worked there a year, the boss had even given him a raise.

Not that she saw any of it, but she'd been glad for his sake. He'd made friends, had fun playing cards and riding his Harley with them. He'd been good to the kids, telling Suanne she was a sweetie pie and laughing at TJ's clowning. Sometimes he even acted proud of *her*—so long as she kept away from the other men. Didn't matter if *he* flirted with any woman that looked his way. Oh, no. To him, that was just a guy thing.

Lately, she'd only had to put up with a little rough play or a slap or two on her behind. But now, was it going to start all over again?

Maybe prayer was worth a try. Lying there in bed next to her snoring husband, Velita squeezed her hands together under her chin and wondered what she should ask for. Finally she whispered, "Oh, Lord, if You're up there somewhere and can hear me, please, please, let me get out of this jury duty."

From then on, Velita had kept the house extra neat, fixed all Ralph's favorite meals, made sure his tan knit shirt was clean in case he wanted to go out with his friends in the evenings. Tried to keep the kids from fighting. If she didn't mess up, maybe this time he really would keep his promise.

By this morning her bruises had pretty much faded, but she put on a long-sleeved blouse anyway. She fixed Ralph's favorite breakfast, pancakes with sausages and lots of maple syrup. Anything to keep him in a good mood. Suanne and TJ were nearly through breakfast when Ralph came to the table, dressed in work clothes. He gave Velita an up-and-down look. "Hey, you look pretty." Then he pulled back, his eyes squinting. "Whatcha all gussied up for?"

"Did you forget? Today I have to go—"

"*Today?*" His fork stopped halfway to his mouth. "No way. The foreman pulled a rush job on me."

Velita kept her face blank. "Oh, no! What'll I do now? . . . Do you s'pose Tom could pick you up and I could take the car? Who knows when I'll get done?" She wet a wash cloth and wiped Suanne's hands and mouth. "Go on kids, get your backpacks ready."

Ralph speared a triple layer bite of pancake and chewed, licking the syrup drips around his mouth. "Yeah, well, I guess just this once. Whyn't you call him?"

She filled his coffee cup, then headed for the phone.

He grabbed her wrist. "You better not be makin' eyes at them lawyers."

"Don't worry, sweetie." Trying not to wince with the pain, she reached over with her free hand and patted his shoulder. "You're the only man in my life."

When Tom drove up and honked, Velita walked to the door with Ralph. Ralph kissed her, then swatted her on the bottom. "Don't forget what I said!" He flashed a big grin. "And be sure to get off."

Showing off cheerful in front of Tom. But his eyes told her, *Just wait until you get home.*

Chapter 4

Sick with worry, Velita peeked out the jury restroom door. Now that she was stuck here, she had to face the other jurors, and even her fresh makeup couldn't hide the puffiness around her eyes. If only she could disappear into the woodwork.

Marsha Lewis stood nearby, looking out the window. She turned and asked Velita, "You all right?"

"Yeah." Velita moved toward her, not meeting her stare. Everyone would think she was a big baby. She turned her back to the others, hoping they wouldn't notice.

Marsha leaned closer and lowered her voice. "Hey, jury duty isn't something you choose for pleasure; it's a responsibility. It's not like you're cavorting around at a night club."

"I guess." *To Ralph, I might as well be dancing on a table.*

"Don't worry. It'll work out." Marsha touched her arm. "Come on, let's have some coffee."

Velita glanced around, but nobody else seemed to notice her. She followed Marsha to the counter.

Marsha poured two cups and handed one to her, pushing the sugar and cream packets closer. "I know how you must feel. It's scary deciding if someone's guilty or not. I'm sure everyone goes home hoping they've made the right decision."

Velita added powdered cream to her coffee, then leaned over the counter and cradled her cup in both hands, breathing in the steam. *Nobody* knew how she felt, that it was her own skin she was most worried about. And that was something she couldn't admit, especially not to this friendly woman.

After a few sips, she said, "Yeah, it's hard enough to figure out what to fix for dinner. How can I decide anything about a stranger's life?" She stirred her coffee and stared into the dark swirls. "I can't do it."

"You can. We'll listen to the witnesses, the judge'll give us guidelines, and then we just do our best. That's all that's expected of us."

A tubby little man in green plaid slacks, Lester Payne, charged toward them, wagging his finger. "Uh-uh-uh, ladies," he said. His voice sounded as friendly as a dentist's drill. "Didn't you hear the judge say not to discuss this case until it's over? Do you want to cause a mistrial?" He poured himself some coffee and walked away, still shaking his head.

Velita felt as though she'd been slapped, but Marsha made a face at Lester's back. "Don't take it personally. We didn't do anything wrong." She set her cup down on the table and pulled out two chairs. "But we'd better talk about other things until it's over."

Velita sank into a chair and sighed. "See? I don't have any business being here. I don't know the rules, all that legal stuff."

"Well, neither do I," rumbled a deep, warm voice. A man sat down in the chair next to Velita and added, "I feel as out of place as a chicken in a church."

The people around laughed real loud, as though they'd been waiting for something—anything—interesting to happen.

Velita didn't laugh. Was he coming on to her? *If Ralph saw me sitting next to this guy, he'd go wild. Claim I was cheating on him.* She smelled a whiff of spicy aftershave and edged her chair away.

Marsha wasn't a bit bashful. She smiled at the man and said, "Let's see, you're Jacob Franzen, right?"

The man raised his eyebrows and gave a little nod. "I'm flattered you remember."

Velita sneaked a glance. His arms looked strong and solid, and his deep blue eyes beamed at her. She gulped and turned away.

"Names are easy for me," said Marsha. "Yours is unusual. *Franzen*, that is."

"It's German. Flemish, if you go back a ways."

Marsha nodded. "I noticed a little accent."

A tall black woman, Geneva Carson, sat at the table, knitting a sweater. She looked up at Jacob and asked, "Did I hear you say before that you were a farmer?"

"*Yah*. Peaches. South of Fairdale."

"What variety?"

He shrugged. "O'Henry, Mayglo, Queencrest. You name it, I've got it."

"Maybe you can tell me—what's the best kind for baking?"

That was something right up Velita's alley. She forgot her nervousness and leaned forward, breaking into the conversation. "Yeah, what's the best for pies, or cobblers?"

"Elbertas. My wife used to can them . . ." Jacob cleared his throat and rubbed his chin.

The smile in his eyes turned into sadness, and of itself, Velita's hand moved toward his arm to touch it for comfort—but she caught herself just in time. "I'm sorry. I remember you saying you . . . were alone." She took a deep breath and leaned back into her chair, telling herself, *I better watch myself. I hope there's no way Ralph can leave work and come barging into this locked room.*

The man nodded and looked down at his hands. They were big and calloused, his nails a little jagged but clean.

Geneva's knitting needles clicked slower. "You farm the land alone?"

"I got a hired man to help out. My sons—they're young yet, but they're learning."

Another woman asked, "What's this about you being a Mennonite? I always thought—"

He laughed, the kind of laugh that made you want to join in. "Yeah, yeah. Beards, black hats, and wide suspenders." He shook his head. "That's the Old Order. Or Amish."

Marsha asked, "What's the difference?"

"There's more kinds than breeds of poodle. Here in the valley, we're mostly MBs."

Geneva turned back to her knitting. "You've lost me."

"MB. It stands for Mennonite Brethren. We don't bother much with the outward look. We figure what's on the inside counts." His cheeks reddened a little as though he was uncomfortable talking about it. "Actually, we're pretty much like Baptists."

Without warning, the door opened, and the bailiff poked his head in. "Please enter the jury box."

Uh-oh, thought Velita. *Here we go. The beginning of the end of my life.* She followed the others into the jury box, her throat tightening. She'd been so relieved that Ralph couldn't come, but now she wondered: if he had brought her here, could he have talked her out of this mess?

She glanced at the people still hanging around—could he maybe have gotten off work, after all, and snuck into the courtroom? But he wasn't there, and she knew it was just as well; she could have wound up in even worse trouble.

The courtroom was quiet. On the platform, His Honor waited; at their tables, the lawyers shuffled through briefcases. It felt weird, as though she had walked into a TV scene.

Then she turned and saw Duane Jackson staring at her. She swallowed hard. This wasn't playacting; this was the real thing. She was stuck here, and this man's life was in her hands. There'd be lots of big words, lawyer talk, things she couldn't understand. *Oh, God, help me,* she breathed silently. Then she remembered God hadn't answered her other prayers; she'd have to get through this on her own.

Judge Trent rapped his gavel and looked over his half glasses. "*The State versus Duane Jackson.*" His voice sounded like it came from a tunnel.

Jackson and his lawyer stood up.

"The charges are one count of aggravated assault, two counts of possession of narcotics, one count of illegal possession of a weapon, two counts of attempted murder, and one count of murder in the first degree with special circumstances. How does the defendant plead?"

The defense lawyer spoke quietly. "Not guilty on all counts, Your Honor."

Judge Trent glanced at the clock, then looked at the jury. "This has been a change of venue. In view of the time, I will allow the attorneys to attend to pressing duties on their calendars. The opening statements are postponed until one o'clock Tuesday. I must warn the jury not to discuss this case with anyone, not even your spouse."

Velita listened carefully. Most of that was plain enough and seemed easy for her to follow as long as Ralph wouldn't bug her about it.

Out of the corner of her eyes, she saw Lester Payne staring at her. As if she didn't already feel out of place, every look from him made her feel guilty. There was nothing she could do about it. She turned so he was out of her sight.

The judge went on: "You are not to watch news of the trial on television or read about it in the papers." He rapped his gavel. "Court is adjourned."

The bailiff motioned, and Velita followed the group back into that little room. Now what? Would she get to go home?

Marsha looked around at the others, her mouth open. "Well, that was short and sweet."

"Yeah," grumbled Lester Payne. "If we do this every day, we might not finish by Christmas."

Horrified, Velita stared at him. *That long?* Then she felt Marsha touch her arm, shaking her head.

"Don't worry," said Marsha. "He's just griping. But it could take a little longer than the judge expected."

Great. That's supposed to make me feel better? But Velita nodded and managed a weak smile.

The bailiff pointed a finger, sweeping it across the group. "Be sure to come on time tomorrow. The Honorable Grover Trent is a fanatic about promptness."

Eunice Phipps, tall, thin, and white-haired, gathered up her purse and a shopping bag full of paperbacks. "What happens if we're late?" she asked.

The bailiff shrugged. "His Honor considers it contempt of court."

Velita turned to Marsha and asked, "What's that?"

Lester Payne gave a sneering smile. "It means going to jail, little lady."

❖ ❖ ❖

Velita left the courthouse, feeling numb. If getting trapped here wasn't bad enough, now she'd have to face her own private trial with Ralph. It wouldn't be just words—he was going to go up in flames! And she would be the one to burn.

If only there was some way she could get out of telling him. As she turned the car into the street, she glanced at the gas gauge. The tank was full. Suddenly she felt a wild notion to drive on and on until it ran out. Leave Springton, maybe even California. Ditch this green bomb Ralph was so proud of, take a bus, end up in some strange little town she'd never heard of and where nobody knew her. Cut her hair short, dye it—black maybe—and use another name. Start a whole new life. Maybe she could get a job as a waitress or cook—she'd sure enough done a lot of serving and cooking these past years. At least she wouldn't starve to death.

She imagined herself in a tiny apartment, alone, scared to even look out the window. A knock on the door, Ralph standing there, wild-eyed, sneering. "Think you're so smart, huh? Told you I'd find you—there's no place you can hide from me. The kids? Wouldn't you just like to know!"

Her pulse raced, fear choking her as though it were actually happening. She pulled over to the side of the road and waited for her pounding heart to slow down. No way could she leave without Suanne and TJ. Love, sorrow, and desperation flooded over her.

She got home just in time to thank Rhonda, start a wash load, and fix a quick spaghetti dinner. When Ralph slammed through the door, she held her breath, all her nerves on edge. *Here it comes.*

She was shocked to see his mile-wide grin—it actually looked real.

Ralph threw his cap on the kitchen table. "Guess what, Vel! That rush job? It turned out to be an MGA. Sweetest little baby I ever did see. Red '56, guy said it had been sitting in an old man's garage for years, just needed timing corrected, points unstuck, that kind of stuff." Happy like that, Ralph looked more like the handsome guy she'd fallen hard for back in Chockamo, and she felt a little thrill bubble into her throat.

She dished up the food as he plopped onto his chair. "By the time I got it running, the engine purred like a big ole pussy cat. And then the best part: I got to test drive it. 'Course that meant," he said, chewing away, "all over town and into the country. Gotta make sure, you know." He winked and rolled up another forkful, then jabbered away while sauce dribbled out of the corners of his mouth.

He hadn't been in this good a mood for ages. The kids slid into their places, watching him, TJ wolfing his food and Suanne nibbling. On the way to her seat, Velita gave Ralph's shoulders a quick massage. At first he leaned back, saying, "Harder." But then he jerked away and looked back at her. "You did get off, right?"

Her arms dropped, all their strength oozing out. How could she tell him?

Ralph went stiff, his face red, his mouth tight. "Vel?"

Her happiness faded. All she could do was stay on alert. "I tried. Honest. I begged. Over and over. But they wouldn't let me go." She still couldn't believe it herself.

Ralph cursed. "For how long?"

"Two weeks," she mumbled. "Maybe three." She couldn't tell him what that awful little man in plaid said about maybe going till Christmas.

"What?" He whacked the table with his fist, and the dishes bounced. "No way. You crazy or something? What kind of trial is it, anyway?"

"The judge won't let us talk about it. Not even at home." She moved aside, but Ralph grabbed her wrist.

"Forget it. You're not going back."

"But I—" She thought frantically. Then she remembered that horrible man again, what he'd said in the jury room, and she rattled off quickly, "They said if I didn't show up, they'd put me in jail."

Ralph's mouth opened, and he pushed her away. He looked around, kneading his fists, and Velita realized she actually had him this time.

"What about the kids?" he asked finally. "We're not paying for no sitter. You'll have to take them along."

She made herself breathe slower. Did she dare push her advantage? "I . . . don't think the judge would let me."

"Well, for sure you can't load them on my mom."

"They'd be in school most of the time. I might be home before the bus drops them off. But just in case . . . the judge said . . . maybe . . . a neighbor could keep an eye on them, if it's later?"

"Yeah!" said TJ. "I could play with Luke again."

"Rhonda next door checked on them today," Velita explained quickly. "Maybe she'd do it again."

Ralph curled his lip. "That bimbo? Don't want her snooping in our house."

"No reason for her to. They could stay in her yard. Once I get home, I'd just pick them up and leave. That's all. I promise." Velita eyed him. "Just for that little bit, she'd probably do it free." Maybe, Velita thought, there was something nice she could do for Rhonda in return. Without him knowing.

Ralph glared at her, his lips curled, but then his shoulders drooped.

From the living room, the TV blared out *The Simpsons* theme song, and Ralph grabbed his half-empty plate and headed for the sofa.

Velita blew out a huge breath. She'd won. For now.

Chapter 5

As Jacob Franzen drove home, his hands clenched the steering wheel. What had he gotten himself into? When the summons had come, he'd wondered if it would be right for him, as a Christian, to participate. The Confession of Faith didn't mention serving on juries—it only frowned on suing others in the church. But swearing was forbidden. Believers were to affirm. He was prepared to refuse to swear, even if it raised a few eyebrows.

He'd seen a few scenes of trials on TV, a witness or two, lawyers arguing, people screaming at a guilty penalty. But this was the first time he'd been to a real one, and he was amazed how quiet and orderly it was and what a long time it took to select a panel.

When they had all been chosen, they'd been asked to raise their right hands, and he had too, not realizing it was the oath. The judge had asked, "Do you solemnly swear..." and all the others had chanted "I do" while his mouth was stupidly open. So now, had he sworn or not? He didn't even know.

Not so long ago, no Mennonites were involved in government; now some of the more educated were elected to city offices; one was actually a mayor of Kingsburg. But what good could *he* do—Jacob

Franzen, a simple farmer? He needed to be out in his fields, doing his own God-given work instead of meddling in strangers' lives.

At least there was still some daylight left. Buck Slayton, his new hired man, should be busy disking the farthest acres.

But as Jacob swerved into his driveway, he saw that Buck's car wasn't in the yard, and he slammed on the brakes so hard the tires spun a wheelie in the soft dirt. There sat the tractor beside the shed, its disc still attached. It was parked crookedly, not neatly in line like he always kept it, so he knew Buck must have used it earlier. How could the man be finished so soon?

Behind the house, his sons looked up from chopping weeds in the vegetable garden. He jumped out of the pickup and hurried to them. "When did Buck leave?" he asked.

"I passed him on my way home from school," said Sammy. "Right outside town. He was driving awfully fast."

Jacob figured the time. It took Sammy about twenty minutes to ride his bike from junior high—that made it about three twenty. "Strange that he'd leave so early." He glanced at the garden, then squeezed the boys' shoulders. "Good work, guys. When you finish, break up the clods around the carrots and radishes, and then you can quit. Everything okay? Becky in the house?"

"Sure." "Yeah," the boys said in duet, twelve-year-old Sammy's voice already lower in pitch than his younger brother Paul's.

"I'll go change clothes, and then if you need me, I'll be out on the north side," Jacob told them.

Inside the kitchen, his fourteen-year-old daughter was at the sink, slicing boiled potatoes, and he snitched a piece. "Hi, kiddo," he told her between bites. "Something smells good."

"Fresh apricot pie," she said. "Still warm."

"Mmm." He reached for the phone and punched in Buck's number. Although he let the phone ring ten times, there was no answer. *"Nah, heyat,"* he exploded in Low German. "What's going on with that man?"

After sprinting upstairs and changing into work clothes, he dashed back down, swung himself onto the tractor seat, and headed out to the orchard. When he reached the north section, he stopped short. Buck hadn't done more than a fourth of the disking. All Jacob could do was finish the work himself.

This section of his farm had been hit by the recent hail, and everywhere he looked, pink petals, leaves, and twigs littered the ground. The trees looked beat up; his mom would say *fe'tsuddat*—messy as uncombed hair—their branches sticking out every which way.

Most of the farmers in the area were thankful for the rains that had come in March, and he was too. There had been enough to irrigate his field of young saplings in the next section. The whole San Joaquin Valley had been praying for the drought to break, and God had answered. But did He *have* to include hail?

Besides, there'd be the nuisance of spraying the trees again, with all the government paperwork that went with it.

This jury duty sure had come at a bad time. The peaches needed thinning, and with the warm weather, they would ripen fast. A million things needed to be done before picking time.

He'd told that to the clerks at the very first roll call. He'd also spoken to the judge. But they'd all said if he had help on the farm, he had no excuse.

He'd thought, *Oh, well, how long will a trial take? Two, three days maybe?* He could probably spare that much time. No reason Buck couldn't handle things for a little while. Although the man farmed forty acres of table grapes five miles east, he'd agreed to help Jacob in the daytime during early tree-fruit season and tend his own place in the evenings.

Buck wasn't a Mennonite but had seemed reliable in spite of that shortcoming. Now Jacob wondered—had he been wrong about the man? He hoped Buck had a good excuse. With this trial lasting so much longer than Jacob had expected, Buck was needed even more.

When he finished disking, Jacob got a shovel from his shed and went to his south orchard, walking between the rows of peach trees and shoring up occasional breaks in the furrows. He examined a cluster of marble-sized fruit, pinching off the pock-marked ones.

The sun dipped lower between the branches, shining through new green leaves and the last few pink blossoms. Jacob breathed deeply, relishing the smell of clean, still-damp soil and fresh new undergrowth. The air was so clear after the rain that he could see the Sierra Nevadas in the east, their snowy peaks rising so high it was hard to tell where they ended and the clouds began. Far to the west, the coastal range looked like a charcoal drawing against the sky.

Jacob hadn't done much traveling, but from what he'd heard, he knew this had to be the best place in the world to live and raise kids. Not like the big cities with their sin and violence. No tornadoes and dust storms like in the Midwest. Just good soil, sunshine, and fresh air after the rains. Farms close enough to know the neighbors well, just far enough apart for privacy.

He'd always loved working on this farm, first as a little boy visiting his grandparents; later as a teenager helping his dad and brothers; and now, especially, since it was his own to cultivate and cherish. Most of his brothers had chosen more worldly vocations in the cities, but for him, it had always been the farm. Like his grandfather and father, he believed there was something holy about working with soil.

He still remembered the thrill of signing the contract for the land when it was deeded over to him. His grandfather's shaky scrawl, *Jacob J. Franzen*; his father's, *Jacob D.*, and finally his own, *Jacob L. Franzen*.

As a kid, he'd been embarrassed by his old-fashioned, biblical name. Why hadn't his parents called him Greg or Steve or maybe Mike? But when he had taken over the farm and had seen those three signatures, he'd realized his name was part of the legacy.

Yes, it was a good way of life. At least it had been when Sharon was healthy. During those years, when the trees were in bloom, he would stand in the middle of his orchard, so overcome with the beauty that he couldn't contain himself. He'd burst into song, lifting his arms to embrace God, his farm, all of mankind.

"*Vas kann es schoen'res geben, und was kann sel'ger sein . . .*" What could be better, holier?

He shook his head. It seemed like a long time since he'd felt that joy. Now, almost two years after Sharon's death, his first wild grief had eased into a numb, gray routine as though he were running on cruise control. He'd have given up long ago if the farm hadn't kept him going.

He took off his Massey-Ferguson cap and, with his sleeve, wiped the perspiration from his forehead. It sure was warm for early April.

"Daddy! Supper's ready!"

Jacob shaded his eyes and looked toward the two-story wooden house. It stood in the middle of the raked yard, square and modest, adorned only by bushes of red and white camellias and shaded by oaks planted by his great-grandfather. A swamp cooler perched on the roof, next to the TV antenna. A small porch reached out onto a patch of lawn, and he could see Becky at the open screen door, waving at him. The rosy glow of sunset shone through her pale hair, forming a halo.

His sweet, uncomplaining angel. She didn't have it easy, keeping house for her dad and brothers.

As Jacob neared the house, he smelled the spicy aroma of ham and fried potatoes, thought of the pie to follow, and his stomach growled. Becky was a good cook in spite of her youth. Sharon had trained her well.

Sharon. It seemed like part of him had died with her. People kept telling him it was time to get on with his life, to find a new wife. His children needed a mother.

Even Buck had kidded him about not having a woman. "You Mennonites don't know what you're missing," he'd said. "You ought to come out with me some night. I'd show you a real good time."

But Jacob had just smiled and shaken his head. He knew what kind of "good time" that would be. Buck might be a hardworking farmer, but he had the morals of a tomcat. The church taught that sex should be sacred, saved for marriage, preferably to someone of the faith. There were plenty of widows and single women in the local congregations. The trouble was, he couldn't picture any of them in his home. Or his bed.

He leaned against a tree and brushed some dirt from his shirt sleeve. The plaid cuffs were frayed, and he'd found a hole in his pocket. Sharon would have fixed them. Without her, everything was coming apart.

"Daddy?"

Jacob shook himself from his thoughts. "*Yah*, Becky, I'm coming."

Chapter 6

Jacob followed his daughter into the house, stopping in the screen porch to wash up in the stationary tub and scrub his fingernails with a brush.

The house seemed too quiet. He dried his hands on the roller towel and called to Becky in the kitchen. "Where are the boys?"

"Upstairs." She took a pan of *tvebocks* from the warming oven, tilting the fluffy, double-decker buns into a bread basket. "Sammy's science project is due tomorrow, and he hadn't even started on it. I'll go call them."

She went to the foot of the stairs and shouted, "Sammy! Paul! Come eat now. Daddy's inside."

The boys clattered down the steps, each trying to elbow into first place. They fell into their chairs, Sammy's foot hooked around Paul's ankle.

"*Nah*, boys," said Jacob. "Settle down."

Sammy, tow-headed and freckled, looked up with an innocent smile, but Jacob could see his younger brother gritting his teeth, wriggling to free his ankle.

"We're not doing nothin'," said Sammy. He let go suddenly, and Paul's knee shot up and bumped the table. The dishes danced and

Paul's glass of milk spilled, sloshing over the table and dripping onto the floor.

Becky ran for a towel. "Now look what you've done. I just washed the floor."

"Sorry," mumbled Paul, pinching Sammy on his thigh.

Jacob sighed. How would he ever raise these boys? He hated to punish them for every little bit of mischief. But they were as opposite and competitive as Jacob and Esau in the Bible.

The milk cleaned up, Jacob bowed his head and the children followed his example. "Father, we thank You for this food. Bless the hands that prepared it, and us in Thy service. Amen."

"Amen," echoed the children.

Sammy ate quickly, his eyes darting to the serving bowls as though ensuring second helpings. Paul, two years younger and darker in mood as well as looks, studied each forkful, checking for a hint of fat or stray bit of vegetable before offering it to his mouth.

Jacob couldn't help grinning and glanced at Becky. She seemed so much happier this year, now that she'd finished at the public junior high school and was attending Maranatha Academy. In the church-sponsored high school, she could take full part in all the activities, without worrying about the three Ds: drugs, drinking, and dancing. The tuition was high but worth every nickel.

He asked her, "Good day at school?"

"Uh-huh. In chapel, a quartet sang, and the pianist could really ripple—"

Jacob slammed one fist into his other hand. "That reminds me! I forgot the special male chorus practice tonight." He glanced at his watch. "Too late now."

He hated to miss. It was his one chance to spend the evening with friends without feeling guilty for leaving the kids. Especially his good friend, tenor Howard Neufeld, who worked at Trager's Farm Equipment and gave him good ideas for replacements. They'd been buds since high school days.

The annual concert would be soon, the combination of all MB male choruses in the valley, and people would come from all over the West Coast to hear them. Five Hundred Mennonite Men, some people called them, although it was nowhere near that many now. It was a thrill to harmonize his bass with all the other strong voices in those powerful songs. A couple of them in High German too. He was glad he remembered enough from his own classes at Maranatha to pronounce the words easily.

His parents often told stories from their childhood about the church services being held in High German. Now the only time he heard that formal language was in the good old hymns.

But Low German—*Plautdietsch*—that rich, earthy language was still great for everyday talk. Even his kids used some of the expressions. Jokes were twice as funny, losing their punch if translated. Some words had no equal in English. They came so naturally to him that he'd had to be careful at the courthouse, not to accidentally slip a few words in. "I'm sorry, Becky, you were saying—?"

"Just that the pianist at chapel was so good. And he didn't even use music. Wish I could play like that."

Jacob felt an ache of regret. But there'd been no other way. They'd had to give up Becky's piano lessons when Sharon was so sick. There'd been no time for practice, and all their money had gone into medical treatments.

He couldn't bring Becky's mother back to her, but if the crop wasn't a total loss, maybe she could go back to her music next fall.

He sighed. Better not make any promises yet. After that hail, he'd be lucky to scrape together next year's tuition.

After supper was over and they all stood up, Sammy glanced at Paul, then darted upstairs, his brother charging after, hanging on to Sam's shirttail. Jacob watched, shaking his head. Where did they get all that energy? He would have to give them more chores, tire them out a little. But then, they would use that as an excuse when their homework wasn't finished.

He went to the phone and tapped in Buck's number again. After six rings, he hung up.

As Becky lowered a stack of dishes into the frothy suds in the sink, she asked, "How was the trial?"

Jacob wished he could talk about it. About the lawyers, that *brumsch* Lester Payne, such a grouch, the big friendly black woman, the sensible, dark-haired nurse. The cute little blond who acted like a spooked kitten.

But he couldn't disobey the judge. "It was—interesting. Maybe I'll learn something."

Becky dried the last few dishes and wiped off the counter. From upstairs, thumps and scuffling sounds leaked through the ceiling transom.

Jacob looked up, then called out, "Guys, get on with your homework!"

The noise stopped, a few giggles filtered down, then, "Ooohkay," "Yes, Dad."

He shook his head. "Why must they always fight?"

Becky laughed. "Didn't you ever wrestle when you were a boy?"

"We were too tired from working all day." But he grinned sheepishly, thinking of the fun he and his brothers had had *tuzzling* all over the floor together.

He went to the hutch and glanced through the mail. Advertisements, bills, a catalog. A postcard from his older sister, Clara, in Pennsylvania.

Heinz and I will be coming to California in May, it read. *We'd like to stop by and see you.*

His heart filled with warmth. Clara had been more a mother than a sister, with Mama so busy with the five other children. Clara had combed his hair, bandaged his small hurts, read him Bible stories. She'd married late, into the Old Order Mennonites, and was too busy helping with her husband's dairy to travel much. It would be great to see her again. He wondered if they were coming by bus or train. Their church didn't permit owning cars, and they surely wouldn't take a plane.

He shuffled the mail back together. "Well, I'd better get back to work."

Outside, the rising moon was nearly full, and a few stars were out. A cricket chirped under the bushes near the back steps. The scent of jasmine drifted from the side of the house and mingled with the smell of rich, moist earth.

As he crossed the driveway toward the storage shed, he felt Midnight, the black cat, rubbing against his leg. He bent over and scratched her ears, stroked her sides. "Hey, *Mietzi* cat, you're getting fat. Looks like kittens one of these days."

He flipped on the yard light and examined the equipment. One of the cultivator points was broken, and several were worn. Looking through the boxes in the back of the shed for replacements, he found only one part. He'd asked Buck to pick some up, but the man must have forgotten.

While Jacob replaced the broken point, he thought again about the trial. Had the defendant really done all that his accuser claimed? How had the man gotten himself into a mess like this, and how had it all started?

He couldn't imagine that kind of life—his own upbringing had been so strict. Oh, sure, like most boys, he'd kicked against the restraints, but good habits had formed early. Going to church and Sunday school, learning Bible verses. Even though he'd sung the old hymns and choruses without thinking of their meanings, sometimes substituting silly words, they still echoed in his head at odd times. Strangely enough, they now made more sense. *"Take it to the Lord in prayer"; "Oh, yes, He cares"; "There's no other way than to trust and obey."*

As a youngster, he'd had a quick temper—ready to throw insults or punches—but he'd been fortunate: his Sunday school teachers and youth leaders hadn't given up on him. They'd set good examples of nonviolence. Without their encouragement and that of his family, might he have ended up like Duane Jackson, on trial for crimes, even for murder? Troubled, Jacob ran his fingers through his hair. What about his own children? How could he pass on the principles of nonviolence without turning his boys into sissies? With TV and VCRs, even cable, the world came right into the living room, and the "shalts" and "shalt nots" weren't so clear anymore. Where to draw the line—that was the big problem.

He remembered the judge's question about what he would do if someone threatened his children. Last year, a visiting minister had brought up a challenge: if one had to choose between an attacker and your loved one, who would you pick? The sinner, or the believer? It would be better, the man claimed, to give the unbeliever the chance to live, to get right with God, while the believer was ready to meet the Lord.

Jacob felt an ache in the pit of his stomach. With his wife gone, he was the only one responsible for his children. *God forgive me*, he thought. *I'll never be strong enough to follow* that *precept.*

He finished installing the new point and realized that it was getting late. Any other work would have to wait until tomorrow. He hung his tools back in place and went inside.

The kitchen was empty; Becky had finished cleaning up and had gone to her room. Jacob could barely make out the strains of Gaither music coming from upstairs, and he figured that meant she was hard at her own homework. Taking his farm account book and calculator from a drawer, he sat down at the kitchen table. The little calculator chittered out totals, and he muttered to himself.

"*Neh, obah*. In March, we spent more on labor than the whole last quarter. How can that be?"

The pruning—had he used that many workers? And the dormant spraying, that was also higher than usual.

Sharon had always kept the farm books and done all the paperwork. They'd been a team, trying to make a success of the farm.

Sharon. When Jacob shut his eyes, he could see her perched up on the tractor seat, her pale, shiny hair swirled into a knot on top of her head. At night, she'd brush it out until it fell in silky waves over her smooth shoulders and rounded arms, covering them like a blessing. When he'd lift the hair aside and whisper their own special nonsense into her ears, her pink cheeks would turn red, and she'd say, "Oh, you naughty boy!" But she would laugh softly, and then . . .

Jacob kneaded his forehead to ease the ache washing over his body, threatening to drown him. He'd give anything to have life back the way it was before cancer had eaten away their future.

Chapter 7

On Tuesday afternoon, Velita hurried up the courthouse ramp. This time she wore jeans, as Marsha Lewis had done the day before, and hoped her frilly blouse was all right. A long line waited at the metal detector in the lobby, and the clock showed five minutes till one.

She'd be late for sure. Was it true she'd end up in jail, like Lester Payne had said? Her heart raced. What about the kids? Suanne hadn't wanted to go to school this morning; she was getting awfully clingy. Without her mommy around, she'd cry her eyes out. What would Ralph do then?

The line ahead moved fast, but the metal studs in Velita's jeans set off a nasty buzz and the attendant had to slide the wand over her before letting her through.

Maybe she'd still make it on time. But only one elevator was running, with a crowd waiting there too. When the door slid open, it was already crowded, and only a few of those in line pushed their way in.

"A lot of guys are coming up from the county parking lot below," said a guy behind her. "I'm taking the stairs."

Others followed him, and Velita wondered if running up to the third floor would be faster. After waiting a bit, she decided to try, even took a first step toward the stairs, when the elevator door slid open again.

I've got to make it, she told herself. Ignoring the gripes of the people ahead, she sneaked past them and pushed her way inside. A few more people squeezed in after her.

Squashed between a fat man and someone's scratchy shopping bag, she tried to move, but there was nowhere to go. The air smelled of mixed perfumes and cheap cigars. She could hardly breathe.

The elevator took forever, and Velita wanted to scream. Why hadn't she gone up the stairs? Nothing was working for her today.

She'd gotten up early, finished her housework with time to spare, the house all neat, the laundry folded. Then, just as she was leaving, the phone had rung. Ralph, calling from work. He'd forgotten his lunch box and told her to bring it to the shop.

It wasn't in the kitchen; she'd have noticed it there. It took a while to find it in the garage, right on the seat of the Harley, and she just bet he'd left it there on purpose.

At the shop, Ralph made her wait while he checked the oil in the car. He'd said it was low and added a quart. "Treat 'em right, these old babies; they'll run forever. Not like them new computer crates, always got something wrong and you gotta take them clear apart to get at 'em."

Ralph fussed over his '78 Dodge more than his own kids, but this time, she knew he was doing it just to aggravate her. She dug her nails into her palms, forcing herself to stay calm until she couldn't hold back any longer. "Honey, I'm going to be late."

He laughed. "What's the big deal? Can't wait to see them pretty law-boys?"

A rock of worry settled in her stomach, but she kept her face cheerful. *If I say anything else, he just like him to dawdle even worse.*

Luckily, his foreman called. "Ralph? I need a lube job on Mrs. Peale's Toyota." Ralph had left her then, looking back, nodding, like he'd be watching her no matter where she was.

She'd driven away as fast as she dared, through yellow lights and just-turned-red ones, praying no cop saw her. But none of that did any good if this stupid elevator didn't move.

With a sudden jerk, the door opened, and she ran into the jury room. The bailiff stood by the door, taking count. Slipping into line, she tried to catch her breath without making any noise and pretended not to see Lester Payne's glare.

In the courtroom, the lawyers sat waiting, and Duane Jackson again scribbled on a note pad. The judge came in, called the court to order, and asked the prosecuting lawyer to make his opening statement.

James Pettigrew stood up and smiled at the jury, his teeth shining straight and even. "Good morning." He looked like Suanne's Ken doll, his suit fitting just right, his socks matching the little hankie in his breast pocket. "I would like to take you back to October 11, 1993, at 9:36 PM." His voice sounded like he was everybody's best friend.

Resting her chin on her hand, Velita stared at him, trying to keep her mind on the trial and follow all the big words. It seemed the undercover police had searched for drugs at a house in Booneville, California. She could just see it, the cops, their angry glares, their guns held out. Her jagged thumbnail scraped against her throat, and she reminded herself to file it down before Ralph noticed it.

"Two gunshots were fired from inside the house," the lawyer went on. "One bullet hit the finger of Sergeant Martin and the other lodged in Sergeant Newburg's leg."

More police had come, someone went around to the back door, and there'd been more shooting inside the house. The police had kicked the front door down and then found a dead body—was it one of the cops? Velita wasn't sure.

Duane Jackson whispered to his lawyer, and it looked like they were arguing.

The prosecutor talked on and on. "There'd been bad feelings between the defendant and the victim—"

"Objection," said the defense lawyer.

"Sustained," murmured the judge.

"Let me rephrase," said James Pettigrew. "We know that the defendant had a violent temper and had bought the gun specifically to kill—"

"Objection! Hearsay!"

"Sustained." The judge looked grouchy. "Mr. Pettigrew, please confine yourself to the facts."

"I'm sorry, Your Honor." Attorney Pettigrew turned back and talked slowly. "Ladies and gentlemen of the jury, the prosecution will show that Duane Jackson, in malice and with full intent to kill, did fatally wound Officer Robert MacDuff and did cause bodily injury to Officers William Martin and Frank Newburg. You can do no less than pronounce him guilty of murder in the first degree with special circumstances." He turned and went back to his table.

If the man murdered a cop, he'd think nothing of killing anyone else, thought Velita. *Especially people on the jury, if we say he is guilty.*

She swallowed hard to calm her nerves, wishing with all her heart that she was back in her house—even scrubbing the bathtub, wiping fingerprints off the walls. Anything would be better than being here. Maybe if she'd fake a heart attack, they'd let her off the jury. Wouldn't Ralph just love that! But someone was sure to find her out, and then she'd be in worse trouble.

Out of the corners of her eyes, she peeked at the other jurors. Some of them scribbled away in the notepads the bailiff had given them, and she wondered what she was supposed to be writing.

The judge called the defense lawyer, and Arnold Torrance stood up. "Duane Jackson is a peaceful, friendly man." He laid his hand on the guy's shoulder. "At 9:36 PM, October 11, 1993, he and his wife were relaxing and watching television when suddenly he heard pounding at his front door. He peeked out the window and saw two strange men on his porch." The lawyer walked toward the jury, looking from one face to another.

Arnold Torrance didn't smile. Velita wondered how he felt, if he thought it was a lost cause. Killing a cop? There'd be no excuse for that. Why did they even bother to have this trial?

"Yes, Mr. Jackson took out a gun," said Attorney Torrance. "He had purchased this gun for his own protection. There had been threats against him and against his family. Thinking the men were there for criminal purposes, he told them to leave. They became abusive. At no time"—he said each of those words hard—"did he realize the men were police officers."

Velita shivered, thinking back a year when policemen had come to her house. They'd shown their badges and shouted so loud she was sure the whole neighborhood heard it. Her nose had been bleeding, her clothes torn, and Ralph had turned all buddy-buddy with them, saying *she'd* gone nuts and attacked *him*. Suanne had screamed, and TJ had shouted, "Don't take my mommy to jail!"

The lawyer went on, and Velita tried to concentrate. Someone charged in through the back door, and Duane Jackson shot again. "In self-defense . . . no malice, no premeditation . . . an act of reflex—a young man of only twenty-two bravely protecting his young wife and himself."

That wasn't anything like what the other lawyer had said. Velita tried to picture it, to make sense of it.

Attorney Torrance talked for more than an hour. All that time, Duane Jackson sat quietly. Sometimes, he nodded, agreeing. Once, his eyes glanced over at the jurors, and when they reached hers, Velita was surprised to see a look of desperate pleading.

In spite of herself, she felt a stab of pity and wished she could tell him, "Look, it isn't my fault I'm here. I hope you have a fair trial."

Finally, the defense lawyer held out his palms in a begging position. "Ladies and gentlemen, my client was completely within his rights to protect his home. He sincerely regrets his role in Officer MacDuff's death. But Duane Jackson is not guilty of murder, and I will prove that fact in the days to come."

He sat down, and Duane Jackson nodded at him but didn't say anything.

The two stories spun around in Velita's head until she thought she'd go crazy. She'd never be able to keep them straight. Both lawyers had sounded honest. Which one should she believe? She looked at the judge, but his face didn't give anything away.

This was too much. It just wasn't fair that *she* had to help decide if Duane Jackson was guilty or innocent. If she was wrong—and as many mistakes as she made, this was sure to be another one—it might destroy the man's life. Bad enough she'd messed up her own.

The judge stroked his mustache and studied a sheet of paper in his hands. After a bit, he looked up and said, "The prosecution will please call its first witness."

The slick lawyer stood and said, "I call Mrs. Charlene Jackson to the stand."

Nothing happened. Everyone looked around, but nobody showed up. The bailiff went out into the hall and came back shaking his head.

The judge beckoned with two fingers, and both lawyers went to his bench. After a lot of whispering, the judge told the bailiff to take the jury out.

Back in the little jury room, Velita sat down at the table. If only she could ask the others what the lawyers had said, but that was against the rules. It didn't make sense to her: now they were all supposed to switch off everything they'd heard and blabber about stuff that didn't matter.

But that didn't seem to bother anyone else; they laughed and talked about their kids, the price of gas, the weather.

She remembered a few of their names now: Marsha and Jacob were the friendly ones, and the black woman who knitted was called Geneva. Laura was the one in a business suit who ran a furniture store. Eunice had a sack full of paperbacks, and Nellie's mouth was shaped like a quarter moon even when she wasn't smiling. Or were the names the other way around? Everyone was more dressed up today—and here she'd thought she'd fit in better wearing jeans! Would she ever get things right?

She wondered what they thought about her, these people who

came from perfect homes and always knew the right things to do. Or were some of them just pretending like her, hiding behind phony smiles and pretty clothes?

Jacob Franzen seemed strong and solid. Dependable. But you never could tell. She'd once thought the moon hung on Ralph, and look where that had gotten her. With him, the only thing she could depend on was a bad temper.

With a knitting needle, Geneva pointed toward the window. "See that tree outside? All those beautiful pink flowers? Reminds me of the Blossom Trail."

"I took the bus tour last March," said Eunice—or was it Nellie? "The fruit trees were gorgeous. Pink, white, red. When you get into the foothills, the wild flowers—poppies, lupine, just masses of color—"

"You don't need to take a bus," said Jacob. His blue eyes shone. "My place isn't on the official route, but come spring, any road in our area is a blossom trail."

Velita had never heard a man talking like that. Ralph had no use for flowers. He'd gotten mad when she'd used grocery money to buy two cuttings of rose bushes for the backyard.

All the stories she'd read, the movies she'd watched had some kind of happy ending. Seemed like there ought to be at least a little joy in her life, with all the hots Ralph had showed before. But her mama had said to put up with him; that was what marriage was like. For sure, Mama had gotten enough clouts herself, but she'd been big and feisty. She could give back as good as she got.

The door opened, and the bailiff walked in. "There are technicalities that need to be worked out," he said. "The jury is dismissed until the following Monday."

Everyone cheered, and one of the men raised his fists in a victor's salute.

Geneva grabbed Jacob's arm and joked, "Come on, sugar, let's go see those blossoms!" They all hurried out the door and pushed into the now-empty elevator.

Chapter 8

Outside, the courthouse lawn smelled freshly mowed. Squirrels shimmied up the trees. A group of old men sat playing cards at a picnic table. Men in suits hurried past, swinging briefcases, and a young couple dawdled arm in arm down the sidewalk, talking and laughing.

Velita wondered what it felt like to be carefree, to spend time just enjoying the spring weather. To go home to a happy place, to a husband who surprised her with a bunch of violets or some candy, like in the soap operas or magazine stories.

Maybe that was the only place it happened—in stories. Ralph and his friends joked about marriage, saying the only way to keep their wives in line was with a swat or a punch now and then. Last night, Ralph hadn't hit her, but what if she couldn't please him tonight?

She'd be home in plenty of time to fix a good dinner, and if the kids behaved well . . .

Dear God, don't let me mess up this time!

She walked down the courthouse steps with the others until she reached the sidewalk, then turned away toward the underpass leading into the downtown mall.

Marsha called, "Where's your car, Velita?"

Without stopping, Velita turned her head. "Underground," she called back.

"Why don't you park in the garage over there?" Marsha pointed to a high building in the opposite direction. "It's much safer."

Velita stopped short and a shiver ran up her back. "What do you mean, safer?"

Walking toward her, Marsha said, "I mean—we'd be all together. Don't worry, you'll be okay. Just stay with people . . . I've got an idea. Where do you live?" She dug in her purse and brought out a pen and paper.

Was it okay to tell her? Velita hesitated. Finally she said, "East Home Avenue."

"What's the number? I'll swing by Monday and pick you up. We can take turns driving."

What should she say? Ralph would never let her get that friendly with a stranger. Velita shook her head. "No. I mean—I can't—" She eyed Marsha, wishing she could say yes, then quickly added, "I gotta go," and rushed off.

"Think about it!" Marsha called after her.

Velita tucked her purse close, holding the railing of the escalator down to the underground parking lot. Ahead of her were older women with swollen ankles and big shopping bags, a man in a leather jacket, and three giggling teenage girls, their hair spiked up in unbelievable colors.

She felt a flash of envy for the girls' freedom and foolishness. At their age, she'd been a married woman tending a cranky kid and expecting another one. She wouldn't trade her two kids for the world, but if she'd had any sense, she sure would have waited.

Stepping off the escalator, Velita looked for her car. Was it in the E or F division? She didn't remember seeing that big heart scrawled on the cement pillar, saying "Sheila loves JoJo," and the gang markings next to them seemed different.

Those awful gangs and their fights! These days, even little kids got mixed up with them. What would she do if TJ started hanging around guys like that?

The three girls got into a car, the women turned the other way, and Velita was left alone with the man. She kept an eye on him in case he might try something.

Then he turned too, got into a little sports car, and drove off. She heard tires squealing and horns honking, echoing like in a big cave. The air smelled of oil and damp cement.

Two skateboarders wheeled and crashed down a car ramp, glanced at her, then jumped back on their boards and zipped away, their shouts floating back to her.

Just stay with people, Marsha had said. But now Velita was all alone. And when the car noises died down, the only sound she could hear was her own footsteps: *click, click, clickety click,* sharp and hollow as gunshots. Trying to muffle her steps, she walked tippy-toed; but then one of her shoes went crooked and her ankle twisted.

Soon as I get in the car, I'll lock the doors, she told herself. Limping, she searched all the way to the end of the F section but still couldn't see the old green Dodge.

She remembered parking near the escalator. It *had* to be here.

Could it be stolen? Velita's ears throbbed to the beat of her heart. If that was true, she'd just as well kill herself. Next to his Harley, that old car was Ralph's biggest treasure.

She heard voices and saw more people coming toward her from the other direction. Was there another entrance?

Oh, sure! Now she realized: late as it had been, the parking lot was so full she'd had to drive farther to find a slot. After coming up, she'd walked a ways in the open-air mall. She'd noticed how shabby the stores looked now that new shopping centers had sprung up north of town and wondered why she hadn't noticed that the day before. That had to be it—today she'd come up a different escalator.

Velita took a deep breath and hurried on, circling more pillars, finally getting her bearings. Pretty soon she'd see her car.

From around the corner, three teenage boys came toward her, moving like they were listening to some private music. Red bandannas swung from their baggy pants pockets. They pointed to her and said something she didn't catch.

She pretended not to notice. *They're just kids having fun.* But her gut feeling told her they were a gang. They were much bigger than she was, and she felt cold all over.

Then she spotted her car, five spaces away, its big green fenders flashy against blue Toyotas and silver Hyundais. She'd always been ashamed of it, the neighbors and Ralph's friends driving newer cars. Now she was so glad to see it she wouldn't care if it was covered with dents.

The boys moved closer and stopped by the car next to hers. They leaned against it, and one of them peeked into the side window. There was no way to reach the Dodge without passing them.

Her heart thumped. Her mouth went dry. Could she fool them if she went to a different car? She stopped by a nearby pickup and grabbed the door handle. If she was lucky, she'd be able to get in. But it was locked.

All she could do was stand there, pretending she was waiting for someone, hoping the boys would leave. Maybe the owner of the pickup would come, and she could beg for help.

No one came. The gang stayed right there, staring at her.

Her legs began shaking. She'd waited too long—they had to know she was stalling, that she was scared of them.

She eyed them through the windows, trying to think. Whatever the guys had in mind couldn't be any worse than what Ralph would do if she wasn't home soon.

Farther on, a couple got into their car and drove toward her. Velita waited until they were close; then with the thin safety of their company, hurried to her own car.

The boys still watched her, grinning, trading sly looks. One said something about a "foxy lady" and the others laughed. Their voices bounced off the cement pillars and curled around the cars.

Just a few more steps. *Oh God, let me make it*. She waved to the people driving up, but they stared at her and went on by.

The tallest boy broke away from the others and slid toward her, bowing like he was real polite. "Hey, lady, you got a, you know, like the time?"

She'd reached her car and was almost to the door. Why hadn't she thought to get her keys ready?

Not answering, she propped her purse on the window ledge, unsnapped it and walked her fingers through it. Compact, tissues, lipstick—all the time keeping the boys in the corner of her eye. Although they were big and acted tough, up close their faces looked maybe twelve, fourteen. Maybe she could talk her way out of this.

Another kid twirled a knife, then flashed out the blade. "Didn't you hear the man? What time is it?"

"I . . . don't have a watch," said Velita. She barely had breath to squeeze out the words.

"She don't have a watch," he repeated, mocking her soft voice.

"Well, let's just see about that," said the first boy. He swaggered over and picked up Velita's wrist between his thumb and forefinger. "Hey, lady, how come you're shaking?"

His touch burned her skin, and she jerked back but couldn't get loose. With her free hand, she fumbled to close her purse, but instead it slid out of her reach and fell to the cement. Her compact fell out and skittered under the car.

In a flash, the boy let go of her wrist and scooped up the purse.

"What you packin' in here? Oh man," he said, "check this out." He opened her wallet, grabbed the bills, and shook out the coins. A five, two ones, a little loose change. She'd saved it carefully, hidden it from Ralph, to buy material for spring blouses for Suanne and herself. She'd brought it along, thinking maybe there'd be time to pop in at Wal-Mart and look through their table of fabric ends. If only she'd left the money at home!

The kid glared at her. "There's gotta be more than that." He tossed the car keys to another kid and pulled out her driver's license. "Okay lady, where's the credit cards?"

Velita shook her head. "Don't have any." Her throat felt raspy dry.

"You lie! Everybody's got credit cards."

"Bet she's got them in her pockets," said the kid with the knife.

He reached for her, but Velita jerked away. "Nothing in my pockets." She tugged them out, empty. "See?"

The tall one shook out the purse, grabbing her lipstick before it fell. Tossing the purse to his friend, he went to the closest pillar, and red-smeared a big X with a circle around it. After a few more scribbles, the lipstick broke. Spitting cusswords, he threw the tube down.

"Come on, you guys!" Velita tried to sound brave, but her voice cracked. "You've got my money. Now give me my keys. Or else—"

"Or what, momma?" The kid with the knife slashed out the lining of the purse, shook out a dime and a stick of gum, then threw the purse down. "You gonna call the cops on us?" He had a scar across his top lip, and Velita could bet he'd been in plenty of fights.

"There ain't no cops down here. No, ma'am," said the other guy. "This here's *our* territory."

"My husband's going to meet me here," Velita lied. "And he's meaner than any old cop." At least that part was true. She needed to get home, and quick.

The gang clowned around, mouthing off, and one kid pretended to shiver. "Aw, man, like we're so scared!"

Velita's legs felt wobbly, and she leaned against the car for support. "C'mon," she begged. "Let me go, okay?" If she could just get her keys back, she would jump in, lock the door, and be home in twenty minutes.

The scarred boy whacked her shoulder with the heel of his hand, pushing her back against the concrete wall. "Lady, you ain't goin' nowhere."

The look in his eyes told her that he wasn't fooling, and she felt sick to her stomach. By tomorrow, she would be just another headline in the newspaper: Unidentified Body Found in the Underground Garage.

Then, out of the corner of her eye, Velita saw some more people come down the escalator and head toward them. Hope flooded through her. *Please, please, come a little closer—close enough so you can see what's happening . . .*

"Don't worry about them dudes," said the tall one. "They won't bother us none."

"Naw," said the guy with the knife. "They'll just think you're one of us."

The others hooted with laughter, and Velita realized that even if she screamed, she wouldn't be heard over all their racket.

Still in the distance, the people got into their cars and drove toward her. She wanted to flag them down, but the tall kid held her against the wall, hiding her with his body. The cars passed, revving up faster.

The boy with the keys unlocked her car door, slid into the driver's seat and fooled with the dashboard knobs. "Man, this heap is old! Does it run?"

"It better," said the tall kid. "Baby doll's got to drive it for us. We wouldn't want to break the law or nothing." They all laughed, their voices echoing.

In the distance, Velita saw a man stride purposefully toward them. Something about him was familiar, but she was too scared to figure out what it was. Trying to keep her voice from shaking, she lied, "That's my husband. He's got a gun. He'll make spaghetti out of you."

The boys all turned to look at the man, and the tall kid let go of her. In her panic, she made a desperate move. "Honey!" she called out, waving both arms. "Over here!"

The boys looked at each other, then back at the man. He was walking fast, looking toward them, and scowling.

The leader tossed his head. "Shoot, he don't scare us." The one with the knife crouched behind the car, testing the blade with his thumb, watching the man.

Velita leaned over to pick up her bag. Just then, the boy in the car swung the door open. The handle cracked against her forehead, and lights flashed before her eyes. She grabbed for support but felt the car door slide away from her. *Oh please, God, if You care at all about me, save me! My kids—*

It was no use. Her legs folded. She crumpled to the ground, her mind sucked into a whirling black tunnel.

Chapter 9

Velita opened her eyes just a slit. Everything looked gray and foggy. She reached out. Her fingers brushed over a cold, rough surface. Where was she? What was that big black circle beside her head?

"Ralph?" Her voice came out in a croak. She heard rustling, murmuring.

"She's coming to."

"Are you all right?"

"Should we elevate her head or her feet?"

"Better not move her; wait till the EMT comes."

She squeezed her eyes tight shut, then opened them again and looked around. The gray turned into cement. Nothing made sense. Why was she on the floor?

A deep voice said, "The paramedics are coming."

"What's going on?" asked Velita. She tried to sit up, but moving made her head ache. Someone kept fanning her, and past that, faces blurred in and out of her sight.

"Remember me?" It was that low voice again. "Jacob Franzen. You know, from the jury? You've had a little accident."

She blinked several times, and then she could see. The big black circle turned into a tire; that was her car beside her. All around, people leaned over her, staring into her face.

With a jolt, it all came back, and cold fear shot through her. *The parking garage.* "Those guys—where—" Her pulse raced like mad, and she craned her neck to see past the people.

"It's all right," said Jacob. "They ran off when I got here. How do you feel?"

"Weird. My head . . ." Memory trickled back, and she scrabbled her fingers around the floor. "Where's my purse?"

"Right here," said a woman's voice. "I think I found everything."

"There's some aspirin . . ."

"I don't see any," said a woman's voice. "Is it in a bottle?"

"A teeny box. Probably fell out. They got into my stuff . . ." The memory made Velita want to throw up.

"Maybe you shouldn't take any just yet. You never know . . ."

The wail of a siren split the air, then stopped with a squawk nearby.

Strange men burst through the crowd, grabbing her, poking at her. Before she could stop them, they pushed down the neck of her blouse and stuck something cold against her chest. She tried to shove it away, but then saw it was a doctor's stethoscope.

What was going on? She tried to talk, but a sharp voice told her to be quiet. Someone whipped a blood pressure cuff around her arm.

Squeeze-squeeze-squeeze, pause. Behind her head someone murmured, "Respiration normal. BP 160 over 90. Pulse rapid, 110. Pupils equal and reactive to light."

Velita tried moving her head a little. This time the pain wasn't so bad, but she was awfully thirsty.

A stretcher slid next to her. Strong arms grasped her and pulled her onto it, and it zoomed up until she was staring into the face of a bearded man. He pulled straps across her, but Velita batted them away before he could tighten them.

"Hey, wait a minute!" She cleared her throat. "What are you doing?"

"Taking you to Emergency. You've got to be checked for concussion."

"Emergency? The hospital? No way, I'm fine!" She sat up, and the people seemed to spin around her.

The other man piled the equipment into a black box, shoved it into the ambulance, then heaved himself into the driver's seat. He started talking into a receiver.

Jacob Franzen came closer. "It'll be okay," he said. "I'll follow in my pickup and meet you there."

Velita frowned and shook her head, and the movement made it throb. If only she could think . . . "You don't understand! I've got to go home."

The paramedic asked Jacob, "Are you the husband?"

"No. Just . . . a friend."

"She needs medical treatment." Again, he pulled the straps across Velita, but she ducked under them, rolled off the stretcher, and staggered back.

"Who called you, anyway?" The cement walls began to sway, and she reached out her hand for balance.

She felt hands grasp her arms, steadying her. A voice whispered in her ear, a deep, soothing tone. "You really ought to see a doctor." Jacob Franzen again.

She tried to move away, but dizziness washed over her. Was she going to pass out again? Closing her eyes, she leaned against him. It felt so peaceful. Just for a minute, she told herself. Just until she could pull herself together.

The ambulance driver got back out and stood with his hands on his hips. "Okay, lady, what's it going to be? You coming or what?"

"No!" Velita backed closer to Jacob and felt his hands tighten around her arms. "I told you. I'm not going to any hospital." She turned to him. "Make them understand!"

"You're sure?" Jacob cleared his throat and looked into her eyes. She stared back at him, her lips tight.

"Sorry," he told the men. "Guess you guys came out for nothing. I'll see she gets home."

Some of the crowd drifted away, glancing back and muttering. The driver went back to the ambulance and made a call. When he came back, he held out a clipboard. "Sign this paper."

Velita glared at him. "I'm not signing *nothing*."

The driver threw his hands up. "Lady, I don't know what your problem is. Either you sign the release, or you come with us. One or the other. It's the law."

Velita squinted at the paper. The words blurred into each other.

Jacob read over her shoulder. "Against medical advice . . . I take full responsibility . . ."

"That's so she can't sue us if she keels over on the way home."

Jacob nodded and handed Velita a pen. "Guess you'll have to. It's all right; it's just to make sure you don't blame them if you have more problems."

Can I trust this man? She studied the paper, trying to make sense of the words. If this was the only way she could get home . . .

The ambulance man crossed his arms against his chest. "Well?"

Finally, Velita scrawled her name at the bottom and pushed the clipboard back at the man.

The paramedics loaded the stretcher back into the ambulance. "Be sure to go see your doctor," said the one with the beard. "And you need to report the attack to the police."

"Sure." *Anything to get rid of them.* Velita rummaged in her purse. Where were the car keys? Did those kids take them? Her heart thumped. The house key was on the ring. Ralph would have a royal fit if they got that.

Maybe they'd fallen under the car. She bent down to look, and blood roared to her head.

Jacob grabbed her shoulders again. "Looking for your keys?" He pointed. "In the ignition."

Velita got into the car and rested her head against the back of the seat. Her blouse was a mess. She straightened it and ran a hand through her hair. She must look awful, but there was nothing she could do about it.

The ambulance drove away, and the last few people left. But Jacob still stood beside the car, watching her. "How's your head?"

"Okay." She rubbed her temples. Even that teeny movement hurt.

"Better let me drive you home." He sounded worried.

If only she could. As long as she got home before Ralph, he'd never know. "What time is it?"

"Five seventeen."

That late? Panic ran all the way to her fingertips. Ralph would be waiting. If she showed up with another man, he'd blow sky high. She closed her eyes. "Thanks for your help." Her voice seemed to come from far away, from another person. "I just need to sit here a minute. I'll be fine."

Jacob frowned, his jaw flexing. "You can't drive like that."

Velita took a deep breath and huffed it out. What would it take to get rid of this man? He'd probably saved her life; she couldn't hurt his feelings. "No, really, you don't need to stick around. I'm okay now. Honest. I'll see you at the courthouse Monday." She smiled, gritting her teeth against the pain in her head.

She started the motor, and Jacob shut the door for her. Backing up, the gears snarled, and she barely missed the van in the opposite space. She slammed on the brakes, and the car choked to a stop.

Jacob came and opened her door again. "Look," he said. "We both know you're in no shape to drive. I don't know how to talk you out of it. But please, first do me one favor. Have a cup of coffee to settle your nerves. You owe it to yourself."

She was so thirsty. Hot coffee sounded awfully good, but she didn't dare take the time. She shook her head and opened her mouth to object.

Jacob wagged his finger in her face. His eyes were sober, and his jaws tight. "I mean it. You'll either kill yourself or half of Springton if you try driving now. There's a coffee shop right on the corner, and it'll only take a few minutes. Move over. I'll drive your car there, and we'll come back for my pickup."

❖ ❖ ❖

Velita leaned back into the corner booth of the café, staring at a menu. This couldn't be happening to her. She shouldn't be here. It was all her fault—she never should have left the house. Why hadn't she listened to Ralph and thrown away the jury summons?

But she couldn't do that. If her mama had taught her anything, it was to tell the truth. She even felt guilty for lying to the gang members.

Jacob Franzen leaned toward her, his strong, tanned arms resting on the table. "Take it easy. Believe me, this will help."

She tried to relax. The mess she was in, what difference would a few more minutes make?

Then she had an awful thought. What if one of Ralph's friends saw her here? She eased her head around and glanced through the room. No one looked at her, and she didn't recognize any faces.

Maybe she should call home. But what could she say? *"Hi, honey, I'll be a little late, I'm having coffee with this nice man."*

Suddenly her stomach lurched. Frantically she looked around for the ladies' room. "Be right back," she gasped, and hurried between the counter seats and the booths, dodging the waitresses. She barely made it into the restroom stall and leaned over the toilet before it all exploded.

Shakily, Velita went to the sink, washed her face, and cupped her hands under the faucet water to rinse out her mouth. The reflection in the mirror couldn't be her; it looked so awful. She felt around for her purse, then realized it was back in the booth with Jacob Franzen. All she could do was rake her fingers through her hair, which didn't help much. Gulping huge breaths, she wondered how she could face that man now.

Finally, weak and drained, she forced herself to go back. On the way to the booth, she passed the exit and stopped. Should she just walk out and head for her car? Trouble was, Jacob also had her keys.

She turned back and saw him watching her, smiling, with two cups and a plate of doughnuts on the table in front of him. She slipped back into the booth and took a sip of coffee. The hot, bitter liquid warmed her, and a few more swallows jolted her back to life.

"Better?" asked Jacob.

She couldn't meet his eyes. "I feel like such a fool."

"It's not your fault."

She looked up, puzzled. *Why is he being so nice to me? What does he want from me?* But his blue eyes were clear and honest, and his voice was gentle. He didn't seem anything like Ralph and his cocky friends.

Jacob started on his second doughnut. He motioned toward the plate with his head. "Try them. They'll give you energy."

She picked one up, thankful that her hands were steadier now. Settling back into the corner, she nibbled at the sugary edges, surprised to find she was hungry. She finished two doughnuts and a second cup of coffee, and told him, "Thanks. I guess I did need that."

Jacob shook his head. "I still don't feel right about you driving. Come on, I'll take you home. Maybe your husband can bring me back to pick up my vehicle."

Velita sat up straight. "No!" *He can't be serious. Ralph would—* "I'm fine now. You've got to believe me. I'll lock the car doors and go right straight home." Then she remembered. "The police. I should tell them—"

He pointed to the pay phone by the entrance. "I called them while you were in the restroom. Told them you'd make a full report tomorrow."

She took a deep breath. This man thought of everything!

Back in the underground parking lot, Velita said, "Thanks. For . . . everything. You've been awfully kind."

Jacob shrugged. "Just lucky I was there in time. Be careful now, okay?"

"Don't worry. See you Monday." Shifting the gears carefully, Velita drove out slowly. She'd show Jacob Franzen she could manage on her own.

He followed in his pickup, waving to her, and she waved back before turning onto the street. Now all she had to do was get home safely.

After several blocks, she stopped at a traffic light and glanced in the rearview mirror. Behind her was a gray sedan; behind that, Jacob's brown and tan pickup.

She stared, puzzled. Why was he still following her? Had she forgotten something? But he wasn't signaling or honking . . .

Maybe he lived around here too. No, that couldn't be right; he was a farmer. Near Fairdale, he'd said. Fairdale was twenty-five miles in the opposite direction.

She didn't see the light turn green, and several cars honked at her. She shifted gears too quickly, and the car lurched. *Darn it! Now the guy's going to get all shook up again.* She looked back and saw he was still following. Swerving into the next lane, she overcorrected and ignored the angry one-fingered salute from the man in the car behind.

At the next intersection, she zipped through on a yellow light and Jacob stayed back, caught by the red. Speeding up, she turned at a side road and lost him. But two blocks later she saw again, far behind, that brown and tan pickup.

Then it sank in. *He's going to follow me all the way home. All the way to Ralph.*

Chapter 10

Right from the start, Velita's mama had said Ralph Stanford was trouble. Deep in her heart, Velita had known it too. But what kid ever listened when she was crazy in love?

Her first sight of him was seared into her memory. It had been one of those rainy November days in southern Oklahoma, when the creek rose over the muddy back road a mile from her family's two-room shack, and the bullfrogs bellowed from the neighbor's reservoir.

The school bus had been stuck up to its axles again. The driver had let the kids out, and Velita had slogged through ankle-deep muck and weeds, reaching Chockamo High wet and dirty just in time for an unexpected assembly.

Assemblies were always noisy, all the kids trying to get the best seats. But suddenly the room went quiet, and Velita turned to see what had happened.

Her older brother, Orrin, and his little gang of rowdies had come in, crowding into the back row with the other seniors. Swaggering in with them, metal taps on his boots clicking, was a new guy in tight, faded jeans and a mocking grin that dared any teacher to tell him what to do. His eyes flashed darkly, and he tossed back the straight black hair falling over his forehead.

A shiver of—what? Thrill, excitement, fear?—went through her chest, choking off her breath. She jerked her eyes away. But the feeling didn't leave. She forgot all about her muddy clothes, and the assembly program—announcements for new dress codes—went right over her head.

She didn't fool around with the guys at school—they'd laughed at her feed-sack dresses and rundown shoes too many times. But this new guy seemed different, with a kind of sizzle about him.

The other girls fell all over themselves, trying to attract Ralph Stanford's attention. Some of the popular girls knew him from before, and whispers said he'd scored high with them.

Velita knew she didn't have a chance, no more than with a movie star. She was barely fifteen, a scrawny little sophomore, so why would he notice her?

But after school, Ralph rode up to the entrance on a beat-up Harley. In spite of the mud stains still on her skirt, Velita joined the circle of admirers gathered on the school yard.

All the other girls squealed, "Oooh!" and begged for rides. Velita remembered Orrin drooling over pictures in borrowed motorcycle magazines and she thought, *Man! Is that a Shovelhead?*

She must have said it out loud, because Ralph turned and gave her a long look. His eyes went all the way from her straggly blond hair straight down her dirty dress to her ragged, muddy sneakers. It was like he could see right through her clothes. Her body tingled. But he didn't laugh.

Finally he said, "You're Orrin's kid sister." He jerked his head toward the Harley. "Hop on."

Velita felt the jealous glares of the other girls, heard their whispers. But it didn't matter. She moved like a fish on a hook to her destiny.

After that, rain or shine, she never rode the bus again. She, Ralph, and the Harley, they were all of one piece. Instead of going home after school and doing her chores, helping her mama with the littler kids, she stayed in town and watched Ralph adjust the steering or fiddle with the carburetor. In the vacant lot behind the general store where his mom, LaDonna, worked as a clerk, Velita handed him wrenches and sneaked him beer out of the cooler when LaDonna wasn't looking.

When he was satisfied with his work, he'd take her home, her arms tight around his waist, her body pressed into his back. Their black and blond hair whipped together in the wind.

Those days, her brain turned to mush. She forgot about studying, and her grades zoomed down. Mama yelled at her, and her stepdad slapped her around, but she paid no mind. In class, all she could do was daydream about Ralph and draw hearts around his name in her copybook.

The other kids whispered, but nobody laughed out loud. She wouldn't have cared if they had. His kisses—they made her melt like lard in a fry pan. And when he touched her . . . her muscles turned to wet string, and all she could do was whisper, "Oh, Ralph baby."

She was still fifteen when her stepdaddy learned she was pregnant, and he had hauled Ralph away from his buddies, out of the middle of a late-night movie. He had woken an old preacher out of his sleep and made him say the marriage vows as she and Ralph stood there, she shaky, Ralph fuming.

Now, nine years later, with two babies, she was stuck thousands of miles away from Chockamo and her family. Tied to a man whose brain was in his britches, who messed around with anything in a skirt, and who settled all his problems with his fists and a six-pack of beer.

❖ ❖ ❖

Turning onto her street, Velita shook so badly she could hardly steer the car. What would Ralph do when he saw Jacob? He'd always been jealous—couldn't stand it if she so much as smiled at a grocery clerk or said "hi" to the mailman. He said it was because he loved her so much, but sometimes she wondered if there was something wrong with him. She'd never cheated on him—wouldn't dare flirt since a guy had winked at her at a party and gotten punched for his efforts.

Now, for sure, Ralph would think she'd been up to something. How would she explain Jacob Franzen being here? How could Jacob do this to her?

She motioned frantically to the man, *Go on by!* But as she turned into her driveway, there came the pickup, right at the curb.

Velita sat frozen, her hands still gripping the steering wheel. The front door of the house opened, and Ralph stood in the doorway, his legs splayed, his arms crossed, his hair damp and slicked down from his shower.

After that, everything seemed to happen in slow motion, her ears ringing, her heart thumping. The TV flickering through the lace curtains, sounds of "dah di di dah di di dah-ah-ah" of a *Star Trek* rerun. The curtains parting; Suanne peeking through the window. Behind the house, the tops of the ash trees glowed blood red from the setting sun. Velita forced herself to open her car door and slide out but couldn't make herself move toward the house.

TJ wiggled out from behind Ralph, shouting "Where you been, Mom? We're starving!"

Suanne came running to her, but stopped and stared at the strange pickup.

Then Jacob stepped out, and Velita's legs almost gave way. Jacob smiled as though everything was normal and said, "For a while there, I didn't think you'd get home in one piece."

"Who's he?" asked Suanne. She hopped from foot to foot, her blond ponytail bobbing.

"A man from the trial," said Velita, slamming her car door and hugging Suanne. "Mr . . . uh . . . Mr . . . what was it again?" *Play it down, make it look like he's a stranger.*

But she knew it wouldn't do any good. She waited by the car, holding Suanne tight.

"Jacob Franzen." Jacob walked toward Ralph. "Just making sure she got home okay. She's had quite an ordeal." He stuck out his hand. "Pleased to meet you—"

"Well, Mr. Friendly." Ralph brushed past him, ignoring the hand. His lips twisted, his eyes blazing into Velita's, he told Jacob, "Now that you brought my wife home safely, you can just go find somebody else to protect. I think I can take care of my own family."

Jacob pulled back his hand and shoved it into his pocket, his face turning red. His eyebrows shot to his forehead, and he looked from Ralph to Velita and back again. "Sorry," he said. "I was afraid she'd have an accident."

Velita shrank against the car. She wanted to tell Jacob to leave, but she didn't dare talk to him. *Oh, God, don't let Ralph start now. Not here, not now.*

Jacob cleared his throat. "Well, I guess I'd better be going."

"Yeah, you do just that." Ralph put his arm around Velita a little too tight and walked her toward the house. "Tell your boyfriend bye-bye, Vel." His voice was oily smooth.

Velita's face burned. *What must Jacob think? What can I say that won't make it worse?* "Ralph, he only—" but Ralph shoved her through the door and closed it carefully behind them.

"I knew it." The fake voice turned harsh. "You thought you'd have yourself a little fun on the side. Didn't you? Huh? Didn't you?" He punctuated his words with pushes at her shoulder, and her purse slid to the floor.

"No, I—" She twisted away and took Ralph's backhand on the side of her head.

"Don't lie to me," he shouted. "I saw the way he looked at you!"

Suanne scooted down the hall to the bedroom, but TJ crouched behind the sofa, his eyes wide.

"Go with Suanne," Velita whispered. But he didn't move, and she didn't have the strength to get after him. Through the window, she saw the pickup was gone, and felt relieved. At least Jacob wouldn't see or hear anything. "It's not what you think," she said to Ralph. "I've been—"

"Yeah? Where've you been? Not in the courtroom all this time. Look at your hair! You been holed up in a motel? Think I'm just a dumb mechanic, that I can't figure things out?" He backed her against the wall, his heavy arm clamped across her chest like a vise. She gasped for air.

"The parking lot—"

"Golly gee!" Ralph's voice was a mocking falsetto. "My wife, making out in the parking lot with Mr. Dream Boy." He pulled her away from the wall and gave her a hard shove. She flew against the coffee table, scraping her shin, and landed on the sofa. Magazines and books slid from the table onto the floor, and a beer can tipped over, leaking into the carpet.

She scrambled up and backed behind the sofa. How could she convince him? "No, Ralph baby, I didn't do anything! There were these kids, a gang, they got my purse."

"Sure. So how'd your purse get here on the floor?"

"That man, the one who followed me. He chased them away." A commercial blared out from the television and Ralph turned it down.

"'Spect me to believe that? You're even dumber than I thought." He started toward her again, and she moved aside, nearly tripping over TJ. The boy scrambled to his feet and ran down the hall.

"It's true!" She picked up her purse and opened it. "See—they ripped the lining. With a knife. Got my money. Knocked me down—"

"Come on!"

"The ambulance driver said I should tell the police." She said it fast, to get it all out before the next clout.

Ralph's arms dropped and his mouth went slack. "Ambulance? Police?"

Velita waved her hands, palms out. "Somebody called them. It was a mistake. But the guy said to report it. It's all in his record, you can check it out. I had to sign something—"

"You signed something? What?"

"It was—a release, I think. They said I had go to the hospital if I didn't sign."

Ralph stared at her, running his hands through his hair. "That better be all it is. And you leave the police outta this. It's none of their business." He kicked at a book on the floor. "Hurry up and get dinner." After turning the sound back up on the TV, he flopped onto the sofa.

She watched him a bit, relieved that he'd backed off but feeling resentment boil up inside her. *If he'd been the one mugged, I would have made over him, babied him. He doesn't care what I've gone through. He says he loves me. That's supposed to be love?*

But she knew better than to let the bitterness show. She went into the kitchen and fried up some frozen hamburger and opened a can of beans, the quickest meal she could think of right now. Her stomach revolted at the smell, but she forced herself to stay at the stove. It'd be crazy to get Ralph worked up again.

Suanne came from the bedroom, dragged the step chair to the counter, and climbed up, squeezing in close. "You were awful late. I thought you'd run away."

Run away? If only she could. Velita gave Suanne a quick hug. "Not without you, sweetie." Little as she was, even her daughter could see this wasn't a good way to live.

Some day. Some day . . .

Suanne swiped a bean out of the can. Her eyes were teary, her chin crumpled. "I hate Daddy."

If the kids turn against him, he'll blame me. Maybe start hitting them too. Can't let that happen. Velita glanced at the door. Ralph was heavy into his TV program. "Don't say that. Sometimes he, um, just can't help it. We have to be careful not to make him mad."

She got tomatoes and cucumbers from the refrigerator and started a salad, the kind he liked. Back home, her mama always said that was the way to settle a man down. Funny, though, the neighbors who'd taken Velita to Sunday school didn't seem to work that hard at it. They'd smiled and laughed a lot. One time, she'd seen the man angry about something he'd heard on the news, and after hitting his fists together, he'd gotten real quiet and gone out into the yard and chopped wood.

What made them different? Her Sunday school teacher had said God was love, but if He cared about people, why did He let her get so messed up? He was supposed to know everything—didn't He know how hard life was for her?

Suanne ate another bean. "We got to play in the sprinklers today. But TJ pushed Luke Avery down hard. Mrs. Avery yelled at him." She looked up at Velita, her eyes squinched. "What's that bump? Did Daddy do that?"

Velita pushed her bangs aside and felt her forehead. "I hit it on the car door."

TJ came in, shoved Suanne off the step chair, and stood on it himself, ignoring her wail when she landed on her bottom. "When we gonna eat?" he asked.

Velita felt a rock settle into her stomach. He was starting to act just like his dad. "In a minute." She took his arm and pulled him off the chair. "Tell your sister you're sorry, then go wash up."

"Sorry," he mumbled, made a face at Suanne, and darted off.

"TJ!" she called after him, but he didn't answer. How was she ever going to raise her kids right with all this hitting going on? She'd have to talk to TJ when Ralph wasn't around. But then he'd tell his daddy she was picking on him, and that would start another go around. No matter what she did, it would all turn out wrong.

She set the table, then told Ralph, "Supper's ready." Maybe after eating, he would be in a better mood, ask about how she felt.

"Bring it to me here," he growled.

Her heart aching, Velita filled his plate with food and set it on the coffee table in front of him. He grabbed it, eyes still on the screen, and dug in his fork.

When she started back into the kitchen, he yelled after her, "Don't think I'm finished with you yet!"

She blinked away the sudden prick of tears. Was this all there was to marriage for the rest of her life? For now, all she could do was try to keep him satisfied, keep him from getting too rough in bed. Later, much later, when he was asleep, she could let go.

Chapter 11

Jacob drove home slowly, his thoughts in a turmoil. As if the trial wasn't enough, now he was mixed up in a stranger's problems. A married woman, yet.

After court had adjourned, he'd planned to go straight home. But then he'd remembered Becky's birthday coming up and instead stopped at a crafts shop at the mall—for only a few minutes. He hadn't seen anything just right for her.

A little sooner, and he would have been gone before Velita had come to her car. A little later—who knows what those punks might have done?

Maybe it wasn't by chance. Maybe he'd been *sent* to help her. Like the Good Samaritan in the Bible.

He sighed. Trouble was, she hadn't *wanted* to be helped. Surely the Good Samaritan hadn't dealt with so much resistance.

The most puzzling aspect was that husband of hers. One devil look from the man's eyes, and Jacob had known he was in the wrong place.

He massaged his forehead. *Lord, what did You get me into?*

A blast from the horn of the car behind jolted him, and he swerved back into his lane. *Pauss opp*, his dad often said. *Watch out.* Especially when dealing with the world.

He'd *better* watch out. Not only was he way out of his league; now he was driving as crazy as Velita had.

As Jacob turned off the freeway and headed toward Fairdale, he studied the peach trees on both sides of the county road. Already, they were starting to set their fruit. His own Queencrests needed thinning, and he'd told Buck to hire a crew for next week. Lord willing, the trial would be over by then, and he'd be around to check on things and make sure Buck got the work done.

He switched on the dash radio. The news had just finished, and a talk show introduced a psychologist. "Improve your love life," she said.

Jacob snorted. What love life? He flipped through the stations, found only rock music and medicine salesmen, and snapped the radio off.

He wished his thoughts would shut off that easily. They kept going back to that underground parking lot. The anger he'd felt at those punks. Velita's trembling body against his, the scent of her hair . . .

It had been an impulse, steadying her. He'd thought she might collapse again. She was so small and frail looking, more like a little girl than a grown woman. He'd been shocked by the sudden stir of response in his body.

Now he gripped the steering wheel until his knuckles turned white. "Control yourself, Franzen," he said aloud. "She's not for you." Not only was it wrong to feel that way about a married woman, but with a husband like that, it was downright stupid.

By the time he drove into his yard, the sun had set. The house was quiet, and he knew the kids had already been picked up for a

Maranatha High baseball game. He'd called Becky from the coffee shop to tell her he'd be late, and she'd left food on the warming tray.

Gathering up the day's mail from the sideboard, he sat down with his plate at the kitchen table, flipping through the advertisements and Reader's Digest contest forms.

There was an envelope from Trager's Farm Equipment. A bill for a dozen cultivator points: sixty dollars, with Buck's signature.

So Buck *had* picked some up. Then where were they?

Jacob finished eating, put his dishes into the sink, and ran water into them. Through the kitchen window, he could see his equipment by the shed, lined up next to his Toyota Camry, exactly the way he'd left it last night. As though not a single piece had been used. Hadn't Buck showed up at all today?

Jacob reached for the phone.

This time Buck answered. He said he'd wrenched his back and couldn't work for a couple of days. "Prob'ly be okay by Sunday. Would've called but figured you weren't home anyway."

Jacob scratched his head and stared at the receiver. "You know I don't work Sundays."

Buck didn't answer, and Jacob sighed. "*Yah*, well, hope it's better by Monday. Work's piling up . . . While you're on the phone, Buck—those cultivator points you ordered. Where'd you put them?"

There was a long silence. Then, "What points?"

"I've got a bill here for sixty dollars from Trager's. Got your name on it."

Another silence. "Oh. Well, uh, yeah, I ordered them, but they haven't come yet."

Unconvinced, Jacob hung up. The store wouldn't have sent a bill if the points hadn't arrived. Not bothering to turn on the yard light, he went outside. Clouds drifted across the moon, and a sudden gust of wind rustled the leaves of the mulberry tree.

The temperature was dropping; that would slow the peaches down a little. After the thinning was done, he'd have Buck stake and tie up the new trees in the section behind the barn.

But tomorrow he'd go into town and get parts for the sprayer. And while he was there, he'd talk to Ron Trager and find out what was going on. Clear up this business of the points.

Midnight rubbed against his ankle, and he looked down, seeing only the black cat's disembodied yellow eyes in the dark.

He stooped and picked her up, running his fingers over her swollen belly, lumpy with fertility. There must be at least four or five kittens in there. "Did Becky feed you?" he asked. "You've got to eat good now, little mama."

Midnight purred in his arms, and Jacob stroked her head. He thought of Velita's soft blond hair and quickly set the cat down.

The next morning, Jacob got up early and went into the shed. He reached out to the wall where his shovel normally hung, then stopped short.

Its place was empty. Had the boys used it and forgotten to put it back? Frustrated, he stomped back into the house. Being away at this jury trial was sure messing up his life.

In the kitchen, Becky was setting out cinnamon rolls and oatmeal while Sammy and Paul sat at the table making faces at each other.

The boys looked up at him and grinned innocently, and Jacob asked them about the shovel.

"No," they insisted, one after the other. They hadn't used it.

Jacob thought a minute, then said, "Go ahead and eat. I'll be back in a bit." He grabbed a few of the cinnamon rolls, put them in a plastic bag, got into his pickup, and drove the six miles to Buck's farm. When he reached the driveway, he cut his engine and coasted in, parking by the shed.

"Lord, forgive me if I'm wrong," he muttered as he pushed open the door.

Buck's equipment was parked every which way, and inside the shed was a rat's nest of rope, old tools, and rusty iron. In a corner, half hidden behind some old brooms and rakes, stood a shiny shovel.

His shovel—he could tell by the markings on the handle.

Jacob looked around. Everything else seemed to be just Buck's normal clutter. Against the far wall, a greasy tarp lay over some large boxes. He lifted a corner, then threw back the tarp. An invoice taped to the first box said *Jacob Franzen. One dozen cultivator points.*

He went back to his pickup, got out the bag of rolls, and walked over to knock at the back door of Buck's house.

After a long time, Buck came to the door, wiping sleep out of his eyes. His hair stuck up wildly, and he smelled of stale whiskey. When he saw Jacob, his jaw dropped.

"Brought you some breakfast," said Jacob, holding out the bag. "Guaranteed to make you feel better. Also, I'd like to borrow some rope, if you can spare it."

Buck quickly put the sack inside and started out the door.

"No, no," said Jacob. "Don't trouble yourself with your bad back. I'll find some." He strode off to the shed.

Buck hurried to catch up. He had no sign of a limp. "Wait, Franzen, you won't know where it is."

"No problem," said Jacob, throwing open the shed door and

looking around. "I think this length will do just fine." He picked up a loop on the floor, exposing the shovel. "Hey, this looks familiar. What's it doing here?"

Buck's Adam's apple slid up and down, and his face looked pasty in the dim light of the shed.

Sadly, Jacob looked into his eyes. "Now, you want to tell me about the points?"

❖ ❖ ❖

On Sunday morning, Jacob listened to the organ prelude at Fairdale Mennonite Brethren Church. Clean-shaven, he wore navy slacks and a sports coat, the design in his navy necktie matching the pale blue of his shirt.

Beside him, Paul sat quietly sober. On the other side of Paul, Sammy grinned and ran his hands through his hair, making his cowlick poke up even higher. Beyond him was an empty space; Becky would sing in the youth choir and join them later.

Three rows ahead sat Jacob's parents, his father sitting straight in a pin-striped suit and tie, his mother small and neat in her Sunday-best purple, her white hair swirled from her usual Friday beauty parlor appointment. Jacob noticed his father's head slowly moving along with the music, probably mouthing the words of the old familiar hymn, "What a Friend We Have in Jesus."

On the platform, the minister and praise team sat waiting. Just below, between two potted plants, a small table held the communion elements covered by a white cloth. The organ music swelled into "Work, for the Night Is Coming."

Work. He didn't need to be reminded to do that. It would be a lot harder now that he'd let Buck go. This time of the year, everyone else was busy with their own farms. But what else was there to do? He couldn't trust the man.

At least the mystery of the cultivator points was solved. Probably Buck had planned to resell some of them. Jacob smiled sadly and nodded, his eyes staring to the side, unfocused.

Suddenly he became aware that in the next row and across the aisle, a woman was smiling back at him.

Uh-oh. Emma Redekopf. He hadn't realized he'd been looking her way. He'd known Emma since elementary school, even taken her to a banquet his junior year at Maranatha High. She'd been a lot of fun, a good friend through the years.

That's all she'd ever been. A friend.

But since he'd been widowed, it seemed every time he turned around, she was there. As though she was waiting for him.

Emma had never married and lived alone in an apartment in town. She was a great cook, had a responsible job in a bank, and wasn't bad looking. A bit on the hefty side, but that was okay. Jacob's friends kept hinting that he'd be smart to team up with her, and he'd even given it a little thought. Just a little.

There was something about Emma. He couldn't quite put his finger on it; it was a certain air of overconfidence, bossiness. A little bit too *dreest*, too forward. Whenever he saw her hungry eyes on him, he wanted to run the other way.

Now she would think he had smiled at *her*, encouraged her. What trouble had he started? He looked down at his hands, suddenly too large and clumsy with nothing to do. He picked up the bulletin and studied it blindly, intently. Sammy snickered and poked Paul, making him bump against his father. The bulletin slipped out of Jacob's hands and slithered to the floor.

He reached for it, butting his head on the pew ahead of them. Emma smothered a laugh, her plump fingers covering a mouth piously free of lipstick. Her shoulders shook, and her lace collar danced above the yellow flowers of her dress.

Jacob cleared his throat and looked around. In the pew ahead a toddler kneeling backward bounced up and down and giggled, pointing at him. The couple across the aisle glanced from Jacob to Emma, then whispered to each other.

Ach, yauma. Rumors would be all over church by next Sunday. They'd have him lassoed and the knot tied, when all he'd done was smile to himself.

Just then, a little red light flashed on above the choir loft, signaling that they were on the radio, and the church went silent. The youth choir marched onto the platform, singing, their voices sweet and true in three-part harmony. Jacob was glad the attention was finally away from him.

Becky stood in the front row of the choir, and although some of the other girls wore slacks or short skirts, she was neat and pretty in a new pink dress she'd sewed herself. The hem modestly covered her knees.

Jacob watched her with approval. Sharon would have been proud of her.

Suddenly he realized he'd thought of Sharon as in the past, without the old familiar stab of pain. At first he felt guilty. Then he wondered: could this be God's way of telling him to stop grieving and move on with his life?

The message started, and Sammy began to wiggle. Watching him, Jacob saw he was playing a follow-the-leader game in reverse, imitating Paul, motion for motion. Now a foot swing, next a finger tap, then a shrug of the shoulder.

What a *vruzzle*. An absolute rascal. He nudged both boys, giving them stern looks. Couldn't they last one half hour?

His parents told of services in the old days, of standing through long around-the-world prayers, each person *out-fromming* the others, trying to be the most pious. There had been two or three sermons, each about an hour, in High German. Church might go on until one o'clock or later. Let the kids try to sit through that now!

Nobody preached in High German anymore, not even the churches in the Midwest who seemed to think Californians were a little too modern. But everyday *Plautdietsch* still hung on. Words one wouldn't dare use in English were somehow acceptable in that beloved earthy language.

A soft rustling sound made Jacob aware that all around him, the congregation was standing. Emma Redekopf was still watching him, her eyes crinkled with laughter. He quickly stood and fumbled through the hymnbook. "Come, Thou fount of every blessing . . ."

Please Lord, don't let Emma be my special blessing. She was a fine woman, but for someone else. Not for him.

He thought back to the little coffee shop in Springton. Velita Stanford sitting across from him, her slim fingers curled around the coffee mug, then reaching up to push back the fluffy hair from her forehead.

But that husband of hers! Jacob could still see the sneer on his face. How had a nice person like Velita come to marry a clod like that?

He twitched his head to rid himself of the memory. After all, he had only helped out a woman in trouble, and that was over.

Jacob felt a nudge from Sammy. They were off the air, and the deacons stood in the aisles, passing the communion bread. He took the quarter-loaf in his hand and hesitated. Was he honestly ready to partake?

Silently he prayed, "Lord, forgive me where I have sinned. Where I have been harsh with the children or been a bad example. Forgive any secret sins."

Velita's face flashed before him again. He had held her close. But just to steady her. Had he taken too much pleasure in that? "Lord, I beseech Thee: rid me of any evil thoughts."

He opened his eyes. People were staring at him. Quickly, he nipped off a chunk and passed the bread on.

Chapter 12

At Jacob's house that afternoon, on Channel 24, the Portland Trail Blazers were ahead of the Golden State Warriors 83–69 at the end of the third quarter. But Jacob didn't realize it; he was napping in his recliner.

Becky was at a picnic with the youth choir, and later, they would sing for the old folks at the church's nursing home. The boys were out in the yard, playing catch and looking for lizards by the shed. Their shouts and laughter floated in Jacob's dreams, mingling with the screams of basketball fans from the TV.

A loud honking jolted him awake. Sammy was shaking his shoulder. "Someone's here!"

Jacob wrinkled his nose, tasting the staleness of sleep. "Who is it?" He looked at his watch; it was too early for Becky to be home.

"Uncle Heinz and Aunt Clara! They've got a car!"

Heinz and Clara? In a car? It couldn't be. Besides, she'd said they were coming in May. Jacob glanced around the living room. Becky had cleaned yesterday, but the Sunday paper was scattered around his chair. He quickly pushed it into a neat stack before going to the back door.

"Jakie!" Clara smothered him in an embrace of soft flesh and the smell of lye soap. Clara was a tribute to her own good cooking. Short, plump, and white-haired, a typical little Mennonite housewife. In *Plautdietsch,* she'd be described as a *mumkya.* Without any makeup, she still had the smooth skin and glowing face of a much younger woman.

Marriage seemed to agree with her, even if it was into the Old Order.

"You're looking good," said Jacob. "Don't you ever get older? I'm catching up with you."

Clara giggled, her voice running up and down the scale. She grabbed a boy in the crook of each arm and planted kisses on their foreheads before they could squirm away. "Such fine *bengyels*, good boys growing into men already."

"Whoa, what gives here?" asked Jacob. "A car?" It was a sleek black Dodge, not new—probably '94 or '95—but well-kept. "Have you two been kicked out of church?"

Heinz's stocky frame was bent nearly double, getting luggage out of the trunk. He set the suitcases down, straightened his wide suspenders, and reached to shake hands. "Nah, der vas trouble mit d'new leader, and d'congregation split. Ve switched over to d'Believers' Church at New Holland. Dey don't get so fired up on details. It vas getting so d'elders frowned if ve so much as used a telephone."

"Sure," said Clara. "They even came around with yardsticks, measuring the girls' hems. And our caps had to be so many inches wide, no more, no less. Now it's so much easier; we don't feel under all that pressure."

Jacob looked at her thoughtfully. She still wore a head covering, but it was more like a short nun's veil, white and flowing to her shoulders. Her cotton print dress reached her black tie-up shoes. He wondered if they'd just traded one set of rules for another.

Heinz closed the trunk of the car and caressed its shiny finish. "Bought her from our English neighbor. Peretti. Got him down to six tousand."

The boys looked at Jacob, and he winked at them, reminding them that the Old Mennonites in that area still thought of all outsiders as "English."

"'Course d'tires had to go," Heinz went on. "D'church don't hold wid vitevalls."

Jacob hid a smile. No problems with details, hmm? "It's a beauty, all right. Get good mileage?"

"Pretty good. Tventy-five on d'freevay."

Jacob looked down the driveway, listening for the sound of a car slowing. Becky better get home soon; otherwise, how would he manage? Sammy's bedroom hadn't been cleared out for guests. And there was nothing prepared, no fresh *tvebocks* or coffee cake, no pie. Should he call his mother, see if she had made extra? But then he remembered: his folks were visiting friends in Reedley.

He picked up the suitcases. "Well, let's go in."

"We would have got here last night already," said Clara. "We wanted to visit your church—"

"But d'fan belt broke just d'udder side of Merced," Heinz broke in. "Ve had to stop over at a Motel 6."

Jacob set the luggage down and held open the screen door. "We didn't expect you till next month. Change your plans?"

"*Yah*, vell. Got somevun to tend the dairy, so ve got avay sooner, and den tought ve stay a vile in Lodi with John and Rosie. But all day, he pokes on his number machine, tax papers strewn on his desk, people comen en goin. No time for family."

Jacob slapped his forehead. "That reminds me! I need to get my tax records to him." Another headache. When would he have time for that?

"D'vife said to call you, but I said, shoot, he's *frindshaft*, relation. Let's go already and surprise him."

"I wish you *had* called." Did they think he just sat around all day and smiled at his farm? "I'm kinda in a bind. My hired man—I had to fire him."

"*Nah yo*, I'll help you, den maybe you have some time free yet."

Jacob sighed. "I'd appreciate the help. But thing is, I've got jury duty. I won't even be home tomorrow. Don't know yet about the rest of the week."

"*Neh obah!*" Clara's mouth pinched. "You're mixed up in a court trial?"

"A long one. I can't talk about it. But it's pretty serious."

She shook her head, clucking at him. "Watch out, Jakie. You know we don't hold with suing. The Bible says to go to the one who's wronged you—"

"I know. But that's among Brethren. I'm just—I'm helping these 'English' to straighten out their problems." It was a good thing he couldn't talk about it. If they knew it was a murder trial, they'd hammer at him all evening.

Heinz slapped Jacob on the back. "Vell, just say vat needs be done. I can help out some, maybe drive tractor." He winked. "Folks back home don't need know it gots rubber tires."

Jacob grinned. What a bother it must be to have all those little manmade rules just to prove that some were more humble than others. "Sure. I'll show you around first thing in the morning. And you could take a few days to sightsee, go up into the mountains while you're here."

"I always vanted to see Yosemite." He pronounced it *YO-sem-ite*. "If you still have the court, maybe your folks'll go vid us."

"They'd like that." Jacob motioned toward the sofa. "Make yourselves at home. I'll take your things upstairs. Becky'll be here soon; she'll get your room ready."

"Heinz, go get the picture album from the car. I want to show Jakie our newest grandson. Only nine months old and walking already."

Half an hour later, Becky rushed in. "I *wondered* whose car that was!" After the hugs and explanations, she excused herself and went into the kitchen.

Clara followed her, and soon Jacob smelled *schnetke* baking and fresh coffee brewing. He could just picture the two of them cutting the thin strips of dough, spreading them with jam, and rolling them into finger shapes. With one ear, he listened to Heinz's rambling account of their trip, and with the other, he tuned into Clara telling Becky about the time he'd beaten up the school bully, getting blood all over his clean white shirt. And about his fourth-grade sweetheart. He was relieved when Becky announced that *faspa*, their usual Sunday light supper, was ready. She didn't need to learn any more of his embarrassing secrets.

That evening, after everyone else had gone to bed, Jacob and his sister sat on the couch and talked.

"They're good kids, your three," said Clara, her double chins nodding in agreement. "You've done a fine job. But you shouldn't try to do it alone. How long's it been already? Two years?"

Jacob stared down at his shoes and nodded. "Nearly."

"High time you married again. Hundreds of nice girls just waiting for a chance at a good-looking widower."

"I don't know about the good-looking part. But so far I haven't found the right woman."

"You're just too picky. *Kyingyas* need a mom. Especially Becky. She'll be courting age soon, needs someone to guide her."

"The women at church, they've been real good to her."

Clara shook her head. "It's not the same. Now, back in Lancaster, I've got a friend who lost her husband last year. Cancer, too. She's about your age, maybe a little bit older, two fine daughters." Clara pawed around in her purse. "You can write her; I've got her address here someplace..."

"Forget it. There are plenty of women around here."

"Oh?" Clara leaned forward, her bright blue eyes twinkling. "Anyone in particular?"

Jacob groaned. "You women, you're all the same. Can't stand seeing a man free and comfortable." For an instant he wondered what she'd think of Velita and was shocked at himself. *Deliver me, Lord!*

Clara hoisted her bulk out of the depths of the couch and headed for the stairs. "You don't fool me. Any man happy like you were with Sharon can't stay alone for long. Just think about it."

If only he could *stop* thinking about it.

Chapter 13

On Monday morning, Velita parked her car on the third floor in the parking garage. Her head still hurt, and she ached all over. Stretching up, she studied her face in the rearview mirror. Her makeup almost hid the bump from the door handle, but high on her right cheek was another bruise. From Ralph.

It would be hard facing the other jurors looking like that. Would Jacob Franzen tell them about last Tuesday, about that gang and all? If he did, maybe they'd think both marks were from that.

But *he* would know that only one bump was from the door. She crossed her fingers, hoping he wouldn't mention it. Pulling a fringe of hair farther onto her face, she looked again in the mirror. If he didn't look close, that other bruise might look like a shadow.

Slowly and painfully, she got out of the car. It was a good thing she was in plenty of time today. Just as she'd headed out the front door of the house, the phone had rung, but this time she'd kept going. Ralph wasn't going to make her late today. If he'd "forgotten" his lunch again, he would just have to pick up a hamburger somewhere.

Velita sighed. He would probably take it out on her tonight, but what else could she do? Going to jail was no picnic, either.

From all over the parking garage, nicely dressed people came from their cars and headed toward the elevator, flowing together like streams into a river. Velita recognized one of them—Laura Crutchfield from her own panel—and hurried to catch up with her. The two of them rode down together with the others, and together they walked the three blocks to the courthouse.

Velita felt pleased to be in the group, pretending to be as good as all the rest. She'd worn a skirt and blouse today, like some of the others. But she couldn't think of anything to say to them, so while they chattered away, she looked around the courthouse grounds. Zinnias and petunias bloomed in beds looped around like big figure eights, bordered with cement tiles. The lawns were a rich green, with benches under the trees and squirrels frisking around, looking for scraps.

Laura coughed, one of those rattling, choky coughs. "I caught a miserable cold over the weekend," she explained.

"I'm sorry," said Velita. TJ'd had the sniffles this morning, had said he felt awful. But his temperature had been normal, so she'd made him get on the bus and go to school anyway. She had to be firm with him; lately, he'd been pulling all kinds of stunts just to stay home.

But now she started to worry. What if that phone call had been from the school, and this time, TJ really was sick? What was she going to do?

He'd had the flu last year and had been so miserable. He'd been weak as a baby and had even let her cuddle him. No Mr. Tough Guy then.

Going up the courthouse ramp, Velita looked around. "Is there a pay phone here somewhere?"

A man pointed. "Next to the main entrance."

She got through to the school quickly, and the secretary sounded relieved. "I've been trying to call you. TJ looks a little pale, and he's complaining about a stomachache. You'd better come pick him up."

Velita caught her breath. "He was okay this morning. Does he have a temp?"

"No."

That didn't sound like the flu. She explained about her jury duty and her son's habit of faking sickness.

The secretary was polite but didn't give an inch. "We can't take any chances. There *is* a virus going around. If he's coming down with it, more children might be infected. Where could I call your husband?"

"No! I mean—not my husband." Ralph would never take off work just to take care of his kids; besides, he'd spit nails if he knew she hadn't answered the school's phone call.

She bit her lip. No way could she leave. If TJ *was* really sick, the neighbor wouldn't want him either.

Velita sighed. There was no other choice. "Call his grandma, LaDonna Stanford." She gave them the number. "Tell her I'll get home as soon as I can."

Dreading what LaDonna would say, Velita went on inside the courthouse and through the metal detector line. Her mother-in-law would be plenty mad. To get her hostess job at the Tenderloin Steak House, LaDonna had lied about her age; and now she worked hard to look young. If she kept TJ, she wouldn't get her beauty nap before going to work at six.

But that couldn't be helped. If something really was wrong, LaDonna would know what to do. Velita circled around the crowd waiting by the elevators and hurried up the stairs to the jury room.

Lester Payne, in blue and yellow plaid slacks, leaned against the whiteboard, arguing with another man. "Well, if those lying politicians would only—"

He stopped and eyed Velita, but she slipped around the opposite side of the table. She didn't need any flak from him.

Marsha wasn't there yet. The other women talked in little groups about daycare centers, school bonds, and the prices at Costco. Laura Crutchfield griped about her furniture store opening; so soon, so much to do, jury duty taking up so much time. And now her wretched cold . . .

They didn't pay any attention to Velita, so she figured they hadn't heard about her run-in with the gang.

Jacob stood by the coffeemaker, pouring a cup. He smiled, handed the cup to her, and poured another for himself.

"Thanks." She took it and sat down at the table. She really wanted to also thank him for his help and apologize for Ralph's rudeness. But what could she say? *"Sorry my husband is such a jerk"*?

The door to the jury room opened, and Marsha hurried in. She looked at Velita, and her mouth opened. But Jacob cleared his throat and shook his head slightly, as if saying, *Don't ask.*

Velita couldn't believe it. This man actually cared how she felt. She thought of how gentle he'd been last Tuesday, even helping her into his car. It seemed so . . . respectful. As though she was worth something. What made him so different? Was he really that nice, or was this just an act?

Ralph used to say she was special. Even after they'd been married, there'd been some good times—parties and shows and days at the flea markets. But after her belly had gotten so big she could hardly walk, he wouldn't take her anywhere.

The first few days after TJ was born, he acted proud of being a daddy and called her "little mama." But that didn't last long after a few nights of hearing the baby cry. Now he just called her "stupid." Maybe she was, for sticking with him all this time. But what else could she do?

It was past nine, and the jury still hadn't been called in. Nellie Kroymire, the white-haired woman with the U-shaped smile, opened a container of oatmeal cookies she'd brought and passed them around.

"Keep this up, we'll all put on twenty pounds," said Geneva Carson, busy knitting. "Lord knows I don't need it. But those cookies look mighty good!"

Velita took one. She hadn't felt like eating breakfast and was a little shaky. Oatmeal was supposed to be good for you; maybe a cookie would make her feel better. She studied her fingernails while she chewed. Why hadn't she brought an emery board along? Here, she'd have time to file them.

Marsha caught her eye and asked, "How was your weekend?"

If the woman only knew. Even if there was time to tell about the gang who stole her money, Velita couldn't go into all the details about Jacob Franzen. And especially not about Ralph.

She faked a bright smile. "Fine. On Sunday, we went to a barbecue at my mother-in-law's. Suanne—that's my little girl—her grandma's going to pay for her gymnastics class."

Since that blowup Tuesday evening, Ralph had quieted down

and acted as though nothing had happened. LaDonna had asked some of her friends from the Tenderloin to the barbecue, and she'd put on a big show of being generous. Velita was sure she was just trying to impress them. Now that her mother-in-law had to look after TJ, she'd probably take it all back, just to get even.

Marsha looked at Velita funny, as though she was studying those bruises, but she only said, "That's nice," and gave a crooked smile. "Mine was normal. At the hospital, it was gallstones, heart attacks, and kidney failure. At home, my daughter and I quarreled. Heather thinks I don't give her enough freedom."

Jacob had been listening in, and his eyes crinkled around the edges. He looked as though it really mattered to him. "Did you solve the problem?"

"I wish. She packed up and moved in with her dad. She thinks he'll treat her better."

"Where does he live?" asked Velita.

"Across town. He'll probably buy her anything she wants and let her run loose. He and his new wife have long work hours. They're also gone a lot of evenings."

Velita thought it must be really awful living in the same town with someone she'd divorced. Passing the kids back and forth, having to call the ex when she wanted to talk to them. She wondered what Marsha's life was like and if her husband had hit her while they were married.

Geneva looked up from her knitting. "What are you going to do?"

"He's her dad, and she's almost eighteen. There's not much I can do." Marsha sighed. "I guess that's how I affect people. My husband split, then my boyfriend walks out, and now my daughter."

Jacob nodded. "That *is* a lot to bear. Didn't I hear you say your friend was a police officer?"

"Yeah. He—" She shrugged. "Might as well tell you. He's been offered a job on the Santa Cruz PD homicide squad. Wanted me to move there with him."

Jacob looked puzzled. "And you don't want to marry him?"

"He didn't . . . exactly . . . mention marriage. But even if he had, I've got seniority at the hospital. Rumors are I might have a chance at head nurse in my department. I can't just drop everything, take Heather away from her school and friends . . ."

Velita stared at her. "But—now she's with her dad."

Marsha shrugged. "Yeah, well, that doesn't mean anything. Who knows how long that will last?" She brushed cookie crumbs into her napkin. "Don't worry; it's not your problem."

Velita couldn't imagine choosing a career over a man. When Ralph wanted to move, she was packed and on the road. She'd left Chockamo, her friends, and her family and wandered through the states from town to town with Ralph and his mother until he'd finally found the job he liked here in Springton.

"Velita?" She hadn't realized Marsha was still talking: "Did you think any more about sharing rides here?"

"Oh. No, I . . . couldn't." Velita set down her half-eaten cookie and toyed with her wedding band. "Ralph wouldn't . . . I mean . . . he thinks it's not a good idea. Because of insurance. You know. Liability?" She shrugged. "I don't understand all that."

Marsha looked at her strangely but said, "That's all right. It's just that we'd both save gas, and it's nicer than coming in alone."

Velita felt the others staring at her. She fluffed her hair and pulled a strand down farther over her cheek. "I guess. But you know how husbands are. They . . . think they have to protect you." She didn't dare look at Jacob. Did he believe her? How much had he seen at her house? Ralph had been so rude . . .

The door opened, and the bailiff came in. Judge Trent had arrived, and they all pushed and squeezed into a line to match their seating order in the jury box.

As Jacob passed Velita, he asked, "Are you all right?"

She looked at him through the curtain of her hair. "Yeah, sure."

"No more headache? Whoa, you still have quite a bruise." He cocked his head. "Hmm. I thought it was on the other side."

She turned away quickly, and a wave of nausea hit her. Could she be catching the same bug TJ had? Luckily, she was next to the wall, and she leaned against it, looking to see if anybody had noticed. They hadn't; they were already marching into the courtroom.

She swallowed several times, felt a little better, and numbly followed them into the jury box.

Chapter 14

The first witness for the prosecution, Police Sgt. William Martin, was big and hefty, had reddish hair, and wore a tweed sports coat. *Looks like a typical cop*, thought Velita. Like the ones that came to the door when the neighbors complained about the noise and yelling. The ones who believed everything Ralph said.

Prosecution attorney James Pettigrew took his time. He smiled, letting his eyes slide across each juror. Then he turned to the big man in the witness seat.

"Sergeant Martin, you have stated you were on duty in Booneville on the night in question. Did you make a visit to a residence at 1002 North Florin Street?"

"That is correct."

"Would you please tell the jury what occurred?"

Sergeant Martin shifted his body and cleared his throat. "Detectives MacDuff and Bayliss went around to the back to stand guard. Sergeant Newburg and I stationed ourselves on the front porch and announced ourselves as police officers. We said we had a search warrant and asked the defendant to open the door."

Attorney Pettigrew flashed the search warrant past the jurors, but Velita couldn't tell what it said. "In your opinion, were you speaking quietly or loudly?"

"We were shouting."

Oh, yeah. They'd be shouting, all right. So all the neighbors could hear.

"What happened next?"

"A gunshot penetrated the door from the inside, and the bullet shattered my finger." Sergeant Martin held up his left hand. The pointer finger was just a nub, half the length of the next finger.

"What did you do then?"

"I went to my car and called for backup."

"Thank you," said Pettigrew. "No further questions at this time." He flashed a smile at the jury. *A bit too cocky,* thought Velita.

The defense lawyer, Arnold Torrance, studied the yellow legal pad on his table. He seemed tired and sad, as though he knew it was a lost cause. Then he raised his eyebrows at the witness. "When you identified yourself, what words did you use?"

"Police officers, open up."

"Was this before or after you broke down the door?"

James Pettigrew jumped to his feet. "Objection!"

"Sustained," said the judge.

"I will rephrase. Was this before or after the door was opened?"

"Before."

"Where were Detectives Robert MacDuff and Kenneth Bayliss at this time?"

Sergeant Martin shifted in his chair. "They went around the house, in the direction of the back door."

"At whose orders?"

"I beg your pardon?"

"Who was in charge?"

"I was. But we made the plans togeth—"

"Thank you. Did you give Corporal MacDuff orders to enter the rear door of the Jackson residence?"

"The plans were to—"

"A simple yes or no, please."

The cop rubbed his chin, then finally said, "No."

Attorney Torrance turned and nodded at the jury. Then he asked, "Were you wearing a uniform at this time?"

"No. We were undercover police on surveillance."

"From your position on the porch, were you able to hear the television in the house?"

"Yes."

The questions and answers flipped back and forth like TJ and Luke playing catch. What difference did it all make if the man was guilty anyway? If they'd just finish up quickly, Velita could go pick up TJ. Maybe he really was feeling bad, and she'd been too hard on him.

"What program was playing? Were you able to distinguish the words?"

Sergeant Martin bit his lip. "I don't remember."

"If it please the court, my associate will go outside the courtroom door and demonstrate."

The judge nodded.

A little later, a muffled sound came from outside the courtroom.

Attorney Torrance asked the jury, "Did all of you understand that?"

Velita hadn't. She glanced at the other jurors and they were shaking their heads no.

Torrance marched to the door and held it open. "Will you please repeat that?"

The aide shouted, "Police officers, open up!"

Velita almost laughed. If the officers could kick in Duane Jackson's door, it couldn't have been as thick as the courtroom's. She'd like to see them try this one—the cops' feet would break sooner than this solid wood. What made them think anyone could hear through it? Were the lawyers dumber than she was?

"No further questions," said Arnold Torrance.

Attorney Pettigrew rose. "I call Kenneth Bayliss to the stand."

"What did you see when you entered the back door?" he asked Detective Bayliss.

Kenneth Bayliss, younger than the others, seemed nervous. He cleared his throat. "All I saw was a flash and MacDuff going down."

"What did you do then?"

"I yelled 'Officer down' and drew my gun."

"Where was Jackson at this time?"

"He was in the hall, struggling with Officer Martin."

"Was he at this time taken into custody?"

"Yes."

"Where was Mrs. Jackson at this time?"

"I don't know. I didn't see her. I was busy trying to revive MacDuff."

"No further questions."

"Cross examination?" Judge Trent asked Arnold Torrance.

Torrance asked Detective Bayliss, "Did you have orders to enter the back door?"

Officer Bayliss admitted that no, they hadn't been given permission to enter the back door. "It was MacDuff's idea."

"No further questions."

James Pettigrew walked to the center of the room.

"If it please the court," he said, "I would like to acquaint the jury with the area in question."

The bailiff wheeled in a projector and pulled down a screen across the room from the jury. The courtroom lights blinked off. Velita closed her eyes for a few seconds and realized she was very tired. How embarrassing it would be to fall asleep! She sat up straighter and stared at the screen.

James Pettigrew showed slides of the house on 1002 N. Florin St. in Booneville. With a stick, he pointed to the white frame house. "As closely as possible," he said, "the scene has been recreated to show the conditions of the night in question."

Velita studied the pictures. The place looked even smaller and shabbier than her own two-bedroom tract house. Four steps led up to a high front porch with a wooden railing, a post at each corner. At the left of the ragged screen door was a light socket with a naked bulb. *Yeah,* she thought, *they could hear through that door.*

The prosecutor tapped the spot. "Notice that the porch light is on." On each side of the door was a window facing the street. Both shades were drawn.

The courtroom was dead quiet except for Attorney Pettigrew's voice and the clicking of the projector control.

At one corner of the house was a camellia bush with faded pink blossoms nearly reaching the eaves and a carpet of rotten petals on the ground. Large, straggly bushes lined the porch. *Duane Jackson mustn't care much for gardening,* thought Velita. *Too bad. With a good pruning, those flowers would really be pretty.*

The next slides looked down behind the house, showing the back door. There was no porch, just a small aluminum awning and steps down to a square cement slab. The last frame showed a telephone pole across the street from the house, but no street light.

James Pettigrew switched off the projector, and the courtroom's overhead lights flashed back on. "I call Officer Frank Newburg to the witness stand."

Using crutches, the man hobbled to the chair. At first he pretty much repeated what the other officer had said but then added he'd heard shouting from inside the house. The curtain had moved, and he'd seen someone peeking out.

"What did you do then?" asked James Pettigrew.

"I held my badge like this"—the officer cupped his palm—"and showed it to the person at the window."

"Do you see that person in the courtroom?"

Officer Newburg pointed. "It was Mr. Jackson."

Then it was the defense's turn. Arnold Torrance asked, "Did the person at the window continue looking out, or did he drop the curtain?"

"He dropped the curtain."

"Before or after you showed your badge?"

"After."

Velita wondered how TJ was by now. She could almost feel the spears LaDonna was throwing at her and didn't know which would get her in the worst trouble—if her boy was really sick or if he was just playing hooky. Either way, she was sure to pay for it.

Attorney Torrance cleared his throat. "Think carefully, Officer Newburg. This person lifted the curtain, you reached for your badge, turned it to the window, and the face was still there, looking out?"

"Yes."

"How long would you say this took?"

"Just a few seconds. Ten, maybe fifteen."

Torrance went back to his table, rummaged through his briefcase, and walked slowly back to the witness. Suddenly he whipped up a cupped hand and waved it in front of Officer Newburg. "What did I just show you?"

Newburg blinked. "A medallion of some sort."

Arnold Torrance turned to the jury and skimmed his hand past their eyes. Something metal gleamed. The lawyer set the object on the railing, and Velita saw it was a brass coaster.

"Officer Newburg, is it your opinion that this person looked out the window, and for fifteen seconds saw armed men in street clothes flashing something metal—and was able to recognize you as the police?"

Newburg hesitated, glancing at the prosecutor. "Yes."

Attorney Torrance gave an "aw come on" look at the jury, then turned back to the witness. "What happened after the curtain dropped?"

Officer Newburg squinted at the ceiling a moment, then said, "I heard shouting."

In spite of herself, Velita became drawn into the trial. Those questions had to mean something, and she tried to remember the answers.

"Could you understand any words?"

"I believe the words were 'Flush it.'"

Velita heard snickers from the audience, and the judge rapped his gavel.

"'Flush it?'" Torrance repeated.

"That is correct."

"Are you sure those were the exact words?"

"Reasonably sure."

"Not positively sure?"

"No."

"Thank you. No further questions."

"Redirect?" asked the judge.

James Pettigrew went up again. "Sergeant Newburg, when you stood on that porch, did you have reason to believe the defendant would recognize you?"

Arnold Torrance jumped up. "Objection!"

"Sustained."

"Your Honor, I believe counsel introduced the possibility himself in cross."

The judge motioned both lawyers, and the stenographer scooted in close. They argued in whispers, with a lot of hand motions and head shaking.

Velita wondered what the big deal was about recognizing the police officer. Unless . . . maybe . . . if Jackson had been in trouble before? That had to be it. She glanced at the other jurors but couldn't read anything on their faces.

Finally the judge announced, "We need to discuss a certain matter in chambers. Court will be recessed until 1:30 PM."

After leaving the courthouse, Marsha and several other jurors walked toward the downtown mall and the little fast-food places, but a few people had brought sack lunches. Velita followed them outside to a bench in the park.

She'd stuffed an apple into her purse but didn't feel like eating it. Instead, she leaned back on the bench and let the talk swirl over her head.

It was strange, she thought, *how people could turn off that murder scene in the courtroom and just laugh and jabber about unimportant things.* Nellie said she had seen an ad for Birkenstocks on sale at Macy's, and Eunice Phipps wondered if there'd be time to rush over there before the afternoon session. One of the men, Gregory something, stopped flirting with one of the alternates long enough to warn Eunice that if she left, she'd lose her parking space and not find another within miles.

Jacob sat chomping on a thick sandwich of ham and homemade bread. Any other time, it would have made Velita hungry, but now the smell turned her stomach. Maybe TJ wasn't faking; maybe he had that bug the teacher talked about, and she was catching the same thing.

She looked up and caught Jacob staring at her. "Didn't you bring a lunch? Here, take part of my sandwich."

A wave of nausea hit her, and she lied, "Thanks. I don't usually eat lunch."

He frowned, his eyes narrowed, still holding out the sandwich. "Try some anyway. It's really good. My sister's visiting; she brought home-cured ham and baked the bread."

"No, honest. I'm . . . not hungry." One bite, and she'd barf all over the lawn. "Where does your sister live?"

"Pennsylvania. She's married to a man in the Old Order. It's like the Amish—the kind everybody else thinks of when they hear the word *Mennonite*. They're helping me on the farm a few days."

Velita swallowed several times, breathing carefully, hoping to settle her stomach. "That's nice," she managed.

"Yeah. It's a big help with me stuck on the jury."

He kept watching her, so she got out her apple and forced herself to take a tiny bite, chewing slowly, making herself smile at him. If he knew how awful she felt, he might get the notion to follow her home again. And then she'd *really* be in trouble.

"Got any steak?"

She stared at him. "What?"

"Steak. Draws out the poisons. Just lay it on that bruise for a while, it'll help."

Oh, yeah. The bruise. She reached up and touched her face. *Fat chance Ralph would let me waste a good piece of red meat on myself!* "I'll be okay."

Geneva Carson was skipping lunch too, and was busy knitting. She asked, "Run into a door, honey?"

"Car door. How'd you know?" If it still showed that much, she'd better put on more makeup.

Geneva raised her eyebrows and nodded. "Oh, I know all about doors. Used to run into one all the time, till I finally got out and slammed it shut behind me. Maybe that's what you need to do."

Had she understood Geneva right? Did the woman mean what it sounded like—to just walk out on her life? If only she knew how many times Velita had thought about it!

Chapter 15

When court opened again, Velita filed into the jury box and took her seat. All she could think of was what Geneva had said. But there was no way to shut the door on her life.

She thought back to the time she actually *had* left Ralph. Back in Chockamo. The very first time he'd slapped her around, she'd taken the baby and gone home to her mama.

Her mama'd said, "What'd you expect? That's the way men are. You wanted him; you got him. Don't come blubbering to me. I got enough troubles of my own."

She'd listened to her folks throwing things and yelling at each other often enough to know that was true. But their fights had been some different—her mama being bigger and stronger than her stepdad.

Before she could mention that, Ralph came roaring up on his Harley, banging on the door. He yelled and moaned, "Don't leave me, Vel, I can't live without you. You know I'm crazy about you. Just come home, and I'll never do it no more. I promise."

Like a fool, she'd believed him, even felt sorry for him. For a while, he was real sweet and loving, and she'd thought everything would be okay. But a few months later when she'd helped the neighbor man plant some pansies, she'd ended up with a black eye and Ralph had told her, "Don't you run off again, or I'll fix you good. No matter where you hide, I'll find you. And then you won't never see your kid again."

If she couldn't do it then, with one baby, no way could she take two kids and leave him. She'd never had a job, didn't even know how to get one. At least now there always was enough to eat, decent clothes for the kids, and a roof over their heads. Wandering the streets with them in tow would only be asking for worse trouble.

Officer Frank Newburg clumped his crutches back to the witness chair, and Velita pushed her thoughts back.

The prosecuting lawyer asked, "After you heard the shouting inside the house, what did you do?"

The officer said he and Sergeant Martin had pounded on the door again. From inside, through the door, had come a blast of gunfire, and he was hit in the thigh.

"Would you please show the jury where you were shot?"

The cop hoisted himself up, flinching as he touched the spot high inside his leg.

Then the questions and answers batted back and forth, fast.

"What did you do after that?"

"I rolled off the porch."

"Over the railing?"

"Yes."

"What happened then?"

"I blacked out."

"What was the next thing you remember?"

"I was at the hospital. They told me I'd lost a lot of blood."

The defense objected. "Hearsay!"

The prosecutor shrugged. "It's well documented. I can subpoena the doctor."

"Overruled," said the judge.

James Pettigrew passed big shiny pictures around to the jurors. Velita stared at the photo of the front door, its screen propped open and two bullet holes near the door knob.

The next pictures were close-ups: the bullet holes, the punctured door from the inside. The screen door's hooked latch. Velita shuddered. It was finally getting to her. This wasn't like watching a crime show on TV—this was the real thing. She looked at Duane Jackson and wondered how he could just sit there every day, doodling away like he was a kid in school listening to a boring history lesson. One would think he'd be freaked out.

The prosecutor sat down, and the defense lawyer stood up. He had only two questions.

"Could you identify the person who fired the shots from inside?"

"No."

Arnold Torrance bent over and looked into Newburg's eyes. "Those were quite large bushes around the porch. In your alleged severely wounded condition, you actually rolled over the porch railing and the high bushes?" He turned and looked at the jury, shaking his head.

Velita wondered the same thing. Officer Newburg was a hefty man. It did seem strange—being shot and all—that he could vault over all that. Maybe he hadn't been as badly hurt as he made out. Maybe he hadn't been hurt at all and that was why Jackson didn't look worried.

But Officer Newburg nodded, his lips tight. "To the best of my recollection, I rolled over the railing onto the ground."

Velita huffed out a little breath. Which one should she believe? She remembered hearing that sometimes people had extra strength when they were desperate.

Maybe—maybe if things got really bad with *her*, there'd be a way out. Maybe.

The next witness came up, and she shook aside the thought. The man worked for the telephone company, said he'd been repairing the lines that evening. Two cars had pulled up, and four men jumped out of them. Two went to the front door, two around to the back of the house. The witness heard shouting and then shots; he'd seen the men on the porch hurdle over the railing to the ground and heard them yell for help. A picture of the pole was passed around, and Velita saw the man perched high, the service truck parked below. The house in the background. There didn't seem to be anything to block the man's view.

"After a little bit, when no one responded, I used the telephone box and called police headquarters. But while I was still talking, a police car drove up and parked next to the other cars, and two men in uniform ran to the house."

Okay, that settles it. This man saw it all. He can back up the cops.

Then Arnold Torrance asked, "How did it happen that you were in front of Duane Jackson's house at that hour of the evening?"

That caught Velita's attention, and she stared at the man. He'd held up his hand and sworn, but was he really telling the truth? Did the telephone company work that late? After nine thirty at night? A while back, *her* phone had gone dead, and she'd had to wait all weekend for a repairman. Ralph had been a bear all that time, even though in an emergency he could have gone next door to call someone.

"I'd started the repair job earlier, then received a call that the wires were down across town and several people were out of service. That evening, I went back to finish up."

Oh, she thought. *Maybe they do things different in Booneville.*

"Were the men you saw on Mr. Jackson's porch in uniform?"

"No."

"What made you think they were policemen?"

The man hesitated. "They . . . acted like cops. Stood straight, walked like cops. Had guns. Held up badges." No, he couldn't identify the badges from where he was. He'd heard them shout but couldn't make out the words.

Velita's thoughts wandered again. Was TJ okay? Was he behaving himself? By now, LaDonna would be mad as a tied-up cat. And when Ralph heard about it, he'd make sure Velita would pay for it. She felt another surge of nausea. *Please, God, let it be only something I ate. I can't afford to get sick.*

Lt. Terry Meacham came to the stand. He was tall and slim, with dark hair and a moustache. He said he and Sgt. Mike Harris had pulled in behind the other cars and approached the house. Newburg was lying on the ground beside the porch, and Martin was assisting him. "Harris and I ran to the front door. We knocked and announced ourselves. There was no answer."

"What did you do then?"

"We proceeded to kick the door open, but the defendant said, 'Don't shoot, I'm coming out.'"

"What happened next?"

"The subject slid his gun through the doorway and came out.

Harris read him his rights and proceeded to cuff him. I went inside the house."

"What did you see?"

"I saw—" Lieutenant Meacham stopped and cleared his throat. "I saw Corporal MacDuff lying on the floor."

"Go on."

"Detective Bayliss was leaning over him."

"Was any other person in the room?"

"Yes. Mrs. Jackson."

"Anyone else?"

"No."

Velita's stomach lurched again, and she took several slow, deep breaths to settle it. One policeman was dead, another almost killed, and the lawyers talked as calmly as if they were reading a recipe. *Oh God, I've got to get out of here, real soon.*

Arnold Torrance stood and looked at the jurors, staring from one face to the next. Velita didn't want to look back but couldn't help herself. What did he expect from her? All she could do was feel sorry for him, defending a guilty man.

Then he turned to Lieutenant Meacham. "Did you see who shot Corporal MacDuff?"

Meacham hesitated. "No."

"What was Mrs. Jackson doing when you came in?"

"She was . . . she wasn't doing anything. She was just sitting on the sofa, her hands covering her face."

"No further questions."

"Attorney Pettigrew?" asked the judge.

"I would like Kenneth Bayliss to return to the stand for cross."

Officer Bayliss seemed more nervous than before, and Velita

wasn't surprised. The man's partner had been shot and killed, right beside him.

"What did you see and hear when you entered the Jackson house from the rear door?"

"The kitchen was dark. All I saw was the flash and the sound of gunshots."

"How many shots did you hear?"

"Two, three, maybe more. And then I heard the other officers entering through the front."

"Did you see Duane Jackson at this time?"

"I was tending to Officer MacDuff, hoping to resuscitate him. I did hear struggle going on in the next room and the click of handcuffs."

"No further questions."

The judge turned to the defense attorney, but Arnold Torrance said, "No redirect," and the judge tapped his gavel. "Court is adjourned."

Weak with relief and dread, Velita picked up her purse from the jury room and hurried out of the courthouse. At the car, she scrabbled for the car keys, her hands shaking. What could she say to LaDonna that wouldn't make her madder? Had she complained to Ralph? Would he say it was all Velita's fault? Was being knocked silly all she had to look forward to tonight?

Chapter 16

Driving to pick up TJ, Velita thought back to that morning. She could have sworn TJ'd been fine. There probably was a math test today. His teacher ought to know by now he'd do most anything to wiggle out of a problem. Velita didn't know which was worse—him faking it or being sick and making a mess at LaDonna's apartment.

Before Velita could ring her mother-in-law's doorbell, she heard the TV blaring, and LaDonna's voice: "Turn that down!"

The door opened. "About time! The kid's driving me bonkers."

TJ sat cross-legged on the floor in front of the TV, eyes fixed on *Batman*, fists punching the air.

Velita hunched her shoulders. "Sorry. I didn't know what else to do." She slipped past LaDonna and went to him.

His forehead was cool. Beside him was a can of soda and a paper plate with the last bit of a hot dog. That meant his stomach was okay.

LaDonna snorted. "Whyn't you get him yourself? I never signed up for babysitting."

"They won't let me off the jury. I *told* the school he wasn't sick, but the secretary wouldn't listen to me."

"Yeah, well, next time leave me out of it. I got better things to do." She went to the television, snapped it off, then turned to TJ. "Okay, buster. Get your backpack and beat it." As he stood up, she swatted him lightly on his bottom.

TJ turned and grinned at her. "I beat Grandma at poker," he told Velita.

Velita sighed. What a con artist. Just like his dad, for sure. She'd have to call the school first thing in the morning, make sure they let him attend with just her signed excuse. They'd better believe her this time.

She made herself smile at LaDonna. "I *do* appreciate it." She nudged TJ. "Tell your grandma thanks for putting up with you."

On the way home, she thought, *Well, that's over.* It hadn't been as bad as she'd expected. But she didn't know whether to be relieved or upset that TJ was okay.

"Listen, kid," she told him. "It's not right what you did, playing sick. That's the same as lying. If you keep doing that, when you're really bad off, nobody will believe you."

TJ looked out the window and shrugged. "Okay." He bounced on the seat and shot imaginary monsters with his thumb and forefinger. "Putchoo, putchoo!" Then he turned to her. "Oh, I just remembered. Teacher says we can go on a field trip. To the aquarium, in Monterey."

The aquarium! She'd seen advertisements. Lots of different kinds of fish, dolphins playing around the rocks, even a little pool for the kids to stick their hands in and feel the starfish. "When?"

"I dunno. It's on a paper. I forgot to bring it home. Putchoo, putchoo!"

Wouldn't you know it? But what a treat that would be, something good for him to learn, too. Velita hoped it wouldn't cost too much. If only she could scrape together enough money. Maybe if she could catch Ralph in a good mood, he'd give her a little extra.

Then she thought again of his stunt to get out of school. She asked, "Did Grandma call your dad?"

"Putchoo, putchoo! Nuh-uh."

Velita blew out a breath of relief. Okay so far. But just in case, maybe she should stop at the grocery store and pick up a steak and fixings for dinner.

"Putchoo! *He* called *her.*"

She nearly missed her turn, and slammed on the brakes. It would take more than a nice dinner to help her now. "What did they talk about?"

"She said you'd better pick me up in time. She had to go to work."

So Ralph knew. At least she'd been warned.

At the meat counter, the smell turned her stomach and brought tears to her eyes. Embarrassed, she blinked them back.

Suddenly, she turned cold. The awful truth, holed up in her mind like a mean little rat, now gnawed its way out.

Raw meat. Twice before, the sight and smell of raw meat had made her sick. When she'd been pregnant.

Numbly, she loaded her groceries into the trunk, made sure TJ was belted in, then put the key into the ignition. Instead of starting the motor, she rested her arms and head on the steering wheel and thought back.

No. No way could she be pregnant. She'd always been real careful taking her pill; Ralph made sure of that. He said he'd had it with squalling brats.

When she'd been pregnant with Suanne, he'd said to get rid of it, and they'd had a really big fight. LaDonna had still been living with them, and for once, she'd been on Velita's side. Tough as Ralph was, he still listened to his mama. After all, whenever he needed money, she was his easiest touch.

Suanne turned out to be colicky and cried a lot at night. Ralph would yell, "Shut that kid up!" and slam the bedroom door, waking TJ. Night after night, Velita had sat up and rocked the baby. Days, she'd cooked many a meal with Suanne at her breast, just to keep the peace.

If she was pregnant now, even LaDonna wouldn't side with her.

She felt a tug at her sleeve. "C'mon, Mom, let's go. I'll miss *Pokémon*."

"Is TV all you can think about? Look, I don't feel so hot, okay?" Her head weighed a ton; she could barely raise it.

TJ groaned dramatically. "Can't you go home first and then rest?"

Velita started the car and headed out of the parking lot. All the way home, she kept thinking, *Please, God, let me be wrong.*

When she pulled into her driveway, Suanne ran from the neighbors' to greet her. "Why's TJ in the car? Where's he been? What did you buy?"

Juggling the grocery bags, Velita unlocked the front door of her house and nudged it open with her hip. "Tell your sister what happened," she told TJ. She set the bags on the kitchen table and went to the calendar, flipping back a page. She counted the weeks twice, three times, dread chilling all through her.

There was no doubt. She was pregnant. But how? Had the kids gotten into the pills, messed them up?

She checked the little pink case. Everything was in order. Maybe when she'd changed brands? The doctor had said there was a one-in-a-million chance. Nothing to worry about. Nothing.

Except Ralph. Velita leaned against the wall, weak in the knees. Why had she bothered to ask God for help? He never answered any of her prayers. Maybe there wasn't any God after all. Why else would she be in all this trouble?

But no matter what Ralph said or did, she wouldn't—*couldn't* get rid of it. Not even if he beat her senseless. No way would she kill her baby.

She rubbed her still flat stomach. "Poor little tad," she whispered. "You sure picked a lousy time to start."

Maybe, just maybe, if she could catch Ralph in a real good mood, he wouldn't take it so hard. He always liked to impress Tom. Tom only had one little girl. If she told him when Tom was around, he might even act proud, like it took a big tough guy to father another kid.

By the time Ralph came home from work, the kids were watching *The Simpsons* on TV. Velita didn't like the program, but Ralph got mad if she fussed about it.

The table was set, and french rolls were warming in the oven. She took them out, turned on the broiler, slid in the steak, and started mashing potatoes. Just as she opened her mouth to greet Ralph, she heard the TV click off and him yelling, "What's this I hear about you playing hooky?"

TJ's voice was pitched higher than usual. "I never! I threw up, and Mrs. Dorsey sent me to the office."

"Your grandma said you were fine."

"She was lying. I had a stomachache."

Velita heard a loud slap. And then, "Don't talk like that about your grandma. And don't ever pull that stunt again, hear? Tomorrow you're going to school. You better not poke your finger down your throat to throw up."

She heard a touch of laughter in her husband's voice. Ralph knew all the tricks. Suanne tiptoed into the kitchen and wormed her head up between Velita and the stove. Her eyes were big and shiny.

Velita gave her a squeeze. "It's okay, sweetie." *If Suanne only knew.*

The steak was crisp on the edges and soft and tender on the inside. TJ picked at his food, sulking, his cheek still red from the slap. Ralph stuffed his mouth full and sopped up the juices with his roll, washing it all down with beer. When he finished, he gave a thunder burp, and Suanne giggled.

"Now that's what I call a good meal," he said and pushed his chair back. Then he squinted his eyes. "What's the catch?"

It was too soon to talk about the baby, even to ask for extra money for the aquarium trip. Velita decided to play it safe. "Just making up for being gone so much. They don't let us take time off from the jury. I know your mama's busy, and I sure hated to saddle her with TJ. But I didn't know what else to do."

Ralph got another beer and sat down in his recliner. "Next time, let me handle the teacher. I'll give that old bat a few things to remember me by."

Chapter 17

The next day, the temperature zoomed into the high nineties, and the air-conditioning in the courtroom didn't seem to be working. In slacks and a long-sleeved blouse, Velita was hot. She'd wanted to make sure no old bruises would show but wondered if it was worth it.

Sitting in the jury box, she fanned herself with one of the writing tablets they'd been given. At least it was good for something. She hadn't bothered to write anything down; remembering was easier than writing.

Across the room stood a big piece of plywood with a square cut out to look like a window, covered with a tan shade. Attorney Pettigrew called Sergeant Martin back to the witness chair, then went to the fake window. "If it please the court, I will demonstrate the visibility of the policemen on the porch."

Arnold Torrance looked at his client and shrugged.

"Would you say," Attorney Pettigrew asked the witness, "that on the night in question, the window shade looking out onto the porch of Mr. Jackson's residence was opened approximately halfway?"

Sergeant Martin ran his fingers over his chin, then said, "More like a third."

The lawyer tried to raise the shade, but it wouldn't move. He pulled again, but the shade just went lower. He yanked once more, and Velita held her breath. This time, the window shade snapped loose and all the way up to the top, whirling sassily around its rod. The audience snickered, and she couldn't help laughing too. Frowning, the judge tapped his gavel, but even he had a twinkle in his eyes. It made him look a little more human, and Velita wondered if he had a family at home. If he worried about all the people he put into prison and the guilty ones who got off scot-free.

Attorney Pettigrew didn't laugh. Soberly and carefully, he pulled the shade down to a point that satisfied him, then turned back to the witness. "Sergeant Martin, you have stated that after announcing yourselves as police officers and while displaying your badges, you saw Duane Jackson's face at the window. Is this correct?"

"That is correct, yes."

"At that time, did you recognize Mr. Jackson?"

"Objection! May we approach the bench?"

They'd already tried that question awhile back. Velita figured it had to mean something. It sure sounded like the guy had been arrested before. Maybe he'd put up a fight. They'd remember him, then. But if that was true, why couldn't they just say so? Shouldn't the jury know about it?

The lawyers and judge argued back and forth in whispers, their hands flashing around, their heads shaking yes and no. Finally, the judge said, "Strike the question."

She thought Attorney Pettigrew would be mad, but it didn't seem to bother him. He just walked behind the piece of wood, bent over, and peeked through under the window shade.

"Is this approximately the position of the face?" he asked.

The witness turned his head to one side. "More vertical."

Pettigrew squatted behind the frame so that his own head was more upright. "Like this?"

"Yes."

This is crazy. Who cares exactly how the man's head was turned?

"Let the record show that the person behind the window appeared to be in a crouched position." It sounded like the judge was bored.

The lawyer got up and came back out. "In your opinion," he asked, "were the police badges easily visible to the accused?"

"In my opinion, yes."

"No further questions."

Arnold Torrance walked slowly to the front, his eyes on the jury. Then he whipped around to the witness. "Sergeant Martin, when you showed your badges to Duane Jackson, was the porch light on?"

The officer scratched his head. "I believe so, yes."

"Is it not a fact that you were in total darkness and that the face looking out was beside a lighted lamp?"

"No, the porch light was on."

"Before or after you showed your badge?"

Sergeant Martin frowned. "I believe it was before," he said slowly.

"But you're not absolutely sure."

He shook his head. "To the best of my knowledge, it was on when we showed our badges."

"No further questions."

Another officer came up and agreed with all that Sergeant Martin had said. Others told about calls made to the station. A gun shop owner showed a receipt for Duane Jackson's 357 Magnum.

Then there was another string of witnesses. A surveyor gave the measurements of the house. The man from the morgue who held a long doctor's title said he'd examined the body and it had been a gunshot that killed the police officer. Someone called a *ballistics expert* talked about the angle of gunfire in the house. He said Officer MacDuff must have been crouching, reaching into his ankle holster, when the shot entered his body. That was why his bulletproof vest hadn't protected him.

Attorney Pettigrew then said he would show the jury *exhibit A*. It turned out to be a marijuana joint found in Duane Jackson's bedroom, and he set it on a tray for the jurors to pass around. Most of them sniffed it, but Velita remembered the smell too well and passed it on quickly.

She wasn't prepared for the next exhibit. The lawyer pulled several big pictures out of a manila envelope and handed them to the judge, then to the jury. The first showed pieces of the bullet he said had shot the policeman. The second was the dead man, all crumpled, his shoulder bloody. The last was a close-up of that wound, the bullet hole itself red, jagged, and bruised.

Close up, they were horrible, and Velita closed her eyes and swallowed several times, trying not to gag. When she looked up, she saw Duane Jackson, still relaxed, his face smooth. He had to know what those pictures were, and he wasn't bothered? What kind of animal was he?

The prosecuting attorney sat down, and Arnold Torrance stood. "No questions at this time," he said. "However, I reserve the right to call the witnesses later."

The day dragged on. There were fingerprint matches, more technicians, and more experts. James Pettigrew read a long list of all their degrees and how famous they were, and Attorney Torrance finally objected, sounding peevish. "The defense acknowledges the competence of the expert witnesses. Now may we please get on with—"

But the judge rapped his gavel, and Torrance snapped his mouth shut. He didn't look a bit happy, but James Pettigrew grinned and kept on bragging.

Torrance didn't bother to cross-examine the experts, but he did object to some of the questions. And every time the lawyers and judge got into a squabble, they sent the jury out.

Lester Payne kept score. Each time they came through the jury-room door, he'd groan and add another mark on the whiteboard. So far today, the count was eleven.

Velita couldn't help wondering about all those secrets. Why shouldn't the jury know what was going on? Anyone could see the man was guilty. The policeman was dead, all right, and Duane Jackson's lawyer hadn't even tried to deny the man had killed him.

But she didn't mind this break. Anything to get away from looking at those horrible pictures. She slipped off her shoes, curled her legs up in her chair, and took out the paperback she'd brought along.

Marsha tapped the edge of the book. "*To Kill a Mockingbird*, huh? That's a good one. Do you like it?"

Velita nodded. "It's kinda sad, though. I wanted to find out about trials, you know? So I stopped at the library, and they picked it out for me. But I haven't gotten very far."

"Do you read a lot?"

"Used to. Don't have much time anymore." *Cleaning up after Ralph and the kids, keeping the yard neat, I'm lucky to have time to sew.*

Across the table, Geneva started knitting another sweater. Pink, with white stripes. Lester Payne, again in green plaid slacks, argued with farmer Wallace Takashi about the grape boycotts.

Jacob doodled on a scrap of paper, adding numbers; Velita figured he was working on his farm business.

Marsha pulled a date book out of her purse and studied it. She sighed. "I've missed five days of work already. My supervisor's going ballistic. It's hard enough to find replacements for regular nurses, let alone those with critical care experience."

Jacob asked her, "Do you work on weekends?"

"Yeah, and sometimes nights and double shifts. That helps some. With Heather gone, there's no one to miss me."

"What about that boyfriend?"

"Haven't heard a peep from him. It's just as well." Marsha acted cool, but her eyes looked sad.

Jacob winked at her. "He probably wouldn't mind if you called him."

Marsha shook her head. "If I'm worth anything to him, he'll have to make the first move."

Velita watched them. Maybe those two ought to get together. They seemed to hit it off well.

The bailiff opened the door, and Velita slipped her book back in her purse and got into line.

James Pettigrew called witnesses against Duane Jackson's character. Past bosses said he'd been late a lot, some days hadn't even shown up, and had had a bad attitude. Former teachers said he'd ditched school and hardly ever turned in his papers. Neighbors complained he was noisy, especially late at night, and always picking fights.

Velita glanced at the man. He still looked calm, as though

nothing mattered. As though the witnesses were talking about somebody else.

She wondered if all those gripes were true. Were the people . . . maybe . . . prejudiced? Or even lying? What if Duane Jackson *wasn't* guilty? She could hardly wait to hear what his lawyer would say to all that.

But Arnold Torrance again asked to "reserve the right to call the witnesses later," and then court was adjourned.

Deep in thought, Velita walked out with Marsha. Back in high school, Ralph had ditched a lot of school. Just like Duane Jackson. What if TJ was starting that same pattern? He'd gone to school this morning without fuss. So far, he'd always seemed to like his teachers, and she'd been able to make him keep up his homework. But after yesterday's stunt, she would have to clamp down on him more.

As they reached the street, Velita didn't see the traffic lights change and started to step off the curb. She didn't notice the car whipping past until Marsha grabbed her arm. Her sleeve rode up, and she quickly pulled it down, hoping Marsha hadn't seen the purple marks.

"Are you all right?" asked Marsha.

Velita blew out her breath, her heart racing. "Yeah. Where's my brain? Thanks for heading me off."

"No," said Marsha. "I mean those contusions. They weren't from the car door, were they?"

Velita shrugged. "I bruise easy."

"On your arms too?"

Velita tugged at her sleeves again. "Can't help it if I'm clumsy. I just . . . keep running into things. I'm okay. Honest."

They walked awhile without talking, but Velita could feel Marsha staring at her. Finally Marsha said, "If you ever feel like talking, I'm a good listener." She stopped, found a pen and an old cash register slip in her purse, and scribbled her phone number. Handing it to Velita, she added, "Sometimes it helps to share your problems."

Velita took the slip and glanced at it but didn't answer. Better to memorize it. First chance she got, she'd throw the paper away. If Ralph found a strange phone number on her, he'd for sure think she was messing around with another guy. He'd fix her good; she'd never make it back to the courthouse.

Chapter 18

On Wednesday, the temperature nosed up another degree, and the air conditioner in the courtroom still wasn't working. All the jurors seemed cranky. Marsha looked tired, and even Jacob was extra quiet. Lester Payne picked fights with anyone who looked at him, and Velita was careful to stay out of his way.

During the trial, the lawyers argued more than usual. The judge kept hauling them up to whisper together, sending the jury panel out to wait in their stuffy little room, where Lester Payne put more marks on the board.

Velita wondered whether they were making any progress. It seemed as though all the lawyers did was go over and over the same picky details. A lot of the jurors, especially Lester Payne, complained how boring it was to sit around wasting time.

But strangely, by now she kind of liked being here. She'd sort of gotten the hang of things—what kind of clothes were okay, where to park, which room to go in. It almost felt like she was somebody important. And because this was something she was forced to do, she could leave the house, and Ralph couldn't do a thing about it.

She could hardly believe how friendly some of the jurors were:

Marsha, Geneva, Nellie, Eunice, and Jacob. Some of the others were nice too. It was almost like being on a team.

Back in school, she'd never been on a team. There was always work to do at home and the younger kids to watch. And once she'd started up with Ralph, he'd taken over her whole life.

But that evening, Ralph grumbled about her new freedom. "That stupid trial's dragging on too long."

No sense arguing; she played along, trying to fit into his mood. "I know. Believe me, it's no fun walking through that run-down old mall with its seedy-looking creeps, just to get to the courthouse."

He eyed her suspiciously, smoothing his hair back, but finally let it go.

Then on Thursday morning, he watched her pick through her clothes for a cooler long-sleeved blouse. "If *I* was on that jury, I'd throw the guy in the clink and flush the keys."

In a way, she agreed with him. Everybody knew Duane Jackson had killed the officer. Why spend all that time arguing about little details?

But she didn't say that aloud. It was kind of nice that she couldn't talk about the trial. For once, Ralph couldn't control what she said or did.

She fixed breakfast, packed lunches, and got the kids on the school bus just like usual, although her stomach was doing loops. All the while, she watched Ralph closely, trying to figure his mood and keep him calm. Waiting for the right time to tell him about the baby.

He followed her into the kitchen, snapping the straps of his work coveralls, grinning his special phony way with his eyes cold and mean.

Oh-oh, she thought, *what's his beef now?* She held still while he squeezed her sore arm and asked in a raspy tone, "Who's the best and the toughest? Me or them pretty lawyers?"

"You, Ralph baby," she said, careful to make her voice lovey-dovey. "You're the only one for me." *As if you could say the same thing!* Just then, the oatmeal started boiling over, and she reached to grab the pan.

He held on to her arm, twisting it. "And don't you forget it." He let go with a little push, but this time he didn't hit her.

❖ ❖ ❖

By Friday, the temperature finally dropped a little, and the jurors seemed more cheerful. Geneva finished knitting her sweater and started an afghan, and Eunice had a new paperback. Wallace Takashi passed around some walnut brownies his wife had made.

Velita loved brownies, but at the first bite her stomach heaved, and she breathed deeply to settle it down, hoping no one noticed.

Nellie took two bars and studied a sales flyer while she ate. She pointed to the pictures on the front page. "Just look at these quilts! Wonder how long it took to make all those tiny stitches."

Glad for something else to think about, Velita set her brownie on a paper napkin and looked over at the advertisement.

Geneva clicked her needles faster. "The one in today's newspaper? That Mennonite sale in Fresno? I read about it. Over two hundred quilts auctioned off this weekend."

Back in Chockamo, Velita's mom had pieced quilts out of old jeans legs and red flannel. Velita had loved them and had sewn little doll blankets from the scraps. But these designs were much more beautiful, with rich colors. If only she could see one close up, touch the material, figure out how they were made. She wondered how much they cost.

As if reading her mind, Jacob said, "Some go as high as eight or nine thousand dollars."

Velita gulped. *Nine thousand dollars! For a quilt?*

Jacob added, "Sometimes a man will buy his own wife's quilt back."

"That's dumb," sputtered Lester Payne. "Why would anybody do that?"

"As a donation. Goes for a good cause."

Lester's top lip curled. "Sure. You can just bet most of the money lines someone's pocket." He stuffed a brownie in his mouth and mumbled between chews, "Says here there'll be a lot of old engines on display . . . antique cars to be auctioned off. Lot of displays, ethnic food . . . flea market. Nobody puts on a show like that without it paying off."

"All donated, and most workers are volunteers." Jacob nodded to the others. "That's run by MCC, the Mennonite Central Committee. Whatever money comes in goes for food and help to developing countries."

"How do you know so much about this?" growled Lester. "You one of them Mennonites?"

Jacob shrugged. "Guilty as charged," he said.

The room turned quiet, and all the jurors at the table stared at him.

"Don't you remember?" Marsha turned to the others. "During the questioning, they made such a production out of the nonresistance thing."

"Oh, so you're the one." Laura reached for the flyer. "But I thought—" She flipped through the pages and pointed to a picture. "You don't look at all like this."

Before he could answer, Geneva said knowingly, "There's all kinds of Mennonites." She wiggled her heavy shoulders, flirty-like. "Personally, I like Jacob's kind."

Jacob's neck turned red. Laura kept looking at him, and he finally said, "Around here, Mennonites look like anyone else. The people in that picture, the caps and wide suspenders, they're Old Order Mennonites." He turned to Velita. "Like the sister from Pennsylvania I told you about. She and her husband dress like that. These in the picture are from Canada, here to help with the sale. No matter what variety, when it comes to a good cause like this, we all work together."

"Says here it's at the Fresno Pacific University. Are you going to be there?" asked Marsha.

Jacob ran his fingers through his hair. "I usually go. But this year I'm too far behind in my work. My sister and her husband plan to be there, though. They're up in Yosemite right now but should be back in plenty of time."

Velita looked from Jacob to the picture and back again. "Did your whole family used to dress that way? Way back when?" She held her breath, surprised she'd had the nerve to speak up.

"No. Well, in my grandpa's day, they were kind of old-fashioned. But not like that. As long as I can remember, we've been pretty ordinary."

Velita felt her face grow hot. In her opinion, he wasn't ordinary at all. He was one special guy.

❖ ❖ ❖

In the courtroom that morning, James Pettigrew showed pictures of the inside of Duane Jackson's house. Something was strange about them, but Velita couldn't figure out what. Then she realized—the rooms were too tidy. With all that had happened in that house, wouldn't it have been a mess?

But the living room looked as though nobody lived there. Hardly any furniture: a sofa, a little TV on a stand, one straight chair, and a bare coffee table. No magazines, no clothes scattered on the floor, no empty beer cans.

She thought of her own house. There was always something lying around. As quick as she cleaned up, Ralph and the kids made more clutter. If anyone barged into *her* house unexpected, they'd see popcorn by the recliner, Barbie dolls and Matchbox cars scattered, and three copies of *Cycle World* on the floor. And always, those smelly old beer cans.

After the pictures had gone around, Attorney Pettigrew called Jackson's wife to the stand. "Let the record show Mrs. Jackson as a hostile witness."

The judge nodded. "So noted."

Charlene Jackson looked around at the jury and the rest of the people as though she wasn't scared of anybody. Tall, slim, with a nice figure, she could pass for a model. Her hair was piled on top of her head, a jeweled comb stuck in it, and tiny beaded braids fell to her shoulders. Her short leather skirt and silky yellow blouse looked classy, and Velita wondered how she could afford clothes like that. And how did she come to be tied to a murderer? Was she cold and hard, or had she, too, made a bad mistake?

When asked, the woman said that, at the time of the incident, she'd been married to Duane for three months. That evening, they'd been watching TV in the living room. He'd seemed nervous, couldn't sit still. Then he'd left the room, come back with a small tin box. She'd seen it before, knew it held stuff for a heroin fix.

The heroin was in a little gray container, like a film canister. No, she hadn't helped him get it ready, hadn't watched. "I just tied a scarf around his arm, that's all." After he'd shot up, he'd put the needle back into the box.

"Did you use heroin at this time?" asked Attorney Pettigrew.

"No. I was tryin' to, you know, kick the stuff."

"Where did Mr. Jackson keep the tin box?"

The woman shrugged. "Don't know."

"You don't know?"

She shook her head and grinned up at the lawyer. "He never told me."

"When he came into the living room, carrying the box, from which direction did he come?"

"Mmmm, maybe . . . from behind me."

"Could it have been from the kitchen?"

Charlene Jackson studied her long red nails. "Who knows?"

Attorney Pettigrew frowned. "Did you not see him?"

"Wasn't watchin'."

The woman has to be lying, thought Velita. *I can tell where Ralph is, what he's doing, even when I can't see him.*

"What happened while he was shooting up?"

"There was this bangin' at the front door, yelling. Me and Duane, we got scared. Wondered what was goin' on."

"Didn't you in fact know that it was the police?"

"No."

Hmm, thought Velita. *Maybe that was when they did a quick tidy-up.*

"And didn't you in fact hear the words, 'Open up, police officers'?"

"Objection," said Attorney Torrance. "Badgering the witness."

"Overruled," said the judge. "Answer the question."

"No," said Charlene Jackson. "I couldn't make out any words."

"What did you do then?"

"Duane gave me the canister and goes, 'Get rid of it.' So I did."

"Exactly what were his words?"

Mrs. Jackson tried to look at her husband, but the lawyer stood in her way. "Answer the question," said the judge.

"I don't remember. Just said to get rid of it."

"Did he not say 'Flush it'?"

She shrugged. "Maybe. Yeah, I guess." She sounded like she didn't care one way or the other.

Velita glanced at the judge. Would he get after the woman for smart-mouthing? But there was no way to tell what the judge was thinking.

Attorney Pettigrew looked toward the jury and nodded slowly. Then he went back to his table, pulled a gun out of an envelope, and held it out to Charlene Jackson. "Is this the weapon owned by Duane Jackson?"

She glanced at it. "Could be. Looks kinda like it."

"Yes or no?"

"Yeah. I guess."

"What did Mr. Jackson do with the gun?"

She flipped her fountain of braids. "I don't know."

"You don't know? Did you not see Mr. Jackson fire the gun?"

"No."

Attorney Pettigrew shook his head, and Velita could see he didn't believe the woman either.

He asked, "Did you hear shots?"

Charlene nodded. "Yeah."

"How many shots did you hear at that time?"

"Two. Maybe three."

"What happened next?"

"There was this crash at the back of the house, and all of a sudden these guys were inside with guns. Then I heard more shots."

"Who was shooting this time?"

"Couldn't tell. I didn't look." Her voice turned flat, like she was reading the words off a paper, and Velita wondered if she'd memorized what to say. Maybe Duane's lawyer had told her ahead of time what the questions would be.

"What happened after that?"

"Uh . . . the front door bashed in. Duane, he raised his hands and said 'Don't shoot, I'm comin' out.' They put cuffs on him, shoved him out the door."

"Remember, you are under oath to tell the truth. Did the police officers strike you or Duane Jackson?"

"Yeah. They bashed me on the head with a gun, cuffed me. Shoved me outside. Duane, he was layin' on the porch, and two guys were kickin' him. They jerked him up, packed both of us down the steps and into the car."

"And then what happened?"

"Hauled us off to the police station."

Velita took a deep breath and let it out slowly. When the neighbors had called the police for Ralph's rampages, he'd said it was just a family quarrel. That they could work it out themselves.

He'd been cool and polite, smiling at her sweet as saccharine, raising his eyebrows. "Can't we, sweetheart?" and all she could do was nod, because she knew what would happen if she didn't.

If the police *had* arrested him, would they have taken her too? Handcuffed them both? Hauled them into court in front of a whole bunch of people like these and then locked them both up in prison?

And the kids—what happened to kids when their folks were arrested? Would they be put in a foster home?

She couldn't do that to them. What *could* she do? Put up with Ralph's beatings, somehow, for the rest of her life?

Chapter 19

Arnold Torrance walked up to cross-examine, and Velita forced her thoughts back to the trial.

The men on the porch had been in regular clothes, Charlene explained. She didn't know they were police. The TV'd been on, kinda loud, that's why she couldn't hear what they said.

Velita frowned. Something was wrong about that. If the police could tell what they'd yelled inside, the part about the flushing, why didn't the woman understand *their* shouting?

Charlene Jackson told about phone call threats and a drive-by shooting. "Someone was after us. Yeah, we called the police, but they never showed. That's why Duane went and bought the gun. For protection."

"You have told the court you did not see the shooting on the night in question. Would you please explain why?"

"I was hidin'. Behind the couch. Had my hands over my eyes, couldn't tell who was shootin' who." She shrugged. "All that yellin' and chargin' around, could be the police shot themselves."

"Objection!" shouted Pettigrew.

"Sustained," murmured the judge.

The defense lawyer went on. "You say that the police, and I

quote, 'Bashed me on the head with a gun, cuffed me.' What happened next?"

"They had me and Jackson down on the porch, kickin' and stompin' us."

Arnold Torrance nodded at the jury, then looked at the judge. "No further questions."

He sat down, and James Pettigrew went up again. "When the police officer approached you, did you not kick and bite him?"

Charlene Jackson glared at him. "I did not!"

Pettigrew's voice was soft. "Isn't it true you were the one who supplied Duane Jackson with heroin?"

"No way!"

"And isn't it true that you were in the business of selling drugs, in fact have a conviction pending—"

"Objection!" shouted Attorney Torrance. "Your Honor, I request a conference."

The judge cleared his throat. "Strike that last question from the record. The jury will please disregard it." He looked at his watch. "Due to previous obligations on the part of both the prosecution and defense, court is adjourned until next Tuesday at 10:00 AM. I will see both attorneys in chambers." He whacked his gavel and left the room.

All that drug business, thought Velita. *What if that was the secret the prosecutor was trying so hard to keep from the jury?*

On the way to the parking garage, Marsha asked her, "Are you going to that Mennonite sale?"

Those gorgeous quilts! If only things were different . . . Velita shook her head. "Ralph and me . . . we don't go out much." Anymore, she hated going places with him. Never could tell when he'd get drunk and pick a fight with someone. The way things were going, she sure didn't need any more trouble.

Back before she'd gotten mixed up with this trial, they'd gone to a barbecue at a friend of Tom's, and someone had made a joke about Okies. Ralph had punched the guy in the nose, getting blood all over the potato salad. Tom had tried to calm him down but finally got him to leave, and she had to collect the kids before they finished eating and rush them to the car or get left behind.

Then there was the time a preacher had come to the door and tried to tell Ralph he needed to get right with God . . .

Marsha touched her elbow. "Why don't I pick you up, and just we two go? Come on, it would be fun."

Velita stared at her. Fun? Never, ever, had she gone off on her own like that, just for a good time. She smiled a little, imagining what it would be like. How nice it would be to do things with Marsha as a friend. To walk around, look at the quilts, maybe even have a snack . . . She shook her head. "I wish I could." Dumb to even think about it. Ralph would never let her. "But I . . . I think my husband has plans."

She drove home, wondering what to do with the whole free afternoon. It was almost as good as going out with Marsha. Ralph didn't know she was out early—she could do anything she wanted. If only that sale was today, she could even have gone there for a little while and still be back in time to fix dinner.

At home, the *Springton Beacon* lay rolled up on the coffee table where she'd put it that morning. She took the flyer and settled on Ralph's recliner, studying the front page of the flyer until she could see the pictures with her eyes shut. Oh, those beautiful quilts!

Then she turned the page and read through the flyer. About

how the Mennonites worked all year getting those quilts and other handwork ready, how all the money from the sale went to Africa and countries she'd never heard of before. Helping the poor by providing materials for them to make baskets and carvings and clothes to sell, teaching them to make a living and feed their families.

Every year, people from all over California—even Oregon and as far as Canada—came especially to Fresno for that sale. They bid on the quilts and a whole lot of old restored classic cars and saw displays of old machinery. Ralph would go crazy over stuff like that—

An awful thought hit her, and she bounced up like a spring. What if the TV news reported that the jury had been sent home early? If Ralph found out later, there'd be real trouble—he'd be sure she was sneaking around on him. She smoothed out the upholstery on the recliner so Ralph wouldn't know she'd been lazing around on his favorite chair, then called the shop and left a message for him that she was home.

Carefully, she tucked the flyer back into the paper and spread it out next to the chair, fixing it so when he opened it, the Mennonite sale flyer would be on top. The part about a flea market, the old machines display.

Maybe he and Tom would decide to go tomorrow. He'd come home in a good mood, and she would cook a special dinner. If that all went smoothly, it might be the right time to tell him about the baby.

Planning the meal, Velita got out the vacuum cleaner and started going over the carpets.

That evening after dinner, Ralph pushed back in his recliner and picked up the *Beacon*. He glanced at the pictures of the quilts on the front of the flyer, then tossed it aside. "Why do they put all this trash in with the paper?"

Velita picked it up and pretended to read it for the first time. She turned the page. "Whatta you know? A '31 Chevy coupe."

"Huh? Gimme that."

He glanced at the page, then settled back in his chair. She went into the kitchen and cleaned up. When she was finished, he was still reading. He looked up and said, "Hey, maybe we ought to take the kids and go see this show."

Velita caught her breath. She hadn't counted on *that*. It'd be nice to see those quilts, but was it worth the gamble of going out with Ralph? "You're sure you want to bother with me and the kids?"

He looked at her sharply. "What's the matter? Don't want to be seen with me?"

What could she say? "I'd love to go with you. If you want me." Then she had a horrible thought. What if Jacob was there? But then she remembered he had said he was too busy to go this year.

Putting on a smile, she said, "I bet Tom would like to see all that stuff. His wife too."

"Yeah, why not? We'll make it a party."

A party. Sure. But maybe, with Tom and his wife along, it might not be so bad. Tom could help keep Ralph calm, and although Velita didn't know his wife well, it'd be nice to have some woman company.

Velita pulled out a card table from the hall closet and set it up in a corner of the living room. On it, she arranged her portable sewing machine and a nearly finished blouse and started hemming.

Chapter 20

A full moon shone over the Franzen farm, lighting up the bright red Massey tractor and reflecting off the disk blades. Jacob didn't need the yard light to see his way around. In the shed, all the tools and ropes hung on hooks or were stacked on shelves, each in its proper place. If Heinz had used any of them, he'd put them back where they belonged.

Jacob nodded in satisfaction. It paid to be neat. Even with his eyes shut, he could stretch out his hand and find what he wanted. He wished it was that easy to keep the farm work organized.

As if it wasn't enough that Buck had been stealing from him, today he'd found out the man had also failed to line up a thinning crew for this week. Jacob had spent all afternoon contacting different crew bosses, even begging, but all had given the same answer—their men were busy on other ranches.

He walked over to the nearest trees and felt among the leaves, his hands confirming what he already knew. The branches were thick with undeveloped fruit. He gave a sharp whistle. It was past time.

Timing was so important. If he thinned much later than this week, the fruit wouldn't size. Nobody would buy golf-ball-sized peaches. Without a good crop, how would he pay for his tractor and disc, the repairs, the spraying, even living expenses?

The principal at Maranatha had been kind enough to give him an extension on Becky's tuition, but it looked like he'd have to put them off again. Worse, there might not be money to send her next year.

That would break her heart; she was fiercely loyal to her class. And how could he face his parents? Three generations of Franzens had attended that small church-sponsored high school.

He had to do something. Starting with the nearest tree, he began culling out the marbles. His fingers fumbled through the clusters, searching, yanking, tossing, faster and faster, until leaves and bits of branches lay at his feet. On to the next tree, and the next, until finally, breathing in rasping groans, he stopped and leaned his head against the rough bark. Even if he pulled the kids out of bed and they all worked all night, the Queencrests wouldn't get done. Not to mention the other early varieties on his eighty acres.

He dropped to his knees on the ground and pounded his fists into the dirt. How could he have gotten himself tied up at a time like this? He'd thought sure they'd let him off, that he'd had a good enough excuse. He should have tried harder, spoken out about the Bible's views on capital punishment. "Whoever sheds man's blood, by men shall his blood be shed." Some in the church held that the verse referred to the death penalty. That the commandment "Thou shalt not kill" just applied to murder. If he'd told that to the judge, the defense would have surely kicked him off. But did he really believe that?

He thought of Duane Jackson, messed up by drugs, half-crazed with fear and confusion, shooting the policemen who had charged into his house. The defense had said the man had thought he was protecting his wife from intruders.

The judge had asked what Jacob would do if someone was threatening his family. Now he knew the reason for that question, and there was a lot to consider.

It was an awful responsibility, deciding a man's fate. Maybe it wasn't too late to tell the judge he couldn't be impartial. But would that be true? If he dropped out, would his replacement be any more fair?

No. That would be the coward's way out. Jacob got up and slowly thinned a few more branches. He'd always been taught that things didn't happen by chance. God must have put him on the jury for a special reason. Just like He'd sent him to the underground garage at the right time to rescue Velita. Of that he was sure.

But then he felt again the sensation of holding her trembling body, steadying her shoulders. Her soft hair brushing against his cheeks. His face burned, and he shook himself to rid the unclean thoughts. Maybe this was the Devil testing him. He had only done what was necessary. Velita was doing all right now, so that should be the end to it. But what about that *fe'rekt*, crazy husband? And why was there a bump on her other cheek?

Jacob sighed. He couldn't get involved in their lives—it would only make more trouble for her. There were others who could help her. Marsha Lewis, being a nurse, would know better how to work things out.

After the trial was over, he could go back to his own routine and the safety of the church. He would never see any of the other jurors again—that chapter in his life would be over and forgotten.

Suddenly Jacob became aware of Becky calling him from the house. "Daddy, telephone!"

He sprinted inside. *Dear Lord, let it be the contractor with a new thinning crew.* Grabbing up the receiver, he gasped for breath. "Franzen here."

"Jakie?"

Clara was the only one who still called him that, but that wasn't Clara's voice. However, their parents and she and Heinz should be driving back from Yosemite about now—Heinz still new at the wheel and all those winding mountain roads around Yosemite—what if they'd had a wreck and someone else had to call?

The voice went on: "I was wondering if you could see your way clear to helping out at the MCC sale tomorrow."

Jacob blinked. This had nothing to do with Clara. But the voice was familiar. Maybe it was some older woman, a friend of his mother's. "I don't know—I've got an awful lot to do on the farm. I've been gone so much . . ."

The voice went on, even while he talked: ". . . the Heiers have the flu, and Roger Martens has to drive to Los Angeles to pick up his daughter, and we were already shorthanded. It's only a couple of hours; surely you can spare that much."

"Well—"

"And what about Becky? We need all the help we can get."

"She'll be in the burger booth for Maranatha High."

"But you can help?"

He shouldn't. The trial, all his work, Buck gone . . . But he *had* been wanting to see the old farm equipment display. Two hours wasn't so long. If the thinning crew couldn't come anyway . . . "I guess so. What time?"

"If you could come at eleven, stay till one, that would be great."

Sam and Paul wouldn't mind tagging along, eating hamburgers at the Maranatha Cougar's stand. The boys went to a lot of their games and would love to fool around there, talking to some of the athletes.

Jacob started to hang up, then realized he'd forgotten to ask: "What'll I be doing?"

"Oh, didn't I tell you? You'll be in the fritter booth." He heard a giggle on the other end of the line. "We need your strong muscles for lifting the heavy pans of oil."

Suddenly he recognized the voice, the laugh, and slapped himself on the forehead. Emma Redekopf. That woman would do anything to get her hooks into him. Like a dummy, he'd fallen right into her trap. *Vout yehfs et noo?* What was he getting into now?

Oh well. The booths were open all day, and there'd be several shifts of workers. If he was lucky, he might not even see her.

But it didn't take a smart man to figure it out. If Emma was in charge, her shift would match his.

Chapter 21

At eleven o'clock on Saturday morning, the parking lot at Fresno Pacific University was crowded. Attendants waved Ralph's old green Dodge on, telling him to go clear to the far end. This area was jammed too, with crowds heading toward the buildings. Ralph cussed, and Velita held her breath, hoping this wouldn't start him off. Just then, Tom pointed out an empty space between a pickup and a van.

After parking, the men didn't get out right away, instead finishing the beer they'd brought along. TJ reached for the door handle, but Velita motioned for him to wait. She wished Tom had brought his wife along—it would have been nice to get to know her better—but Tom said she was at work. She managed the kitchenware at Wal-Mart, and they had some big stuff on sale.

"Yeah," said Ralph, looking back at Velita. "Some women are smart enough to get jobs."

She had to bite her lip. *He* was the one who kept her from doing anything that smelled like freedom. She wouldn't even be on that jury if he had anything to say about it.

Ralph looked around, then took another gulp from his Coors. "I don't see no antique cars."

In the distance, between two buildings, a long banner hung with huge hand-printed letters: "MCC Sale." From all directions people—big, little, young, and old—kept moving toward it.

Tom pointed to it. "Pro'lly over there."

Velita watched the men, hoping they'd find lots to do. On the way over, Ralph had been real chipper, going on about old engines, motorcycles, and vintage cars. This was only his second beer, so if nobody looked at him wrong, Tom should be able to keep him from blasting off.

As quietly as possible, Velita opened her door just a crack. The sun felt warm with a nice cool breeze and no sign of rain. She'd put on the new flowered blouse she'd finished the night before, and from the way Tom had eyed her, she knew she looked nice.

"Hold your horses, woman!" Ralph tilted his head for the last few swallows.

I'd better walk a tight rope, just in case. Velita crossed her fingers and closed her eyes. *Just a few hours, dear God, is that too much to ask?*

Slowly and lazily, Ralph got out of the car and tossed the empty can under the van next to them. He stretched his arms and twisted his back as though he'd been driving for hours instead of forty minutes, then hitched up his Levis. "Well, let's get this show on the road."

Tom grinned. "Yeah, must be *something* to see, all those people heading out there." He and Ralph swaggered off between the parked cars. Velita hustled the kids out and hurried after the men.

Even before she passed under the sign, she could smell onions, cinnamon, and hot oil. Over the thump of music and the laughter and chatter of the crowd came the heavy throb of engines. Between the buildings on a stretch of lawn, a line of booths advertised food, drinks, and crafts.

Around the corner from the entrance, a large, roped-off area held machines of all sizes and shapes, chugging away. Old tractors lined up four deep, and people swarmed over them like ants on a cookie crumb.

Ralph stopped short, and Velita nearly ran into him. "Oh, yeah," he breathed. He sounded as though he'd just walked into heaven.

TJ pulled on Ralph's arm and pointed to a model airplane in a nearby stall. "Can I buy one? Only a dollar."

Ralph frowned, but Tom laughed and said, "Come on, tightwad. It'll get him off your back."

Ralph reached in his pocket, then glanced at Suanne. She stared up at him, her eyes begging like a puppy dog.

"Ohh-kay," he said, and gave them each a dollar. TJ whooped and ran off to the counter. "Wait for me right here," Ralph told Velita, then heaved himself over the rope barrier and headed for the machines.

Velita and Suanne stood watching the crowd. People greeted each other, hugging and laughing like long lost friends. Everybody seemed to know everyone else. Were they all Mennonites? She scanned the faces, wondering how you could tell. They looked the same as people you'd see in Von's or Target.

She wondered if Marsha or others from the jury were there but didn't see anyone familiar. Once she thought she spotted Jacob after all, but it turned out to be someone else. That was a relief. But kind of disappointing.

Past the engine display, the grounds were fixed up like a carnival. Couples and families swarmed about, little kids ran around on the lawn, and long lines waited at little decorated booths. Brightly colored signs announced Russian Pancakes, German Fritters, Funnel Cakes, and *Beerocks*. Farther on were hamburgers and tacos and several ice-cream stands. The longest row of people, two deep, snaked into a big building marked with an arrow pointing to a sign: *Verenikya* dinner. Velita wondered what that was.

On each side of the booths, long tables with benches were filled with people eating all kinds of goodies. Velita glanced at their plates, wishing Ralph had given her some money for a snack. If those punks in the parking lot hadn't helped themselves to her wallet, she could have bought a rolled-up Russian pancake dusted with powdered sugar. A whiff of engine exhaust joined the smell of hot cooking oil and salty nachos, bringing back Velita's queasy stomach, and she figured it was just as well she had no money.

Back among the engines, she saw Ralph grinning like a kid in a toy store. That was a good sign. Tonight, she would cook steak, and Tom might stay for dinner. *If* nothing went wrong, and *if* she got up the nerve, she would tell Ralph about the baby.

Suanne jiggled Velita's elbow and held up her dollar. "I'm thirsty. Can I buy a soda?"

Velita's throat was dry too. A cold drink would feel so good. But Ralph had said to stay right here. "Wait, sweetie," she told Suanne. "When your daddy's done . . ."

Tom had climbed on top of a diesel tractor, and Ralph was studying an old pump at the far end of the display. Velita waved, but neither of them looked her way.

Farther down the sidewalk, a hot dog stand sold Pepsi. Did she dare? It would only take a minute; Ralph wouldn't miss her.

The line wasn't long, and she was served quickly. Before handing Suanne her drink, Velita took a sip, but the sweetness went against her. She looked around for a drinking fountain. Finding none, she started back to Ralph, looking through the open doors of the buildings on the way. Some had shelves of canned and dried fruit, some baked goods, and others had handmade crafts, like wooden candlesticks and carved animals. She saw a rack of scarves, T-shirts, and strings of beads. One building was filled with tables full of used books, with a display on a stand outside the door. She picked up a book and leafed through it, trying to get her mind off her uneasy stomach. It didn't help, and she set the book down.

Across from the engines, another building was marked Auction, and people streamed in and out its double doors. Velita peeked in and saw a drinking fountain. "Come on, Suanne," she said. "I gotta have some water."

Once inside, she sucked in her breath. Racks and racks of quilts—she couldn't believe how many. Even more beautiful than they'd looked in the newspaper. Drawn as though by a magnet, she started toward them. Then she remembered Ralph, quickly took a drink of water, and went back outside.

The men had moved on to the antique cars, and Ralph sat inside a shiny Model A. The hood was open, and Tom and some other men were examining the engine.

Velita smiled. Ralph was happy. He could be there for hours. TJ was still near the airplane booth, playing with another little boy. It would be safe to take a quick peek at the quilts.

"Wait for me here," she told TJ, and pulled Suanne along into the building.

"Would you care to sign our guest book?" asked a young woman in a black cloth bonnet and a long black dress. Her blond hair was pulled back into a tight bun.

The woman lifted her skirt just enough to show high-top buttoned shoes. "This was my great-great-grandmother's wedding outfit," she explained.

Velita signed the book, then looked around. Suanne pulled loose and ran to a table full of crocheted dolls, aprons, and knickknacks. Beyond that, in a corner of the building, propped on sawhorses, was a brightly colored patchwork quilt tightly stretched on a wooden frame. A group of women sat around it, busily sewing swirls of tiny stitches in a fancy design.

"That's the Dorcas Circle from the Bethel Mennonite church," said the guide. "They pieced it together at home and are giving a quilting demonstration here. All together it takes about two hundred woman-hours to finish."

Velita watched the needles dipping and rising, following a penciled-in pattern. The women laughed and talked as they worked, as though they were at home in someone's living room.

They seemed to be having a lot of fun. *Amazing,* she thought, *that strict church people like Mennonites would laugh so much.* She asked the guide what it took to belong to a group like that, and the woman said anyone could join. She told Velita about the many different sewing circles and their meeting times.

Velita thanked her, knowing Ralph would never let her join up. But as much sewing as she had done, and with all the scraps she'd saved over the years, maybe she could piece a coverlet at home.

She wandered over to the racks of finished quilts. One in particular caught her eye. A pinned-on sign said "Wedding Ring Pattern."

Twined circles of yellow, orange, and brown colors were highlighted with a chocolate brown border. It was so rich-looking that her heart ached. Wouldn't a bed look gorgeous with a covering like that!

Cross-section samples of quilting lay on a card table nearby. Velita picked one up and studied it. She'd need to buy batting for a filler and material for the back. If she kept a little bit out of the grocery money each week, maybe someday she'd have enough saved up.

The shout of an auctioneer blared over the crowd noises. Someone brushed against Velita, and she turned to see people filling up tiers of bleachers on the other side of the room. The auctioneer stood on a low platform at one end, and while helpers on one side held up the quilts, a woman in the center described it and told who had made it.

Velita could hardly believe it. She was actually seeing the quilt auction Jacob had mentioned! Before long, almost all the bleacher seats were taken, and as the auctioneer warbled his spiel, yipping at each rising price, his helpers moved among the people, waving in the bids. There was a lot of joking and teasing, and again Velita wondered if all the people knew each other.

She glanced at her daughter. Suanne had found a bin of stuffed animals nearby and was setting them up in a row, talking to them while cuddling a bunny in her arms.

Velita peeked out the door again and saw Ralph still deep in the machines. Staying close by the door, in case he got through, she watched the fast-moving auction. One beauty after another was taken off the racks, held up, and sold.

She couldn't believe the prices. She'd thought Jacob had spread it on a little thick, but it was true. Twelve hundred dollars, thirty-five hundred dollars, seven thousand dollars. An especially gorgeous king-sized quilt went for twelve thousand dollars!

She sighed. *Imagine having enough money to buy such a treasure!* That would be something to pass down to your children and grandchildren. A real heirloom. She looked back to the line of racks to see if her favorite had been sold. It was still there, waiting for her.

In her mind she traced the twining rings, envying the lucky woman whose husband would buy that for her. Someday she would make one just like that. But first she would practice on small coverlets, maybe an airplane design for TJ's room, kittens for Suanne. Then the wedding ring quilt for herself. If she got very good at it, maybe she could make another one and sell it.

She was busy figuring out yardage in her head when she heard a whistle.

Ralph! She had forgotten about the time. She got up and hurried to Suanne. "Put back the bunny," she whispered, grabbed her daughter's hand, and rushed to the entrance.

Ralph's face was dark with anger. "What you doing, hiding in here?"

"I'm just . . . just looking at the handwork. You ought to see the pretty—"

"Where's TJ?"

Velita pointed. "By the model planes."

But he wasn't there.

"Can't even keep track of your kids," growled Ralph. "Get on outta here." He and Tom marched off.

Velita hurried to catch up. "He was there a minute ago. He can't have gone far."

"He better not." Ralph whistled again, this time loudly enough to be heard over the crowd noises. "Hey, Tiger!" he yelled into the air.

People turned to stare. There was no sign of TJ.

The joy of seeing the quilts shriveled to a hard lump in Velita's throat. How could she have been so stupid as to lose track of the time? And where could TJ have gone? Now, for sure, the day had gone bad.

She followed Ralph down the sidewalk and past the food booths. He stopped abruptly, looked up at a sign above one of the counters, then fumbled in his jeans pocket.

He told the pretty young waitress, "Be a sweetheart and gimme a beer and a ham sandwich."

The girl smiled. "All we have is Pepsi."

Ralph pointed with his thumb. "The sign says—"

"*Beerocks.*"

"Shoot, I thought you just couldn't spell. What's a bee-rock?"

A man moved up beside the girl and said, "It's a bun filled with ground meat and cabbage. Really tasty. Here, try a piece." He cut one open and held out a chunk.

Ralph backed off. "No way, man. Smells like—"

Tom threw his arm across Ralph's shoulders. "We'll pass. Thanks anyway." He pointed past the booths. "S'pose your kid went that way?" The two walked off.

The man's hand was still stretched out, holding the piece of bun. Velita didn't want to hurt his feelings, but after what Ralph had said, she didn't dare take the food. She shook her head and followed her husband.

It's good that Tom is along, she thought. Who knew what Ralph would have done without his friend to calm him down. Now if they could just find their boy and get out of here . . .

TJ knew better than to go off with strangers; she'd drilled that into him, and his teacher had talked about it in school. No, he *had* to be here, somewhere. All the fun stuff going on, he was sure to be in the middle of it.

A little farther on, a lot of kids were jumping in a huge, blown-up plastic tent. Ralph shoved past the children waiting in line and looked inside, then shook his head.

Velita swallowed the bile rising in her throat. It was all her fault. She should have stayed right there by the machines and not moved an inch, no matter what. Then she thought of those beautiful quilts, the thrill of touching them, planning one. It was nice to have that memory. But was it worth it?

Tom had gone on ahead and now came back. "Nothing to drink in this whole crazy zoo! Soon's we find the kid, let's go to a liquor store and then—"

His words were drowned out by a drum roll. Farther on was a portable stage with amps and speakers blasting out the whine of electric guitars. A teenage girl swayed and sang, cuddling the mike.

Velita caught a few of the words. "On Christ, the solid rock, I stand." Right now, she sure could use something solid to stand on.

Chapter 22

Wearing a long denim apron, Jacob swung a huge metal tray of hot, raisin-studded fritters over to the counter of the booth. Two latex-gloved girls waited to roll them in sugar. He nodded at them and turned back to his station at the portable stove. Across the vat of hot oil, his partner ladled in more blobs of batter, and slowly, the fat white lumps turned into golden nuggets.

Wiping his sweaty forehead with the back of his hand, Jacob pushed up his Massey-Ferguson cap, then turned the fritters with a long slotted spoon.

Why had he let himself get talked into this job? He'd promised to work two hours, eleven to one, but here it was one thirty and he was still at it. A fresh crew had come to relieve the baggers and the sales girls, but his own replacement hadn't shown up. It wouldn't be so bad if he didn't have to listen to the twittering of Emma Redekopf and her friends. So far, he'd heard all the latest gossip: who was pregnant, who was seen coming out of Shorty's Saloon, which were new couples, and which marriages were in trouble.

Sharon had never been one to gossip. Once she'd heard a group of older church women chew over a juicy bit of scandal, and she'd dared to scold them. "You're just like vultures, enjoying rotten things," she'd told them. Later she had apologized—after all, they were her elders. But she'd only apologized for the name-calling, not the criticism. Like Jacob, she'd had no use for people who condemned smoking, drinking, movies, and dances but thought nothing about the hurt caused by spreading rumors.

Now, as if the gossip wasn't enough, Emma fluttered around in the crowded booth, giving him unnecessary directions, brushing against him. He leaned his hot, tired body closer toward the cooking oil. Was she *that* man-hungry? Or was he just imagining things?

"Hey, *Yoacob*, what you doing in there—frittering away your time?"

Jacob turned to see an old school friend, also a farmer, at the counter. He laughed at the pun and waved the spoon at the man. "There's no rest for the weary," he countered.

The man carefully chose the fattest in the pile of sugar-covered fritters on the tray. "How are the peaches sizing?" He helped himself to coffee from the urn at the corner of the booth.

"Not so good. Know any thinning crew that's not busy?"

"I'll let you know if I hear of any."

"Thanks. Have you seen my sister around? Clara?"

"No, she's here? With this big crowd, I've run into a lot of old friends. I'll keep an eye out for her."

The man moved on, and Jacob turned back to the hot oil, glancing at his watch. Clara and Heinz were sure to have eaten already, and were probably at the quilt auction. He needed to find the boys and get some lunch. Becky would probably have a hamburger with her friends, but the boys might not have the sense to save a little money for food.

He was scooping up some more fritters when he heard a voice from behind. "Did my kid come by? Eight years old, about so high, dark hair?" Something about that voice was vaguely familiar. Something unpleasant.

The sales girl answered, "By himself? There *was* a boy—shooting a little airplane and chasing after it—"

"Yeah, that's probably him."

The girl pointed. "Last I saw, he went that way."

"What are those, fried rats?"

Where had he heard that flat, sneering tone before? Jacob craned his neck.

A black-haired man. Next to him, her back toward him, a blond. That fluffy hair—

Of course! *Velita.* And that skunk of a husband. Another man was with them, and a little girl looking like a miniature Velita.

"Hello," said Jacob, putting on a polite smile. "Enjoying the sale?"

Ralph stared at him. "You!" He spit out the word, and turned to punch Velita's shoulder with the heel of his hand. "Hey, babe, no wonder you got all gussied up! You knew your boyfriend would be here."

Velita didn't meet Jacob's eyes. She touched Ralph's arm and said, "Come on, honey, let's go."

Ralph shrugged her hand away. "Now I get it. You planned this whole thing!"

In the vat, the next batch of fritters turned dark brown. Quickly, Jacob flipped the fat nuggets over. What could he say without making things worse?

❖ ❖ ❖

Velita watched Ralph's jaw tighten, saw the anger building up in him. Her face grew hot, her hands cold. Why did Jacob have to come, after all? She'd spotted him first, had desperately hoped they'd get past the booth before he turned around, before Ralph noticed him. "Tom went on to the Sno-Cones," she said, forcing her voice to stay calm. "Maybe TJ's over there."

"TJ can wait. He's a big boy. I want to see what this fancy-man is making."

The salesgirl looked at Jacob, her eyebrows raised.

"Bag up a half-dozen," Jacob told her. To Ralph he added, "My treat. They're good, you'll like them."

Ralph laughed as he took the bag, and his eyes glittered. "Well, by jiggers," he said, glancing at Velita. "A present from your sweetie." His voice lowered to a husky whisper. "Know what I'm going to do with it?" Slowly, he spread his fingers over the sack, and Velita was sure he'd smash it into Jacob's face.

Tom came up and muttered, "Cool it, man." He reached for the bag but wasn't quite fast enough. Ralph had squashed it flat onto the counter.

All the workers in the booth stared, and Velita felt like crawling into a hole and disappearing. How could she ever face Jacob again?

Then she heard a woman's shrill voice, with a hint of German accent.

"If you don't want it, fine. There's plenty more that would. We don't need trash like you littering up our booth. Now get out of here and stay out."

Velita turned and saw a stocky woman with short permed hair glaring at Ralph, her fists on her hips. What would her husband do to someone who dared sass him like that?

Ralph looked the woman up and down, his mouth slightly open. "Hey, this broad's got spunk," he said. "More than you can say for that turkey in an apron."

Velita felt confused. Would he actually back down? To a woman? She wondered what would happen if *she* tried holding her ground. At home, her mama had always fought back, but then, mama was big and tough.

She turned to go, but Ralph stayed where he was. "Hey, lover boy!" he purred. "Come on out of your pretty little cage. Let's see what kind of man you are."

His back to Ralph, Jacob kept turning the fritters. He lifted his chin. "Be glad to oblige," he said, "but my shift's not over yet."

"Shift, huh? Okay, I'll be waiting. I'll shift your gears so fast you won't know them from a hole in the ground." Ralph turned to Tom and motioned with his head. "C'mon, let's go find my kid."

Tom hesitated, then got his wallet and pulled out a ten-dollar bill. He slapped it down on the counter. "Keep the change."

Velita, her nerves jangled, held tightly to Suanne's hand and followed the men in the direction the salesgirl had pointed. Finding Jacob in the fritter booth had been bad enough—if Tom couldn't persuade Ralph to leave before Jacob finished working, she'd rather die than watch what would happen.

Jacob looked strong and muscular. He could probably hold his own against most people. But he seemed such a kind, gentle man, and Ralph liked to fight dirty.

Ahead of them on the portable platform, a new group of musicians had set up their equipment, and more people gathered to listen. This close, each thump of the drums stabbed through Velita's head, and she closed her eyes for a minute. Then she felt a tug at her arm.

Suanne pointed toward the stage. "Look, Mommy."

A crowd of kids stood in front of the stage, clapping and rocking with the beat. Right in the middle was TJ, singing with them, his shoulders twitching along.

Velita tried to get his attention, waved for him to come, but he didn't look her way.

Then Ralph came over and spotted him too. Her husband's face flushed, and he growled, "I'll teach that punk to run off."

But Tom laughed. "Hey, look at that rhythm. Your kid's a natural. Bet he'll be a famous rock star some day."

Ralph hesitated. "Yeah, well . . ."

"Get him a guitar and some lessons. He could make you rich."

"Yeah?" Ralph cocked his head, watching TJ jerk and twist.

"Sure!" insisted Tom. "That's how most singers get their start. Even ole Elvis. Good old gospel rock."

Ralph's face relaxed into a grin, and Velita went limp with relief. Now maybe they could leave peacefully.

❖ ❖ ❖

In the fritter booth, Emma swept the crushed sack off the counter and into the garbage can. "What was that all about?" she demanded. "Do you know those creeps?"

At first, Jacob didn't answer. How could he explain Ralph's crazy jealousy? One by one, with his turning spoon, he fished out an entire batch of burnt fritters from the vat and threw them into the trash. "That woman—we're on the same jury panel."

Emma's eyes narrowed, and her head tilted to one side. "That's it?" She didn't look convinced.

Jacob nodded. He didn't owe her any explanation. Whatever he said would get spread all over church by Sunday. Besides, he couldn't explain it to himself. He thought back. Had he done something that could be misunderstood? Anything improper?

He'd just followed Velita home to make sure she was all right. Nobody in his right mind would be that jealous over a small act of kindness.

Again he remembered the sensation of Velita in his arms. But that had only been an innocent gesture of help, and anyway, Ralph didn't know about that. Or did he? Could he have wormed it out of Velita?

As Jacob worked, he felt Emma's eyes on him. When his replacement finally came, he took off his apron with relief and handed it to the man.

Then he drew in his breath in a soft whistle. In the distance, near the bandstand, he could see Ralph and Velita standing at the edge of the crowd. Was the man actually waiting for him? What would the guy do?

Ralph's bluster didn't scare him. As a kid back in school, he'd had his share of fights, winning most; since then, farm work had kept him strong. But he'd always been taught there were better ways to solve a problem. Nonviolence—that was what set the Mennonites apart.

He could still hear his youth leader quoting from the Bible: "A soft answer turneth away wrath." Trouble was, soft answers seemed only to make Ralph madder.

He turned and walked in the opposite direction, toward the Maranatha High booth to check on Becky and the boys and find something to eat. It was easier to think on a full stomach. And if Velita and her husband were still around by then, the Lord would show him how to calm the guy.

When Jacob found Becky, she told him Sammy and Paul had eaten there earlier. They'd found friends and were now chasing each other with water balloons behind the buildings.

Becky held out a wrapped bun. "Want a 'super-'Natha-burger'?"

After smelling hot oil for hours, Jacob didn't want anything greasy. He wandered from booth to booth, trying to decide what to eat.

"Well, hi there! I wondered if I'd see you here."

He turned to see Marsha Lewis grinning at him. She looked cool and refreshing in white jeans and a pink T-shirt, like a vanilla cone with strawberry topping. "Quite a crowd here," she said.

"Ever been to one of our sales before?" he asked.

"Never. I don't know where to start. Are there any guided tours?"

Maybe this is the answer, thought Jacob. He really ought to go find Clara and Heinz, but maybe if Ralph saw him with another woman, he'd realize there was no threat to his marriage. "I've got a little time. I can show you around."

As they looked at the exhibits, Marsha seemed interested in everything—the food, the crafts, the quilts. She bought a few trinkets from the crafts booths. Jacob found himself enjoying her company, pointing things out, explaining, being a regular Mennonite tour guide.

"Before we go on," he told her, "let's get something to eat."

"Great," said Marsha. "I worked the day shift today, and it was so hectic there wasn't time for lunch."

Jacob ticked off the food options: German, Russian, American, Mexican. "*Yah*," he answered her puzzled expression, "there are several Hispanic Mennonite churches around here. Even some Chinese, and one Hmong. But they don't have a booth this year."

"Chinese and Mexican I can have any time. I'll go for the German experience." Marsha pointed to the *verenikya* sign. "What's that?"

"*Verenikya*? It's like a big ravioli, only filled with hoop cheese—that's like a dry cottage cheese. It's served with ham and onions and gravy. Real tasty. Want to try some? Let's see if they're still serving."

The dining hall was at the far end, and they passed the bandstand on the way. The gospel rock group had left, and now a teenage girl swayed and crooned along with a small combo. "Would you live for Jesus and be always pure and good?" Jacob didn't see Ralph and Velita in the crowd and let out a breath of relief.

Jacob and Marsha had almost reached the dining room when he heard that unmistakable harsh voice. "All done playing house?"

Ahead in the path, Ralph stepped from around the corner of the building, splay-legged, thumbs hooked into his hip pockets. Beside him stood the other man, watching, his face expressionless. Velita was off to one side, the children behind her.

A shiver ran up Jacob's spine, and the hair on the back of his neck prickled. Marsha looked surprised. "Velita? I thought you weren't coming."

Velita gave a quick, nervous smile but didn't answer. She took Suanne's hand and started to walk away.

Ralph grabbed her by the arm, pulling her back. "Where you

think you're going? I want you to see this. I'll show you who calls the shots around here."

Velita stood still, looking down, her mouth tight. She draped her hands over Suanne's shoulders and toyed with the little girl's long hair. "Please, Ralph," she murmured. "Let's go home now."

Ralph ignored her and turned back to Jacob. His lips twisted into a sneer, and he leaned his head to one side, nodding slowly.

The air seemed to crackle. Jacob wondered how to defuse that hatred. *A soft answer* . . . He shrugged. "Hey, I've got no quarrel with you."

Ralph snorted. "Well, now, that's a matter of oh-pinion. And mine says you've been messing with my wife. What do you say to that, pretty boy?"

Marsha looked at Jacob, frowning. "What's going on?"

Jacob shook his head and motioned for her to stay back. Turning to Ralph, he said, "I don't know what your problem is. But it's got nothing to do with me." He put his hand on Marsha's back and gently but firmly urged her into a detour.

"Don't you run off on me! I'm not through with you." Ralph's fist shot out and slammed against Jacob's shoulder, spinning him around.

A crowd started to gather, and someone shouted, "Call security!"

The song from the bandstand echoed in Jacob's head. *Would you live for Jesus* . . . He raised his palms and told Ralph, "Look. You've got a nice family. Don't make things—"

A fist exploded in his stomach, and Jacob gasped. Blood pounded in his temples, and a red haze of anger clouded his eyes.

Time rolled back, and he was a boy on the playground again, facing the school bully. His hands clenched, and he struggled to calm himself.

Velita's voice seemed to come from a distance. "No, don't! You'll just make it worse."

"Shut up, stupid," said Ralph. He gave his wife a shove, knocking her off balance and against the building.

In reflex, Jacob's fist shot out and punched Ralph on the jaw.

Ralph staggered back. Gasps and murmurs came from the crowd. The music from the bandstand stopped, and there was a silence so thick Jacob could hear his ears ring. He stared at his hands, not believing what he'd just done.

Then he felt an iron grip on his shoulder, and turned to see Ralph's red twisted face just inches away. The man's eyes looked wild and evil. "Nobody hits Ralph Stanford and gets away with it."

The punch caught Jacob just under his ribs. As he twisted, nearly doubling up, he saw Velita sitting on the ground, head bent, wiping her eyes.

Suddenly he lost all control. His arms moved with a strength of their own, hitting, punching, jabbing. He felt Ralph's teeth against his knuckles and something hot and sticky spurted between his fingers. Then someone grabbed his arms, holding him back. Voices chattered around them.

"It was him, he started it."

"No, it was the other guy."

Jacob tried to catch Velita's eye, to tell her he was sorry, but she wouldn't look at him.

Two hefty men came running, wearing security badges. One was a retired police officer from Dinuba who attended the Mennonite Church there, and Jacob recognized him.

The man nodded to Jacob, and asked, "What's going on?"

Jacob pulled away from his restrainer's hold and wiped his hands on the sides of his pants. What could he say? It was all so complicated.

Before he could explain, Ralph's friend stepped forward. "Just a little disagreement here. Got kinda out of hand, but I think it's settled now. We'll be on our way." He helped Ralph up, and Marsha held out a wad of tissues from her purse.

Cursing under his breath, Ralph ignored the tissues and ran his arm across his bloodied face. "I'll get you for this," he muttered to Jacob. "You're gonna be plenty sorry. You can't always have your buddies looking out for you."

The guards cleared a way through the crowd and followed Ralph and his family to the exit. As the crowd closed after them, the last thing Jacob saw was TJ's face turning back to stare at him.

He felt a stab of sympathy for the little boy. It must be awful, seeing your dad beat up. But there was no hatred in TJ's eyes. Instead, they held an expression of awe.

Chapter 23

After a quick cleanup in the restroom, Jacob found Marsha waiting for him at the cafeteria door. A tantalizing aroma of sizzling ham and onions filled the room, mingling with the sound of bits and pieces of friendly conversation among those still eating. He motioned to the entrance and asked, "Ready to take a chance?"

She looked at him a few seconds, her eyes puzzled, but then said, "Sure. Why not?"

He guided her through the food line, greeting the other people, introducing her to friends behind the counter, acting as though nothing unusual had happened, as though the cut on his lip and the stubborn smudges of blood on his clothes were no big deal.

It was four thirty, and they were the last ones to be served. The kitchen crew was busy cleaning up. Here and there, small groups still visited, lingering over their empty plates, and Jacob found a quiet spot at a far table.

"Okay," said Marsha, staring at him over her plate of *verenikya*. "Are you going to tell me what's going on with you and Velita's husband?"

Jacob put down his fork and stared into space, chewing a

mouthful of ham. When he didn't answer, Marsha asked, "That *was* Velita's husband, right? Why was he so mad?"

Jacob swallowed, wiped his mouth with his napkin, and took a deep breath. "Oh, yeah. That's him, all right. He's a ve-e-ry troubled man. It's a long story, and I hardly know how to start."

Marsha kept her eyes on him, waiting quietly.

"I think I told you about Velita meeting that gang in the underground parking lot." He went on to tell her about his part in the incident, following Velita home to make sure she got there okay. Ralph's strange reaction.

"I couldn't just leave her there. The way she drove, I thought sure she'd plow into somebody. Wouldn't you think he'd be grateful that someone looked out for his wife? But that one!" Jacob shook his head and blew a soft whistle.

"That's it?"

He nodded. "Yep."

"And because of that, he thinks you two have something going?"

Jacob gave a short, bitter laugh. "Seems so. Worse yet, looks like he's taking it out on her."

"I've wondered about that. Those bumps on her forehead . . . I also saw some bruises on her arm. Have you noticed she always wears long-sleeved blouses, even when it's hot? As though she wants to hide something."

"One bump was from the car door handle, down in the parking lot. But only one. The others must be from later." Jacob thought a minute. "I got so aggravated at her that day. She wouldn't go in the ambulance, wouldn't let me drive her home. I thought she was just stubborn. But that explains it. She was scared to death of what that snake would do."

"You'd think women wouldn't stay with that kind of guy. But in my line of work, I've seen battered wives. A lot of times, they think it's their fault. The husband says he won't do it again, and they want so badly to believe him. They think if they do everything just right, he'll straighten out." Marsha shook her head. "But it only gets worse. Tell a person often enough that they're stupid, and they get to believe it themselves."

Jacob rubbed his forehead. "And now I've pushed him even further. Who knows what he'll do to her?" He lowered his head and stared at his half-eaten food. "This has got me puzzled. I've always believed marriage was sacred, that it was a sin to break that bond. Now I wonder if there could be exceptions."

Marsha frowned. "You mean all Mennonites have perfect marriages?"

Jacob felt his neck get hot, and he gave a crooked smile. "Well, no. I can't say that. Used to be, you never heard of divorce among us. If there was trouble, the couple patched it up. But some never did. They stayed together because they'd promised and just kept out of each other's way."

"Oh, come on! How could they do that?"

"One man didn't speak to his wife for years. Just worked his fields from dawn till dark, ate his supper, then slept in the barn. At church, they'd sit at opposite sides. But they stayed married."

"You've got to be kidding."

"Well, that was in my parents' time. Now lately, there've been a couple of divorces in our congregation. Both because the man got mixed up with another woman. And then he left the church. The new people, though, some were divorced already when they became saved and joined our church, so that was different."

Marsha looked at him sideways. "You know *I'm* divorced, don't you?"

Jacob raised his eyebrows. "Me and my big mouth. I hadn't remembered . . . I guess you've been through some tough times, too."

"It took a while to recover, but I'm doing okay now."

"At least there won't be another fierce husband to work me over. One's enough to last a while."

She chuckled. "I'm glad you trashed him. Maybe it'll knock some sense into him."

Jacob shook his head. "I don't know what got into me." He planted his elbows on the table and leaned his head into his hands. "I'm ashamed of myself."

Marsha stared at him. "Ashamed? Why? He had it coming."

"Maybe. But it's not our way. Our whole history is built on nonviolence. What kind of example am I to my children now?"

"I don't get it," said Marsha. "This idea of nonviolence. How does it fit in with the death penalty?"

"We shouldn't talk about the trial."

"I'm not. I mean in general. Do you mean nonviolence is only for you? It's okay to kill a person, as long as someone else does the dirty work?"

"In the Bible, long before the Ten Commandments, God told Noah, 'Whoever sheds man's blood, by men shall his blood be shed.' Otherwise, evil will take over."

"Isn't that what you did today? Took care of the evil?"

Jacob groaned. "I don't know. Probably just made things worse. I wish I hadn't come here." He'd cleaned his plate and glanced at the food still on Marsha's. "That all you're going to eat?"

"It was a big helping. But the—veronicas—is that how you say it? They're very good."

He laughed. "*Ve-REN-i-kya*. With a rolled *r*. You don't have to finish them. Not everyone likes them." He pushed the small dish of *pluma mos* toward her. "Prunes and raisins. I can live without it, but a lot of Mennonites seem to think it's commanded in the Bible."

Marsha tasted a small spoonful of the thin purple pudding. "Interesting texture. Kind of grainy. The flavor's not bad if you like prunes."

"The whole meal is a traditional Sunday dinner, because it's all prepared in advance. In the old days, our women cooked and baked all day Saturday so on Sunday they'd be free to go to church and still serve a big noon dinner. Probably invite another family over and visit until time to go to church in the evening."

"What about now? Don't Mennonite women work—I mean outside jobs?"

"Now, yes. Around here, a lot of them do. Back in my grandpa's day, they raised big families and all worked on the farm. Baked, canned, sewed most of the clothes. In Pennsylvania, my sister still does. But remember, she's Old Order. Even in my folks' generation, a few here worked out, especially summers in the cannery and packing sheds. Now, things are changing. Most of the sheds are mechanized so there aren't as many jobs to be had. Quite a few women are teachers, secretaries—I even know one who's a doctor and some who are real estate agents. Friend of mine has her own store."

"Do they still keep up with all that canning and baking?"

"I doubt it. At least, not regularly. They think all the good stuff is fattening. They just prepare it for special occasions like this." He laughed and shook his head. "I don't usually jabber like this. I sound like an old woman at sewing circle."

"But it's very interesting," said Marsha. "What about your wife? Did she work?"

"Just on the farm. She did the paperwork, helped me outside, raised the kids. She liked the old-fashioned way. Taught Becky to cook and clean, kept up that German work ethic. Now that she's gone, Becky knows how to take care of things."

"I'm sorry." Marsha patted his arm. "That she died, I mean. Sounds like you had a really good marriage."

"Wasn't yours? At least, for a while?"

"We argued a lot. Philip griped about the messy house; I yelled at him for not helping. But I thought we were pretty normal. Until he decided to leave."

Jacob nodded. "Must have been real hard on you."

"Yeah." Then she smiled and shook her head.

"What?"

"I'd never make a good Mennonite."

"Why not?"

"My Sundays. First thing in the morning, a load into the washer, then vacuum the floors. Shopping in the afternoon. For me it's a day to catch up on everything that got left during the week."

"No church?"

She looked down for a minute, then shrugged. "We used to go. Every Sunday, to Grace Community Church. I haven't been since Philip left."

"I'd miss it. Helps me through the week's problems."

"Yeah, well, I hear my husband and his new wife still show up at

Grace once in a while. I don't want to take the chance of running into them."

"That can happen." He moved his fork through the gravy on his plate, drawing lines. Marsha had always acted cheerful at the trial, and he'd thought she was happy and satisfied with her life. Now it seemed that Velita wasn't the only one with problems.

"You think I'm a heathen," she said.

He looked up and smiled. "No. But I remember a couple of weeks ago, our pastor said to keep our eyes on the Lord, not on other people."

"I hadn't thought of it that way."

He winked at her and gave a little nod. "Try it sometime. If nothing else, maybe you could find another church." Then he remembered something else the pastor had said. "A Christian without a church is kind of like . . . um, like a football player without a team. A soldier without an army. The Bible says people need to encourage each other. Prop each other up when we need it." He was surprised how easy it was to talk about spiritual things. As though God had given him special strength.

Marsha nodded. "Maybe a different church would help. Now that I'm single again, the whole atmosphere at Grace has changed. Seems the only friendly people are the older widows. My married friends shy away from me—as though they're afraid I'd want to steal their husbands."

To Jacob, that was a new thought. Were men that way, too, shielding their wives from him? Did they all think like Velita's husband? But his couple friends still invited him and his kids over, and him being widowed only seemed to cause his church family to close in tighter.

Before he could mention that, he heard snickering and looked up to see Sammy and Paul peeking through the open door. He grinned and pointed with his chin. "My sons. I need to go find the rest of my family and take them home." He wondered how he would explain his cut lip to them. The spots of blood on his shirt. "I haven't even finished showing you around."

"Don't worry about it. You've helped a lot. I think I can find my way around. But first, I have a question. How is it that you know so many of these people? They don't all go to your church, do they?"

Jacob laughed. "Part of it is being related. The saying is if you dig far enough back, we're all somehow related. But the churches also get together for song festivals and conferences, and somehow, we all just feel a common bond."

"It must be nice to have so many friends," said Marsha.

Jacob nodded and rose from the bench. "Well, thanks for the pleasure of your company. I hope you enjoy the rest of the displays."

"Thanks for the advice."

Jacob looked at her questioningly, and Marsha explained, "You know, about the church. I'll think about it." She gathered up her purse and belongings, and they left the building. "See you Tuesday. And don't feel bad about Velita's husband. He needed that."

But Jacob left the relief sale depressed. He suspected his fight with Ralph had only begun.

Chapter 24

Ralph cut off a big chunk of steak and chewed it slowly. Suddenly he stood up and spit it onto the table. "'Spect me to eat this garbage?"

Velita froze, holding her breath, staring at the yellow wheat design in her plate.

He slammed his palm on the table. "Well?"

"It's top sirloin," she said, her throat tight with dread. "You always liked it before."

She'd watched him boiling all the way home from the sale, his jaw clenched and twitching, his hands squeezing the steering wheel. She knew it wasn't the fight itself that ate at him. It wasn't even jealousy, not really.

It was the shame. She'd never known him to back down from a fight before; it was always the other guy who got clobbered. Tom had tried to cheer him up. Kept Ralph going with slugs of the whiskey they'd picked up at the liquor store. Told him it was all a fluke; any day, he could take on even the toughest dudes. If the security guards hadn't shown up, it would have gone the other way. Told him what a jock he was, how all the regulars at Casey's Pool Hall looked up to him. Even the women, especially the redhead—but then Ralph made him shut up. They never did stop to eat any food, and Velita'd hoped all that booze would knock Ralph out and he'd sleep it off.

Instead, it had made him meaner. She'd hurried dinner onto the table, hoping that would settle him down. But this time, even steak hadn't done it.

"Want me to fix you a hamburger instead?" she asked him.

He imitated her soft voice, waggling his head. "No, I don't want a hamburger." He speared the meat with his fork and dangled it, dripping, in front of her face. "I want my steak rare, not bloody. Can't you get that through your fool head?"

She pushed her plate toward him. "Here, take mine, it's tender."

He took the plate and slammed it back down on the table. The stoneware broke jaggedly in half, its stalk of wheat split crosswise. Mashed potatoes and peas dribbled down between the cracks.

Suanne started whimpering, and Velita motioned for the kids to leave the room.

"But Mom," whined TJ.

"Go!" she mouthed, and he followed Suanne out of the room.

Ralph's lips bulged in a sneer. "Really thought you could get by with it, didn't you? You and your lover boy."

Velita stumbled to her feet. "No, Ralph. I swear—"

Before she could finish, he whipped around the table, grabbed one of the plate halves and shoved the mashed potatoes into her face. The rough edge scraped against her cheek and food plopped onto her blouse and down her neck.

She staggered away from the table, and Ralph came after her, pinning her to the wall. "Say it. You've been makin' it with him!"

She shook her head. "No, never."

"Liar!" He tore at her blouse, and a button popped off. "I'm not enough for you, huh?"

She reached out to him, but her jagged thumbnail scraped his arm.

He snarled, "Oh, so you wanna fight dirty? I'll show you dirty." His knee kicked up hard.

Velita gasped and doubled up. "Oh no, Ralph, please don't." Her stomach cramped, and her eyes blurred.

He bunched up her blouse at the shoulder, grabbing along a handful of flesh. Shoving her toward the living room, he cracked her head against the door jamb. Nearly blinded with pain, Velita slipped loose and eased back into the kitchen, behind the open door.

Ralph gave a strange, high giggle. "Oh, now it's hide-and-seek? Okay." He staggered through the doorway. "Ready or not, here I come!" He grabbed the knob and whipped the door out at arm's length. Velita scrambled out of the way just before it slammed back against the wall. Tripping over his foot, she sprawled onto the floor.

Ralph swung his leg, jabbing the toe of his boot into the soft flesh of her belly. "Clumsy idiot."

Coughing, Velita got on hands and knees and scrambled to the cabinets. With the help of the drawer pulls, she dragged herself upright. Ralph stood watching her, swaying a little. His face was red, his eyes like slits.

Another cramp hit her stomach.

The baby! If Ralph knew she was pregnant, maybe he wouldn't . . . No! That would only make him worse. Mad as he was, he'd never believe the baby was his. She'd just have to ride this one out and hope for the best.

Weak with pain and nausea, Velita stared up at her husband. She'd never seen him *this* crazy, never seen that wild-eyed, red-faced maniac before.

The neighbor! If I could just slip out the back door, catch Rhonda's attention, get her to call 911 . . . Edging along the wall, she gauged the distance.

But Ralph darted ahead of her and stood blocking the door with his arms. His eyes glittered. "Forget it. You're not going nowhere."

Velita blinked. *He's going to kill me this time.* Glancing at the stove, she saw the iron skillet still on the burner. If Ralph respected people who stood up to him . . .

She reached over, grabbed the handle, and swung with all her might.

Ralph dodged, seized her wrist, and brought her arm back on herself. The skillet cracked against her head, and all she could see was a spray of lights.

As she slid to the floor, she heard the mocking echo of his voice. "Now, why'd you do that to yourself?" She felt him pulling her arm, dragging her to the bedroom, and wished she could black out.

❖ ❖ ❖

In the middle of the night, Velita woke up. Waves of pain gripped her naked body. She tried to get up, but her head felt as big as a watermelon. Her skin was sticky, and she ached all over. Easing herself onto her side, she closed her eyes again.

The next thing she knew, it was morning. The pains in her stomach throbbed and tugged at her. The alarm clock on her nightstand said seven thirty.

Beside her, Ralph was snoring, his face flushed, drool running from one corner of his mouth. His breath smelled sour and rotten.

The terror of the night before flooded back to her. Weakly, she inched her way out of bed, feeling as though she was slogging through mud.

Ralph still breathed deep and even, and she worried about him being late to work. But from the living room came the sound of cartoons on TV and the voices of the kids, and she realized it was Sunday. Using all her strength, she dragged herself to the bathroom.

Drops of blood marked her path. Then more and more blood, clotted and dark. *Oh, dear God—my baby.* She felt a terrible sorrow, and her arms went weak. But mixed with the sadness was a flood of relief. This was hard enough on Suanne and TJ. It was no life for a sweet, innocent baby.

She staggered into the shower and gasped as the first icy water hit. Her legs gave way, and she slid down into a corner of the stall. The water, now warmer, soothed her only a little as she watched it carry away part of her life.

It's all my fault. If she hadn't baited Ralph with that sale flyer, none of this would have happened. Ralph and Jacob wouldn't have fought, Ralph wouldn't have beaten her up, and she'd still be pregnant.

But who was she trying to kid? Once he found out about the baby, it would have been the same thing. He was the way he was, and nothing she did would change him. Dried and swaddled, she scrubbed at the blood stains on the floor, using her whole body to add strength to her arms. The spots finally left. Now she would never have to tell him. She pulled her robe down from its hook on the door and started brushing her hair, but stopped when she saw the mirror.

That face couldn't be hers. She looked closer. Her forehead was swollen, her eyes purple, and a red welt ran along her left cheek. She traced the line gently, then bathed her face in cold water and turned away from the mirror. Farther down, her stomach and thighs were covered with bruises.

I ought to see a doctor. But how would I explain the way I look? Covering up with her robe and tying the belt, Velita shuffled into the living room.

The kids sat on the sofa, watching TV and eating dry cereal out of the box. They stared at her, and Suanne put her thumb into her mouth. She was still in last night's clothes, wrinkled and covered with dust bunnies.

Velita brushed her little daughter's back. "How'd you get so dirty?"

"Under my bed," said TJ. "You look weird. Want some Frosty Pops?"

Velita shook her head. All she could stand was black coffee. In the kitchen, she found that the kids had put last night's dinner dishes into the kitchen sink, and streaks on the floor showed they'd cleaned up the mess as best they could.

When she went back into the living room with her coffee mug, Velita gave them each a thank-you hug, her eyes swimming with tears.

They didn't deserve this kind of life. *She* didn't deserve it. Somehow, someday, she was going to take them away from this. If only she could figure out what to do.

She heard footsteps and saw Ralph coming down the hall, looking groggy. He plopped down on a chair at the table. "Dry toast and black coffee," he said, and held his head in his hands.

"Look at me," said Velita.

Ralph glanced up, looked away, then did a double-take. "You look awful."

She took a deep breath. "Yeah, and you know why."

"You're accusin' me of doing that? Come on!"

"I can't take it anymore. We've got to do something."

"Like what?"

"Like maybe see a counselor, get help."

"Forget blabbing to a shrink; no way would I go."

"If you hate me this much, maybe we ought to just . . . split up."

"Aw, Vel, you know I don't mean anything by it. I don't even remember nothing. It was just the booze. I swear I'll never hurt you again."

Sure. Along with her pain and grief, Velita felt a flash of anger. Maybe he didn't remember what he did, but it was a lie that he'd never hurt her again.

The phone rang, and when Ralph answered, perking up real quick, Velita could tell it was Tom. When he hung up, he said, "Get me a clean shirt. We're going to the rally."

Velita remembered seeing it in the paper: all week, all the bikers getting together in Settler's Grove, listening to music, and partying. It'd be about a four-hour trip each way, so they'd be back late.

Just before Ralph left, he grabbed her by the shoulder, his finger pointing at her nose. "Don't you run off on me while I'm gone, y'hear? Won't do you no good. I'd come after you, find you."

All day, the kids hardly squabbled at all. Velita lay on the couch, read her book, and napped while they played and watched TV. In the middle of *World's Funniest Videos*, a news flash came on, and she saw Duane Jackson's face.

"Change channels," she told TJ. "I'm not supposed to hear this."

"That the guy in your trial?"

"I can't talk about it. Find something else."

If only she *could* talk to someone about it. She had so many questions. It still blew her mind that *she* had been chosen for something as important as a murder trial.

Now that she'd been reminded, she couldn't stop thinking about it. Once Duane Jackson had been a little boy like TJ. What had turned him into a criminal?

Her children sat on the floor, playing the game of Life and laughing at their fates. She watched them, wishing real life was that easy. How could she make sure they had a chance to turn out okay? Would they be better off without a daddy, or staying with a violent one? He had never hit them, except to whack TJ when he got in the way. What would she do if she left Ralph? Would she and the kids end up on the streets like the homeless people, begging for handouts?

She glanced at the television screen. TJ had switched channels, and a young woman sang, "*There is a place of quiet rest, near to the heart of God.*"

Velita took in a sharp breath. She could sure use a place like that. "*A place where sin cannot molest, near to the heart of God.*" She sat up, staring at the singer. The woman seemed to be looking straight at her. How could she know about Ralph?

Then a man spoke. "Jesus said, all of you who are weary, you who carry heavy loads, just come to Me, and I will give you rest."

Was there really a chance she could get some relief? Maybe start over with a life that wasn't full of slaps and kicks and cussing?

Just then Suanne yelled, "No fair! You moved my marker!"

TJ made a face at her. "Did not. You can't always have good stuff."

Get real." He kicked the game board, and the tiles, cars, and money scattered.

Velita sighed and got up to settle the quarrel. The game was really too old for them, but it was a gift from LaDonna, and she didn't always choose appropriate toys. "Clean up the mess, both of you, and I'll fix you something good to eat." *Get real.* That couldn't be true—a quiet place where God would protect her. If there actually was a God, He sure didn't care about her—He hadn't answered any of her prayers.

That night after the kids were in bed, Velita felt a little stronger. It was good, she thought, that she hadn't gone to a doctor. Ralph might have found out she'd been pregnant.

Had it been a boy or girl? She thought of TJ and Suanne when they were babies, their soft skin, fuzzy scalp, and chubby creased legs. The smell of warm milk and baby powder.

She went into the kitchen, took a pair of shears and a flashlight from a drawer, and went out the back door. By the fence, a rose bush had a few pink buds, and she made a tiny bouquet.

In the far corner of the yard, Velita knelt down on the ragged Bermuda grass, gathered a few pebbles together and laid the flowers down on them. "Sleep well, sweet little angel baby," she said. "You'll be happier in heaven." Only then did she let go and allow herself to mourn the death of her baby, her love, and her marriage.

Chapter 25

"Appreciate your disking for me," Jacob told Heinz at the Monday evening dinner table. "With me chasing off to the courthouse and Buck gone, it's been hard to keep the farm going."

"Sure runs easy, dat rubber-tire tractor," said Heinz between chews of a mouthful of pot roast. "Vish I could sneak it into my car and take it home vit me." He glanced at Clara next to him, his face sober, his eyes laughing.

She shook her head at him. "The bishop would have something to say to you about that."

"Vell, I vunder vat he'd say about you using an electric sewing machine." He playfully pinched her ear.

Jacob and Clara's parents, sitting on the other side of the table for this farewell meal, smiled at each other. Jacob was glad they'd been able to go to Yosemite with Clara and her husband and get better acquainted with him. They'd always been leery of traveling to Pennsylvania, and Clara had only come this way once, years ago, by train, bringing the two oldest children. They'd often wondered aloud what the Old Order strictness would do to Clara's natural cheerfulness. It looked to Jacob like Heinz's good humor reassured them.

"I guess it's like a phone," said Becky. "It's okay to use it as long as you don't own one. Right?"

Clara blushed and whispered loudly behind her hand, "Heinz has a telephone in his barn. Been a lifesaver, too, that time Phoebe nearly died."

"Phoebe?" Jacob couldn't remember a niece by that name.

"Our best milk cow," said Heinz. "By de time ve vould have gone to town to call the vet, it vould have been too late."

"What's the difference?" asked Paul. "I mean having a phone in the house or the barn."

"Vell, dis vay it's only used for business. Not for *schnattering* vit de neighbors or flirting vit your girlfriend."

"*Schnattering*? What's that?" asked Paul.

Jacob's father laughed. "Gabbing. Talking a lot about nothing. Like teenagers."

Paul, seated between his grandparents, raised his eyebrows and aimed both forefingers at Sammy.

Sammy's face matched his reddish hair. "She only called last night to ask about our math homework."

"Uh-huh," Paul said dryly. "For forty-five minutes."

"That's enough, boys," scolded Jacob. At least Paul was across the table from Sammy, too far apart for them to kick each other and spill food.

Jacob's mother patted Paul on the shoulder. "Just wait till you're older. You'll understand." She turned to Heinz. "Did you enjoy the relief sale?"

"Oh, *yah*, lots of good food, things to see. Even some of our own kind of people dere."

"I think the best part was watching all the different kinds of Mennonites working together," said Clara. "One doesn't always feel that communion when you only stay with your own kind. I think this trip did us good."

Jacob watched Heinz's face and was relieved to see him nod. He was also glad the man didn't bring up the fight with Ralph. It had been hard enough to talk his way out of that on Saturday—just a misunderstanding, he'd told them, hoping they wouldn't mention it to his parents. To change the subject, he asked, "I'm glad you could stay for the male chorus concert yesterday afternoon. Did you enjoy it?"

"Oh, my, yes," said Clara, beaming. "Such good harmony." She glanced at Heinz, but his face was neutral.

"Must be hard to fit the voices togedder," he said.

It was only then that Jacob remembered many of the Old Mennonite churches still only sang in unison. He smiled and shook his head. "It's a gift." He dared to add, "And I believe when God gives us a gift, we need to use it to His glory."

Heinz looked surprised, but then shrugged. "Maybe you are right. It vas a glorious sound. I vill remember it long."

"We'll have a lot of good memories from here," added Clara.

"What did you think of Yosemite?" Jacob said the name carefully, to give Heinz the right pronunciation.

"Big," said Heinz. "That vun vay up high, split in half, vat vus it?"

"Half Dome," said Jacob's father. He told Jacob, "We hiked up to the bridge at Yosemite Falls, all except your mom—"

"My legs. They don't like to walk that far," she said.

"And then we drove all the way up to Glacier Point."

Clara sighed. "Brought back memories of when our family camped there in the valley. That was fun, wasn't it?"

Jacob nodded, still seeing her as a teenager dressed in jeans, climbing the rocks. *She must have some regrets over leaving California and an easier life,* he thought. His mind filled with early memories of Clara playing with him, guiding him through his growing years. When he was seven, he'd taken a dare and run barefoot through a pile of ashes in the field, only to find embers still burning underneath. Clara had cleaned his feet, soothed them with balm, kissed him, and prayed for his quick healing and wisdom to resist foolish risks. The recollection still made him choke up, and he blinked back the burning in his eyes.

He passed the bowl of mashed potatoes to Heinz. "Ready for some more?"

Heinz rubbed his comfortably large belly. "Tanks, but my bread basket says it's full. I tink dere's room for Clara's *eiyah* pie, though."

Becky got up to cut the egg custard pie. "I'm sure going to miss you, Aunt Clara. I can't believe how much work you've done around the house. My mending basket is emptier than it's ever been. And thanks for sewing the collar on my new dress. For the life of me, I couldn't figure out those instructions."

Jacob smiled at Clara. "We'll all miss you." The whole time they'd been visiting, Clara had cooked, baked, and even sewn the boys new Sunday shirts. Today she'd canned early peaches from the neighbors, some to take home with her but plenty to leave here. At their parents' place, she'd washed the windows and curtains and scrubbed out their oven. Without chemicals.

"*Yah,*" said their father. "She's like the description of a good wife in the last chapter of Proverbs. Keeping everyone clothed and fed, staying up late to get all the work done. A good example to follow." He nodded at his wife. "You trained her well."

She tilted her head. "I imagine she learned to work even harder in her community, isn't that so, Clara?"

Clara smiled and shrugged, and Jacob knew she must have made a lot of adjustments after marriage. Struggles she didn't want to admit in front of Heinz. But she seemed happy now, so there was no reason to dwell on it.

Jacob shook his head slowly. "Wish you two could stay longer."

Clara passed around the slices of *eiyah* pie, richly golden and sprinkled with nutmeg. "Well, Jakie, you know what that means. You need a wife, not a sister."

Jacob glanced at his mother. She'd been so close to Sharon; talk like that might bother her. He hung his head. "Someday, Clara. Someday. I'm . . . just not ready yet."

But a flash of memory slid back into his head—the feel of Velita leaning against him when he'd chased off that street gang.

He shook himself. The woman was married, for Pete's sake. And so different from the women in his church. But he couldn't help wondering what Clara and his folks would think of her. Just as a friend, of course.

After dinner, he got out his camera and took several pictures of them all: his folks with Clara and Heinz, Sammy taking one of all the adults, then showing Clara the settings to snap Jacob with the kids. Jacob wondered what had happened to the camera she'd owned before marrying Heinz.

The next morning, Jacob woke extra early to the smell of coffee, and dressed quickly. Downstairs, he found Clara scrambling eggs and toasting leftover *tvebocks*. The table was set, and in the middle, sliced bananas waited in a bowl; beside it stood a pitcher of freshly squeezed orange juice.

Clara tossed some hash browns into the eggs, stirred them in, then turned and gave Jacob a hug. "Thanks for putting us up. Come and visit our home sometime soon."

"Maybe next year after peach harvest."

She winked at him. "You might even find a nice woman in Pennsylvania."

Jacob sighed and shook his head. "You've got a one-track mind. Don't worry about me. When the time comes, I'll surprise you."

Heinz came down the stairs, black hat on, suspenders in place, and lugging two suitcases. "Nah, Yoakob, ve didn't vant to bodder you. Taught ve'd yust sneak off and leave a tank-you note."

"You're all ready to go? I better wake the kids. They'll want to say goodbye."

"We need to make it through the Mojave Desert before it gets too hot," said Clara.

"Don't you have air-conditioning?" asked Jacob.

"No," said Heinz. "De church says ve can drive cars, but cold air is too fancy."

Jacob felt like arguing that with Heinz but knew it would be pointless. Each of their churches had certain rules—some taken from God's Word, some from traditions through the years. As long as they all believed in Jesus' sacrifice on the cross for them, His resurrection, and that He meant what He said: He was the way, the truth, the life, the only path to God. That was what was important. The rest—well, each one had to get along in their own community. And in his, clothes and electricity were no big deal. If some thought otherwise, that was their business. He had no quarrel with them.

Sammy came down the stairs in his pajamas. "I smell toasted *tvebocks*." He shuffled over to Clara and looked into the pan of eggs.

"You be good now and obey your dad," she said, giving him a hug. "Do your chores and study hard."

He nodded against her arm. "Sure."

"And not so much *schnattering* vid de girlfriend," added Heinz, his eyes twinkling.

Sammy pulled loose, suddenly wide awake. "She's *not* my girlfriend!" He ran back up the stairs, pushing past Becky on her way down.

Becky hugged Heinz and kissed Clara. "I wish I could spend a summer at your place sometime. You could teach me so much more than cookbooks and patterns do."

"Say, that's a wonderful idea." Clara dished up the eggs and crumbled the crusty brown *tvebocks* into bowls. "We've got a lot of young people for you to meet, too."

Jacob wondered if that was such a good idea. Becky was pretty, and the Old Order boys were sure to fall for her. From what he'd heard, the young were held in tight reins until age eighteen, then allowed to run free for a year. *Rumspringa*, they called it. Jumping around. A lot of the guys turned loose and tried everything, smoking and drinking and what not else, till they felt guilty enough to come back to their church.

He preferred the Mennonite Brethren way—to let the children mix with the world all along, learning right from wrong under supervision as they grew. Vacation Bible school and youth group Bible studies gave them a strong foundation in the Word. He'd have to explain that to Becky. After Heinz and Clara left.

They all sat down around the table, and Jacob gave a hearty prayer of thanks for the good food, the hands that prepared it, and a plea for a safe journey for the travelers.

Then Clara asked, "You want coffee or hot milk on these *reschte tvebocks?*"

Sammy and Paul elbowed each other down the stairs, shouting, "Hot milk!"

The rest took coffee, and Clara settled down to enjoy her own meal. "You know the story about *reschte tvebocks*, don't you?"

"You mean about when our forefathers escaped from Russia?" asked Jacob. "Sure."

Paul looked puzzled, and Clara explained, "Toasted *tvebocks* don't spoil—they just get harder and harder. When the families were in danger from the Communists, they escaped in the middle of the night, crossing the Amur River into China. They didn't know how long it would be till they could buy food, so the women baked lots of *tvebocks*, toasted them, and carried them along in pillowcases. They saved our people from starving."

"Wow," said Paul. He dug his spoon into a large chunk, breaking it up, and crunched on a bite. "Where did they get the milk? Did they have cows along?"

"No, they didn't dare," she told him. "They just ate them dry. Sometimes one half was all they had for a meal, so they nibbled very slowly, crumb by crumb."

Jacob smiled into his boys' wide eyes. "So now you know some Mennonite history."

"Yah," Heinz added. "Ve have it so easy now. It's goot to remember the past."

While Clara and Becky cleaned up the kitchen, Jacob helped Heinz load up his car with the suitcases, canned fruit, and a battery radio Heinz had bought at the relief sale auction. For the barn, of course, so he could get the news and weather reports.

The goodbyes were tearful, and Jacob wondered when he would see his sister again. Even though he'd talked about visiting, the chances were unlikely. Especially when it came to Becky.

Sammy didn't shed any tears. He'd enjoyed the food Clara had made, but after hugging her and giving Heinz a quick handshake, he backed away.

Jacob grinned, sure that was just to avoid more girlfriend teasing.

As Heinz eased into the driver's seat of the car, Clara gave Jacob one last hug. "I hope you'll soon be done with that old trial business."

Jacob sighed. "Me too." But he thought again about Velita and wondered if he really meant that. Waving goodbye, he went back into the house to get ready for court.

Chapter 26

By Tuesday morning, the swelling on Velita's forehead had gone down some. And under her eyes, the dark circles were fading. Lots of makeup helped hide the scratch on her cheek. She fluffed her hair low over her forehead and across her cheeks and walked into the jury room wearing a pair of dark glasses. She still felt depressed and shaky but figured just sitting in the courtroom wouldn't be too hard.

Most of the other jurors paid no attention to her, the women gabbing about a new mall to be built northwest of town and how all of Springton was shifting in that direction. Lester stood near the window with his back to her, arguing with Wallace Takashi again—water rights this time. But Marsha looked at Velita funny.

Trust a nurse to notice something wrong. Velita said, "Hi," then sat down at the table and took out her book, turning the pages from time to time without reading the words. Geneva asked Jacob how the relief sale had been. "I was planning to go, but we were out of town."

He smiled. "It went well. Haven't heard the figures yet, but I think we beat last year's total." His voice sounded warm and comfortable. "It was a busy weekend. Sunday, we men sang in the People's Church in Fresno. About a hundred of us, I guess, from a lot of different churches. That program always goes along with the sale."

"Yeah? What'd you sing?"

"Hymns. Male chorus songs. Some knee-slappers, some more reverent. All kinds."

"Mmm, mmm," said Geneva. "Wish I coulda heard it, that many guys. Your audience like it?"

"They said they did." He glanced at Velita, and she quickly looked down at her book. She couldn't imagine Ralph ever singing a hymn. Especially not a reverent one.

Jacob came over and leaned next to her ear. "You okay?"

She hunched her shoulders, then gave a little nod.

Marsha put a cup of coffee in front of her, and whispered, "You don't have to say anything now. But you can't tell *me* everything's all right. I just want you to know, when you're ready to talk, I'm here for you."

Jacob touched Velita's arm and murmured, "I'm sorry about Saturday."

It would have been easier if they'd kidded her about the way she looked. She could have toughed that out. But with them being so kind, all she'd have to do was open her mouth, and she'd blubber like a baby.

Geneva made a funny face and looked at her with squinted eyes. "You better take those blinders off before we go into the courtroom," she drawled out of the corner of her mouth. "The judge'll think you're the Mafia." She gently squeezed Velita's arm.

That was better. Velita gave a watery little laugh and took off the glasses. In spite of her misery, she couldn't help giving a tiny mental cheer. It was nice to have friends, to have people treat her like she was worth something.

❖ ❖ ❖

Henry Crawford, a neighbor of Duane Jackson, sat in the witness seat. He had gray hair and bifocals and smiled at the jury. He told the prosecutor that he knew Jackson slightly, and they'd talked a few times. He'd seen the wife once or twice through the window but had never met or spoken to her.

Mr. Crawford and his wife had been in their living room that evening, reading and watching television. "We heard shouting, and I looked out the front window. There were two cars at the curb. Then I heard shots and saw someone jump off Jackson's front porch. I heard more shots and saw some activity by one of the cars."

Another car had driven up, and two men got out, ran to the porch, and kicked in the door. After a while, they brought Jackson and his wife out, yelling and kicking. An ambulance came, and paramedics brought a stretcher with a body out of the house and took it away.

He must have stood and watched for a long time, thought Velita. *I wonder how much our neighbors heard Saturday night. What would they say about us if the police questioned them? Ralph insists that what happens in our house is nobody else's business, but maybe people know a lot more than he realizes.*

"Did you see the officers kick or beat the suspect or the woman?" asked the prosecutor.

"No."

The defense lawyer took over. "What kind of cars were at the curb?"

Henry Crawford didn't know. "I just noticed they were unfamiliar."

"Unfamiliar how?"

"I know all the neighbors' cars. These didn't belong to anyone around."

"Were they police cars?"

"Not at first, just that last one."

"You mentioned activity by one of the vehicles. What did you mean by that?"

"Well, the men moved around it, kind of hurrying, with one door opened. They talked real loud."

"What did they say?"

"I don't remember. Something about backup. Sounded like a two-way radio going, sort of scratchy. I couldn't make out the words."

Arnold Torrance rubbed his chin. "Your house is next to Mr. Jackson's, is it not? On the same side of the street?"

"Yes."

"From your front window, were you able to see around the bushes surrounding the porch?"

Mr. Crawford hesitated.

The judge peered at him. "Answer the question, please."

"No. Not from my front window."

"Then isn't it possible the men might have beat and kicked Mr. and Mrs. Jackson before they came down the walk?"

Crawford shrugged. "I suppose. But I would have—"

"No further questions."

James Pettigrew called more neighbors to the stand. Lorenzo Garza, on the other side of Jackson, had been friendly with the defendant. "We'd say hi, rap a little, you know, but we weren't exactly buddies. Sometimes we'd borrow stuff, you know, like a wrench or a hammer." That night, he'd been listening to music and hadn't heard the shots. But he'd seen the cars drive up and wondered what was wrong. He hadn't gone outside. Hadn't wanted to get involved.

Since this trial started, Rhonda's been a real good neighbor, keeping the kids and all. Hope I can keep in touch after this is over. It would be fun to trade recipes, borrow stuff. Velita suddenly realized that she dreaded the end of the trial. She would love to hang on to this little bit of freedom no matter how mad it made Ralph.

Florence Everly, across the street from Jackson, had also noticed the activity. But she hadn't seen any mistreatment. She'd looked out the front window just in time to see Jackson and his wife taken to the car.

That time last year when someone called the police on us—did Rhonda see them? Was it she who called them? She's never said anything. I wonder what she thinks of us.

"I wasn't surprised," said Florence Everly. "I figured something shady was going on in that house. The police had been there before—"

"Objection!" shouted Arnold Torrance.

"Sustained," said the judge. "Strike that remark from the record."

How many things are the lawyers keeping from us? Would it make a difference if we knew all that stuff?

The defense attorney glared at his opponent, then turned to the judge. "Your honor, may we approach the bench?"

The panel was sent out again, and Lester Payne added his mark on the board.

Velita sat down at the table and picked up her book, but Marsha took the seat next to her.

"Look," she whispered. "I know I'm being nosy, but I've got to ask you." She motioned toward Velita's face. "Did your husband do this to you?"

Velita closed her book and eyed the woman. How much did she dare admit? That Ralph treated her like trash? Finally she sighed. "He—when he gets drunk, he hits." She dropped her glance to her fingernails and mumbled, "Since I've been on this jury, he's been drinking a lot more. I knew I shouldn't have come here."

Marsha pressed Velita's hand. "Don't blame yourself. If it wasn't this, it would be some other excuse. Men who abuse women can be triggered by any little thing."

"I try so hard. Thought if I did everything right, I could make him happy. But no matter what I do, it turns out wrong."

"Would he be willing to see a counselor?"

"I wanted to, but he said no. It just made him madder."

"Have you ever thought of—leaving him?"

Velita shuddered, not looking up. If Marsha only knew how many times! And how scared she was of being on her own. "I tried, once. First time he slapped me, I took the baby and went home to my folks."

"Did they call the police?"

"Didn't have a phone. Mama had her own problems, said she couldn't bother with mine." Velita stared into space, remembering. "Ralph came to their house, said he was sorry, swore he'd never do it again. Fool as I was, I believed him." She bit her lip, fighting back tears.

Marsha turned and looked her in the eyes. "But he has."

Velita shrugged, then nodded. "He's not always like that. Sometimes months go by—"

"And then what? Hasn't it gotten worse each time?"

Velita couldn't answer, and Marsha leaned closer. "There are places," she whispered. "You know, shelters, for battered women. You could take the kids there. You'd be safe."

Velita thought of the TV program, the song about a quiet place. But that had to be in a dream world, and she shook her head. "I'll be okay, at least for a while. He went to the Settler's Grove rally Sunday, partied with all the bikers, and probably thumbed his nose at the police. That'll keep him happy for a few days."

"He was gone? Why didn't you call me? I could have helped you work out something."

"I was . . . sick." She couldn't tell anyone about losing the baby. Not even Marsha. Just thinking about it tore her up all over again.

Just then, the bailiff opened the door and announced, "Jury is dismissed until tomorrow at ten."

Velita shook her thoughts free, grabbed her things together, and hurried out the door. Was she crazy to spill out her problems? What would Ralph do if he found out?

Chapter 27

When Velita pulled into her driveway, the kids saw her from the neighbor's house and came running. Suanne hugged her and TJ said, "It's about time. I'm starving."

"You're always starving." Velita unlocked and opened the door, TJ squirming under her arm and darting inside. He tossed his backpack onto the sofa and pulled a crumpled paper from his pocket.

"You gotta sign this. I need twenty bucks by Friday."

She looked at him blankly. "Twenty dollars?"

"The field trip. Remember? The aquarium?"

She *had* forgotten. *Twenty dollars by Friday!*

Velita figured in her head. She always shopped carefully and usually stretched the grocery money to cover a few extras. But with that gang stealing the last of her allowance, she was still short. This week, she'd stocked up on canned stuff on sale and bought Suanne new shoes. No way could she scrape up another twenty dollars. By the time Ralph came home with Friday's paycheck, it would be too late. She'd have to ask him special for the money. But how could she, after everything that happened Saturday?

Now that he was in a good mood, she wasn't about to knock him off balance.

She shook her head, yearning for TJ's sake. "I don't know. Don't count on it." Then she thought, *Wait a minute.* Since Tom had bragged up TJ singing along with that gospel music, Ralph had seemed real proud of him. "*You* ask your dad," she told him. "He might give you the money."

TJ looked at her sideways, frowning, his head pulled back doubtfully.

"Trust me," she said, with the thin hope that Ralph would agree. She took the paper into the kitchen and stuck it to the refrigerator door with a cookie-shaped magnet. TJ followed her, grabbed a popsicle from the freezer, and went into the living room. He plopped onto the couch and punched the TV remote control.

Velita smiled. He was so easily satisfied. Give him cartoons and a snack, and he was happy. If only Ralph would let him go on that trip; it would be so special for him.

Suanne clung to her. "I hate staying at the Averys'. There's nothing to do."

"Won't TJ play with you?" Velita smoothed Suanne's long blond hair from her face, and noticed a small bruise near one eye. "What happened, sweetie?"

"TJ and Luke Avery put ice down my back, and I fell."

Velita stuck her head around the kitchen door. "TJ?"

The television noise blurred TJ's answer.

"Where did you fall?" Velita asked Suanne.

"On the coffee table. I cried." Her face clouded, and she snuggled her head against Velita.

Velita turned cold. Just when she'd thought TJ was behaving better! She'd have to get after him again.

Suanne sniffed. "I wish you could stay home."

Velita knelt to look into Suanne's eyes and dabbed at the dried tear tracks with her thumbs. "Well, sweetie, it won't be much longer. And then you don't have to go to the Averys' anymore, unless you want to. Okay?"

Suanne hung her head and sighed. "Oh-h-h-kay."

"That's my girl." Velita got up and tied on an apron. "Want to help me squish up a meat loaf?"

At bedtime, while Suanne was in the bathroom, Velita settled TJ in his bed and rubbed his back. "You don't have to hit to prove you're tough," she told him. "Especially people smaller than you are. Only bullies do that. If you want to be a superhero, you protect them against the bad guys."

TJ's eyes were nearly shut, but then he opened them. "Is Daddy a bad guy?"

Velita caught her breath. Anything she said could get back to Ralph. She massaged TJ's neck and shoulders, then said, "I'm talking about you kids. Go to sleep now." She hoped her scolding wouldn't backfire.

❖ ❖ ❖

On Wednesday, the prosecution called Roger Bosnell, police dispatcher for Booneville, to the stand. Officer Bosnell had taken all incoming calls the night Charlene Jackson claimed there'd been a drive-by shooting.

Officer Bosnell checked his files and said, yes, there had been such a call from 1002 N. Florin St., although no name had been given. According to his records, Sgt. Louis Moseda and Cpl. Dan Poole had responded to the call.

Louis Moseda was called next. He studied the record and nodded. "Yeah, we went out. Rang the doorbell. Nobody answered." They'd gone around the outside of the house, shone flashlights on the doors and windows, but found nothing. "There were no signs of violence. No shells, empty casings, nothing like that." They'd gone to several neighbors' houses, asked the occupants if they'd seen or heard anything, but none had.

Velita remembered Jackson's wife saying she'd called the police, but they hadn't come. *Who's telling the truth?* she wondered.

James Pettigrew's next witness described the gun used by Jackson, and the lawyer passed it in front of the jury on a tray, along with the bullets and their casings in a little plastic bag. Velita shuddered, glad there was no gun in *her* house.

Then a man talked about examining the bulletproof vest Corporal MacDuff had been wearing, and the prosecutor held up a stained, gray object that looked like an ugly life preserver jacket for boating.

Velita leaned forward. *That* was a bulletproof vest? She'd imagined them to be metal, sort of like the suits of armor knights wore in fairy tales.

The witness pointed out the stains and explained how his tests showed whose blood it was, as well as that on the floor and the front porch.

Blood. Velita closed her eyes. *All that blood.* She felt as though she was back in the shower, shivering, washing away the last signs of her baby's poor, cheated life.

She felt a touch on her arm and jerked. Next to her, Nellie mouthed, "You okay?"

She nodded and told herself to pay attention. The man was still talking about DNA and the way stains were tested. He said the shot had to come from above, at a slant, to miss the bulletproof vest.

"In your expert opinion," asked James Pettigrew, "what would this mean?"

"The victim was crouching and was shot by someone in a standing position."

When it was Arnold Torrance's turn, he asked if the bullet could have bounced off the ceiling or wall.

Dr. Scruggs said no, not the way the bullet holes were angled.

Attorney Pettigrew went up again and asked if any bullet holes had been found in the house.

"One."

"Where was this?"

"In the floor, approximately two feet from the body."

That afternoon, more doctors were called. One had examined the Jacksons and had found only small traces of heroin. Another had checked their arms for needle tracks and found only old ones. He'd shone light into Jackson's eyes; the pupils were normal.

"What does this indicate?" asked Attorney Pettigrew.

"During narcotic use, the pupils are pinpoints and do not dilate in light. Duane Jackson's eyes dilated, indicating he was not on drugs at the time."

Arnold Torrance asked how long it had been between the time of shooting and the examination, and the doctor said it was about three hours. He admitted that was probably long enough for the eyes to adjust back to normal.

After several more technicians testified about lab tests and measurements and more doctors gave their expert opinions, finally

James Pettigrew nodded to the jury and judge. "Your Honor, the State rests."

The defense lawyer called his first witness, the Reverend LeRoy Hargrave from the Bethany Community Church in Booneville. Reverend Hargrave, white-haired with a short white beard, had been Duane's pastor and had baptized him. He said a lot of nice things: "A fine boy. Attended church regularly, sang in the choir, served as an usher. Helpful, friendly kid, always smiling."

Velita couldn't believe it. The two sides of Duane Jackson didn't fit. How could a good boy go and kill someone?

When Attorney Torrance finished, the prosecutor asked, "Has Mr. Jackson attended your church recently?"

"Well . . . I don't recall seeing him lately. But he could have—"

"How long has it been since you have seen Mr. Jackson?"

"About . . . four years."

"No further questions."

All day, the defense called witnesses up to the stand. Relatives, old friends and neighbors, an ex-girlfriend, former teachers way back from elementary school. They all testified what a friendly and caring person Duane was. Always looking out for the other guy. But when the prosecuting attorney questioned them, they all admitted the same thing. They hadn't seen him for at least four years.

The last witness of the day was Duane's mother, Mrs. Flora Jackson. A heavyset woman, she wore an orange flowered dress covered with a flowing jacket. Her hair was pulled tight up on her head, then caught in a band and let out in a short spray of frizz. Mrs. Jackson said that for the last ten years, she'd worked as a cook in a nursing home. She also cleaned offices uptown. Had to work double, after her husband left.

Duane was the oldest, and he'd helped her raise his four brothers and sisters. "He's always been a good boy, done well in school. At sixteen he got himself a job and brought his pay home to me."

James Pettigrew leaned his head to one side and smoothed his sleek hair. "How long was Duane in school?"

Mrs. Jackson looked puzzled. "How long?"

"Yes. How many years? Did he graduate?"

"Yeah, he graduated from eighth grade and went on to high school. Did real well there, too."

"Did he finish high school?"

"No. He was big for his age. Strong. He worked—"

"When did he drop out?"

"He—" She glanced at Arnold Torrance. "In tenth grade."

Eyeing Jackson with a new interest, Velita chewed on her thumbnail. Just like her, in his sophomore year. Had he also grown up too fast? Did he regret those lost years?

"Is it not true," asked Pettigrew, "that he was expelled for skipping too many classes?"

Uh-oh, not the same after all, thought Velita. She'd *wanted* to finish school. Would have, too, even after getting married, if the pregnancy hadn't made her so sick.

"Yes. But he was so tired from his job—"

"What type of work did he do?"

"At first, around the neighborhood, mowing lawns, washing windows. Then he got on as a box boy at Big T Groceries."

"At the time of the arrest, was he still working there?"

"No, he got laid off."

"Why?"

"Objection," said Arnold Torrance. "Irrelevant."

"Your Honor," said Attorney Pettigrew, "Defense has already introduced Mr. Jackson's job record."

"Overruled."

"Is it not true," Pettigrew went on, "that he was fired for beating up a customer in the parking lot?"

"That's what *they* say." Mrs. Jackson's eyes flashed. "But he—"

"Thank you. What was his next job?"

"Um, that would be night watchman. In a lumberyard."

"At the time of the arrest, did he still work there?"

She sighed. "No."

"Can you tell us the reason he left?"

Arnold Torrance yelled, "Your Honor, I object to this line of questioning. Calls for hearsay."

Pettigrew shook his head. "Your Honor, I submit that this witness has firsthand knowledge of her son's work record."

"Overruled," said the judge. "Please answer the question."

Mrs. Jackson's eyes flicked to the judge and back. "Well, he was sick a lot. They wouldn't—"

"Was it not because he had a history of tardiness and unauthorized absences due to heavy drug use?"

Mrs. Jackson's shoulders sagged. "That's what *they* called it. He couldn't help—"

"I have no further questions."

On redirect, Attorney Torrance asked, "Was there an event in Duane's life that was especially traumatic to him?"

"Yes." Mrs. Jackson nodded slowly, glanced at the jury, and then looked back at Torrance. "He was fifteen when his daddy left. He never got over it."

"How did this affect your son?"

"He was pretty messed up. Couldn't keep his mind on his studies. Got further and further behind."

"No further questions."

Velita thought about Ralph growing up without a father. What an empty hole that had to make in a boy's life, no matter when it happened. No matter how mean the dad was.

James Pettigrew wasn't satisfied and went up again. "Before your husband left, how did he and your son get along?"

Mrs. Jackson tried to look at the defense lawyer, but Pettigrew stood in her way.

Judge Trent said, "Please answer the question."

Velita could barely hear Mrs. Jackson. "They . . . uh . . . mostly good."

"But not all the time? Isn't it true that on the day your husband left, your son attacked him?"

Mrs. Jackson glanced at the judge and hesitated.

The judge nodded at her, his eyebrows raised in question.

"Yeah." Velita could hardly hear Mrs. Jackson's voice.

"With what did he hit his father?"

She dropped her head and wiped her eyes. "A baseball bat."

"Thank you."

Duane Jackson sat perfectly still, holding his pencil straight up on the tablet as though he'd been tagged in a game of freeze.

Sitting there cool as you please while thinking about clubbing his own daddy, thought Velita. *Now I know how I'll vote. Duane Jackson's got to get the worst punishment the law will give.*

Attorney Torrance cleared his throat. "Your Honor, I respectfully request a recess before I call my next witness."

Judge Trent looked at his watch, then rapped his gavel. "Court is adjourned until tomorrow at ten."

Then Velita noticed something different about Duane Jackson. His lips were trembling.

Chapter 28

All the way home, Velita thought about Duane Jackson. She could see him swinging a bat at his father and wondered how badly he'd hurt the man. What made him do that? And why, up till now, hadn't he shown any feelings? Had the lawyer warned him to keep quiet? Those trembling lips . . .

The kids chattered around her as she fixed dinner, but she hardly heard them. She wished she could talk to someone about the trial, but Ralph wouldn't be any help. He'd just say it was her fault for getting into something she was too stupid to understand.

To her surprise, Ralph came home grinning. It was hard for her to snap out of her mood, but by now she'd learned to pretend. It was safest to go along with him.

"A guy brought in a Beamer that kept overheating," he told her. "Couldn't figure out why. He'd taken it to Rhode's Repair across the street, and they wanted to put in a new radiator, all kinds of other parts. Labor and all, be about six hundred, they told him.

"His wife got mad, said take it to Carter's, and I could see right off all's it needed was a new radiator cap. Twenty bucks, plus labor. Guy was so tickled he gave me another twenty, told the boss I was a keeper." Smugly, he blew on his fingernails, then polished them across his chest.

"Guess that made points with the boss," said Velita. "Maybe he'll give you another raise." She glanced at TJ and motioned with her head. This might be a good time to ask for the field-trip money.

TJ's eyes grew big. "Teacher wants to take us kids to the aquarium," he said, watching his dad's face. "But it costs a lot of money." He chewed his lip and waited.

"How much?" asked Ralph, ruffling TJ's hair. "I can give you a dollar."

TJ flipped his hair back. "I hafta have twenty. By Friday."

"What? You want to clean me out?" Ralph scowled down at TJ, but Velita noticed a twitch of a smile. When TJ hung his head and turned away, Ralph grabbed the boy's arm. "Okay, okay. Remind me tomorrow after work. Right now I gotta make some phone calls." He picked up the receiver and punched in several numbers, calling Tom and a couple of other guys to meet him at Casey's Pool Hall for a poker game.

Velita felt let down. Why couldn't he for once spend his good mood with the kids? Now he'd probably lose a week's wages and come home fighting drunk. *There goes the field trip!*

After helping TJ with his math homework and putting the kids to bed, Velita got out her work basket and caught up with her mending. She kept the TV on but didn't pay much attention to it, always listening for the old Dodge pulling into the driveway. When her eyes wouldn't stay open any longer, she went to bed.

Sometime in the middle of the night, Ralph came stumbling into the room and shook her awake, raving about the game. He'd won the pot, not real big but enough to send him high. Velita reminded him of TJ's field trip, and he said, "Sure, sure. I'll take care of it." She hoped he'd still remember in the morning.

To her surprise, when he wound down, he didn't touch her but just rolled over and soon snored. At first, she was relieved and snuggled back into her pillow.

Then she noticed something different. A faint whiff of perfume, one she'd never smelled before. She sniffed again, not believing, but there it was. Probably just one of the waitresses at the pool hall, flirting with him, she told herself. But Tom had let slip something about a redhead there, and Ralph had cut him off. Why?

Was Ralph fooling around with another woman? The more Velita thought about it, the wider awake she became, and a worm of suspicion crawled through her mind. As if her mind wasn't smart enough for Ralph, now had he lost interest in her body too? If that was true, she must be completely worthless, and for sure there'd be no pleasing him at home.

❖ ❖ ❖

The next day turned muggy, and the courthouse air conditioner didn't seem to help. While waiting in the little room, Geneva grumbled at the dropped stitches in the blanket she was knitting. Nellie held her paperback open but didn't turn the pages. Lester Payne picked a fight with Oliver Banks, a plumber from Sanger.

Even Jacob seemed different. His hair stuck out in places, like he hadn't taken much time to comb it, and his collar curled up on one side. Velita itched to straighten it for him but didn't dare. Absently, she smoothed her own turtleneck, its long sleeves already too hot.

When she followed the jurors into the courtroom, she wondered what was going on. All the seats were filled, and people whispered and stared as though they were expecting something. The air seemed to buzz with electricity.

Then the defense called Duane Jackson to the stand. Shoulders slumped, his jaw muscles working, the young man darted a scared look around the courtroom. He didn't look like the cool murderer Velita had watched for two weeks.

After Jackson was sworn in, Arnold Torrance said, "Would you please tell the court what happened the night of October 11?"

Jackson talked slowly, as though carefully choosing each word. "That night, me and Charlene, we was just, you know, watchin' TV. All a sudden, we hear poundin' at the door. Someone yellin'." He flicked a glance at the jury. "We was real jumpy by then, and Charlene, she started, you know, shakin'."

"Why were you jumpy?"

"We knew someone was, you know, out to get us." He told about owing money to the drug dealers, a contract out on their lives, the drive-by shooting. "I got the gun for, like, protection." He shook his head. "Don't know why the cops didn't find shells. Pro'lly under the bushes."

He also didn't know why the police had come to his house. Neither he nor Charlene were dealing anymore. They kept a little marijuana in the house, but only for themselves. He admitted taking heroin that night, but said it was a bad scene and he'd been trying to quit. He knew it only messed up his brain.

Velita remembered most of his story, told in bits and pieces of testimony by the lawyers and witnesses. The men on the porch, MacDuff charging in through the back door.

"I didn't know he was the police. All's I knew was he was comin' at me, and I got spooked. I never meant to kill nobody."

"Do you have any further words for the jury?"

Duane Jackson rubbed his forehead and nodded. "I'm sorry for what happened. I never did it on purpose. I swear to God, I ain't no killer. You gotta believe me."

Velita studied the man. Could she really believe him? Was he sorry for shooting the policeman, or for getting caught? Ralph was real good at making up lies to weasel out of things he didn't want to do.

James Pettigrew stood up and looked at the jury, smiling, his eyebrows raised. As though he was saying, *We all know he's faking.*

While the prosecuting attorney cross-examined Duane Jackson, he stuck to his story. Because of threats to his and Charlene's lives, he had been spooked. When the men came, he'd only wanted to protect his wife.

"Is it not true, Mr. Jackson, that you had met these officers before, and you recognized them as they stood on your porch?"

"No, sir, I didn't."

"And is it not true that after you killed Officer MacDuff, you shot him again, and then again?"

"I don't remember. I just freaked out."

"Just like you did when you nearly killed your father?"

"Objection! Counsel is badgering the witness."

"I will rephrase. Mr. Jackson, do you admit beating your father with a baseball bat?"

"Yes."

Attorney Pettigrew walked back to his table, then wheeled around. "How long have you been addicted to heroin?"

"About . . . three, four years."

"Four years." The lawyer looked at the jury.

Velita could see what he was getting at. All those people who said how good Jackson was, they'd lost track of him about four years ago. A lot could happen in that time. People could turn rotten.

Ralph had never been a choir boy, but he hadn't been real mean until TJ was born. He'd started drinking more, and everything seemed to make him mad. Her being on this jury really got him boiling. Maybe once this was finished, he'd settle down. But what if Marsha was right, and he turned even worse?

Attorney Pettigrew sat down, and Arnold Torrance walked up to the jury box. He stared at each juror, slowly, one by one, as though he was trying to read their thoughts. Velita felt uncomfortable and didn't want to meet his eyes, but his look pulled hers. Finally he turned back to Jackson. "Tell us about your father."

"Objection! Your Honor, that is irrelevant to the case."

"If it please the court," said Torrance, "the matter has already been introduced by the State. It has a bearing upon a previous witness."

"Overruled. Proceed."

Duane nodded slowly, then shook his head. For a long time, he talked about his childhood and how poor they'd been. "We was always hungry, had to wear raggedy clothes. The other kids, they made fun of me. Called me names." He told about little bits of success at school—good grades on art projects, a part in a play—and lots of big disappointments. "My dad, he wasn't around much. Mostly he was, you know, out boozin'. At home, he just yelled at us kids. We git in his way, he hit us."

"Did he ever play with you, take you to ball games, things like that?"

"No, sir. When I was in school programs, he'd said yeah, he'd come, but he never showed."

"What was your relationship with your mother?"

James Pettigrew jumped to his feet again, but the judge waved him down.

"Okay," said Duane Jackson. "She done her best. But after my dad left, she had to work all the time. Day and night, cookin', scrubbin' office floors. Me and my sister, we watched the littler kids."

Velita could imagine the children running around in torn clothes, not having enough to eat. Just like her own childhood, her helping with the babies, the school kids making fun of her feed-sack dresses.

If—*when* she left Ralph, would TJ and Suanne have to be on their own while she worked day and night to keep them fed and clothed? What would their life be like without a father? Could she do that to them? Was it worth it?

Ralph could be mean, but he always brought home enough money to feed his family, give them decent clothes. Now that his kids were bigger and didn't squall all night, he was proud of them. Probably loved them, in his own way. A while back, he'd bought TJ a bike at a yard sale and now had promised him the field-trip money.

"What happened the night your father left home?" asked Attorney Torrance.

Jackson rubbed his forehead and eyes. His voice was thick, and Velita had to strain to understand him. "He was—he was beatin' on her."

"Your father was hitting your mother?"

"Yes, sir."

"Objection! Leading the witness."

"Overruled."

"Did he do this often?"

Jackson nodded. His voice was flat. "Yes, sir."

"How did that make you feel?"

"Real bad. Us kids was always scared. Never knew when he'd come after her. Or us."

Velita stared at him, living the event, feeling his fear. And her own children—was that how they felt too?

"And this particular time in question, what happened?" asked the lawyer.

"She was on the floor, and he was, you know, kickin' her. Hittin' her with his belt. It had this—this big buckle. Metal, you know, real heavy. She kept screamin' and tryin' to get away. There was blood—blood all over." A tear trickled down Jackson's cheek.

"What happened next?"

Jackson brushed his cheek with the back of his hand. "My sister, she called 911."

"And what did you do?"

The judge handed Jackson a tissue, and he blew his nose. "I thought Momma'd be, you know, dead before anybody came. I grabbed my bat and yelled for him to quit."

"Did your father stop then?"

"No, sir. He just look at me quick. His eyes were like, crazy. He kept kickin' and hittin' at her. So I slugged him with the bat, and he went down to his knees." Jackson stopped, took a long breath, and let it out slowly.

The judge motioned to the clerk, and she brought Jackson a glass of water.

He took a sip and set the glass down carefully. The courtroom was dead silent, everyone watching him, waiting for him to go on.

Velita's heart pounded. Her thoughts switched to her own home. TJ's Little League baseball bat was in his closet. The season hadn't started yet—maybe she ought to hide it, just in case.

Attorney Torrance asked, "What did your father do?"

"My daddy, he tried to get up and come after me. I hit him again and again until my momma had crawled out of his reach. I told him, 'Get out, or I'll kill you.' I never meant it, I—I just wanted him to stop hurtin' my momma."

"Go on."

"Then he cussed and kind of, you know, got up and staggered out the door. Took the car and split."

"Did you see him after that?"

"No. He never came back. People said he was shacked up with some woman 'cross town."

"Did this affect your school work?"

"Objection! Conjecture."

"Overruled. You may answer."

Duane Jackson rubbed his forehead. "I lost it, man. Couldn't think straight."

"Your grades went down?"

"Yeah."

"How old were you at this time?"

"Fifteen."

"Seven years ago, right?"

"About that, yeah."

"And you still remember it clearly?"

"Oh, yeah. Sometimes I get, you know, nightmares."

"When did you next see your father?"

"I didn't. After a coupla years, the police called. Said my daddy'd shot his woman and himself. Both dead."

"How did you feel about that?"

"He was mean, but he was my daddy, you know. And I never got a chance to tell him I was sorry for hittin' him." Jackson wiped his eyes.

"Is that when you turned to hard drugs?"

"Yeah. I knew it was wrong. But once I started, I couldn't quit. Been tryin' to, though."

Attorney Torrance bowed his head. "No further questions."

It was eleven thirty. Judge Trent cleared his throat, rapped his gavel, and said, "Court is adjourned for the noon recess. We will convene again at one thirty."

Her thoughts spinning, Velita followed the other jurors out of the courtroom.

Chapter 29

On the way out of the courthouse Marsha said, "Hey, Velita, let's go get a chicken salad for lunch. My treat."

She's going to ask me about Ralph, thought Velita. *I've already talked too much.* "No, thanks," she said. "I . . . I've got some errands to run."

Walking fast, she headed for the mall, trying to blot out the pictures in her mind—the beating, the belt buckle. The baseball bat.

People stood lined up at the little snack shops on each side of the plaza, jabbering and laughing, but the smells of pastrami, chili dogs, and soy sauce didn't tempt her. She passed the Dollar Tree, a wig store, and a pawn shop, pretending to look at the displays in the windows. For all she knew, they could be filled with dirty rags.

Two blocks ahead, the north end of the mall was nearly deserted. Most of the stores there were closed and run-down. Still she walked, the clicking of her steps telling her: *Don't think, don't think.*

Two men in suits hurried past her and disappeared into an office building. She reached the far end of the mall and, looping around, started back on the opposite side.

A group of teenage boys in fat men's pants and backward caps came out of a video store. They followed her, matching their steps to hers.

Suddenly, she realized how alone she was and felt cold. She'd been crazy to come here. She didn't need any more problems. If these guys tried anything, it would be all her fault. This time Jacob wouldn't be here to rescue her. *Oh God*, she breathed, *You're my last chance. If You can't help me, no one can.*

Just ahead, in the middle of the pavement, was a fountain with benches around it. An old woman in ragged clothes sat there leaning on a wooden cane. Next to her was a beat-up shopping cart full of lumpy plastic bags.

Velita hurried to the bench and dropped down next to the woman. The boys gathered around them, poking into the bags. One asked the woman, "What you got in this limo of yours, Miss Piggy? Christmas presents?"

Cussing and spitting, the woman switched her cane at them, but they just laughed and shuffled away, carrying off a watch and a knit cap they'd found in the cart.

Velita turned to the woman and said, "I'm sorry. I thought they'd be the end of me."

The woman just stared off into the distance. Finally she muttered, "It don't got no end. It just keeps on rolling and rolling. Till you stop it."

That didn't make sense, and Velita watched her for a minute. Then she realized: the woman was right. That was the way with trouble. There wasn't any end. Unless *she* did something about it.

She'd always figured she had to take the knocks until the kids were old enough to be on their own, hoping somehow by then Ralph might ease up.

If Marsha was right, that wasn't going to happen. Last night, he'd been in a good mood; this morning she'd gotten by with only a squeezed arm. But knowing Ralph, anything could set him off again.

She couldn't hold back the pictures anymore. Duane Jackson's angry father swinging his belt; the mother, bloody and screaming; the boy getting the bat, hitting and hitting—and growing up to bury those memories in hard drugs. Then it was herself on the floor, Ralph swinging at her, and TJ, her little TJ . . .

What should she do? She saw only two choices. Leave, go who-knows-where, maybe end up on the streets. Or stay with Ralph, get killed, her kids growing up like Duane. Either way seemed hopeless.

Heartsick, Velita got up and slowly headed back to the courthouse. From the distance, she could faintly hear the old woman still mumbling, "Rolling and rolling . . ."

She walked into the jury room just as the bailiff announced, "Request the presence of the jury."

As the afternoon session began, Attorney Torrance had one question for his client. "Did you intentionally kill Robert MacDuff?"

"No, sir. I did not."

"The defense rests."

The judge looked from one lawyer to the other. Finally, with both hands, he motioned them to the bench. They whispered a while; then he announced they would meet in chambers and told the jury to wait in their room for his decision.

Back at the table, Marsha asked Velita, "Are you all right? You look a little pale."

Velita bit her lip. What could she say without getting herself in worse trouble? "It's just . . . I worry about my kids. Especially TJ. He's starting to push Suanne around."

"You mean because they see Ralph abusing you?" whispered Marsha.

Velita felt like the wind had been knocked out of her. She hadn't expected Marsha to be so outspoken. She glanced around, but the others didn't seem to be listening in.

Marsha pushed on. "How does TJ react when it happens?"

"I know he hates it, but seems like each time he's getting more used to it."

On Velita's other side, Jacob cleared his throat. "Does this, uh, happen a lot?"

So Jacob knew too! Velita felt so ashamed. Finally she admitted, "When he's drunk, yeah."

"Does your husband's mother know?" asked Marsha.

"Sure. She told me it was my fault—I was the one who got pregnant and tied him down." Velita couldn't believe she was telling this to people she'd known only a little while. But maybe they'd suspected all along—what with her bruises and the way Ralph had treated Jacob when he'd followed her home. And then that fight at the relief sale . . .

She bit her lip to keep from blubbering. "Ralph says I drive him crazy. That if I'd just quit messing up . . . I try so hard to do everything just how he likes it, but once he gets in that mood, there's no stopping him." She closed her eyes, feeling again the kicks, the pain.

"That's so typical." Marsha shook her head slowly. "The women I've seen—they all think if they just push the right buttons, everything will be okay. But that's not the way it works; the abuse only gets worse."

Velita hunched her shoulders. "My folks used to scrap a lot. Hit, throw things. I thought . . . Mama used to say . . . this was what marriage was like."

Jacob caught his breath, and his face looked angry. "No! It isn't—it shouldn't be." He plowed his fingers through his hair as though itching for a fight himself. "God planned marriage for a man and woman to be helpmeets to each other."

Marsha stared at him a minute, then turned back to Velita. "Is there any way you could get your husband to change his mind about counseling?"

"Ralph? Not a chance! If the whole world was against him, he'd still be the only one right."

"What about the kids?" asked Jacob. "Does he—?"

"Not Suanne. TJ might get a whack if he's in the way. Most of the time, he knows enough to go hide. But I don't know how long that'll work." Now that she'd opened up, she couldn't stop talking. She told them about trying to defend herself with the frying pan and how that had backfired.

Marsha gave a soft whistle. "Believe me, I know about men like that. I've seen too many of their wives end up in the hospital. Or worse."

"There's got to be some way we can help." Jacob's voice was husky. "It's hard to stand by when someone you . . . when you see someone get hurt."

It was too much. Velita couldn't hold back her tears any longer, and Jacob reached into his back pocket and handed her his big handkerchief.

She buried her face in it, and felt Marsha's gentle touch on her hand.

All around, she heard the other jurors laughing and telling jokes, but when she opened her eyes, Geneva was looking at her, and Eunice had closed her book.

Marsha glanced at them and turned so her shoulder blocked their view. She whispered, "You've got to tell the police. It could save your life."

Velita took a shuddering breath and wiped her face. "The neighbors called them a couple times. By now, Ralph knows most of them. He weasels out of it, makes it look like it's my fault. Gives me that warning look, so's I won't tell on him. If I did, if I pressed charges, afterwards I'd get it even worse." She blew her nose into the handkerchief, remembering Saturday night, the evil in his eyes. "Even if they did lock him up, wouldn't take long he'd be out. Ready to get back at me."

Jacob's jaw tightened, and his eyes looked sad. "Couldn't you get a restraining order?"

"That wouldn't stop him. Just make him madder."

Marsha shook her head. "I still think the shelter is the best idea. It's not a luxury hotel, but it might be the only smart thing. For your own sake. And for your children. Trust me. You'd be safe."

"You don't know Ralph. I wouldn't be safe anywhere." He'd drilled that into her, over and over. *"Don't you run off again. No matter what, I'll find you."*

Jacob tapped his fingers together, staring at them. Then he looked up suddenly. "You know, when you see black clouds, it's a warning that a storm is coming. All the things that happened to you—maybe it's God's warning to you that you need to leave. You have to trust that He'll protect you."

Velita sighed. "So far, trusting hasn't done me much good. I don't think God hears my prayers. But I guess you're right—one of these days I'll have to just up and leave. I can't now, with this trial going on."

Marsha shrugged, holding out her palms. "Hey, we've got alternates. I could talk to the judge for you."

"If he starts up again, I'll call you. I promise." Now that all the bottled-up misery had finally come gushing out, Velita felt like a dry, empty shell.

She thought of what Jacob said, about a storm warning. Could that be why God hadn't answered her prayer to get off the jury? Had there been a reason she was called here? After hearing Duane Jackson and his mother, she could see clearly it wasn't just her that Ralph hurt; it messed up her kids' whole lives. And like the old bag lady said, only *she* could end it.

She started to hand the handkerchief back to Jacob, then noticed all the makeup and mascara smeared on it. What a sight she must be! She headed for the little restroom to redo her makeup and wash the hankie; by the end of the session, it ought to be dry.

Just then, the door opened, and the bailiff stuck in his head. "Jury is dismissed until tomorrow at ten."

The jurors cheered, grabbed their belongings, and filed out. Velita hesitated, but the bailiff waited, motioning her to follow the others.

She would just have to give the hankie back to Jacob, stained as it was. Velita hurried after the last of the jurors, but by the time the elevator reached the bottom floor, Jacob had disappeared.

She didn't dare take that hankie home. As she passed a trash bin, she wondered if she ought to throw it away. Jacob probably had plenty of them and might not miss it. Then she noticed his initials, hand-embroidered on one corner, all fancy and swirly. His wife must have sewed it for him; now that she'd died, it would be a treasured memory. Velita felt a tightness in her chest, an envy of such love and devotion that she herself would never have.

She thought hard. Last time she'd looked at the clock on the wall, it was only two thirty. If she was very careful, she could have it washed, ironed, and hidden under the spare sheets in the hall closet long before Ralph got home. And Jacob would get his clean hankie tomorrow. Stuffing it deep into her purse, Velita hurried to the parking garage.

Chapter 30

Limp and shaky, Velita drove home from the courthouse. She still couldn't believe she'd poured out her heart to people she'd known only two weeks—had said things she'd never dared tell anyone else.

In a way, it was a relief. Now she wouldn't have to pretend to them anymore. She just hoped her gut feeling was right, that she could trust those two. And that this all wouldn't somehow get back to Ralph.

She thought about Duane Jackson's mother. The woman had been brave, raising those five kids alone, working day and night. It must have been awfully hard, but she'd proven it could be done.

Yet there was one big difference between Mrs. Jackson and herself. That woman's husband had left her. *She* didn't have to worry about being found.

At home, Velita met TJ and Suanne running home from the bus stop, and they bounced around her, trying to outtalk each other. TJ had made a fish out of aluminum foil, and Suanne begged for a special kind of pencil the school had for sale.

"It gots the school name on it! Only a quarter, Mommy, please?"

Velita pawed through her purse, looking for stray change.

TJ came over and frowned into the open purse. "What's that rag in there for?"

Velita thought quickly. "I needed to clean something up," she told him. Finding two dimes and a nickel, she motioned toward Suanne's backpack. "Put the money in the side pocket, and don't lose it."

At the kitchen sink, Velita scrubbed at the stains on the handkerchief and thought about Jacob. Strong, solid—like a rock. Tough enough to get the best of Ralph, but so gentle that he'd offer his handkerchief to a crying woman. A man who believed in God and wasn't ashamed to show it.

Ralph would say that was sissy stuff. He was the red bandanna type, rough and coarse. He never would have comforted her. He'd just say, "Quit your yammering," and give her the back of his hand to make sure she understood.

There were still smudges on the cloth, so Velita went into the laundry room, rubbed some stain remover on the hankie, and put it into the washing machine, adding clothes from the hamper to make a full load. It would be done in plenty of time.

TJ had homework and spread his papers on the kitchen table. At the other end, Suanne shaped Play-Doh into cookies and fruits. While drilling TJ on spelling words, Velita peeled and sliced potatoes for a casserole and fried pork chops to simmer with it. Then she took berries from the freezer and spread them on a pan for cobbler. Ralph loved warm fruit cobbler.

When TJ finished his homework and ran outside, Suanne put away her Play-Doh. She washed her hands, then helped Velita sprinkle sugar on the berries. "Mommy, can you stay home tomorrow?" she asked.

Velita crumbled topping on the berries and popped it into the oven. "Sorry, babe, I can't. But pretty soon, it'll all be over. I promise." *All over. And then what?*

With Suanne trailing after her, Velita went back and forth, getting down plates and setting them on the table. The washing machine spun to a stop, and she went and scooped out the clothes and threw them into the dryer.

She glanced at the clock. Ten minutes, and the hankie would be dry. Ralph wouldn't come home for another hour.

An awful hoarse screeching sound came from outside, and Velita ran to the window, then out the door. In front of the house, a car sat skewed across the street, and a man slammed out of it, charging across her lawn. TJ's bike sprawled in the gutter, its front wheel spinning.

"Lady!" the man yelled. "That your kid? Teach him to stay off the street!"

Velita ran past him, her heart thumping. "What happened? Where's my boy?" Then she saw him crouched on the curb, hugging a bloody knee.

The man was still shouting, but Velita had TJ in her arms and asked, "Did the car hit you?"

TJ glared up at her. "He ran into my bike!" His lips quivered, and he wiped his nose with the back of his hand.

Velita felt his arms and legs, had him wiggle his fingers and toes. Neighbors all around stood watching, and Rhonda came over with salve and Band-Aids.

The man quieted down a little and shook his finger at TJ. "You're lucky I got good brakes," he said. "You coulda been killed." He turned to Velita. "I wasn't going over thirty. He just flew out in front of me without looking. I slammed on the brakes, stopped as soon as I could." He picked up TJ's bike, straightened the back fender, then set it up on its kick stand.

"That's right," said one of the neighbors. "I saw it all. The car barely nicked the back wheel of the bike. Your kid okay?"

TJ got up, limped a little, then saw Luke and ran off to tell him the story.

Velita huffed and nodded. "Yeah. I hope he's learned a lesson."

The man nodded. "See that he does." He got back into his car, straightened the wheels, and drove away, and the neighbors walked off, whispering together.

When Velita opened her front door, she caught a whiff of something burning, and rushed into the kitchen. But it was only the juice from the cobbler, bubbling up through the slits in the golden crust, and running over in the hot oven. She took the cobbler out and set it on a rack to cool. The sweet smell of the berries mixed with the spicy scent of pork chops and the buttery casserole, and she hurried to cut up greens for a salad.

The front door slammed. Ralph stomped in, threw his lunch box onto the counter, and tossed his cap on the table. "Dinner not ready?"

Velita looked at the clock, stunned. Was it that late?

As calmly as she could, she said, "In a jiff." Would he blame her for TJ's accident? "Be on the table by the time you've showered." With the handle of a spatula, she snagged his greasy cap and hung it on a hook by the back door. She tossed the salad and prettied it up with a circle of tomato slices on top. "Wash up, kids," she called.

TJ ran in from outside. "Dad, guess what! I got hit by a car! Flew out of the way just in time. Am I Superman or what?"

Ralph frowned, and Velita held her breath. But all he said was, "Yeah, guy 'cross the street told me. Next time, look both ways. Don't want no hospital bills on a squirt like you." Then he swatted TJ's shoulder and grinned. "Superman, huh? Think you're a big shot, don't you?"

TJ ducked out of his reach. "Don't forget—I gotta have my aquarium money for tomorrow. You promised."

It had been a good idea, Velita thought, the boy asking his dad for the money. But Ralph had agreed almost *too* easily. She hoped he wouldn't back out now.

But he dug into his pocket and pulled out a twenty. "You wanna go see those fish, huh? Well, don't let the sharks get you; they'll chew you up and spit you out."

TJ stuck the money in his backpack. "You gotta sign a paper, too."

Ralph headed for the bathroom. "Remind me in the morning." The water pipes sang, and Velita poured milk into the kids' glasses. She took the casserole from the oven and set it in its cradle in front of Ralph's plate. Some of the sauce had run over the edges of the dish. Ralph would gripe about that, so she grabbed a dishrag, scrubbing the sides carefully.

Too soon, the pipes screeched, signaling the end to Ralph's shower, and he came out of the bathroom in jockey shorts, toweling his hair. He asked, "Where's my tan shirt?"

Velita froze. Flipping the dishrag into the sink, she darted toward the laundry room. "In the dryer. I'll get it."

Ralph pushed ahead of her and reached into the dryer. He gave a yelp, then cursed. "It's all stuck together!"

She eased behind him and saw her nightie clinging to the knit shirt. Relieved that he had found it so quickly, she butted the dryer door shut and said, "I'm sorry. I forgot the fabric softener."

She tried to take the clothes from him, but he held them out of her reach, tearing the nightie loose. "You know I hate when it snaps at me." He was silent a moment. Then, "Vel?" His voice was soft, but flat. "Who's J. F.?"

She stared at him, her mouth dry.

"And how come his hankie's stuck to your nightie?"

How could she have been so careless? There was no way she could explain.

Ralph reached into the dryer and pawed through the rest of the clothes, tossing them on the floor. "What else are you hiding in here? Some of his underwear?"

"I just borrowed it—"

He straightened up. "It's that Dutchman, isn't it? Isn't it?" With each question he slapped her face, backing her into the kitchen.

"Yes. No! It's not what you think—"

Suanne starting screaming and ran into the bedroom she shared with TJ.

TJ tugged at Ralph's arm. "Don't, Dad!"

Ralph shouted, "Shut up!" and flung the boy against the refrigerator. Velita reached out to TJ, but he'd already darted after Suanne.

Ralph turned back to Velita, his eyes glittering. He flexed the large square of cloth, then suddenly whipped it around Velita's neck and crossed it tightly over her throat, locking it with his thumbs. "Let's see what good your Mennonite does you now."

"Please, no," Velita tried to say, but she could only croak. Her windpipe closed, and she gasped for air. She clawed at the handkerchief, at Ralph's hands, his arms. *Oh God, help me!*

She felt her eyes bulge; then her legs gave way. Darkness swallowed her up.

Chapter 31

"Wake up, Mom. Wake up!"

Velita opened her eyes. She lay sprawled on the kitchen floor, with TJ patting her cheeks.

She blinked to clear her vision. Her throat burned, and her head ached. Next to her, Suanne sat crying. In the middle of the floor, the casserole dish sat cracked into halves, the creamed potatoes in a mound beside the pork chops. The salad bowl tipped crazily in a chair, and lettuce and tomatoes dribbled down the side.

Then she remembered what had happened and felt cold all over. She looked around and whispered, "Where's your daddy?"

"He took off," said TJ.

She crawled to the window. The car was gone. She tried to pull herself up, but waves of dizziness forced her to slide back to the floor. Why hadn't God protected her? At least she was alive; next time she might not make it. Leaning against the wall, her head on her knees, she moaned, "Oh, Lord, this has got to stop. What can I do?"

Suanne ran and got a glass of water. "Mommy, you want a drink?"

Velita took it gratefully and sipped. "Thank you, sweetheart," she murmured. "I'll get up in a minute." She looked for Jacob's handkerchief; not seeing it, she figured Ralph must have trashed it.

"What'll we do with all this stuff?" asked TJ, picking up the broken casserole. He bit into a pork chop and chewed while rescuing the salad bowl. "It tastes okay."

Slowly, Velita got up and helped him clean up the soggy mess on the floor. He filled a plate for himself with potatoes from the top of the pile, but Suanne said she wasn't hungry. "I don't want yuck from the floor."

Velita fixed her a peanut butter sandwich, but she herself couldn't eat. The rest of the evening, her hands and mouth worked numbly through the kids' baths, stories, and backrubs while her mind was in a fog.

When TJ and Suanne were finally tucked into their beds, she sat on the sofa, trying to pull herself together. She thought all the way back to the start of her married life and tried to figure out how she had gotten herself into this fix. What could she have done different?

All she could come up with was never to have laid eyes on Ralph, for sure not to have married him, even though she'd been pregnant at the time. The only way she could see to undo that mistake was to leave her husband. It would be awful to take the kids away from their daddy, but if she didn't and he killed her, what would happen to them? Would TJ end up like Ralph, beating up the wife he was supposed to love?

If Jacob was right and this was another warning from God, it looked like this could be the final one, and God sure meant business.

If only she could push the years back and be a little girl in Chockamo again! She felt like running back to her mama anyway, kids and all—except she didn't have the bus fare. And after not hearing from her folks for so long, who knew where they lived now or if they'd even take her in?

The shelter Marsha had talked about? It was hard to believe there was any place here in town where Ralph couldn't find her. LaDonna was no help; she'd just call Ralph. The neighbor, Rhonda Avery? Why, Ralph would break down her door.

Maybe the best thing, after all, would be to hide in a big city like LA or San Francisco. Change her name and looks and those of the kids. She had a few dollars left in her wallet; enough to get out of town and hitchhike the rest of the way. Maybe some truck driver, seeing the kids, would take pity on them. But then, how could she tell if the guy could be trusted? From the news she'd seen on TV, there were a lot of perverts out there.

Then she realized she had no idea what the bus schedules were or if they ran this late. And what if Ralph came and found her waiting at the bus station? No, she couldn't take that chance.

Her thoughts ran in a jumble: Ralph beating her senseless; Duane Jackson's mother on the floor, the boy swinging his bat at his father. TJ growing more like Ralph, ending up in prison just like Duane. Her in a cheesy motel, leaving the kids alone while she looked for a minimum wage job.

By eleven o'clock, Ralph still hadn't come home. Velita was sure he'd picked up Tom and they were going from bar to bar, boozing until they got kicked out. It could be as late as the 2 AM closing time before he dragged in. He probably was with that redhead Tom had mentioned, staying out all night just to get even.

Velita thought about the hymn she'd heard on television—"There is a place of quiet rest."

The shelter. It *had* to be the only way out. Marsha had insisted it was safe. Velita gritted her teeth and held her breath for just a moment, then picked up the phone.

Marsha answered on the third ring. Velita asked, "That place you talked about, can you give me the address?"

Marsha's voice had sounded groggy at first, but it turned sharp. "Where's your husband?"

"He's—out."

"Wait for me. I'll be there in fifteen minutes. What's your house number?"

Velita heard a car turn onto the street. "No," she said quickly. She stood paralyzed, the receiver in her hand. The car slowed, then turned into a driveway across the street, and she blew out her breath.

"Velita?" Marsha sounded worried.

"It's okay. I thought he'd come home. But it's just the neighbors." If Ralph knew what she was planning . . . "I don't know. It's too risky. He could be here any minute." She thought a bit. "Why don't you tell me the address? After he comes home and is asleep, I'll have the car."

"I don't know," said Marsha. "What if he gets violent again? Velita, you're not safe!"

"Safer than if he sees you here. That would really set him off. Please—it's the only way."

Marsha gave the address to Velita, along with the phone number, and had her say it back. "Got it?"

"Yeah." Velita repeated it. She'd better remember it. No way could she write it down and let Ralph find out about this place.

"Call me as soon as you get there. No matter what time it is. Promise?"

"Sure." Velita hung up the phone and hurried to her closet, whispering the information over and over. Reaching up to the highest shelf, she pulled down an old battered suitcase. After throwing in some things for herself, she went into the kids' bedroom. She checked to make sure they were asleep, then took a flashlight and groped in their closet. Two changes of clothes for each of them, Suanne's stuffed dinosaur. TJ's favorite shirt and comic books. An extra blanket.

She stuffed everything into the suitcase, then tiptoed back into the living room. The street lamp outside was just bright enough for her to punch the numbers on the phone.

"Safe Harbor," said a soft voice.

Velita cleared her throat. "I need . . . I mean, do you have room—"

There was a scrunch of tires in the driveway, the squeal of brakes. She fumbled down the receiver and ran into the bedroom.

The filled suitcase lay open on the bed. Velita slammed it shut and tried to lift it back onto the shelf in the closet.

It was too heavy.

She looked around frantically. Where could she hide it? She tried to shove it under the bed, but the bed frame was too low. She started to drag the suitcase across the hall to the kids' room. Just then, the front door knob rattled.

Running backward, she tugged the suitcase back into the bedroom. Using every ounce of her strength and then some, she lifted the bed frame a little bit and, with her foot, shoved the suitcase beyond it under the bed. Then she tore off her clothes, threw them into the closet, and snapped off the light. Sliding into bed, she burrowed deep into the covers. Her heart pumped fast as a thumping engine, and she held her breath to slow it down.

She heard Ralph stumbling past the living-room furniture, singing and laughing. Then she heard a chair fall, and he swore.

She took a big gulp of air and forced herself to breathe long and deeply.

The familiar odor filled the room: sour whiskey, sweat, urine. There was something else this time—a strong burnt smell. At least it wasn't perfume, although by now, the redhead could have him for all Velita cared.

The bed rocked as Ralph bumped into it and then sat down. A thud, then another, as his boots dropped onto the carpet. The bed shook again, and she heard him head toward the bathroom.

Then he was back. Still in his smelly clothes, he fell onto the bed, half on top of her. She moved just a bit and murmured, pulling the covers tight around her. *Please, please, God, let him fall asleep.*

Ralph's heavy arm pinned her down, and he giggled. "Hey, Vel, you shoulda seen it. We had us a great barbecue!" He coughed, rolled over, and threw up all over the bed. After that, he lay still.

He'd left her alone. *Thank You, Lord.* Now she could breathe normally—as normally as she could with the horrible odor choking her. She lay still, waiting for him to snore. When the first rasping breaths rose and fell, she lifted up on one elbow and studied him. Years ago, right after they were married, sometimes she'd lie awake and watch him sleep. He'd looked like a cute little boy then, so innocent and peaceful, like he'd never hurt a flea. She'd been crazy in love and would have done anything to keep him happy.

Now she could only see the monster in him and smell the filth. All she felt was disgust and a deep sadness for the love that had been crushed out of her.

The snores came louder. Velita eased herself out of bed, slipped back into her clothes, and cleaned up the worst of the mess.

The car was home now; she could use it to escape. She looked for the keys. Ralph usually kept them on the dresser, and she felt all over the surface and the floor below.

They weren't there.

They must still be in Ralph's pocket. She tried to ease her fingers into one, but he moved onto his stomach. There was no way to get them without waking him. And with his weight on the bed, she couldn't pull that suitcase from under it. *Tomorrow. It's gotta be tomorrow.*

Chapter 32

Over at the Franzen farm that night, the moon was a thin sliver. At ten o'clock, Jacob parked his Massey-Ferguson tractor between the cultivator and sprayer in the shed and turned off the headlights. There was a lot more work to do, but he'd better call it a day. He lined up his shovel and rake in their proper places and set his floodlight on the shelf.

Clumps of sawdust crunched under his feet, and he noticed a hammer and some scrap wood on his work table. Sammy must have been making something and forgotten to put things away. He'd have to remind the boys to clean up after their projects. He laid the hammer in the tool chest and scooped the wood into an odds-and-ends box.

Before turning out the lights, he took one last look around the shed. Everything was in place.

Midnight meowed a greeting and curled around his ankles. She was skinny now, with four kittens hidden somewhere in the shed. He reached down and petted her. "Did Becky feed you?" he asked. She raised her back in answer to his touch, then darted off into the darkness. A glow in the northern sky outlined the town, and Jacob remembered he hadn't bought nozzles for the sprayer.

The house was dark except for a light in the upstairs bathroom.

It reminded him of Sharon waiting up for him. She'd be fresh from her shower, her hair shiny and sweet-smelling, her body soft and silky. The familiar ache of loneliness swept over him as he went into the silent house.

Becky had left the coffee pot on, and he poured himself a cup. Between sips, he shuffled through the day's mail stacked neatly on the kitchen table.

The water bill was sky high again, and his allocation had been cut still more. He shook his head. He'd finally found a crew to thin the peaches, barely in time. But unless the trees got enough water, it wouldn't do much good—the fruit still wouldn't size right.

He scribbled on the back of an envelope, adding, subtracting. How much would the bank lend him until the crop was sold? A new manure spreader would have to wait until next year. Maybe he could borrow one.

He was so tired. Working late, night after night. Then getting up early, out into the orchard until it was time to clean up and go to the courthouse.

He'd be glad when the trial was over. The worst was still ahead—deciding the verdict. He'd thought he had it all figured out. Sin had to be punished, especially murder. The death penalty was consistent with the concept of nonresistance, of living peaceably. Doing away with hard criminals made nonresistance possible for the rest of the world.

That was before it had touched his own life. Now, after looking into the eyes of the convicted man, listening to his defense, things took on a different light. It just wasn't that cut and dried.

Marsha's words nagged at him. *It's okay to kill a person, as long as someone else does the dirty work?*

He rubbed his aching shoulders and yawned. That was tomorrow's worry. Tonight, he had to get some sleep. He put the mail away and went upstairs to bed.

❖ ❖ ❖

"Dad, Dad!"

Jacob woke up suddenly. Sammy was pulling at his arm. "The shed's on fire!"

He looked toward the window and saw a red glow, much too bright for city lights.

Grabbing his jeans, he pulled them on over his shorts. "Call 911," he said and ran down the stairs.

Flames shot out the window of the shed and licked the surrounding walls. The blaze crackled and snapped, and the acrid smell of smoke filled his nostrils.

He raced toward the fire, his heart pounding. Sammy and Paul, still in pajamas, ran to join him.

Jacob shouted, "Stay back," and yanked the shed door open. A blast of heat propelled him backward.

"The kittens!" screamed Paul. "They're in there!"

Becky, tying her flapping bathrobe, ran to him and pulled him back to the lawn.

Jacob grabbed a hose and tried to squirt down the walls. The flames sizzled, then roared louder. He dragged the hose around behind the shed to his bin trailers. They hadn't caught fire yet; maybe they could be saved. The spray hissed against the metal and wood, and smoke enveloped him, choking him.

His mind whirled, trying to figure out how the fire had started. A problem with the wiring? A spark from the tractor?

Sammy shouted, "The trucks are coming." Sirens wailed in the distance, getting louder and louder.

An explosion rocked the building, knocking him to the ground. The blaze thundered to the roof and lit the whole sky. He scrambled to his feet and backed away.

Two fire trucks shrieked into the yard. The chug of water pumps and shouts of firemen mingled with the angry hiss of flames. A police car pulled up, followed by a few of the closest neighbors in pickups.

The officer walked up to Jacob. "Any idea how this started?"

Jacob shook his head. Sammy had been in there earlier, he thought. But he wouldn't have had reason to light a match. Would he? Sometimes boys think they have to experiment with smoking—

"Got insurance?"

"Some. Not a lot."

The neighbors gathered around, and someone patted his shoulder. "Hang in there." At last the blaze fizzled down. The firemen coiled their hoses and wiped their faces. All that was left of the shed was a sad mess of soggy, jagged boards.

Jacob stepped carefully near the hot debris, his boots crunching on cinders. By the light of the engines, he could see the charred remains of his tractor and cultivator.

The policeman pointed to a tipped gasoline can under the window. "That yours?"

Jacob looked around. His empty cans still stood, warped and blackened, on a steel shelf. He shook his head. "I don't recognize it."

"Got any enemies?" asked the officer.

Jacob rubbed his forehead. "Not that I know of," he told the officer. Then he felt a chill slice through the heat from the fire. "You think . . . it might be arson?" That would rule the boys out but carry other implications.

The policeman shrugged. "Could be. Probably vandals. Been a lot of that this spring. Kids with nothing else to do, looking for kicks. Better call your insurance agent first thing in the morning."

The fire engines and police car left. The neighbors said, "Anything we can do, just holler," and they too drove away. A breeze lifted the leaves of a sycamore tree and flapped the fringes of the awning at the back door.

Jacob looked up at the moon. Stars twinkled in the smudged sky. "Why me, Lord?" he groaned. "And why *now*?" Beyond his pain and despair formed a knot of worry. *Who was this unknown enemy? Would he come back again?*

Paul stumbled toward him and burrowed a wet face into Jacob's stomach. Sammy hunched on the ground under the tree, and Jacob reached for him. Becky joined them, and they wept together, arms twined in a family hug.

Suddenly, Paul wrenched away and ran toward the shed. He picked up a small black object.

"Midnight!" cried Becky.

The cat jumped down from Paul's embrace and ran back toward the shed. But instead of going in, she darted behind the building. Jacob and the children ran after her and saw her leap into the farthest bin trailer. There, in a dark corner, squirmed four tiny kittens.

Jacob rubbed the cat's head and told her, "At least we both still have what's most precious." He hugged his children again, ashamed of even considering the boys as suspects in the fire. "Thank You,

Lord," he prayed aloud. "Thank You for sparing our lives and those of the kittens. We don't understand why this happened, but we trust You to help us recover."

It was three in the morning, but nobody felt like sleeping. They went inside, and Becky made hot chocolate. They sat around the kitchen table, each in their own thoughts.

Finally Paul spoke up. "What now, Dad?"

What now? Good question. Replacing the equipment, rebuilding the shed. Insurance. Borrowing money until the insurance came through. Paperwork.

Jacob dropped his face into his hands and rubbed his forehead. Sharon had always done the paperwork. She had been quick with figures and a good reader. She could take a legal notice and make sense of it in the time it took him to read the first paragraph. How was he ever going to get through this without her? He'd thought he missed her before, but now his need reached far beyond the physical yearning.

Sammy, always the practical one, shrugged his shoulders. "I guess first we got to clean up that mess."

"Good thinking." Jacob clapped him on the back. "But it's still an hour till sunrise. Let's get back to bed so we'll have energy to work."

Lying alone upstairs, Jacob's eyes felt gritty and heavy, but sleep wouldn't come. He planned his workday. Tow out the ruined equipment, tear down the charred boards. Throw away what couldn't be salvaged.

Then he remembered. First he had to put in his day at the courthouse. He punched his fist into the pillow. If only he could ask for a day off like the lawyers did. When they had things to do, they didn't mind making the jurors wait around. And the judge—Jacob suspected he worked his courtroom appearances around his golfing schedule.

But a farmer was a slave to the elements, to the government, and now, to the unknown crook who had destroyed his property. And right now, there wasn't even time to fight back.

If only Buck was still working for him. Too bad he had to be fired.

Buck. Suspicion shot through Jacob's mind, growing stronger by the minute. Could he have done this for revenge?

Jacob's worry and frustration turned into deep sadness. It was even worse when the enemy had a face.

Chapter 33

A streak of morning sun in her eyes woke Velita up. Confused, she looked around. After cleaning up Ralph's mess, she must have spent the rest of the night on the sofa. She stumbled over to the living-room window and pulled the drapes tighter. Even this early, the sun felt hot.

Today was Friday. The day she'd promised herself she would leave Ralph. She looked around the room at her furniture, her little sewing machine—all bought at flea markets and yard sales, but so familiar and comfortable—and her throat tightened. She'd have to leave everything behind, and what would be ahead of her?

Then she balled her fists. *Remember the kids and what Ralph's meanness could do to them. I can't lose my nerve and back out. Not now.* But she couldn't leave her sewing machine. She got out its case and boxed it up, then filled a plastic bag full of thread and fabric remnants, ready to go.

The suitcase was waiting under the bed. As soon as Tom picked Ralph up for work, she would haul it out and take the kids over to that shelter. It better be true—that she'd be safe. That Ralph couldn't get to her. It was an awful big chance to take.

She went over the address in her mind again, making sure she had it right. As soon as she got there, she'd call Marsha, see if she really could fix it up with the judge to use an alternate.

If not, she'd be in even worse trouble. If the judge held her in contempt of court for not showing, if she got away from Ralph only to end up in jail, she'd be a wide-open target for him.

Velita breathed deeply, trying to slow down her racing heart. All this was too scary to think about. If Jacob was right about Ralph's attacks being God's warnings, she was standing at the edge of a cliff. One wrong step, and she was done for. All she could do was hope that Jacob's God wouldn't let her down.

Jacob and Marsha had been so nice to her; maybe they could help her figure out what to do next.

Then Velita remembered the trial was almost over. She might never see her new friends again. She could be in for a really, really lonesome life. But at least she'd have the kids.

She tiptoed down the hall and cracked open the bedroom door. Ralph still slept, his face red and his mouth open, drooling. His matted hair stood on end. The room smelled of sweat, booze, and vomit, and she turned away, holding her nose.

So many mornings, she'd babied him through his hangovers, watching his moods, scared to say or do one wrong thing.

This would be the last time. She swallowed hard. *Only one hour more. I must be extra careful, act the same as always so's not to give away my plans. Soon as Ralph's gone to work, I'm off.*

Ralph groaned and rolled over onto his back, shading his eyes with his arm. "What time is it?" he mumbled.

"Six thirty. Want breakfast?"

"Ugh, no. Don't make me puke."

Velita wanted to say, *You already did—can't you smell it?* Instead, she went to the closet and took out her slippers.

Ralph raised up, but flopped back down. "My head feels like it's caught in a cement mixer."

"You'll feel better after a shower." She went to the kitchen and started the coffeemaker, then woke the kids.

Ralph crawled out of bed and staggered to the bathroom, and Velita hurried to strip the bed. She couldn't leave the house in that kind of mess.

When Ralph made it back into the room, he fell onto the bare mattress, groaning. "Gimme a beer. I'm dying."

Velita knew it wasn't just put-on. He *was* hurting. *Act gentle*, she thought. *But don't cave in. Remember the kids. Remember what you've got to do.*

She took the sheets and mattress pad into the laundry, started the washing machine, and went back into the kitchen. The kids were spooning extra sugar into their cereal, and she put the sugar bowl back into the cupboard and poured milk for them.

The coffee was ready, hot and strong. It would help sober him up and get him going. She filled two mugs, sipping one while she took the other to Ralph.

He snarled, "I said *beer!*" and swatted at the mug. Velita jerked back but not soon enough. The hot liquid splashed over her legs and Ralph's bare stomach.

Ralph yelled, and Velita screamed. She ran to the bathroom and turned on the cold water in the shower, bathing her legs. Her robe got soaked, but she barely noticed.

Ralph followed her, still bellowing.

Velita was sure he would trap her in there and bash her head against the tile. She jumped out of the shower, grabbed a towel, and ducked under his arm. "Put cold water on those burns," she told him. "I'll get some salve from the kitchen." *Only one more hour. Please, God, don't let him start again.*

The kids had finished eating, and Velita hurried them into their clothes. TJ tossed aside the T-shirt she handed him. "I don't want this green one." He scrabbled through his drawer. "Where's my Sooner shirt?"

It was in the suitcase, but Velita didn't dare tell him that. The less the kids knew, the better. She tried to think what to say, when Ralph called. "Where's that salve, dummy?"

"I'll find your shirt later," she told TJ. "Just put on the green one for now."

In the bedroom, Ralph was sprawled on his back on the mattress. She offered him the tube of salve, but he said, "You put it on," his face puckered like a hurt child.

Velita took a cotton ball from a container on the dresser and, as gently as she could, dabbed the medicine on the red welts. As she worked her way up his chest, he grabbed her wrist and twisted it. The cotton ball fell onto the bed, and she dropped to her knees beside him.

Ralph's pout had turned into an ugly sneer. "Think you'll get away with it because I'm sick? Just you wait." He let go with a shove, pushing her backward off the bed. "Call Tom. Tell him not to pick me up today."

Velita's knees nearly gave way. She hadn't counted on him staying home from work.

"Go on," he said. "Say I got the flu. Tell him to call that new foreman, what's-his-face."

She couldn't risk riling him now. Taking a deep breath, she went to the phone.

Tom was sick, too, his wife said. He wouldn't be at work, either. *Oh, great. The boss will never believe both of them have the flu.* Velita's throat and chest felt tight and heavy, and her stomach seemed loaded with rocks. There was no way she could go through with her plans now. Ralph would get fired and be home all day, every day. Then, for sure, there would be no escape.

Was Jacob wrong about the warnings? Didn't God want her to leave? Confused and miserable, Velita helped the kids find their books and papers and get their backpacks ready.

She forced down some dry toast and drank her coffee, now lukewarm, then cleaned up the kitchen. The washing machine finished spinning, and she put the load into the dryer.

Ralph got up and shuffled to the refrigerator for his beer, then sprawled on the couch and clicked on the TV.

Velita put fresh sheets on the bed and tugged the bedspread down on Ralph's side as far as it would go. She set his boots out so he wouldn't poke under the bed and notice the suitcase. Then she looked around the room, hunting for signs that would give her away. She didn't see any. Relieved, she slid open the closet door and took out a skirt.

"What you think you're doing?"

Velita jumped. Ralph stood leaning against the door frame. "You're not going anywhere."

She forced herself to speak sweetly. "Ralph baby, I *have* to. It's . . . the trial's practically over."

"Forget the stupid trial. Do what *I* tell you."

"Hey, I can't help it. If I don't show up, the cops'll come get me."

Ralph squinted at her, his forehead wrinkled, his eyes unsure.

She shrugged, head against one shoulder, as if saying, *What can I say?*

He let out a huge burp and went back to the sofa, cussing under his breath.

"Mama?" Suanne called from the living room. "The bus is coming."

Ralph answered for her. "Well, get on out there. You better not miss it."

Velita closed her eyes. *Please, please, Lord. If You help me get out of here before it's too late, I'll trust You the rest of my life.*

Chapter 34

That morning, Jacob walked into the jury room, feeling numb. With all that was on his mind, how would he be any use to the job ahead?

In the courtroom, he had just listened to the closing statements from both lawyers and the instructions from the judge: "On charges of the wounding and dismemberment of Sergeant Martin and Sergeant Newburg, you as a jury must consider assault with a deadly weapon, aggravated assault, or self-defense.

"Regarding the charge of homicide of Robert MacDuff, there are four possible verdicts: first-degree murder, second-degree murder, or manslaughter, voluntary or involuntary." Innocence wasn't a choice. Duane Jackson had never denied firing the shots that had injured Martin and Newburg and killed MacDuff.

The judge had taken a long time spelling out the guidelines: Malice aforethought. Premeditation. Special circumstances. Heat of passion. Credibility. They'd seen the evidence again: several glossy photos, the marijuana cigarette, the gun, the bulletproof vest.

The jury members slowly gathered around the deliberation table, their faces sober, obviously dreading the job ahead. Next to Jacob, Velita looked worried, and he supposed she was struggling with her thoughts about the trial. In the next chair beyond her, Marsha looked cool in a yellow sundress, a brown scarf knotted across one shoulder. But her eyes looked droopy. Jacob heard her whisper to Velita, "Why didn't you do it?"

"He came home too soon."

"I waited all night for your call."

Jacob saw tears in Velita's eyes and realized she had more on her mind than Duane Jackson. He wondered what had happened. His heart ached for the woman; her problems were so much worse than his burned-down shed. *Lord Jesus, ease her pain*, he prayed silently.

"Then you didn't get much sleep either," he heard her say. "I'm sorry. I'm more trouble than I'm worth."

Marsha frowned. "Don't talk like that. We'll get you through this. But you've got to grab your chances when they come."

Lester Payne cleared his throat. "Well, this is it."

Jacob pulled his thoughts back and nodded. Finally, they could discuss the trial and share their opinions and doubts. They would have to decide the future of another human being and live with that decision the rest of their lives. He ran his hand through his hair and sighed.

Both lawyers had been believable. Pettigrew was clever and had a good case against the defendant. In spite of Attorney Torrance's soft, tired delivery, he could squeeze tears out of a lump of iron. Which picture of Jackson was the real one? The cold-blooded murderer or the victim?

Geneva spoke first. "Sure don't make sense. That judge, with all his smarts, leaves the final decision to ignorant people like me."

"It's the law." Lester Payne spoke slowly, as though explaining to a child. "Has to be decided by a panel of peers."

Velita whispered, "I don't feel like a peer."

Jacob smiled and nodded at her. "Join the club."

Lester cleared his throat and stood up. "I guess we'd better pick our foreman." No one said anything. He shrugged. "Well, if nobody else—"

"I nominate Jacob Franzen," said Marsha quickly.

"Second it," said Wallace Takashi. "All in favor?"

Ten hands went up. Lester's lips twitched; then he sat down and barely raised two fingers.

Jacob leaned back in his chair. He, a leader? On this of all days, how would he ever be able to think clearly enough?

He held his palms up. "Hold on, hold on. I don't know anything about law."

"None of us do," said Geneva, "but I think you'll be fair."

Slowly, he shook his head in disbelief. He, a dumb country boy, a *waarlooss*, nonresistant Mennonite, was supposed to be a jury foreman? He didn't even know how he himself would vote.

But fair? Yes, that he thought he could be. With God's help. The others urged, and reluctantly, he took his place at the head of the deliberation table.

"I'm not sure how to start," he said. He'd been on church committees for this and that, and they'd always opened with prayer. But now, when he needed guidance the most, he felt awkward, not knowing how the group would react to that. Whether it would even be legal.

Then he remembered a verse in the Bible that said not to worry about how to speak when in court, that the Holy Spirit would give one the words. He bowed his head and silently asked God for help.

When he opened his eyes, Lester was standing again, and said, "We need to take a poll. See where everybody stands." He tore up twelve pieces of paper and handed them around. "First the assault. Simple or aggravated? I think we can rule out self-defense."

"No," said Jacob. Lester would need careful handling, or he'd take over for sure. From what he'd noticed, the man wasn't much for fairness. "We don't rule out anything yet. Just put down what you think."

When the votes were in, it was unanimous. Assault with a deadly weapon. Everyone said Jackson knew it was the police at his door, but nobody thought he'd meant to kill them.

"Well, that was quick," said Lester, passing another round of paper scraps. "Now for the biggie." He settled back into his chair, a smirk on his face.

Jacob's stomach churned. This one wouldn't be so easy. For three weeks, they'd sat around this table jabbering about politics, peaches, and quilts. Everything but the trial. Now that they could speak up, nobody seemed willing to talk.

He glanced around the table at the others. Marsha rubbed her forehead, Velita twirled a strand of her hair, and Geneva wiped a tear from her cheek. Eunice blew her nose, and Wallace stared at his scrap of paper, his mouth pinched tight.

"There's nothing final about this vote," Jacob told the group. "I understand that after we discuss it, we can still change our minds. Maybe several times." He wondered how many times he would change his own mind.

Before this trial, he would have had no problem condemning a murderer. *"Whoever sheds man's blood, by men shall his blood be shed."* It had been as simple as that. People who killed, maimed, raped should be put away. Swift and final punishment. It would make others think twice before committing such crimes. The Old Testament was full of harsh laws against crime.

But after listening to Duane Jackson on Friday, looking into his pleading eyes, Jacob knew it wasn't that cut and dried. The judge had made it clear: whatever their decision, it should be beyond a reasonable doubt. And right now, he had so many doubts.

Jackson was only twenty-two. Had he fully understood what he'd done? Drugs in his system didn't excuse him, but they could have clouded his judgment.

If a person had been threatened and feared for his life, what would a natural reaction be to someone charging through the back door?

Jacob closed his eyes and sent up another quick but fervent prayer. Then he scribbled on his paper, folded it, and pushed it to the center of the table.

The votes showed five murder ones, three second degree, two voluntary manslaughters, and two blanks.

"I don't believe it!" Lester's voice was shrill. "The guy's a killer. Can't you see that?"

"The preacher talked like he was a pure little choir boy," said Wallace.

"You bet," said Oliver Banks, the plumber. "Until the last four years."

Lester got up and started pacing. "Who do we believe? Him or the police officers? Credibility. That's the key."

Geneva shook her head. "It's sad, really sad. Mess with drugs, and life goes down the toilet."

Jacob thought about his own boyhood. He'd done stupid things, been as much of a *schuzzel* as any kid. But he'd had a Sunday school teacher, Mr. Schultz, who'd gotten through to him and his friends, shown them the reality of God, and guided them into commitment to the faith and baptism. Almost all of the boys in that class were still with the church, now solid family men. If only there was a way to push time back, give Duane Jackson a Mr. Schultz, maybe his life could be salvaged.

There was a program he'd heard of—Impact, or something like that. For young people in trouble. It might be too late for Jackson, but it could keep other boys out of trouble. It might be good to get involved with something like that.

"Mr. Foreman?" Lester's voice was sarcastic.

Jacob saw that everyone was looking at him and realized he'd missed a question.

"What's the main difference?" Eunice repeated. "Between first- and second-degree murder, I mean."

"It all boils down to malice," Lester answered for him. "Intent to kill. And you can just bet he had plenty of intent."

Jacob frowned, thinking. "Way I see it, murder in the first degree means he planned to kill MacDuff, with hatred in his heart. Second-degree murder, the hatred's there, but he didn't plan it ahead of time. Voluntary manslaughter means there was no hatred. It happened suddenly and without plan, but there was some reason for the killing."

"What about that other choice?" asked Nellie Kroymire. "Involuntary manslaughter. What if he didn't mean to do it at all?"

"No way," said Wallace. "Why else did he have that gun in his hand?"

Lester snorted, and several others shook their heads.

Laura Crutchfield spoke up. "I just don't see how, in that short time frame, Jackson could have planned to kill MacDuff. It *had* to be reflex. And the reason was he was scared. He was protecting his home, his wife."

Lester shifted in his chair, and his lips twisted. "He bought that gun weeks before. Don't tell me that was reflex."

"A 357 Magnum explodes inside its target," said Oliver. "Designed to maim and destroy. Just the fact he bought it proves he meant business."

"I'd believe that if it had been an Uzi," said Wallace. "But a revolver, I don't know. It might have just made him feel tough."

"Aw, come on!" Lester scraped his chair back and stood up. "It wasn't his first offense. He's a hardened criminal. He hated the police."

"But that's not admissible evidence," argued Laura. "Remember, the prosecutor tried to sneak that in, but the judge ordered it stricken."

"Yeah well, he'd already shot the ones on the porch," said Oliver Banks. "He saw MacDuff coming at him, grabbed his chance. And he was prepared."

Wallace Takashi said, "I don't know. He was running scared. What would you do if someone drove by and shot at you? And a few days later, someone stormed up and beat your door down?"

"I'd have been scared silly," murmured Velita.

Jacob felt his chest tighten. She'd been through so much. He had a sudden urge to hold her close and erase her pain, like he would comfort his daughter, Becky.

The others were still arguing. "And you want him just slapped on the wrist."

"The special circumstances will take care of that. No matter what, he'll be put away for a long time."

"What about the way he sat there, all through the trial, as though he didn't care?"

"I'm sure his lawyer told him not to make waves. Didn't you see his eyes when he was on the stand? Like an animal caught in car lights. He cared, all right."

"Seemed like it was a relief for him to finally let his feelings out."

Jacob looked at his watch. "It's nearly lunch. Are we ready for another vote?"

The papers came back slowly. Three first-degree murders, two second-degrees, and seven voluntary manslaughters.

The bailiff brought sandwiches, and then they all settled around the table again.

"If I remember right," said Wallace Takashi, "the officers behind the house were only supposed to guard the door and wait for further orders. MacDuff shouldn't have barged in the way he did."

"We'd better make sure of that." Jacob buzzed for the bailiff to bring them the records.

Lester splayed his fingers over his chest while looking at his notes. "The shot entered from the top, *over* the vest. The only way that could have happened was if MacDuff was hunkered down." He got on one knee to demonstrate.

"The top would slant out," added Oliver. "Jackson's tall, the shot would have been at an angle." He jabbed his finger down toward Lester. "He'd have to be awfully close, aim real carefully, to get him in the heart like he did."

Jacob wondered how Lester could be so cold-blooded as to act out a dead man's part, and looking around, he could tell the others felt the same way.

He was trying to decide what to do when Geneva said, "Get up, man, you give me the creeps."

Lester shrugged and stood, looking smug that he'd made his point.

Jacob thought about it while the others talked.

"Yeah, a dead shot like that, how could it be an accident?"

"Unless the bullet ricocheted."

"Nah, they didn't find any holes in the wall, did they?"

"According to his partner, there wasn't time to aim."

Marsha studied her notes. "His partner said MacDuff was wearing an ankle holster. Maybe he was reaching for his gun."

"Which means," said Lester triumphantly, "that he was still unarmed when Jackson shot him!"

Velita spoke up for the first time. "I always thought cops had their guns out when they kicked down the doors. That's the way they show it on TV."

Oliver laughed, and Velita blushed.

"Can't go by TV, girlie," said Lester. "Gotta go by the evidence."

Jacob stared at him in sudden anger. Velita was finally starting to open up. It would be just like Lester to bully her back into her shell.

It was hard to keep his voice even. "What *Mrs. Stanford* said is worth considering. Why would MacDuff charge into the kitchen unarmed? He must have heard those first two shots."

Geneva shrugged. "Maybe he was crouched behind a door and just getting up."

The bailiff came in and laid the records on the table.

Wallace read through the copies. "Here it is: 'Torrance: After the backup officers arrived, where did Detectives Robert MacDuff and Kenneth Bayliss go?

"'Martin: They went around the house, in the direction of the back door.

"'At whose orders?

"'I beg your pardon?

"'Who was in charge?

"'I was. But we made the plans togeth—

"'Thank you. Did you give Corporal MacDuff orders to enter the rear door of the Jackson residence?

"'The plans were to—

"'A simple yes or no, please.

"'No.'"

Wallace smacked his palm onto the table. "So they had no orders to charge the house from the back door."

Laura nodded. "That's the way I see it."

Almost everyone agreed.

Geneva raised her hand. "I'd like to talk about the character witnesses. Not the preacher, but his teachers and former bosses. His mother tried to give her side of the story, but the prosecution blocked it. Seems to me there could have been extenuating circumstances."

Nearly an hour later, they voted again. Eleven voluntary manslaughters, one vote for murder one.

Chapter 35

Jacob looked around the table. Lester had to be the one holding up the vote. And Lester was hard-nosed. If this went on much longer, they'd have to be sequestered. Or end up a hung jury, all this time and the taxpayers' money wasted.

He leaned his elbows on the table and listened to the discussion around him. At least it hadn't come to the death penalty. He was at peace with his own decision and impatient to be done and out of there. The farm work was waiting. The shed needed to be rebuilt and the insurance settled before peach picking.

But was he supposed to just walk away from Velita when she was in such trouble, probably even danger? He needed to stay in contact, to make sure she was safe.

Ever since boyhood, his dad had warned him to be careful, especially with things of the world. *Pauss opp,* he'd say. But sometimes a person could be too careful, too detached from people outside of church. Sometimes a man had to use his own judgment.

He ran his fingers through his hair. *Stay awake, Franzen. Now's not the time to daydream.*

Time for another vote, though it probably wouldn't do any good.

Marsha asked, "What happens if Jackson gets first-degree murder, and the judge gives him the death penalty?"

Lester snorted. "Automatic appeal. A new trial."

"And he could get off?"

Lester shook his head. "No way." But his eyes shifted, and he rubbed his chin. "I see what you're getting at." He pushed back his chair and went and stared out the window. Finally he returned to the table. "Okay. Let's vote again."

Jacob stared at Marsha. That woman was clever. If she could get stubborn old Lester to think . . .

This time, it was unanimous. Voluntary manslaughter. Jacob filled out the forms and buzzed for the bailiff.

As he walked with the others into the jury box, he glanced at Jackson and saw the naked fear in his eyes. Jacob wished he could tell the man, "We did the best we could."

While Jacob handed the judge the paper, Duane Jackson stood waiting for the verdict, looking down, his shoulders slumped.

"Assault with a deadly weapon. Guilty."

Jackson nodded, as though he'd expected that. But when the judge read "Voluntary manslaughter," his head snapped up, and he stared open-mouthed at the jury.

Flora Jackson shrieked, "Thank You, Jesus, hallelujah!" There were sobs and hugs, and someone began singing "Amazing Grace."

The judge rapped his gavel, and the courtroom quieted down. "Sentencing will be determined by the court on Tuesday at 10:00 AM." He thanked the jurors for their service, told them they were free to go, and that they were not obligated to speak to the press.

In the lobby, reporters swarmed around, shoving microphones

in the jurors' faces, but only Lester, looking eager, stopped to talk to them.

❖ ❖ ❖

Velita hurried with the group to the parking lot. Jacob seemed especially relieved to get out early. He said he had a lot of things to do.

"Don't we all," grumbled Oliver Banks.

"Yeah, well," said Jacob, "we had some excitement out at my ranch last night. Someone burned down my shed."

"What?" Marsha stared at him. "You mean—arson?"

"That's what the police think. They asked if I had any enemies."

The other jurors told him they were sorry and offered advice. They'd reached the elevator, and Oliver Banks punched the up button. "I'd set a trap for the sucker," he said. "Catch him in the act."

Geneva shook her head and stepped into the elevator. "Wouldn't do no good. Guy like that, you never know who's his next target." She held the door while the others followed her in.

Velita couldn't believe what had happened. A nice man like Jacob wouldn't have enemies, would he? Now, if it were Ralph, he'd stepped on plenty of toes; there might be someone mad enough to hold a grudge—

Ralph. Coming home in the middle of the night. That strong burnt smell, all that weird giggling about a barbecue. She shivered and closed her eyes.

The elevator door opened at their level. She felt the other jurors brushing past her, but she couldn't move.

Marsha grabbed her arm. "What's the matter?"

"I've got to tell you something. Last night, Ralph went real crazy. He—" Velita looked around. The other jurors had scattered to their cars, and only Jacob had stayed with them. The elevator door slid shut and the three moved up to the next level.

Velita pulled down her collar to show her friends the welts on her neck. She told about Ralph's attack on her and about packing up to leave for the shelter.

Jacob sucked in his breath, and Marsha hugged Velita. "You know what you've got to do," she said. "It's like Jacob said, a warning. You *have* to get out before he kills you."

Velita sighed. "There's more. When he came home, besides the smell of liquor, there was this awful strong smell like smoke. Something burning. Then, I was just trying to hide the suitcase and keep out of his way, so I didn't think anything of it. But now—" She dropped her face into her hands.

Marsha gasped. "You think *he* burned down Jacob's shed?"

Velita nodded without looking up. "It just fits." She wiped away tears with the back of her hand. "I feel so awful. It's all my fault."

"No!" Jacob touched her shoulder. "Even if it is true, you're not to blame."

"This proves it," said Marsha. "The man's dangerous. He's got to be stopped." She stared at Velita, then at Jacob. Then she slapped her fist into her other hand. "I've got an idea. Where are the kids?"

Velita frowned. "At school. Why?"

"Go to the shelter. Right now. I'll pick up the kids and meet you there."

"They're supposed to take the bus home."

"They get out at two? I can just make it."

Velita shook her head. "The school won't let them go with anyone that's not on their list. It's got to be me."

"What if Ralph sees you?"

"He never comes to the school. Not even for open house."

"How about this?" said Jacob. "I came in my Toyota today. Leave your car here, and *I'll* take you to the school."

"If someone saw me in your car and told Ralph, he'd kill both of us."

Marsha unknotted her brown scarf. "Here," she told Velita. "Wear this over your hair. Keep your face hidden while you're in the car. And call me as soon as you get to the shelter. Remember the address?"

Velita nodded and got into Jacob's car, then turned back to Marsha. "What about the suitcase? It's still under the bed. Ralph didn't go to work . . . "

"Forget the suitcase. I'll lend you anything you need. Just get going."

❖ ❖ ❖

Jacob took the freeway through town, swerving in and out of traffic. He glanced at the clock on his dashboard. Almost two o'clock. *Please, Lord, let us make it to the school before the kids get on the bus.*

He took the next exit and squealed around a corner onto Toller Street. "Still with me?" he asked.

"Yeah." Velita hung onto the armrest. Her blond hair was tucked out of sight under Marsha's scarf, and she wore her dark glasses. Hopefully, no one would recognize her from a distance. Especially not in a strange car.

A few blocks farther, beyond a row of sycamore trees, Jacob saw a chain-link fence. "Turn right here," said Velita.

It was two ten, and buses were waiting in front with children lined up at the first one. The curbs were packed with cars.

"Where can I park?" asked Jacob.

Velita grabbed the door handle. "Just let me off. Circle around; I'll meet you right here."

Jacob drove around the block and back to Toller Street. There was no stop light, and traffic was heavy. It was several minutes before he could merge and get back to the school.

He double-parked and stared into the mass of children. They all looked the same to him, so he concentrated on looking for Velita. But that wasn't much better; he didn't know whether to look for a brown scarf or blond hair.

Next to him, the parked car honked, and the driver motioned for clearance. Jacob moved forward, then started around the block again. Maybe he could get that parking space.

By the time he got through the traffic and made it back to the school, the first bus had left, and long lines of children waited at the second and third. The parked cars had shifted up, filling the spaces emptied by those leaving.

He double-parked again. Velita was still nowhere in sight. What had gone wrong? Had she changed her mind? Should he get out and go look for her? But he wouldn't know where to start, and they might completely miss each other.

Finally he saw her, hurrying toward the gate, glancing around, looking nervous. The scarf was tied around her waist. With one hand, she pulled Suanne along, and with the other, she gripped TJ's arm, nearly dragging him while he turned back to yell and wave at his friends.

Jacob got out and motioned to her, then opened both doors on the curb side.

Velita maneuvered between the buses and parked cars and shoved the kids into the backseat, ignoring their squeals of protest.

"Just do as I say," she told them, reaching over to lock the doors. "Put on your seat belts. Quick." She fumbled with the scarf, trying to put it back on.

"Hey," said TJ. "Isn't this the guy who—"

"Shush!" said Velita. "Put your heads down now. Let's play Seven-up."

"I don't wanna play. Open the window, I gotta say 'catchya later' to the guys." He waved furiously. "Hey, Ger!"

Jacob turned into the traffic just as the second bus pulled out. He jammed on the brakes, yielding the right of way, pounding the steering wheel in frustration. When he looked through the rearview mirror, he noticed a red Mustang convertible, three cars back, also moving into the street.

"There's Dad," shouted TJ, waving out the back window. "He's got Tom's car. Stop! I gotta get my paper!"

"What?" shouted Velita. "How could he be there? Oh, dear God, we're done for. Duck down! Don't let him see you."

Jacob spun out, but he was still blocked behind the slow-moving bus. He glanced back and saw Ralph at the wheel of the convertible. Beside him was the friend who'd been with him at the relief sale. Ralph's face was red, his mouth twisted, his teeth bared. Blasting the horn, he shook his fist and yelled at them, his words garbled by traffic noises.

Chapter 36

Jacob slammed his foot on the accelerator and swerved around the bus, barely missing an oncoming pickup. He shot a glance at Velita in the backseat. "You said Ralph never comes to school."

Velita's face was pale, her eyes huge and dark. "He doesn't!"

Jacob swung down a side street, then another. The red Mustang still followed.

TJ reached over the seat and punched Jacob's shoulder. "You gotta stop! I want my paper!"

Jacob turned another corner, then shot through an alley, crunching over empty cans and spilled garbage, barely missing a cat. "What paper?"

"My permission slip. You know, Mom, the field trip. I hafta turn it in today."

"Didn't you take it this morning?"

"The money, yeah, but I forgot the paper. Tell this guy to stop!"

Velita screamed, "No! We can't!"

TJ kicked the back of Jacob's seat. "But Dad'll get mad if I don't."

They were out on Toller Street again, darting from one lane to another. Brakes screeched. Cars honked. Angry looks and gestures followed them.

So did the red convertible.

Velita frowned. "How come he's got your paper?"

"I called him."

"You *what*?"

"He said he didn't care, it was my fault. And anyway, he couldn't bring it 'cause you had the car. But then Tom said he could borrow his. If he came all for nothing, he'll whop me."

"Oh, Lord," moaned Velita. Through the rearview mirror, Jacob saw her arms crossed tight, rocking herself back and forth. "What'll we do now?" she asked. "He'll kill us all."

"Not if I can help it," Jacob said between clenched teeth. He could hear Suanne whimpering. "Hang on, everybody." He swerved into the on-ramp for the southbound freeway through town, cutting off a huge semi, and was rewarded with a blast from its horn.

"Sorry, buddy," he muttered. *Maybe the truck would slow the Mustang down, buy a little time.* He shot off the freeway again and drove along an access road. A quick glance in the side mirror showed no sign of the convertible, and he blew out a breath of relief.

TJ banged on the top of the seat with his fists. "What's going on? Let me outta here!"

"Hush," said Velita. "We've got to get away quick. We have to find some place where your dad can't hurt us."

"You mean—we're running away?" TJ turned onto his knees and stared out the back window. "He sure looked mad . . . But Mom, what about my paper?"

"Turn back and sit down," she told him. "I'll . . . I'll talk to your teacher, get another paper. Or something. You've got to trust me."

"Sheesh." TJ crumpled back onto the seat. "For sure, Dad'll beat our brains out for this."

Jacob kept watching the mirror. He still didn't see the Mustang, but he couldn't take any chances. Without signaling, he changed lanes and swung back onto the freeway. *Lord, why did You get me mixed up in this?* Three weeks ago he didn't even know Velita existed, and today, he could get killed for trying to help her.

He ran his hand through his hair. Crazy, that's what it was. Maybe his dad was right after all. *Pauss opp.* He was getting in too deep. If he could just get Velita settled in that shelter and safe from her husband, then he could wash his hands of this whole business.

He caught Velita's glance in the mirror. "What's the best way to get to the shelter?"

Her mouth dropped open, and she stared at him. "I . . . don't know. All I have is the address: 4687 Crandall Street. Don't *you* know where that is?"

"*Ach, yauma.* Crandall . . . Crandall . . . I think it's somewhere south of town." Why hadn't he asked Marsha for directions? "Look in the glove compartment; there might be a city map."

Velita reached over the front passenger seat and pulled out the smog certificate and insurance papers. "I don't see one."

He scratched his head and sighed. "We'll have to play it by ear." He could kick himself. His kids had been pestering him to get a cell phone, but he'd laughed that off. *"Why would I need to drag a phone around with me? I get enough calls at home."* Now he wished with all his heart he'd listened to them.

Then he had an idea. "If we've lost him, we can go to the hospital and get directions. Big parking lot like that, we'd be hard to spot."

Then the truck on his left dropped back, and across the median Jacob spotted the red Mustang, speeding north. Ralph looked straight at him, shouting something, his face nearly purple with rage. The convertible skidded to a stop and fishtailed across the sandy divider strip. Right toward Jacob's car.

Jacob tried to accelerate but was blocked by a garbage truck ahead and a van in the center lane. The left lane was clear, and the Mustang picked up speed, gaining on them.

Then the van pulled ahead of the truck, and Jacob slammed down the gas pedal and veered into the center lane. The Mustang sped up and cut in behind Jacob, jolting his rear bumper. The man with Ralph seemed to be trying to calm him down, his hand on Ralph's shoulder, but Ralph pushed it away.

"Hang on, everyone," Jacob shouted, and he swerved to cut in between the cars on his left. But the driver in the second car accelerated and blocked his path.

The Mustang crept closer, and Jacob felt another jolt, this time stronger. He looked around; couldn't the other drivers see what was happening?

Then he saw the car behind the convertible moving over into the outer lane, and then another, and another. If he could just pick up enough speed to get a couple of cars between them, then veer off that exit on the next overpass, maybe he could lose him again.

A small spot opened up in the outer lane, and he squeezed into it, ignoring the driver's obscene gesture. He passed the clog of traffic just far enough, switched lanes, drove slightly past the exit, then yanked the steering wheel and zipped off the ramp. *If I can just make the curve and straighten out without skidding too much . . .*

Then he felt a crash at his left rear bumper, pushing, pushing. His car went out of control, and he struggled to correct. But he overcorrected, and in the middle of tires squealing and the smell of burnt rubber, as if in slow motion, his world went upside down. *Oh, dear Lord, please keep Velita and the kids safe.*

As though from a distance, he heard screaming and shouting, felt himself bouncing and smothering. Then his mind went blank.

❖ ❖ ❖

Velita stared at Suanne, lying limp across her, and she tried to loosen her daughter's stuck seat belt. TJ was jammed under her, yelling and struggling to get out. Blood ran down his cheek, and his right arm hung crooked. The window below him rested on the ground, and weeds poked through the jagged pieces of glass.

Before she could help her children, the door opened above her and arms reached in. "Jacob?" she whispered.

An angry face appeared between the arms. *Ralph!*

"No! No!" she screamed, but he grabbed her hair in one fist and batted at her with the other, yanking her up past Suanne. Out of the corner of her eyes, in the front seat, she saw a collapsing air bag and Jacob's head lolling to one side.

"The kids—" she started, but Ralph slapped her across the mouth and snarled, "Shut up. What made you think you could run off from me?"

I'm dead for sure. Why had she been stupid enough to think she had a chance in life? Now she'd ruined everything for herself, the kids—for Jacob too, if he was even alive. So much for trusting in God.

Ralph had a hold of her arms now, tugging, twisting, and her body scraped against a jagged edge of the open door. She heard other voices, then a siren, and saw red and blue lights flashing. The siren stopped, but more voices yelled around her.

"That's him!"

"That's the guy who chased them!"

"Watch out, he's crazy!"

Ralph gave a yelp, let go of Velita, and disappeared. She fell back against TJ; he squawked, and Suanne whimpered, "I don't feel good. My stomach hurts."

Grateful for whatever had stopped Ralph, Velita held Suanne close and kissed her forehead. "Shh, sweetie. Take a great big breath and let it out slowly."

Both doors on top opened, and a friendly voice said, "Are you all right?" A policewoman slit Suanne's seat belt and lifted her up. Suanne cried out and grabbed Velita's hand, but Velita gently pushed her on. "Go ahead, babe, I'm right behind you."

An ambulance had parked beside them, and as Velita climbed out and eased herself to the ground, she saw people carefully brace Jacob and lift him onto a stretcher. He opened his eyes and tried to sit up, but one of the men strapped him down firmly. "Don't move," the man told him. "We need to make sure you're okay."

"Velita?" Jacob called in a weak voice. "Is she all right? The kids—"

Did she dare answer him? Her heart pounding, Velita looked around for Ralph but couldn't see him in the gathering crowd. "Tell him we're okay," she said to the attendant. "But how is he?"

"We'll take him to the hospital and check him over," said the man.

Police were measuring skid marks, talking to people in the crowd, and Velita heard someone on a cell phone calling a towing company. She saw Tom limping around, running his hands over his convertible, shaking his head at the crumpled front fender and dangling bumper, the broken headlight.

He looked up, saw her, and lifted his palms in apology. "I'm so sorry, Vel. I tried to stop him, but he wouldn't listen . . ."

She could smell liquor on Tom's breath and nodded. "He's drunk, too, isn't he?"

Tom hung his head. "Yeah, we had a few. I shouldn't have let him drive, but he said it was just to the school."

Another ambulance pulled up, and attendants helped Velita and the children in. A woman checked their blood pressure and heartbeat, patched up TJ's cheek, and put his arm in a sling. Then the policewoman came inside and asked, "Can you tell me what happened?"

She heard Ralph shouting from somewhere, "Don't listen to her; she's a liar!"

Then she saw him swinging at the officers, trying to get away. They got him spread-eagled on the ground, with a policeman patting him down. He still tried to turn, to fight his way out, but the man slipped a pair of handcuffs on him, then pushed him to his feet and into the police car.

TJ pulled on Velita's arm. "What are they doing to my dad?" he asked. "Where are they taking him?"

She put her arm around TJ. "Looks like they're taking him to the police station."

"They won't put him in jail, will they? Not my dad!"

"The man says you're his wife," said the policewoman. "Is that true?"

Velita sighed. "I'm afraid so. Don't know what he'll do to me now." She brushed away tears with the back of her hand, but they kept coming.

"He says the driver of this car was kidnapping you."

"Kidnapping me?" An attendant handed Velita a tissue; she wiped her eyes and stared at the officer. "No! He was taking me to a shelter."

"A shelter?"

"You know, a place where women can go when their men beat them up. And now he's hurt bad, all because of me."

"So your husband was chasing you?"

"Yeah," TJ chimed in. "Kept bumping the car. Made us roll over." He bared his teeth. "He was awful mad!"

The officer nodded, then turned back to Velita. "Has your husband been abusive before?"

"Oh, yes." She glanced at TJ; he shrugged, then nodded. She pushed away her collar and showed the officer the marks where Ralph had choked her and showed the fading bruises on her arms.

"Are you willing to press charges?"

She looked over at the police car where Ralph still sat, glaring at her. "I don't know. I'm scared of what he'll do to me then. He'll just get worse."

"Ma'am, you wouldn't have to worry about that. We've got enough on him to put him away for ten, fifteen years. Be for his own good, and you'd be safe. All you need to do is sign a complaint."

"You can do that? You're sure he won't come after me?"

"We've already got him for drunk driving, assault and battery, and child endangerment among other things, but if you'd be willing to come with us to the station and sign for the abuse, that would make sure he couldn't get at you. You can also get a restraining order, in case he gets out on bail."

Velita rubbed her sore scalp, feeling where some of the hair had been torn out by the roots. "I got to get my boy to a doctor first. I think his arm's broken."

"You're going to Mercy Hospital? I'll send someone over there to pick you up. Do you have family, someone you can call?"

Family. LaDonna would be the last one she'd want to see; Ralph was sure to give his mother a call. Without Jacob's strength, Velita felt all alone. Except—there was one person who would know what to do. "Could somebody phone Marsha Lewis?"

"Here in town? You have her number?"

Velita tried to remember it but finally shook her head. "Don't know if she's home anyway; she might be at work. She's a nurse there at Mercy."

"I'll check the hospital," said the officer. She went to her car, and Velita saw her talking on her radio. The other police car took Ralph and Tom away, and the ambulance drove Velita and the kids to the hospital.

As they sat in the emergency waiting room, Velita could hear footsteps out in the hall, bits of sentences from beyond the walls, and in the distance, sirens that froze her mind and body.

A hand clutched her shoulder, and she shrank back in terror. But it was Marsha. Seeing a familiar face was too much, and Velita broke into wild sobs. Suanne cried with her, and TJ hid his face against her shoulder.

Marsha brought a cup of water from the drinking fountain and handed it to Velita. "There, there; it's okay." While Velita sipped, Marsha asked, "You didn't make it to the shelter? What happened?"

Wiping her eyes, Velita told Marsha about the chase, the car bumping Jacob's, the rollover off the ramp. "You should have seen Ralph's face—he looked like a . . . a maniac!"

"But . . . how could he have chased you? And how did he find out?"

Velita explained about TJ's permission slip, Ralph driving Tom's car to the school and spotting her.

"How awful," said Marsha. "Where is he now?"

"The police took him away. But who knows for how long? They said I should go to the station and sign a complaint, get a restraining order. Much good that'll do."

"When you're done here, I'll take you over there. Sounds like there's enough to put him away for quite a while. Long enough for you to put your life back together."

As mixed up as Velita felt, it didn't seem possible that her life would ever get straightened out. She started to say that, but Marsha gave her a hug.

"Listen, you can do it. I'll back you up all the way, help any way I can."

Chapter 37

By the time TJ's cheek was stitched, his broken arm set and cradled in a fresh sling, and she and Suanne had been checked and released, Velita was exhausted. But she was frantic with worry about Jacob. "Can you check on him?" she asked Marsha. "Nobody will tell me if he's dead or alive."

"Better yet," said Marsha, "I'll take you up to his room, and you can see for yourself. I already asked; he's alive, all right, and I'll bet he's just as worried about you."

Velita shrank back. "He probably hates me by now—it's all my fault that he's hurt and his car got wrecked. I should never have gotten him involved—"

"Yeah," said TJ. "And you made my dad real mad, too."

But Marsha shook her head. "Don't blame yourself. I'm sure Jacob doesn't. But now you know there's no limit to what Ralph will do." She led the way to the elevator.

On the fifth floor, down one corridor and around the corner from the nurse's station, Marsha tapped on an open door and peeked through.

"Want some company?" she asked, then walked in.

Nervously, Velita followed with Suanne. TJ hung back, scowling, and leaned against the doorway.

Jacob's bed was slanted up, and he was talking on the phone. A bandage on his head looked like a white turban, and an IV dripped into his hand. When he glanced up, his eyes grew wide, and he motioned them to come closer.

"Someone's here," he said into the phone. "Let me call you back." He hung up the phone and looked at Velita, his eyes sober. "Are you okay? And your kids? I'm kicking myself for not getting you to the shelter."

Velita couldn't believe that with all the trouble she'd caused him, he'd still be concerned about her. She felt an ache of warmth for the man and envy for whatever Mennonite woman might win a prize like him. "I'm fine, just a few bruises. Suanne got the wind knocked out of her, but she's better now."

"Looks like TJ got the worst of it. Broken arm?"

"Yeah," said TJ, brightening up and edging nearer the bed. "And I got twelve stitches in my cheek!" He sounded as proud as if he'd won a trophy.

Jacob grinned at him. "The kids at school are going to think you've been in one big fight. You'll have to tell them, 'You ought to see the other guy!'"

"What about you?" Marsha asked Jacob. "Concussion?" She pulled up a chair for Velita.

Jacob shrugged. "A slight skull fracture. And a few cracked ribs. I'd just as soon go home, but the doctor says he wants to keep me a day or two. Thinks he has to keep an eye on me." He huffed a short laugh, then turned to Velita. "I'm glad Marsha found you; I didn't want you and the kids left unprotected. Where is that—your husband?"

Velita hesitated. "He . . . the police arrested him. I guess he was . . . pretty drunk."

Jacob blew out a long breath. "My prayers were answered. That'll keep you safe for now. But what happens next?"

Velita shuddered. The thought of going back to her house made her sick to her stomach. What if the police just questioned Ralph and then let him go? That restraining order wouldn't stop him from getting to her. Maybe Jacob's prayers were answered, but she didn't know if she could depend on God to keep Ralph away.

"After we finish at the police station, you can come stay at my apartment," said Marsha. "And then we'll figure out what to do next." She touched Velita's arm. "Okay?"

"No!" wailed Suanne.

TJ kicked the chair. "I want to go to my own house."

Velita shushed them. She stared at Marsha. "I couldn't impose on you." Then another thought hit her. "What if he tracked me down at your place?"

Marsha's eyes narrowed. "Have you ever mentioned my name to him?"

Velita thought hard. "No. Never."

"Well, then. I've only seen him once, at that Mennonite relief sale. As mad as he was then, I doubt that he even noticed me. He's got no way to know who I am or where I live." Marsha glanced at the telephone. "We'd better leave and let this nice man finish his call. I work here tomorrow, Jacob, and I'll stop by your room sometime."

Later, the police reports done, Marsha led Velita and the kids into her apartment living room. "TJ can take the sofa, and you and Suanne can use Heather's bedroom," she said. "I can pretend she's back."

Velita took Marsha's hands in hers. "Oh, gee, I'm so sorry. Here I've been blubbering away about myself, when you've got enough problems of your own."

Marsha shrugged. "Let's just concentrate on getting you squared away." She pointed out the bathroom door. "Would you like a shower? It might help relax you. Towels are in the cabinet. TJ better wait until the doc says it's okay." She reached for a robe on the back of the bathroom door. "Here, you can borrow this; I'll find T-shirts for the kids."

After Velita and Suanne finished cleaning up, they went into the kitchen, where TJ, in a floppy Cowboys T-shirt, was watching Marsha heat up some canned soup. He seemed in a better mood, and Velita knew he was glad to get out of bathing.

Marsha asked, "All settled?"

Velita nodded. "Thanks. That was real nice. You're so good to do this for us."

"Oh, hey, that's what friends are for."

After Suanne and TJ were tucked into bed, Velita sat in the kitchen with Marsha.

"What am I going to do now?"

"I've been thinking. I know a lawyer who specializes in abused women."

"I can't afford a lawyer."

"This one takes some pro bono cases. No charge, if you don't have money. She'd help you make a fresh start. Without Ralph."

Velita dropped her head into her hands. "I hate the idea of divorce. What if prison straightens him out?"

"Can you take that chance? Hasn't he promised it'll never happen again, and instead it gets worse? The way I see it, you only have two choices. Leave him now and protect yourself and your kids while you can, or hang on and maybe get yourself killed. Without you, what would happen to your children?"

Velita thought again of Duane Jackson's mother and of Duane, now waiting to hear his sentence. "How do you know so much about it?"

"You won't believe how many beat-up women I see at the hospital. Black eyes, teeth missing, jaws broken, or worse. Problem is, they usually go right back for more. Sometimes Child Protective Services takes their children away."

"You mean there're others dumb as me?" Velita gave a crooked smile. "We ought to make a club."

"Those clubs exist. They're called 'support groups.' Women get together and share their stories. I'll give you a number to call. It'll help you get through this."

Velita went to her and gave her a tight hug. "Marsha Lewis, you're the best friend anybody could have. I'll think about it." But all she wanted to do now was go to sleep and wake up to find it was only a horrible nightmare.

The next morning, Velita woke with a start and jumped out of bed. And smashed into a wall. Her heart racing, she sat back down and looked around. Ralph would have a fit if breakfast wasn't ready when he finished shaving!

Then she saw Suanne still sleeping in the bed, realized she was in Marsha's apartment, and memories of the day before rolled through her mind. Speeding down the freeway, Ralph's look of fury, the taste of fear rising in her throat. She felt again the thump of Tom's bumper against Jacob's car, the car rolling over and over, TJ crushed under her and Suanne on top. Ralph grabbing her by the hair. And now, a confusing emptiness.

All her life, someone had bossed her around. First Mama and Daddy, then her stepdad, then Ralph. They'd told her how to act, what to wear, what to think. Until the trial started, all she'd had to figure out was how to keep the house clean and what to fix for dinner.

Today was up to her, and she had no idea what to do. A terrible pressure pushed and tore at her until she thought she'd explode. Leaning her face into her hands, she let silent sobs rock her body.

She didn't hear Marsha come into the room but felt the bed sag beside her and arms hugging her. "It's all right," whispered her friend. "You're entitled. Don't hold back, you'll feel better if you let it all out."

After a few minutes, Velita brushed the tears away. "I'm such a fool."

Marsha squeezed her shoulders. "No. There'd be something wrong if you *didn't* cry. When I finally faced up to the problems with my ex, I was a total disaster."

"You? I don't believe it. You're always so cool."

"That's just on the outside. I've had some bad times, too. I know what it's like."

"Yeah?"

"Philip never hit me. He was one cold fish. When he was mad, he could freeze a raging bonfire. But was he ever charming to the ladies! At parties, he'd come on to them right in front of me, daring me to object. When I'd finally had enough, I learned real fast to take care of myself. And you will too."

"I don't know. I feel so . . . so helpless. Like a little kid."

"Trust me. I'll help you get it together. Right now, we'll have some breakfast. I've got three kinds of cereal and some Pop-Tarts. After the kids are up and running, we'll go pick up your car."

❖ ❖ ❖

At the parking garage, Marsha drove slowly through the second level.

"Right there," pointed Velita. "J 48. I've learned to keep track of where I park."

"I don't see it," said TJ.

Velita frowned, confused. Instead of the old green Dodge, a shiny silver Ford Taurus sat parked in the spot.

Marsha asked, "Are you sure this is the level?"

Velita looked around. By now, she wasn't sure of anything. "Maybe it was the next one."

Marsha drove in and out of the rows, through all the levels. The Dodge was definitely not in the garage. "Do you suppose Ralph's friend came and got it?"

Velita felt a rush of relief. "That's got to be it." Then she reached into her purse and felt cold metal. Shaking her head, she pulled the keys out and dangled them in front of Marsha. "This is the only set we've got. Besides, how would Tom know where it was?"

Marsha stared at her. "Are you thinking what I'm thinking?"

"Stolen?" whispered Velita.

"I don't know what else it could be."

"Dad's *really* going to be mad now," said TJ.

Velita turned cold. How well she knew that. Her running away from Ralph was nothing compared to losing his precious car.

Then she realized that in jail, Ralph couldn't do anything about it. It was *her* problem now. She thought a minute. "I guess I should report it to the police."

"Tell them they better get it back before my dad finds out," said TJ.

Marsha drove them back to the apartment, and Velita phoned the station.

That afternoon, Marsha changed into her uniform and left for work, saying her shift was over at eleven that evening and she'd be back soon after. She told Velita to feel at home in the apartment, to relax and baby herself. "Better stay inside, just in case. Don't take any chances. There are games in the hall closet and some of Heather's old videos the kids might like to watch."

After Marsha left, Velita started *The Lion King* for TJ and Suanne, then sat down on the sofa and paged through a magazine. She tried not to think about Ralph but kept seeing him in her mind, tugging at her, trying to yank her out of the car. Imagining him in jail, cussing at her. Blaming her for the missing car. She couldn't stop shaking.

Noticing a photo album on a side table, Velita picked it up. She saw snaps of Marsha in an above-ground pool, holding a little girl, wet-haired and grinning; the same girl, a little bigger, riding a bike and waving; a teenager kneeling on a pyramid of cheerleaders, then in a long dress, standing beside a grand piano on a stage. School pictures all the way through high school. *What sweet memories Marsha has of her daughter,* Velita thought enviously.

Ralph never spent money on the kids' school pictures. They didn't even own a camera. All Velita had of their babyhood was one free photo from some photographer off in a corner of the grocery store. Three-year-old TJ, making a silly face, holding little Suanne, who was ready to cry.

Velita closed the album and looked around. An upright piano stood beside the sofa. She went to it and looked at the music on the rack, with all the little black circles and pokey stems, and wondered how people made sense out of it. She touched a key softly, then another and another. How nice it must be to know how to play it.

Suanne looked up at her. "That sounds nice, Mommy. Do that again!"

If only the kids had a chance to learn an instrument! Once TJ brought a little recorder home from school, but after just a few peeps, Ralph had grabbed it, smashed it against the wall, and cussed up a storm. They'd had to pay the school thirty dollars, and the wall was still chipped in that spot.

Velita went into the kitchen and looked around. All this thinking was driving her crazy. She wished there was something to do, something useful.

Next to the dishwasher, she noticed a closet with folding doors slightly open. Peeking inside, she found a washer and dryer; on the floor, piles of laundry. She started a load in the machine, fixed the kids some tuna sandwiches, and played several games of Uno with them. After they went to sleep, she still couldn't sit still, and by eleven thirty that night when Marsha came home, Velita had vacuumed and dusted the apartment. A casserole bubbled in the oven, a coffee cake cooled on the counter, and a salad waited in the refrigerator. The kitchen and bathroom floors were scrubbed, and clean laundry hung over door frames or lay folded on the kitchen table. Her own clothes and those of the kids', tossed into the loads, were ready for the morning.

Marsha said, "Mmm, something smells delicious!" She glanced

at the clothes hanging, and added, "Hey, you were supposed to take it easy!"

"Yeah, well, I got tired of doing nothing. Thought you might be hungry after working all evening."

"Fantastic. It was so busy on my floor, I didn't have time for a supper break." Marsha reached into the cupboard and took out two tea bags. Instead of the usual muddle, the cereal boxes stood neatly together, and all the spice jars were lined up in a double row. She shook her head. "Velita, you're too much. Ralph doesn't know what a treasure he's thrown away." She heated two mugs of water in the microwave, dropped in the tea bags, then picked up an armload of folded towels and took them into the bathroom.

Velita set two places on the cleared end of the table and got out the casserole and salad. When Marsha came back, Velita noticed her eyes sparkling and asked, "Did something special happen? It'd take more than a clean house to make me look like that."

Marsha sat down at the table and didn't answer right away. Staring at her plate, she said, "Jerry stopped in at work."

"Your cop friend? Are you getting back together?"

"He wants to get married."

Velita shrieked her congratulations, but then sadly realized, "I guess you'll be moving to Santa Cruz?" Being independent was one thing, but losing her best friend was more than she could handle.

"No," said Marsha. "That's the best part. When the police chief learned Jerry was considering that job, he mentioned an opening in homicide here. Said Jerry was too good a cop to lose.

"Jerry applied, passed the tests, next week goes for a second interview. Looks like he'll get it."

Velita sighed in relief. "I'm so happy for you. Is he nice? Will he be good to you?"

"Oh, yes. Nice and good. Not bad-looking, either."

"Did you set a date?"

"Not exactly. Just sometime next spring."

Velita hugged her friend. But she couldn't help feeling a lump of envy. Back when she'd first met Ralph, her whole body thrilling just to be with him, how impossible it had been to stay away. And look where it had gotten her. Would she ever have that kind of happiness again? Did God really care what happened to her, with all the baggage she carried?

It couldn't hurt to try praying again. Tonight when she went to bed, she would ask God what to do about Ralph and if there was any chance of her life getting better.

Chapter 38

Jacob lay in his hospital bed, aching for sleep but too troubled in mind to drift off. As soon as he'd settled in his room, he'd picked up the phone on the table next to him and talked to his children, telling them not to worry. He'd called Howard to get his car out of the wrecking yard and check if the fruit-thinning crew had shown up. They had.

Then came the dreaded call to his parents. How would he ever explain this accident?

All his life, he'd tried to follow the precept: honor thy father and mother. God had told the Israelites that it would even extend their lives.

It was more than that, though. For Mennonites, the church was also their entire social life, and when any of the brethren seemed to be slipping away, mixing with outsiders, others would warn them. And pray for them. And sad to say, there would be gossip. *What will people think?*

Jacob wanted to be open and honest with his parents, but they wouldn't understand the strange connection he'd developed with Velita, a married woman, not even a born-again Christian. He didn't understand it himself. Although he tried to stay level-headed, there was something about her that pulled on his heart.

Now that he knew she was all right and her husband safely behind bars, Marsha firmly in charge, he should close that chapter. But how could he, knowing how needy she was, how unsure of herself?

When his dad heard his first words, that he'd had an accident and was in the hospital, there'd been no time for more details.

"We'll pick up the children and be there as soon as possible," said his dad and then hung up.

Barely a half hour later, he'd heard footsteps, raised his head from his bed, and seen his parents, still in work clothes, coming through the door of his hospital room. His children were right behind them.

His father took off his straw hat and smoothed his thick white hair. "*Nah, Yoakob*, what lands you in this godforsaken place?"

Jacob laughed. His dad called all public places "godforsaken." He hugged Paul with his good arm and looked over the boy's shoulder. "Oh, a crazy driver ran into my car. I know one of the nurses—they'll take good care of me here. But I sure didn't expect to be lying around just when the fruit needed thinning. I'm just glad the crew showed up when it was supposed to."

"How did it happen?" asked his mother. "The wreck."

Jacob sighed. It was no use trying to keep the whole story from them; it might even come out in the newspaper. Better they heard it firsthand. "This woman from the jury panel—her husband nearly killed her. I was driving her and her little children to a safe house, where they keep people like that. Somehow, the guy got wind of it and chased us."

Sammy wormed his way around his grandparents and stood by Jacob's bed. "You mean that guy you fought with at the relief sale?"

"What?" gasped his mother. "You said you'd taken care of a troublemaker. Now he's after you for that?"

Jacob took several long breaths. "I guess I better start at the beginning."

His dad nodded, his eyebrows raised. "Please do," he said dryly.

Jacob watched their shocked expressions as he told about Velita's assault by the gang in the underground parking lot, his following her home to make sure she made it safely, her husband Ralph's jealous reaction. The encounter at the relief sale. "Turned out, the man's been beating his wife, and Thursday night, he nearly choked her to death. Marsha, another jury member who's a nurse, caught on to what was happening. She persuaded Velita to take the kids and hide out in a shelter for abused women."

His mother drew back, her mouth puckered. "But—why didn't you just let the police handle it? Why did *you* have to get mixed up with all that?"

Why, indeed? He'd never intended to get involved in Velita's life. "I don't know, exactly. On the jury panel after being together that long, we got to be friends, most of us. Marsha knew where the shelter was, and I—well I sort of volunteered."

Becky looked pale. "Did you get the woman to that—shelter?"

"No, the man rammed into us before we got there. Our car's pretty well totaled. It got towed away; Howard's going to check on it."

"Neh, obah!" said his mother. "What now?"

"Will that man come after us?" asked Becky. "Does he know where we live?"

Oh, he knows where I live all right, thought Jacob. *Does he ever!* No point in mentioning that Ralph might have started the fire in their shed—that wasn't proven yet. And it wouldn't do to scare his children. "Last I heard, he's in jail."

"What about the woman?" asked his dad.

"She and the kids are at Marsha's place."

Jacob's father frowned, and his fingers worried the brim of his hat. "Are you sure there's not something more to this? *Beta pauss opp,* better be careful. You might be in deeper than you think."

"I couldn't let her get beat up again. She's been through too much." Suddenly Jacob felt very tired, and he closed his eyes for a moment. He'd already berated himself, over and over, for the attraction he felt toward Velita. He didn't need any more scolding. To change the subject, he asked, "Anything in the mail from Heinz and Clara?"

"Not yet," said Becky. "They're probably only halfway home by now."

"They might stop somewhere on the way. I think Heinz has a cousin in Kansas." Jacob turned to his mother. "Don't you think Clara looked good?" he asked her. "She seems so happy."

"*Yah,* I'd wondered a little, her marrying into the Old Order. They don't think the same. But it seems to be working out."

His dad asked, "Trial about over?"

"We finished this afternoon." Jacob saw Becky smile and Paul clap his hands silently, and he felt his love for them well up. They were all such good kids.

"*Nah yo,*" said his dad. "It's time you got back to normal."

"Yeah. Hot as the weather's been, it won't be long till the first picking."

"The fruit size okay?"

"Surprisingly good. Some are starting to color. Price is up a little too. Not as high as I'd hoped, but better than last year."

They were quiet for a few minutes. Then his father asked, "That woman—the one you helped. You say you got to be friends?"

Jacob scratched his head. "We all did. Why?" He hoped his tone was casual.

When his father didn't answer, he turned to see the older man studying him, his eyes squinted.

"She's—*ach*, Pop, you can't imagine what she's been through."

His father's look still bored into his eyes. "You know what it says in Proverbs, not to be snared by the wiles of a strange woman."

Jacob felt prickles on the back of his neck. "She—Mrs. Stanford isn't like that."

"Is she a believer?"

He had to admit that he didn't know. "But I heard her say she'd prayed." He felt his face get hot, knowing that wasn't the whole truth. She'd also said she didn't believe God answered her prayers.

His father slowly shook his head. "I just don't understand how a man like you, raised in the church, knowing right from wrong, can still get mixed up with a married woman. I knew you should never have gone into that trial. One step into the world, and a person can get dunked into a muddy pit." His dad put his straw hat back on, a signal that he was ready to leave.

Jacob glanced at him, then looked away. "Yeah, well, don't worry. Now that the trial's over, we'll all go our separate ways and never see each other again." But after they left, he stared at the ceiling for a long time, knowing he couldn't let that happen.

❖ ❖ ❖

On Sunday morning, Velita got up early, made coffee, warmed up the rest of the coffee cake, and whipped up some eggs. By the time Marsha came into the kitchen, the eggs were scrambled and ready.

She squeezed Velita's shoulders. "You're spoiling me. I don't know when I've had a nice breakfast like this."

"Well, you've been so good to me. I know we're just in your way."

"Uh-uh. You're not in anybody's way. I'm happy to do what I can. You're worth it. Remember that."

Marsha kept telling her that, but it was hard to believe she was worth all this bother. If she was, why had her life turned out this way? "I ought to go home and clean my house," said Velita. "I'll bet the men left it in a horrible mess."

"Huh!" laughed Marsha. "You sure you're ready to tackle something like that? If it were me, I'd put it off as long as possible."

The phone rang, and she said, "That's probably the hospital. We're always shorthanded, and the head nurse keeps begging for us to come in extra." She answered, then nodded at Velita. "I can't get away right now," she said into the phone, "but what about nine thirty? Will that help?"

By the time she hung up, TJ and Suanne had come into the kitchen, dressed in the clean clothes Velita had set out for them.

TJ grinned at the coffee cake, smacking his lips. "Can we go home after we eat?"

Velita looked at Marsha. "I guess we better. That way I'll have plenty of time to get the kids ready for school tomorrow."

"I can drop you off and then go on to work," said Marsha. "But first, I want to call the police station, see if Ralph is still locked up."

He was, with bail set high, and Velita sighed in relief. No way could he get hold of that much money.

When Marsha pulled up in front of Velita's house, TJ threw open the car door and ran to the front step. Suanne started to follow him, but Velita sat and stared, her heart pounding. Did she dare go in?

Suanne looked back, a puzzled look on her face. "What's the matter, Mommy?"

"Nothing, sweetie," she said. "Are you glad to be home?" She got out of the car, not wanting her own fears to spook the kids.

"Yeah. I bet my dolls missed me."

The hose and sprinkler zigzagged across the ragged lawn, and Velita stooped to roll them up. *I should have cut the grass. Trimmed the daisy bush . . .*

Marsha asked, "You want to pick up your mail?"

Velita felt strange, reaching into the metal mailbox and taking out the wad of bills and flyers. "Ralph always brings it in. He's got to be the first to look at it." She bit her lip and glanced at Marsha. "But sometimes I peek." She stood shuffling the envelopes, wondering which were bills and what to do about them.

TJ ducked under her arm and tried the door. "It's unlocked," he said. "Maybe he's home." Pushing the door open, he called, "Dad?" then immediately backed away, holding his nose. "Man, something stinks!"

Heat and an odor of beer, rotting food, and sour vomit hit Velita, and she hung onto the door frame, trying not to gag.

A spilled Coors can left a sticky mess on the coffee table, and empties cluttered the floor. In the kitchen, half a loaf of bread lay open on the table, the dried slices shuffled out of the wrapper. Crusts, part of an apple, and an open box of Cheez-Its sat next to a half-empty package of bologna. How awful to have Marsha see her house like this!

"I'm sorry," said Velita. "He and Tom must've had themselves a big party Friday." She looked around the room, wrinkling her nose. "Said he was sick." She huffed out a breath. "Sure."

Marsha pushed past Velita and told the kids, "Help me open the windows. Every one."

Velita found a garbage bag and started to sweep the trash into it. Memories, good and bad, flashed through her mind. Babies crying, Ralph yelling, kicking the furniture. Cheering when the kids did something smart, slapping her if she talked to the mailman. Smiling one minute, boiling the next.

She saw Marsha watching her, and she whispered, "I swear he's around a corner somewhere, ready to get me."

Marsha hugged her. "He isn't. I've been all through the house. And we just called the station, remember? . . . Look, you don't have to do this now. I can take you back to my place. You can stay as long as you like."

Velita stood by her bedroom window and gulped in the welcome morning breeze. "No, I better get it over with." In spite of the wash she'd done before leaving for the courthouse, the sour smell hung on, and Ralph's dirty clothes lay tangled on the floor. She could almost hear him say, *Get busy, stupid, and clean up this mess!* But then she realized: Ralph couldn't boss her right now.

That was a strange feeling. A . . . good feeling.

"If you're going to stay, you ought to change the locks. Add a couple of dead bolts."

"That wouldn't stop Ralph. If he couldn't get in the door, he'd be mad enough to break a window."

"I hate to leave you here," said Marsha. "But they really need me at the hospital."

"Oh, gee, you've already put yourself out so much."

"Call me if you need anything. Anything! Promise? If you freak out, I'll be over like a flash."

Velita gave Marsha the bravest smile she could manage. "I'll be okay. Honest. Thanks for everything. You're the greatest."

As Velita washed the walls, wiped the furniture, and sprayed all the rooms, she thought about Marsha. She'd never had a friend like that. Never. And if she hadn't been chosen to be on the jury, she wouldn't even have met the woman. Was it just luck, or was this the reason God didn't answer her prayer? Or was this His own way of answering?

She'd just finished scrubbing the kitchen floor when the phone rang.

Velita froze. What if it was Ralph, steaming mad? Or LaDonna—that would be almost as bad.

Finally TJ picked up. "Hey, Mom," he called. "It's your friend. She says turn on the radio."

"The radio?" Velita took the receiver from him. "Hello?"

"Turn on 1130," said Marsha. "Station KRDU. I'm at the hospital in Jacob's room; he's listening to his church program, and their male chorus is singing. He says he usually sings in it. You've got to hear them; you won't believe how good they are!"

Puzzled, Velita frowned. Over the phone she could hear men's voices singing but couldn't make out the words. "Jacob's church is on the radio?"

"Yes! He says they broadcast every Sunday morning. Tune in—I think you'll like it!"

When Velita found the station, the men's rich harmony filled the room. "Are you weary, are you heavy hearted? Tell it to Jesus, tell it to Jesus!"

She sank onto the sofa. The words seemed meant just for her. She was awfully tired, and her problems were a heavy load.

When she was about ten, her folks had taken her to a revival meeting in a big tent with rough wooden benches and sawdust on the floor. The people looked gloomy, their mouths pinched as though going to church was a punishment, and they sang scary songs about sin and blood.

The preacher's hair and beard were white, but his eyes were black and fierce. She hadn't understood much of what he shouted, but from the way he looked at her, she knew whatever it was, was her fault.

When the sermon was over, the people stood up and sang, "Sad, sad, that bitter wail—almost, but lost." That preacher's black eyes had stared right at her, and she knew she was supposed to walk up there to him. But she was more scared of him than of the hellfire he threatened.

Her stepdad must have felt the same way, because he'd said, "Let's get outta here," and they'd left. That had been the end of religion for Velita; he'd even made her give up Sunday school.

But this was so different. When the song ended, a preacher started talking. He didn't shout. He didn't threaten. Instead, he quietly said, "In Matthew 11:28, the Lord invites all you who are weary and carry heavy burdens to take His yoke instead. Team up with Him, and He will give you rest. He'll help you carry those burdens. He'll give you security and peace of mind."

Velita dropped her head into her hands and let the tears bathe her fingers. "Oh, dear Jesus," she prayed. "I'm at the end of my rope, and I really need Your help. Please take my burdens, and give me that peace."

Chapter 39

The next morning, Velita woke to rain tapping against the window. She'd thought she wouldn't be able to sleep, but she had, deeply, and now felt rested. In spite of her worries about Ralph, there seemed to be an invisible net around her, keeping her safe. She thought about the verse Jacob's preacher had quoted: "Come to me, I will give you rest." Was it just her imagination, or had her prayer worked?

She'd let Suanne sleep with her, partly to soothe her little girl's fears, but also for her own comfort. Now, after sliding silently out of bed, Velita glanced down the hall through TJ's open door. He stood by his dresser, holding the little balsa airplane he'd bought at the Mennonite sale. One wing was broken, and he fingered the loose piece.

He looked up and saw her coming. "Dad broke it," he said. For a few seconds he looked sad, then said quickly, "But he didn't mean to. Said he'd fix it. When's he coming home?"

Velita felt a rock settle in her stomach. What could she tell him? With the restraining order, Ralph wasn't supposed to come near the house. And if he ignored that, if he sneaked over here, it would be to break things, not fix them.

Finally she said, "We'll just have to wait and see. The cops know he hit Mr. Franzen's car on purpose. They said that made it assault and battery."

He shrugged. "So?"

"People have to pay for the wrong things they do. That's the law. He might have to be in prison for a while to keep him from hurting others."

TJ's shoulders slumped. He turned away and stumbled to the window, kicking over his metal wastebasket on the way. "I guess that means he won't never fix this for me." He straightened the wastebasket, then dropped the airplane into it. The *clunk* echoed in Velita's ears.

She went to him and stroked his dark hair, so like his daddy's. How could she heal all his hurts, make things right for him? She'd have to ask God to help her be tough, and make sure TJ'd stay out of trouble in the years ahead. "You and me and Suanne, we've got to do things for ourselves now. We've got to be brave and stick together. Take care of each other."

She could only hope the police would put Ralph away for a long time. But who knew what a tricky defense lawyer would pull? The way Duane Jackson's trial had gone, each lawyer telling such a believable story, anybody could be fooled. If her husband had his say, the whole thing could turn around, and they could blame *her*.

The thought was too awful, and she started to leave the room.

TJ pulled on her arm. "Can I go see him? Maybe he still has my paper."

Velita had forgotten the permission slip for the field trip. "I'll talk to your teacher; I'm sure she'll give you another one, and I can sign it."

Suanne woke up, and peeked out the door of Velita's bedroom. "Is Daddy here?" Her voice trembled.

"No, sweetie," said Velita. She glanced at TJ, her eyebrows raised in a "See what I mean?" look. "The police have him locked up."

"For a *long* time," added TJ, scowling. "My arm hurts."

"Sure it does. It'll take a while for the bone to heal. But you can still write with your other hand, and the kids in school can see how tough you are."

That made him cheer up. "Yeah. Nobody else in my class ever had a broken arm."

After he and Suanne ran through the drizzle and got on the school bus, Velita washed the breakfast dishes, wondering what to do next. With jury duty over and Ralph gone, she was on her own. She could do anything she pleased.

But the house was clean, and it was too wet to work in the yard. Without a car, she had no way to go anywhere. Even if she walked eight blocks to the grocery store, without Ralph's weekly paycheck, she couldn't buy much food.

She started a load of laundry, then rummaged through her cupboards, trying to figure out what to make for supper. As she pulled out a package of rice, she heard a car turn into the driveway.

Her heart jumped into her throat. *Ralph!* Had he gotten out this quickly? Should she sneak out the back way and run to the neighbors?

Before her feet would move, through the window she saw Marsha coming up the walk. Weak with relief, she threw open the front door.

Marsha looked around the living room and nodded. "Looks a *lot* different now. You're some housekeeper! I need to take lessons from you."

Velita shrugged. "Working hard keeps me from screaming." The coffee pot was still hot, and she poured them each a cup.

As they sipped, Velita noticed Marsha watching her. Finally Marsha said, "You seem more relaxed today."

Velita smiled. "You know that radio program you told me about? Jacob's church?"

"Yeah? Did you enjoy the music?"

"It was beautiful. But more than that, what the preacher said—it was just what I needed."

Marsha stared at her with a puzzled look. "I guess I missed that part. I didn't stay for the whole thing."

Velita told her about the message and how she'd prayed for peace. "And you know what? I do feel more peaceful. Like God is really going to help me through this."

"Hmm. You know, I could use some of that myself. Guess it's time for me to '*have a little talk with Jesus.*' You ever hear that old gospel song?" When Velita shook her head, Marsha said, "Next time I have a Sunday off work, you and I'll find a good church. Take the kids to Sunday school. Jacob said I should get back, and I'm sure he's right." She stared into her coffee, then asked, "Have you thought any more about that divorce lawyer I mentioned?"

Velita dropped her head into her hands. "Oh, man, what would Ralph do? I know it was a big mistake to marry him . . ."

"Don't wait too long to correct that mistake. You know what they say at weddings? 'What God has joined together.' I don't think God put you two together."

"But if I—leave Ralph, how will I feed the kids? With him in prison, he can't pay child support."

"I was wondering about that," said Marsha. "I don't want to be nosy. But how are you for money, right now?"

Velita shook her head. "Friday was payday, but he didn't go to work."

"So the check's still at the shop?"

"Probably. You think they'd let me have it?"

"They'd better. I'll take you over there tomorrow, and we'll ask. You're on his account, aren't you?"

Velita stared at her. "What do you mean?"

"You know—you can sign checks?"

"He always took care of the money. Said it was *his* job. He put his pay right in the bank; I never saw it. He just gave me enough cash for groceries." Velita chewed on her lip and stared at her fingernails, embarrassed. "I hate for anyone to know how dumb I am. I've never even written a check. I never . . . learned."

"No problem. We'll cash it at his bank." Marsha touched her arm. "Hey, don't ever be afraid to ask for help. We'll get you through this." She was quiet a minute. "What about groceries? I could help you out a little . . ."

Someone pounded at the front door, and Velita jumped. A voice screeched, "Will somebody tell me what's going on?"

"LaDonna," whispered Velita. She closed her eyes and felt all her energy drain out.

Her mother-in-law burst through the door, marched into the kitchen, and stood looking down at them. Her face was pale against her dyed black hair, and red spots shone high on her cheeks.

"Where've you been all this time? I've been trying and trying to get ahold of you."

"We've . . . been in an accident."

"Yeah, yeah, I heard about that. Ralph called me. Collect. Said you'd left him. Said you told all kinds of lies to the police so they'd put him in jail." LaDonna spit the word out. "He's my only kid, all I have. Had to raise him without a daddy, make up for that louse of a husband running out on us. Least you could do was give my boy the love he needed, but no, you just trash him." Her voice cracked, and she brushed away tears with her fingers, still glaring at Velita.

Velita felt like a rabbit trapped by a wildcat. What could she say that wouldn't make the woman even madder? "He . . . dragged me out of the car by my hair, cussing at me. The police charged him with abuse."

"Well, you asked for it, running away from him like that. The police arrested the wrong person. I'll make sure they find that out."

Marsha touched Velita's hand and whispered, "Be strong." Then she spoke quietly but firmly. "I know you're upset, Mrs. Stanford. But Velita has been through a very hard time and—"

LaDonna came closer. In spite of her smeared mascara, she looked powerful. "Who are you?" she demanded.

"Marsha Lewis. Velita's friend."

LaDonna lifted her upper lip and waggled her shoulders. "Well, your highness Marsha Lewis, you just butt out. This is between Vel and me."

"No." Velita faced LaDonna's angry eyes. She couldn't let her friend leave. "This is my house, and I want Marsha here with me."

She gulped, shocked that she'd actually had the nerve to say that out loud. But she stared the woman down.

"*Your* house?" LaDonna snorted. "You wouldn't even have a place to live if I hadn't helped Ralph with the rent. That sofa, the coffee table, this nice kitchen set—they're all mine. The recliner. I paid for them. If you're splitting up with him, I want them back."

Velita felt her courage leave. *Help me Lord*, she prayed silently. "The beds," she whispered. "The kids need their beds."

"Shoot, I got no use for their beds. But the good dishes, that sewing machine—"

Velita gasped. There was no way she'd give up her sewing machine. Before she realized what she was doing, she stood up, placed her palms on the table, and faced her mother-in-law. "That Singer is mine, and you know it. Ralph traded for it, way back in Chockamo. For my birthday. You're *not* going to take it away from me." She glanced at Marsha, and saw her friend give a thumbs-up.

LaDonna blinked. She opened her mouth, but Velita barged ahead. "You knew how it was between Ralph and me; you saw his tantrums. How he hit me. Yeah, he was still your little boy; you always stuck up for him. And *that's* what put him in jail."

LaDonna clenched her fists and leaned forward. Her whole face was red, and her eyes shifted from Velita to Marsha and back. "You—you—"

Marsha held up her hands. "Look, what's happened has happened. Nothing can change that. It's best if we can talk things over calmly."

"Easy for you to say. It's not your baby that's locked up." LaDonna turned back to Velita. "You haven't heard the last from me. I can't afford a lawyer, but I'll hit on everyone I know for that bail money. And you'll pay for this, in more ways than one."

She started out the front door, looked around, then asked, "Ralph said he'd been driving Tom's car. Where's the Dodge?"

Velita felt as though her breath had been punched out of her. "It got stolen." She could barely get the words out. "From the parking garage."

LaDonna's mouth flew open. "What? You know how much he loves that car. Does he know?"

"Uh-uh. I just found out yesterday."

"That does it. You just wait and see." LaDonna left, slamming the door.

Velita stumbled to the sofa and sank down on it. Her head ached, and she felt shaky. Where had all that peace gone to? Bad enough that Ralph nearly killed her. Now she had to put up with LaDonna's threats. It was too much. *Oh, Lord, show me what to do!*

Again, Velita felt her hair being torn from her scalp, the scrape of the jagged metal against her body. Heard the cussing, saw the fury in her husband's eyes.

Marsha was right. Ralph would never change—he'd only get worse. And TJ could turn out just like him. This had to be another warning from God, giving her the chance to start her life over.

"Okay," she told Marsha. "Ask that lawyer if she'll see me."

Chapter 40

The next day went by in a whirl. Velita thought she'd never keep up with all Marsha had planned. Marsha had even helped her make an appointment with the divorce lawyer. "The hospital has piled on the hours since I missed so much work during the trial," her friend had explained. "I've only got one day off to help you, and it's best to get the wheels turning."

Velita knew that was right. By herself, she wouldn't know where to start.

As soon as the kids left for school, Marsha took her to Carter Machine Shop to pick up Ralph's check. The sun shone brightly, and in the distance, Velita could see the Sierra Nevadas looking fresh and clean, the highest peaks frosted with snow. It seemed to be a good sign of the new life she was starting, and she felt a little tickle of excitement.

In the shop's cluttered office, the gum-chewing bookkeeper in jeans shuffled through papers and files and found Ralph's check. "You say he had a wreck? Sorry to hear that. Thought he'd called in sick. Will he be in tomorrow?"

Sure hope not, thought Velita. She glanced at Marsha, wondering how much she should tell the bookkeeper.

Marsha answered for her. "He'll have to get back to you about that."

Next, they went to the bank to cash the check.

"Ralph Stanford's account?" asked the teller. "What's the account number?"

Velita stared at her. "The number?"

"Yes, the number on the checks. You say you're his wife? Is this a joint account?"

"It better be," said Marsha.

The teller narrowed her eyes at Velita, then tapped her computer keys, frowned, and tapped some more. "Sorry, just his name on it. He'll have to come in with you for you to cosign before you can cash the check."

Velita's world crumbled. She couldn't tell this snippy stranger that Ralph was in jail, and even if he wasn't, no way would he agree to let her get to his money. The rent was paid up for the rest of the month, and the stuff in her cupboards might last a week or two, but then what? Would she and the kids end up on the streets after all? Numbly, she followed Marsha to the car.

Marsha tapped her fingers on the steering wheel, staring out the windshield. Finally she asked, "Is there a store where they know you, know you're Ralph's wife? They'd probably take the check."

Velita thought a while. "The grocery store, maybe. But I've always used cash, that's what Ralph gave me. He goes to Casey's Pool Hall—they know him all right. On L Street, near the Chinese Buffet."

"Hmm. Maybe that would work."

At Casey's, a shapely, red-haired waitress took one look at the check, glanced at Velita with a strange curl of her lips, and said,

"Ralph too lazy to come in?" She rang open the cash register and counted out the money.

Velita remembered Tom mentioning a redhead. Was this the one Ralph fooled around with? Suddenly she felt ugly and worthless and turned away with the bills in her hand.

Marsha stepped up. "You're ten short there."

The redhead turned to Marsha with a glare, added the ten, and slammed the cash drawer shut.

Embarrassed that she herself hadn't caught the shortage, Velita breathed her thanks to Marsha. How would she ever make it without such a good friend? It seemed like God had sent an angel to help her. And if Velita was leaving Ralph, he was welcome to the redhead; maybe she could give him a good fight.

By ten thirty, they'd shopped for groceries and were back in Velita's kitchen, putting them away. "By the way," said Marsha, "I called the hospital, and they're releasing Jacob Franzen this afternoon. It'll take a while for his ribs to heal, but the CT scan showed no brain damage. All he needs is a couple of follow-up appointments."

Velita smiled big. "I'm so glad." But secretly, she felt let down. That meant she would never see Jacob again. It had felt good to be around a man who treated her nice. Now, with the trial over, there'd be no reason for their paths to cross.

Marsha took a notebook and pencil from her purse and sat down at the table. "Okay. Unless you want to go on welfare, we have to find you a job. What can you do?"

Velita sighed. She'd tried to put this scary part out of her mind. "I've never worked outside of home. Nobody'll hire me without experience." Ralph had drilled that into her often enough. "I can't type. I don't know how to work a cash register. Let's face it: I'm just dumb!"

Marsha thumped the table with her fist. "You're not! We'll draw on the things you do best. You're a good mother, you keep house like a pro, and you're a great cook. We could try a restaurant or a bakery. And a lot of women would be delighted for someone to clean their house." She thought a bit. "But I think we could try for something that pays a little more. Do you take the newspaper?"

Velita went outside and found the *Beacon* still rolled up under a bush. She took it inside, and Marsha turned to the classifieds. Running her finger down the help-wanted ads, she circled a few, then looked up. "You sounded pretty attached to your sewing machine. Do you sew a lot?"

"Well, yeah, I make Suanne's and my tops, some dresses."

"Anything else?"

"Made these drapes. And—" Velita looked around, then pointed. "That chair was awfully ragged, so I made that cover for it."

Marsha ran a double circle around another ad and smiled. "Perfect. We're going to pay a visit to Strader's Drapery Shop on Blackstile Avenue."

The showroom of the store was lined with shelves holding bolts of fabric and bins full of tassels, fringes, and lace. In the center stood free-hanging rods of sample drapes and curtains in rich brocades, silk, velour, and sheers. Velita could hardly keep her hands off the lush material.

"May I help you?"

She looked around. Next to the drapes, behind a shiny desk stood a slim woman in a classy navy suit.

Marsha nudged Velita, and she cleared her throat. "Are you Mrs. Strader?"

The woman smiled. "Strader's retired. I'm the manager, Janet Wilson."

Velita swallowed the lump that threatened to choke her. "I . . . um . . . I saw your ad in the paper." She glanced at Marsha, and Marsha nodded encouragement. "I'd . . . like to apply for a job. Sewing."

"Do you have experience?"

Her courage fled. No experience was the story of her life. She'd just as well turn around and walk back out.

"She's sewed for years," said Marsha. "Everything from children's clothes to drapes and upholstery covers."

"Have a chair and fill out this application," said the manager. "When you're finished, I'll take you to the back room for you to show me what you can do."

After Marsha had helped her fill in the blanks, Marsha waited in the store while Velita followed Janet Wilson into the next room. Three other women sat at huge, noisy machines, sewing long, gold brocade panels. They glanced up but didn't stop working.

The manager led Velita to a vacant machine. "Have you ever worked one of these before?"

Velita thought of her little Singer bought at the flea market and shook her head. "But I can learn real fast, if you just give me a chance." The notion of working with those gorgeous materials made her fingers itch.

Janet Wilson studied her, frowning, then turned to one of the other women. "Trish, why don't you show Mrs. Stanford the ropes, then give her some scraps to practice on. I'll be back in a few minutes."

When the manager left the room, all three of the machines stopped. The woman called Trish came to Velita. She wore a cotton smock over slacks and a red T-shirt, and her brown hair was held back with a sparkly comb. She smiled and introduced the other two women, Nikki and Stephanie. "Don't be afraid of this monster." She pointed to the machine by Velita. "All you have to do is baby it along, and it'll purr like a kitten."

Velita sat down, listened carefully to Trish's instructions, and fed in a square of material. When she started the machine, it ran so fast she thought it would gobble up the fabric, her hand, and start up her arm. There was no way she could handle this job!

But after several tries, she got the speed to settle down and managed to run a straight seam. By the time Janet Wilson came back into the room, Velita had sewed several pieces together to look like a cushion cover.

Janet looked at the fabric and nodded. "Neat work." She was quiet a bit, then said, "Tell you what. I'll give you two weeks probation, with pay, and if you can handle the job, it's yours. Can you start tomorrow?"

Tomorrow? What would she do about the kids—about all her problems with Ralph? But this was her big chance, and one way or another, she'd grab it. Pretending to be brave, she told the manager, "Sure. What time?"

Back in the car, Velita hugged Marsha and squealed with joy. She could hardly believe it. "I've got a job! A real job!" Maybe she could make it on her own, after all.

Then reality sank in, and she stared at Marsha. "But—without a car, how will I get to work?"

"We'll call the police and see if they've located it. If they haven't, tomorrow I'll drop you there on my way to work. I can take you on my days off. The rest of the time, you can use the city bus. It runs regularly, and I think there's a stop a block or so from your place. There's a schedule in the newspaper." Marsha was quiet for a while, then said, "The car's registered to Ralph, isn't it? Even if it's found, you'll eventually want to get one of your own."

Velita was determined not to depend on Marsha all the time. But how could she pay rent, support the kids, and save up enough money to buy a car? What if after the two weeks probation, the manager decided to let her go? Her new life seemed crowded with impossible road blocks.

But Marsha said, "Don't look so worried. We'll take one step at a time. You're going to make it. I promise!" She glanced at her watch. "We better pick up a burger at a drive-through. Don't want to be late to your appointment."

Attorney Theresa Farnsworth was a stocky, middle-aged woman with a square chin and looked like she could tackle anybody dumb enough to cross her. She eyed Velita, her face stern. "You're sure you're ready to go through with this?"

Was the woman trying to talk her out of it? Velita glanced at Marsha, took a deep breath, and blew it out. "I'm sure."

A sudden smile brightened the lawyer's face, and her eyes shone with kindness. "Marsha told me about your case, so we'll get right to it." She pulled out a folder with a stack of papers and slid them over to Velita, explaining each page. "As soon as you fill these out and sign on the marked lines, I'll send them over to the jail for your husband to sign."

Velita felt cold wash over her. "He'll never do it. Like as not, he'll just tear up the paper."

"Tough," said Ms. Farnsworth. "You've got all the grounds you need. If he won't sign, we wait. The divorce will come through by default."

"And then what?" asked Velita.

"Then I'll get you a court date, have you tell your story to a judge. If your husband shows up, he'll try to weasel out. My guess is that he won't come. He'd be pretty stupid to fight all these charges."

Velita thought again about the redhead. That could be another charge. But she didn't know for sure, and it was too embarrassing to mention.

When Velita waved goodbye to Marsha and opened the door of her house, she heard the phone ring. Hurrying inside, she picked up and heard a female voice. "This is a collect call from Ralph Stanford in the Springton County Jail. To accept this call . . ."

Velita nearly dropped the receiver. Should she take it? What would she say to him? She could almost hear his voice—at first soft, buttery, but if she didn't cooperate, a little louder, then threatening, shouting, cussing . . . She let the receiver slide out of her hand and back into its holder.

When Suanne and TJ came running from the school bus, Velita hugged them, listened to their problems and escapades of the day, and fixed them some Kool-Aid and crackers with peanut butter. She told them about her job and that she'd talked to Rhonda next door. The woman was willing to keep them after school until Velita got home from work.

TJ shouted, "Yay!" but Suanne's face crumpled. "I thought you were going to stay home now."

Another road block. Was it fair to the children for her to get a job and be gone so much? Maybe she should have taken Ralph's call.

If she could just swallow all her hurts and put up with him, if she would take back her complaint, maybe he would get out of jail free. Now that the jury trial was over, life could go back to normal, and Ralph would have nothing to be jealous about.

Or would he? He'd had no reason before. And now, he'd never believe that she and Jacob didn't have something going on between them. Her heart ached. How would she ever handle all these decisions?

Then she remembered the radio sermon she'd heard. Something about *"If a person would come to the Lord, He would give them rest."*

Even if it looked like there was no way out?

"God will help you carry those burdens. He'll give you security and peace of mind."

Oh, Lord, Velita prayed silently, *show me what to do.* To Suanne, she said, "Let's try it for two weeks and see how it goes. If it doesn't work at all, we'll do something else."

Suanne chewed her lips, then finally gave a corner of a smile and nodded. Velita hoped it would work out; she had no idea what something else would be.

Chapter 41

That evening, the police called and told Velita they'd found her car. Her relief was shot down when they went on to say it had been stripped and the frame burnt.

What was Ralph going to say? It was a good thing he was behind bars; for sure, he would blame her.

She wondered how he was getting along in jail. Probably going crazy, locked up day and night. Would he think about what he'd done to her, all the slaps and punches? Knowing him, though, he'd end up being the leader of a pack, getting meaner by the day.

Without the car, she'd better get used to taking the bus. Marsha'd been a big help, but it was time to stop taking advantage of her friendship.

After work the next day, Velita walked the three blocks home from the bus stop, her shoulders and back aching, but her heart singing. The other workers had been friendly, and the manager had praised her work.

When she reached the neighbors', TJ and Suanne came running out, and she hugged them. "Did you have a good day?"

"Yeah," said TJ. "Me and Luke made a hideout in their backyard. We're gonna have a club." He made a face at Suanne. "Boys only."

Suanne stuck her tongue out at him. "I got to help make cookies. So there."

Rhonda, standing at her door, nodded. "We girls have to stick together."

Velita laughed and thanked her for keeping the kids. But inwardly, she sighed, wondering if staying here would just drive her two children farther apart. If only there were some little girls nearby for Suanne to play with.

She took the kids home and went into the kitchen to fix supper. As she picked up a pot to cook spaghetti, the phone rang.

Ralph! Velita set the pot down carefully, silently, as though any sound would get through the phone line. After the fourth ring, TJ ran to answer, but Velita shouted, "No! Don't pick up."

"Why not?" he asked.

"I . . . we don't know who it is."

He looked at her like she was crazy. "Course not! You gotta say *hello* first."

"It might be a collect call. Promise me you won't accept any collect calls."

"Sheesh. I don't even know what that is."

The rings finally stopped. "An operator calls and asks if you'll accept. You have to say no and hang up right away. Promise?"

"I don't get it." TJ frowned. "Do you mean like if it's from jail? Can't I even talk to my dad?"

"Don't you know why he's in jail?"

TJ's shoulders slumped. "I guess. 'Cause he nearly got us killed."

"You've seen how he can be. We don't know what else he might do."

The phone rang again. Very slowly, Velita lifted the receiver but didn't say anything.

She heard only silence. Then a voice barked, "What's going on?"

LaDonna. Velita felt only slightly relieved. "I . . . was busy."

"Ralph said you hung up on him the other day. Wouldn't take his call. Don't you care what you've done to him?"

"The police don't want him calling here. He's got to stop bothering me."

"Oh, aren't you the sly one? You really think you fixed him good. Well, it's going to backfire on you."

At supper, TJ and Suanne gobbled up the spaghetti but Velita could hardly eat, worried about what LaDonna was up to.

An hour later, a truck parked in front of her house, with LaDonna's car right behind it. Two husky men came to the door.

"We're here to pick up a dining set and a sofa," said one of the men.

So that was it! Velita looked past the men and saw her mother-in-law, jaw stuck out, fists on her hips, and a smug look on her face.

There was no use arguing. Without a word, Velita opened the door wider, and the men marched in. Before they lifted the sofa, Velita grabbed the cushions. She'd made those herself—no way could LaDonna claim them.

TJ and Suanne watched open-mouthed while the men also carted away Ralph's recliner and the coffee table. "Why does Grandma want all that?" asked TJ. "She's got better ones."

Velita shrugged. "Ask her."

He ran over to LaDonna and tugged on her arm. "Grandma, you can't take away our stuff! We need it."

She gave a short laugh and pushed him aside. "Hey, your mom never paid for them. Freeloading time's over."

The kitchen and living room looked empty without the furniture, but Velita tossed the cushions on the floor, pulled out her card table, and set a vase on it. If her job lasted, she decided, she would find some remnants and make bigger cushions to sit on. At least she wouldn't have to beg for money to buy what she needed.

Saturday morning, Marsha called and asked how Velita was getting along at work. After hearing Velita's good report and cheering her on, Marsha said, "I read in the papers that Duane Jackson had all kinds of previous convictions. Gang involvement, drugs, that kind of thing. But I still think we made the right decision about him."

"I guess," said Velita. "All I know is I wouldn't want my boy growing up to be like him. I hope prison straightens him out."

That night, exhausted after her full day, Velita finally drifted off into a sound, dreamless sleep.

Suddenly, the flash of the overhead bedroom light woke her, and something heavy thudded onto her bed.

Blinking her eyes, Velita saw straight black hair and lips twisted into a snarl. "Ralph?" she whispered. Chills flooded through her, and she shook uncontrollably.

"Where's my car?" he growled. "Don't tell *me* it's stolen. It's a classic. You just thought you and your boyfriend could sell it and get rich."

"The . . . the police." Velita's mouth went dry, and she could hardly speak. "They f–found it in the foothills. Ask them. They'll tell you."

"The police?" He laughed, and the sound grated her nerves. "Oh no you don't. You just want to get me in trouble again." He leaned his face close to Velita, and she nearly gagged at the whiskey fumes on his breath. "Baby, you can't get rid of me that easy." Rearing back, he swung his fist at her.

She rolled quickly, protecting her face with her arm, and the blow caught her elbow. Pain shot up to her shoulder, and she fought to block out her feelings. But her mind raced, trying to find a way to settle him down. "How did you get out?"

He snorted. "Ever heard of a bondsman? Guy only needs to put up ten percent. Thanks to you, I had to hock my Harley. But your nice furniture helped too."

Velita drew in her breath. So that's why LaDonna wanted it! "The restraining order—" It was supposed to keep him at least a hundred yards away from her.

"Dumb broad. Did you think a lousy piece of paper could keep me out of my own house?" Then he noticed Suanne, now awake and wide-eyed, in the bed beside Velita. "What's the kid doing in here? Go to your own room!"

Tears rolled from Suanne's eyes, and she pushed closer to Velita, her fingers clamped to her mother's nightgown.

"You hear me? Git!" he shouted.

Velita's heart plunged into despair. Had all her efforts, all her prayers been for nothing? Would this be the end?

Velita kissed Suanne and whispered in her ear, "Go find a safe place."

"Yeah," said Ralph. He pushed them apart. "Crawl under your bed."

Suanne tumbled to the floor, then ran into TJ standing in the doorway.

"Dad!" said TJ. "When did you get home?"

Ralph turned and stared at him. "What you doing up? This a party or something?"

"How come you're here? I thought—" TJ came closer, but Ralph shoved the boy against the wall. "Get back to bed if you know what's good for you." Then he mumbled to himself, "Leave them alone, and they think they rule the roost."

TJ got up slowly, favoring his injured arm. He eyed Ralph fearfully, then sidled out the door.

Ralph watched him go, then turned back to Velita. "What you try'na pull, sending me divorce papers?"

She thought fast. "You don't need me and the kids hanging on you. This way, you can find someone good enough for you." She almost said, *like the redhead,* but stopped just in time. He'd probably hit her for mentioning the woman.

Ralph drew back and squinted at her. "That don't sound like you . . . Oh, I get it. The Mennonite put you up to it. Wants you for himself."

"No." Velita rolled farther away. "He's got his own people. He was just—"

"Shut up!" Ralph grabbed her hair, and her already tender scalp burned with the tension. She knew if she resisted, he would tear it out by the roots. Twisting it around his wrist, he pulled her head up and glared into her eyes. "I shoulda thrown you into that guy's shed before I burned it down."

He pushed her back onto the bed and said slowly, "Yeah. Now I'm gonna make up for that. I'll teach you a lesson you'll never forget."

By the third punch in her face, the metallic taste of blood filled Velita's mouth, and warm liquid rolled past her cheek. Her ears rang, black dots swirled in front of her eyes, and she fought to stay conscious.

Dear Lord, she prayed silently, *You're the only one who can get me out of this. If You can't help me, I'm dead. For my kids' sake, please, please save me.*

The noise in her ears grew louder and louder. Suddenly, the blows stopped. She tried to open her eyes but could only see through blurry slits. It seemed like the whole room was full of Ralphs, but they were bustling around and not hitting her anymore. Then firm but gentle hands lifted her up, whirled her into cool air, and back into a closed place. *Is this what dying feels like?*

She woke to find someone patting her cheek. "Velita, it's okay. You're safe now."

Safe. That's what she'd thought before. "Suanne? TJ?"

"They're fine. They ran to the neighbors', and Rhonda called the police. Velita, look at me. It's Marsha!"

"Marsha?" This was confusing. Had Ralph killed Marsha too? Velita managed to peer between swollen eyelids. The beige curtains circling her looked familiar.

"You're in Emergency. And this time, with Ralph breaking the restraining order, the judge will make sure he doesn't get bail."

❖ ❖ ❖

In the morning, after a lot of tests, poking and jabbing, and doctors asking all sorts of questions Velita hardly knew how to answer, the nurses finally helped her into a wheelchair and moved her upstairs to a hospital bed. "For observation," one doctor told her. She felt as though she'd already been observed too much, having to tell all the things Ralph had done to her.

If it hadn't been for Marsha helping and encouraging, she wouldn't have been able to open up at all. She was sure the doctors would sneer at her; say, "Why did you put up with it this long?" But they didn't, and their eyes were kind.

She'd worried about the cost; after all, she hadn't worked long enough to get healthcare benefits. But Marsha checked with Carter's Machine Shop, and Velita was still listed on Ralph's insurance. Not for long, though, she knew. Not if that redhead had anything to say about it.

Marsha had said TJ and Suanne were fine too. Her daughter, Heather, was home again, and between the two of them and Velita's neighbor Rhonda, the kids had around-the-clock sitters.

"Don't spoil them too much," Velita told her. "We've got to really cut back when I get home."

When Marsha brought them to see her that afternoon, Suanne cuddled up to Velita, crying, wanting to stay, asking when Mommy would come home. But TJ burst in full of excitement. He'd spent the night with Luke, played with his electronic games. "Mom—he's got Nintendo! Me and Luke killed off all the bad guys—" Then he stared at Velita's battered and blackened face and missing tooth, and he tiptoed closer, his eyes big with shock. "Dad did that to you?" he whispered.

Velita nodded. "Do you understand now why he was arrested?"

TJ rubbed his own shoulder. "Yeah, he hurt me too. Why does he do that?"

"Sometimes—he just goes crazy. That's why we can't live with him anymore."

He leaned over, and she held him tight. It would be hard raising the kids without a father. It would take a lot of help from Marsha—and God—to make a home for them.

She was supposed to rest, but there were too many people in and out. The police, also asking questions, and reporters from the paper and TV. She hadn't wanted to be on the news, but somehow they knew how to worm things out of her. She hated to think what LaDonna would say to the stories they would cook up.

That evening after the aide took Velita's dinner tray away, things quieted down a little. No nurses came in, and she fell asleep.

She woke suddenly to find a warm hand brushing the hair back on her forehead.

Jacob? Velita wanted to pull the sheet over her head. She'd fixed herself up for her kids and the reporters but knew her face was still swollen and puffy, her hair messy from sleep. "I hate for you to see me like this," she told him.

He smiled down at her and shook his head. "Don't talk that way. No matter what, you're still beautiful."

Had she heard correctly? Beautiful? She squinted up at him and couldn't believe what she saw. There were tears in his eyes, and his lips were trembling. "When Marsha called and told me what had happened, I thought for sure we'd lost you. I . . . couldn't stand that. I've been praying so hard . . ."

Velita had never before seen a grown man cry. Her heart was beating so fast she could hardly breathe, and blinking back her own tears, she turned away.

"Velita, look at me. You have to know how special you are to me."

She did look at him then, saw the glow in his eyes, so strong she could hardly stand it. She was free now—at least, she would be when her divorce was final. But then her heart sank. "Jacob," she whispered, "Marsha told me Mennonites don't believe—"

Before she could finish, Jacob placed his finger lightly across her mouth. "None of this was your fault," he said. "*None* of it. I believe God has been watching over you and gave you the courage to leave Ralph before he killed you."

Velita couldn't control the tear rolling down her cheek, and Jacob gently thumbed it away. Then she heard quick footsteps, and a nurse came into the room with a tray of medications.

"Sorry," said the nurse. "It's time for our patient to get some rest."

Jacob cleared his throat. "Get well quickly," he told Velita. "Your children need you." Leaning close to Velita, he kissed her on the forehead and whispered, "I'll come again when you're better."

Velita caught her breath. "I'd like that." She watched him back out of the room, his eyes locked on hers.

God had brought Marsha and Jacob into her life; that was for sure. Being rescued from Ralph was a huge miracle.

Thank You, God, she prayed silently. *I don't know much about You, but I want to learn more. And trust You for whatever happens.*

Chapter 42

May and June passed in a heat wave, ripening the fruit all over the valley. Packing houses worked day and night.

By the middle of July, Jacob's Elegant Lady peaches were ready, with the John Henrys ripening fast. He'd already called the foremen of his two picking crews from years before, and they'd agreed to come at dawn. Based at a government housing camp in the nearby small town of Parlier, the seasonal workers usually arrived in April and stayed until October, when they left to work in apple orchards in Oregon and Washington.

"We know you treat us good," Lupe Alverado had told him. A seasonal worker from Mexico, he and Jacob had become friends. "You give us water and portable toilets, all ready when we come."

Jacob's former helper, Buck, hearing about that, called and laughed at his efforts. "You're just babying the pickers. No way will you get your money's worth." But Jacob ignored him, believing that comfortable men made good workers. The fact the experienced help kept coming back was proof enough for him.

The first morning, as soon as the rays of the rising sun came through his bedroom window, Jacob jumped out of bed and slipped into his work clothes, already hearing the two vans drive into his yard.

Without stopping to eat, he went outside and greeted the men, supplying them with buckets and ladders. But before starting work, he led them in a prayer of thanks for the ripe and healthy fruit, for the hands that labored, and for their families, and in a petition for a successful harvest.

Some of the men crossed themselves, but all bowed their heads and rumbled a hearty, "Ah-men." He knew not all would understand what he'd said but could get the idea by the tone of his voice.

By that time, the lights were on in his house, and he knew Becky was up fixing breakfast. Howard drove in to help, and soon after that, Jacob's parents. After his mother had gone into the house, Sammy and Paul came straggling out sleepily.

As the more experienced men climbed the ladders for the highest fruit, Howard, Jacob, and his dad stationed themselves to train the younger men and boys how to handle the peaches carefully and how to recognize the culls—over-ripes, split-pits, and pocked fruit.

When everyone seemed settled, Jacob went over to his dad in the middle of the orchard. "Want some breakfast, Pop?" he asked.

"No, your mom insisted we eat at home, make it easier for everyone. You go ahead."

Jacob got the same kind of answer from Howard, so he headed toward the house alone. He was hungry and knew Becky would have a plate warming for him.

With Sammy guiding the tractor-trailer full of padded bins between the rows of trees and Paul and one of the older workers checking for culls, Jacob stopped to watch the pickers carefully roll their full buckets into the bins. "Good job," he told them, picking out an especially ripe cull for his breakfast.

Becky came out of the house, her hair pulled back into a ponytail, her shorts and T-shirt covered with a flowered apron. "Got some culls for me?" she asked.

Paul nodded and pointed to two filled boxes on the ground. Jacob helped Becky carry them into the house.

Inside, his mother was sterilizing mason jars and spreading out utensils and ingredients on the kitchen counter. "We'll can some but mostly freeze them sliced this year," she told Jacob, reaching into the warming oven for his food.

"What about pies?" he asked, his mouth full.

"Don't worry," said Becky. "I'll make at least four so Grandma can take one home with her."

He finished quickly, washed the fuzz off his peach, and sliced it in half. On his way out, he ate it, peel and all, licking the juice that trickled onto his chin. Glancing heavenward, he murmured, "Nothing better in all the world."

The morning went fast, and at noontime, Jacob blew a whistle. The men emptied their last buckets and gathered around the picnic tables Jacob had set up under the large shady oak tree. They'd brought their own tortillas and beans but gave cheers of *"Bueno!"* and *"Gracias!"* when Jacob and Howard brought out a tub full of soda cans in ice.

Before his own lunch, Jacob drove the load of peaches ten miles to Lehrman's Fruit Packing shed where the packers were nearly finished with their last load of plums from another farmer. He heard some groans and knew the women had hoped to finish early in today's heat. But he smiled at them, greeted the ones he knew, and told them, "What can I say? God gave us this sunshine, and all we can do is take advantage of it."

When he came back, he heard singing. A melody he recognized, although the rhythm was slightly different, the words in Spanish. The music came from several trees, and when he caught the words *"El Salvador,"* he knew it meant "the Savior" and realized they were singing a hymn. When they started *"En la Cruz,"* he joined with them in English, "At the cross, where I first saw the light." Heads turned, and hands waved.

At the end of the song, he asked the nearest singer, "You go to that Spanish-speaking Mennonite church in Reedley?"

"Si," said the man. *"El Faro* Church."

By three o'clock, the sun high, the pickers folded their ladders and left in their vans.

"Be back early tomorrow," Lupe told Jacob. "Finish maybe in four, five days."

Jacob used some of the few words he'd learned in Spanish. *"Vaya con Dios,"* he told the men. Go with God. They grinned, nodded, and waved as they left, tired and sweaty.

Jacob was sweaty too. As he and the boys washed out the buckets and put equipment away, he took out his handkerchief and wiped his forehead. Then a thought occurred to him. This was like the hankie he had lent Velita to wipe her tears. The one Ralph had used to choke her. He'd never gotten that one back—never wanted to see it again. But he did want to see Velita.

Yes, he argued with himself. *I know she's not a born-again Christian.* Not yet. But I need to know how she is. I can't lead her on by taking her out on a date, but there has to be some way I can see her again. Some way . . .

"Dad," said Sammy. "I was pretty good with the tractor, wasn't I?"

"Smart aleck," grumbled Paul.

Jacob threw Paul a look, then said, "Yes, Sam, you did very well. I'm proud of both of you. You both earned a good day's pay."

"Well," Sammy went on, "don't you think I could start driving the car around the yard sometimes? That way when I'm old enough for driver's training, I'll be that much ahead."

A light went on in Jacob's head. "Car, huh? I'll have to give it some thought."

Sammy snapped his fingers in frustration, and Paul grinned.

But Jacob went into the house with new determination. A car. That was what Velita needed. Now that she was working, maybe she'd want to look at some inexpensive used models. And he knew just where to find some to show to her.

Chapter 43

Three months later, on a Saturday morning in late October, Velita sat on her sofa in a small, low-income apartment, quilting brightly colored patches she'd sewn together for a doll quilt. From the unit above, she could hear giggles and footsteps pounding, and she smiled. Upstairs was a family of three kids, two of them girls near Suanne's age, and the mother had agreed to keep TJ and Suanne for several hours.

No way could Velita stay in the house she'd shared with Ralph. Even with him sixty miles away in Corcoran State Prison on a ten-year sentence, she would always worry about him being released early.

Marsha had again helped her with all the paperwork for this move and had mentioned it to Jacob when he came to the hospital for a final checkup. Velita had known he was kind but felt overwhelmed when he brought his pickup to help move whatever furniture LaDonna hadn't taken.

"I feel bad about what you went through," he'd said. "All the pain, the divorce and all. I hope this helps you start a new life."

Then he'd asked if she'd be interested in looking at a car he'd found for sale. "I've been hunting all over, finally found a cute little model. I think you'll like it. You must be pretty tired of taking the city bus by now."

Actually, she hadn't minded too much, except on rainy days, and thought she couldn't afford a car. But if it meant seeing Jacob again, what could it hurt just to look?

"Sure," she said, feeling herself blush. It felt good to have someone interested enough to go to all that trouble for her.

"I'll pick you up next Saturday morning, okay?"

Now, as she pulled her needle through the tiny stitches on the quilt, she remembered all the times she'd prayed and thought God hadn't listened. Actually, she was thankful He *hadn't* answered them the way she'd hoped, because He'd come up with even better solutions.

She heard an engine purring outside, and glancing out the window, she saw a tan SUV pull into the parking lot across the way. Her heart gave a little plop, knowing it was Jacob's new vehicle, and she stuck the needle through a bit of the quilt and hurried to put it in the hall closet. The doorbell rang. Velita took several slow breaths, counted to ten, then opened the door.

Jacob's hair was crisp and curling at the edges, like he'd just showered, and he smelled of spicy aftershave. He wore pressed Dockers and a blue shirt that matched his eyes. Looking into the apartment, he said, "You've fixed the place up real nice. Do the kids like their new home?"

"I was worried about that—TJ moving away from the neighbors. But they've already made friends here. And they both seem happy. More . . . relaxed." *Without Ralph around, the whole world's calmer.*

"How's your job?"

"Love it. And I'm hired for good now." She sighed, shaking her head, hardly believing her good fortune. "Sewing's my favorite thing. I'm having so much fun working with such beautiful material."

He smiled. "That's sort of how I feel about farming. Best work in the world."

"How did your peaches turn out?" asked Velita.

"Big and rosy. The price went up higher than I'd expected too." Jacob nodded, smiling. "It was a good year for me. All around."

"I'm glad." He deserved every bit of it. Velita grabbed her purse, and together, they left the building.

Outside, the fall air was breezy cool, and the leaves in the sweet gum trees along the sidewalk had turned shades of glowing gold, orange, and red. Velita shivered with pleasure at the freedom of doing something just because she wanted to.

"Where are we going?"

"A farmer near Fairdale is getting a new Bronco, says he'll let you have his old car for the trade-in price. It's a really good deal."

"You already talked to him?"

"Yeah, I've been nosing around. It's a little Honda, low mileage, very clean, silver with maroon interior. Quiet engine. You've got to see it. If you don't like it, we can go somewhere else."

"Sounds great."

For a while, they rode in silence, passing farmhouses, vineyards, and fruit trees. Velita felt shy and tongue-tied and knew he must think her a real klutz.

Then he started talking about his children, and she could tell he loved them a lot and was proud of them. He mentioned his sister, Clara, and her husband, how he'd appreciated their help on the farm during the trial, and how good it was to get better acquainted with Heinz.

When Jacob told about some of the mischief he had gotten into when he was a kid, she couldn't help laughing until her eyes watered. "I'd hide behind doors, and when my friends came hurrying through, I'd jump out and scare them. Chased them with wires, pretending they'd get shocked."

Velita was surprised. "I thought Mennonites grew up naturally religious."

He nearly choked, laughing so hard. "No, I had to confess a lot of sins before committing myself to the Lord." He sobered and glanced at her. "Now, I don't know how I could live without His help."

"You seem so strong," she said. "Not the kind that would need any help."

Jacob shook his head. "'My strength comes from the Lord.' That's a quote from the Bible, you know."

Velita thought of the verses she'd heard over the radio. *"Come unto me, all ye that are heavy laden."* She studied Jacob's calm face and hoped someday God would give her that much strength.

The car slowed, and Jacob turned the SUV into a farmyard. An older man in work clothes came out of the shed and greeted them. Jacob introduced him as Mr. Richert, calling her *Mrs. Stanford*. Mr. Richert showed them the car Jacob had mentioned, pointing out all the features.

It *was* a cute car.

Mr. Richert handed her the keys. "Take it for a test drive."

"Me?" She looked up at Jacob, shrinking her neck into her shoulders.

"You're the one that has to be satisfied," he said and held the door open for her.

She slid in, feeling awkward at the wheel. This would be a lot different from the old Dodge. Jacob got in on the other side.

Velita pulled out of the yard slowly, hoping she wouldn't crash into anything. Jacob guided her out onto the road, and before long, she felt easy and sailed along like a pro. She sped up a little, rolled down the window, and let the fresh breeze sift through her hair. It felt good to be in control. Not only of the car, but of her own decisions.

"Handles pretty well, huh?" he asked.

Velita smiled. "Yeah. I like it. I love it! . . . As long as I can afford it."

"He's only asking twelve hundred dollars. Can you handle that?"

"I've saved up a little. Would he let me do the rest in monthly payments?"

"Probably. We'll ask."

She turned, headed the car back to the farm, and parked in the driveway.

"Well?" asked Jacob.

She nodded. "I'll take it. You picked a winner, Mr. Franzen."

He laughed. "Smart move, Mrs. Stanford. After we finalize the sale, how about I take you into Fairdale for lunch? To celebrate. Your first car and my good harvest."

Velita remembered sitting across from Jacob for coffee and doughnuts after the first day of the trial, when she had still been shaky from the gang assault. Lunch with this man would be so nice. But . . . "You've already done too much for me. I owe you—"

He shook his head. "Hey, I'm hungry. You'd be helping me out, keeping me company."

She caught her breath, only half believing, but he smiled her down. Before she could say anything, Mr. Richert came out from behind his house and asked, "What do you think?"

Velita took a deep breath. "I'll take it, as long as I can pay by the month."

"No problem," said the farmer. "Come inside, and we'll do the paperwork."

Loaded with papers and a service manual, Velita stepped into her car—her own car!—and followed Jacob's SUV to lunch.

They sat in a tiny café nestled between a thrift shop and an insurance company, eating spicy German sausage and sauerkraut with brown sugar, and Jacob filled her in on all the legal stuff she still needed to do.

Dizzy with details and heady with ownership, Velita sighed. "I just don't know how to thank you," she told Jacob.

"No thanks necessary. Glad to help." He looked down at his coffee cup.

It was time to go; she'd left her kids long enough. "Well," said Velita, "I guess this is goodbye."

Jacob ran his hand through his hair, then looked up and shook his head. "I don't like that word. How about *opp vadasehn*? That's Low German for 'until I see you again.'" He took her hand in both of his, stroking it with a thumb. "If that's okay with you? Just as good friends?"

A bubble of excitement tickled all the way down to Velita's toes, and her knees felt weak. *If it was okay?* Did he really mean it? She swallowed hard, then said, "I'd like that." She knew she could never enter his world, but his friendship was a treasure she cherished.

They stood up to leave, and Jacob drew her into a gentle hug.

If I were to die right now, thought Velita, *it would be enough*. This was the best kind of life. A life where God gave you even more than you asked.

Low German Glossary

Note: These Low German (*Plautdietsch*) words have been spelled phonetically to assist with pronunciation.

ach, ach du lieber, ach, yauma—All are expressions of frustration, wonder, or disgust. Used like the English *tsk tsk, oh dear, too bad, oh shucks*, etc. Actual translations wouldn't make sense in English (e.g., *oh you love*).

beerocks—large buns filled with cooked ground meat and cabbage

bengyels—boys, with just a hint of rascals in the meaning

beta pauss opp—better watch out

brumsch—grouchy

dreest—forward, bold

eiyah—eggs

faspa—light meal, usually on Sunday evening, consisting of tvehbock, coffee, maybe lunch meat and fruit

fe'rekt—crazy, insane

fe'tsuddat—messy as uncombed hair

frindshaft—relatives, relations

kyingyas—children

Mietzi—pet name for cat, kitty

mumkya—little married woman

nah, heyat; nah yo; neh, obah—All are expressions of frustration, wonder, sympathy, surprise, or disgust. Used like the English *tsk tsk, oh dear, too bad, wow, shucks,* etc. Actual translations wouldn't make sense in English (e.g., *now yes*).

opp vadasehn—until we see each other again

out-fromm—outdo in piety

pauss opp—watch out

pluma mos—plum pudding that contains prunes and raisins

reschte—toasted

rumspringa—Old Mennonite or Amish teenagers' running around, a period of time to experiment with the world before joining the church

schnattering—chatting

schnetke—dough similar to pie dough, spread with jam, rolled up into finger-sized portions, and baked

schuzzel—someone who acts silly

tuzzling—wrestling

tvebocks—double-decker buns

"Vas kann es schoen'res geben, und was kann sel'ger sein. . . ."—"What could be better, and what could be holier," taken from an old German hymn

verenikya—a cottage cheese–filled dough pocket, similar to but much larger than ravioli

Vout yehfs et noo?—Literally, What gives now? which means, What will happen now?

vruzzle—rascal

waarlooss—nonresistant, against participating in war

yah—yes; in German dictionaries, *jah*

yauma—misery

Yoacob/Yoakob—Jacob